6/78

Northeast Harbor Library

Northeast Harbor, Maine
04662

REGULATIONS

Annual subscribers may take, on a family ticket six books, only two of which shall be new books, or on a personal ticket two books, only one of which shall be new.

———

New books must be returned in one week. Other books may be kept two weeks.

———

For the retention of books beyond the time limit, *five cents* per day will be charged.

———

Books lost or seriously injured must be replaced by the borrower.

———

All books must be returned to the Library and not passed from one subscriber to another.

NHL-8

NOCTURNE

NOCTURNE

(FROM THE NOTES OF LIEUTENANT
AMIRAN AMILAKHVARI, RETIRED)

BY BOULAT OKUDJAVA

Translated from the Russian, *Dilettantes'*
Travels, by Antonina W. Bouis

HARPER & ROW, PUBLISHERS
New York, Hagerstown, San Francisco, London

When moving, try to avoid pushing anyone.
—*A Book of Etiquette*

This work was first published in Russia under the title *Putishestvie Diletantov (Dilettantes' Travels)*.

NOCTURNE. English translation copyright © 1978 by Harper & Row, Publishers, Inc. All rights reserved. Printed in the United States of America. No part of this book may be used or reproduced in any manner whatsoever without written permission except in the case of brief quotations embodied in critical articles and reviews. For information address Harper & Row, Publishers, Inc., 10 East 53rd Street, New York, N.Y. 10022. Published simultaneously in Canada by Fitzhenry & Whiteside Limited, Toronto.

FIRST EDITION

Designed by Gloria Adelson

Library of Congress Cataloging in Publication Data

Okudzhava, Bulat Shalvovich, 1924-
  Nocturne.
  I. Title. II Title: Dilettantes' travels.
PZ4.04143No   [PG3484.2.K8]   891.7'3'44   77-11544
ISBN 0-06-013289-2

78 79 80 81 82 10 9 8 7 6 5 4 3 2 1

1

I WAS PRESENT AT the duel as Prince Myatlev's second. The prince was shooting it out with an officer from the Horse Guards, a foolish and shallow man. I won't describe now what led them to resort to pistols; the time for that will come. In any case, the real reason was their not having anything to do; duels had long lost their cachet, and therefore the entire incident was like a game and almost ludicrous.

The Guardsman puffed and preened and looked threatening, and for a minute I was afraid that the pistols were loaded and that that turkey-cock would actually shoot in earnest. However, both combatants shot into the autumn sky, and the duel was over. The rivals shook hands. The Guardsman still looked threatening, while the prince tried to smile, twisting his lips and blushing deeply.

It was time to go. People might turn up in this desolate spot, no matter how desolate it was; and since people always want to know what is going on, an encounter boded ill for us.

The touching stillness of an October morning filled the air. The duel seemed an empty fantasy.

We sat down; the coachman urged on the horses; and the carriage moved slowly and silently in the yellow grass.

2

WE HAD BEEN FRIENDS for many years, a decade to be precise, probably more, ever since that infamous year when a young but already famous poet fell in a duel in the Caucasus,

1

shot by a friend over a misunderstanding.*

Prince Myatlev had been a second to one of them. I won't be more specific, but that tragedy somehow broke his spirit. They say that before that incident he had been a rake, and a duelist, and a hothead, but when I met him he was different. Not that the impulse to carouse had died in him completely, but it wasn't constant, as it had been in the past; now it merely flared up once in a while and resembled nothing more than the death agony of youth.

The prince avoided talking about the dead poet, hardly ever mentioning his name, and if someone unwittingly intruded his thoughts and condolences, I could see how my friend suffered. That's why I won't mention the victim's name, either, in keeping with the unspoken agreement between the prince and myself.

3

OUR CARRIAGE SLOWLY APPROACHED Saint Petersburg. We were silent. The prince was thirty-five. His youth had long passed, and everything associated with it had disappeared, too. As they say, the bloom was off his cheek and his ringing laughter had faded. He had been considered handsome in his youth, and even now he had a fairly large crew of female admirers in whom he still inspired rapture. He was taller than average, not very broad in the shoulders, and his rather long face was now adorned with spectacles, which did not conceal his bewildered soul. His dark chestnut curls had thinned and faded slightly.

I loved him, pitied him, was enthralled by him, and suffered for him.

Gentlemen, please remember that Myatlev derived no pleasure from the evil he did, but lamented it bitterly—in our times that is a great virtue—even though his kind of evil, unlike yours, was miserably minor. In his youth you enjoyed him, and by the

*The poet was Mikhail Lermontov, killed in 1841.—Translator.

time he was thirty you forgot him. But that was just when he blossomed for me, when twilight enveloped his spirit and he rushed here and there, trying to find himself, and cried out, like a wounded buck in a glade, not understanding what you wanted from him.

4

WE FINALLY REACHED THE dusty outskirts of Petersburg and were surrounded by two-story buildings. I glanced over at the prince once more. He was still motionless. I remembered him on the smoky morning meadow with the incongruous pistol in his hand: a black frock coat, gray trousers, his tie in his left hand for some reason, the collar of his white shirt undone, something intense, refined, and strong in his stance even though his hand raised the pistol indolently and his lips seemed thin and dry. And now he was sitting, stooped and still not wearingseis tie, which was crumpled up in his fist.

The carriage wheels reached the first wooden paving blocks. The prince's hands rested in his lap. Thin wrists, long fingers, a ring with a baroque emerald—a memory of bygone days. The prince was particularly fond of this ring and thought about it often, staring at it attentively in pensive moments of spiritual upheaval. There was a tiny rust-colored spot on the stone, either a drop of iron or the trace of an ancient creature. Myatlev told me that over the years he had learned to distinguish special markings and lines in the spot and he maintained that they were subject to changes that varied with the season and even, I think, with his moods. He called it Valerik in memory of the famous place of our sad glory and of the man who put it on his finger.

There by the Valerik River the prince had been one of a group of volunteers who launched an attack. Their sortie was successful, but at the last moment a native tribesman's bullet hit him. Gravely wounded, Myatlev was brought back across the river with almost no hope for his survival. His life hung by a thread for a long time. When he fell on the rocky shore he was wearing the emerald ring, which had been given him before the attack by old Raspevin, a soldier of the line. That poor old man with his drooping mustache and his thin face! Extraordinary circumstances had forced him to ask to join the group of volunteers. In fact, his whole future depended on the outcome of the attack. Formerly a brilliant lieutenant, a pleasant man with an expansive soul, full of rosy hopes and the most noble morals, he fell prey to his heart's whims and his duty as a man, grappled with evil, lost, and was broken, stripped of all his rights and privileges and, with the other men involved, was put into chains. His enemies took care of him. They gave him his life—that is, the chance to survive physically—thereby deepening his humiliation. God only knows how much iron ore he dug from Siberian soil in that limitless treasure trove of our resources until finally he was pardoned. He was transferred to the Caucasus to serve as a soldier in the active army until his first important battle. When they came to the Valerik River, he had no thoughts of death. On the contrary, he was simply delirious with the prospect of victory and a swift return to his rank. But fate moved secretly. It was fate that urged him to give sweet trifles to all his friends, in joyous anticipation of victory, as a memento of victory, but it turned out that these gifts became mementos of him, for he was killed at the very beginning of the attack.

We made a small detour, going along Kamennoostrovsky Prospect, then turned slightly left, along the Malaya Neva. There was another stretch of surburban houses, which were, however, part of the city. They were luxurious buildings from the reign of Catherine, when the harmony of wealth and taste and Russian expansiveness and Western refinement was at its peak. The magnificent structures floated by, one after another, witnesses to the recent brilliance of the capital, half-hidden by trees but still visible through the lace of falling leaves. And finally, around a bend, we could see a wonderful wooden

4

building, three stories high and with a cupola, surrounded by tall bushes. Somewhat faded with time and inclement weather, it was still astounding in its strict lines and simultaneous lightness and cheeriness.

The carriage pulled into the iron gates and stopped.

Prince Myatlev's house was known throughout Petersburg. Evil tongues said that ghosts had moved in during the reign of Alexander I the Blessed and still lived there. But this in no way diminished the house's reputation, and actually lent it some mystery, which many people like in their heart of hearts.

Marvelous copies of ancient masterpieces surrounded us as usual in the entry. But we moved on upstairs, even though they extended their cold arms to us. Several dark, ancient canvases, hung God knew when, deepened the darkness that ruled in the downstairs hall. The inhabitants of the house never tarried there, and I, as a frequent visitor, had learned to rush up the broad stairs, up, up to the third floor and the large room where Sergei Myatlev chose to live. Any of our sybarites would find it a very uninviting place: a wide couch that also served as the prince's bed; armchairs covered in worn chintz with wild exotic birds staring in the same direction, which were very comfortable and conducive to conversation; a small oval table with Oriental encrustation; and a redwood grand piano with yellowed keys, a repository of sad memories.

This piano appeared in the house when the prince was five, and it was then that he first touched the cold white keys that suddenly moaned under his fingers. The dead polished box wasn't so dead after all. You had only to excite it and life reappeared and the box became a three-legged, warm creature that shivered when touched, screamed with pain, murmured, and moaned, and whistled, sometimes wild and sometimes placid, like an old dog.

The boy invented a game: he would walk carefully through the quiet house, forbidding his tutor to follow him, creep up to the living room, and throw open the doors. The strange, terrible, three-legged monster, huge and silent, stood motionless in the middle of the room, its grinning face turned to the window. The boy would stick his hands into its jaws and it would roar in a basso voice from anger and pain, and the tutor's pale face, like the moon, would appear suspended in the doorway. The boy grimaced with fear but wouldn't let go. A careful touch, a light caress, a few soothing words, and the monster would be transformed. It would encircle the boy's neck with its long tail, bare its huge teeth in a smile, purr, quiver with pleasure, sing a song without words. "Oli, li-li, la-la, li-la-loo-li." The tutor's face would turn pink and disappear.

The child's interest was noted. Adults' playing increased his passion, and soon a music teacher, training the boy, taught him in turn to train the three-legged monster. Having mastered the difficult art in a very short time, he often amazed his music-loving friends and even tried composing, which he did very well. A sad, strange piece in the style of the German masters of the last century with a troubled andante and a turbulent finale, which broke off unexpectedly on a piercing exclamation, brought him acclaim in a small circle. Everything, it seemed, augured future greatness. At officers' parties people liked to sing to his accompaniment; when young ladies pleaded with him to acoompany them, he always did so with alacrity, and their nervous, mannered, trembling sopranos were tortured in the then-fashionable "Bells."

Once a famous European genius visited Petersburg. He played in several houses, until the time came for him to perform at the palace. The genius was short, broad-shouldered, unkempt, and his apoplectic butcher's face exploded with a cold, sensitive smile; his tanned, wiry hands with the abnormally long fingers lashed at the keys as if they were the face of an enemy. His composition amazed the listeners with its magnificence, and there was no end to the exultations. Then the ball began.

Toward the end, tired and played out, Myatlev made his way to the small hall and sat at the piano, taking advantage of his solitude. Several weary guests stopped in the doorway, smiling condescendingly. The genius joined them. He was ready to leave when suddenly his eyebrows flew up, white spots appeared on his red face, and his eyes narrowed. Finally he whispered, "Whose composition is that?" They pointed at Myatlev. "Who is that heavenly musician?" "Prince Myatlev." "An officer?" At the end of the piece, he walked up to Myatlev and embraced him. The prince blushed, thanked him, and went to the buffet for some vodka. A half hour later he overheard the genius rapturously telling someone about the prince's outstanding talent, to which the man replied, "Undoubtedly, maestro. But the prince is the representative of a very noble family, and it would be much better, with his name, if he served society, well, in the political sphere or, say, proved himself in the military arts." Myatlev went back to the buffet and soon fell asleep.

He almost never played after that night, and when he was asked, he would frown and refuse, making sure that his unwillingness in no way resembled coquetry.

And the polished animal with the yellowed teeth stood motionless and silent, living out its final days with no hope of a tender caress.

A small door led from Myatlev's room to the room that had belonged to his older brother, Alexander, who now lived in Modena with his Italian wife. The prince had set up his library in there, bringing together his favorite books and leaving space for a couch, a large desk, and an escritoire.

Besides the piano, a landmark in the main room was a huge canvas in a heavy gilt frame, painted by some minor artist, either Kravtsov or Kopeikin, a very realistic depiction of the landing of the first conquistadores on American soil. The conquerors hold spears and swords, an obvious sign of their ignorance. The natives, with open, trusting faces and numerous gifts, stand on the clayey shore. In the distance behind them, on the twilit horizon, you can barely make out bonfires, where the rest of the tribe is waiting, with no thought of their swift and inevitable death. Poorly executed and in poor taste, the painting in its incongruous frame certainly did not belong with the room's modest but refined furnishings. But it had been gracing the premises for some twenty years now, eliciting the mute surprise of the infrequent visitor. From the very first time that I saw it I had been fascinated by the face of one of the natives who stood in the back of the crowd. It was lighter than the faces of his brothers, less broad and with lower cheekbones; its penetrating gaze, filled with power and suffering, caught your attention; a higher nobility permeated his tall, lithe body. Despising the artist's abilities, I was yet enraptured by that one portrait which seemed to have sprung to life without its creator's intercession. That figure inspired many sad thoughts, but at the same time pride in the human race flared up within me as soon as I saw it. I knew who the man was, even though his name had not been mentioned aloud in many years.

5

ONCE UPON A TIME the house had glittered and resounded with the noise of a large family and even more guests. Adjutant General Prince Myatlev was very close to the tsar, and the imprint of belonging to the highest caste was on everything in the house. Fortunately, the desire to shine was not limited to hospitality and frivolity. Everything was perfect in the Myatlev household: the best tutors, a marvelous library, and frequent trips abroad. That is why when the time came, which was as soon as he graduated from the Corps of Pages, the young prince was assigned as a cornet to nothing less than the Horse Guards. There he immersed himself with all his youthful passion in the violence and free living habitual in that milieu. His work was not overtaxing, and his diversions and pranks became more and more exotic. The tsar got angry, but not very, since he was very well disposed toward the old prince, and, for a time, the pranks kept a proper distance from the palace. But it all changed quickly after the notorious business with Countess Baranova. The countess was not young, not beautiful, and not bright. Her position as lady-in-waiting to one of the grand duchesses gave her great leeway. Unfortunately, she often used that position to get even with people who displeased her. The people who displeased her primarily were beautiful, young, and smart. And one day two handsome men—our young prince was one of them—wrapped in white sheets, crept into the wing assigned the ladies-in-waiting, hid under the countess's bed, and so scared her when she came in that she fell into a deep faint. But their imagination didn't stop there, and they took the poor lady to the bowels of the palace—I think into the *corps de garderie,* which was empty—and propped her up on a bench with an ancient halberd in her hands. And it didn't end there, either, because their curiosity outweighed their fear of possible consequences, and they hid in a dark corner while the staff physician, Rebrov, came in—and passed out, too. The pranksters got away safely but were soon exposed. The case was handled quickly, and Sergei Myatlev was reassigned to the Life Guards of the Grodnen Hussars Regiment, quite far from Petersburg, and even the old prince was powerless to intervene.

The circumstances of his punishment were revealed, as usual, much later. They say that the tsar, when he learned of the prank, said only, "It wouldn't hurt to remind the prince that he is no longer a boy." He said that and left, but his faithful servants, and perhaps some enemies of the old prince, rushed to fan the flames, so that even Sergei Myatlev began to believe a catastrophe had occurred.

The capital, as they say, was far behind; the hamlet where young Myatlev was stationed with his squadron was repugnant: there was nothing but a filthy old tavern and several officers' daughters, who had grown stupid with boredom. The commander of the regiment, Baron R., a human machine, held almost daily inspections with guaranteed demerits. The meadows around the town were dug up by the horses' hooves, crudity flourished and was supported, and the officers' daughters were ready to do anything with anyone who barely resembled a man. The older officers drank until they passed out, played whist

9

until their brains frazzled, and, with the help of their wives, plotted intrigues against the young officers. *La maladie éternelle.* The baron, obviously, had an *idée fixe* about inspections. The young aristocrats, unaccustomed to provincial soldiering, rebelled. One fine day a funeral procession wended its way through the town. A closed coffin lay on a simple wagon. Several officers walked behind it, led by Myatlev, who was followed by half a squadron of dismounted Hussars. The regimental band accompanied the sad procession. The locals crowded around every gate. Suddenly a carriage bounded around a corner, and everyone saw the commander's familiar face.

"What is this funeral?" the baron inquired.

The procession stopped. The band stopped. Everyone turned to Myatlev. Prince Sergei, his lips bitten white, walked ceremoniously—as ceremoniously as the mud permitted—to the baron's carriage.

"Cornet, what is the meaning of this?" the regimental commander asked in a whisper. "What is it—who is it—whom are you burying?"

"You, Your Excellency!" the young prince replied loudly. "We're all greatly saddened. Please accept our condolences."

The storm broke immediately, but either the commander was not one of the tsar's favorites or else the distance to Petersburg softened the blow. In any case, the thunder rumbled on high, and Myatlev was given a new assignment, got in a carriage with his cook and his servant, Afanasy, and headed for the Caucasus. He didn't like talking about military affairs, but I knew from others how he had played with death down there. His severe wound brought him a pardon. The sudden death of the old prince moderated the wrath of the gods, and Sergei Myatlev, just like the Prodigal Son, returned to the Horse Guards' fold.

By the way, about his grave wound: I think it brought on the sudden attacks of dizziness that occurred unexpectedly and without warning, overwhelming Myatlev from time to time. It was impossible to predict them, no matter how we tried. The doctors who attended him in different periods unanimously rejected the possibility of epilepsy. And the course of the attacks in no way resembled that well-known and disgusting disease. They began with a pallor that spread instantly over his face, a guilty smile appeared on his lips, his gaze grew dull, and his limbs refused to respond to his will. He spoke in *non sequiturs,* walked where he did not mean to, agreed with everything that was said to him, and at the same time insisted on giving his interlocutor whatever money he had on his person. These attacks rarely lasted more than a minute and disappeared without a trace, if you discount the feeble desire to be alone with a carafe of vodka.

In perfect health myself, I pitied the prince and recommended that he go on leave and come down to my beloved Georgia, but he merely laughed in reply, while not refusing the ministrations of useless and ineffectual physicians.

I began frequenting his home. Through inertia the circle of hospitality still spun there, but its gyres were more and more infrequent. The old generation dropped that world or grew weary of it, and the new one had other inclinations. Myatlev and I soon became friends. My duties in the Life Guards of the Paul Regiment didn't tax me overly, either. There was nothing shocking in a friendship between a Guardsman and a Paulist, and we directed all our energies to slowing down life as it flowed past and somehow holding onto our youth. I will not maintain that our thoughts and our time were occupied only with entertainment and pleasure. No, age had indeed caressed us, making us wiser and calmer. Only once in a while, breaking our leashes, we would spend some time trying to make our fantasies come true, but not in any excessively wild way, until we came to our senses once more. But this happened more and more rarely, and the prince appeared in public less and less frequently.

The golden tribe of high society had long ago shown him its empty soul and sharp claws, and Myatlev found no solace in its comforts. What could an extraordinary man do when only ordinariness was accepted and was immune to persecution by that gang? Lose himself in it and leave his fate in its hands? The prince couldn't do that. He was, without realizing it, trying to swim out of it, struggling in the soulless sea, avenging himself on it when and how he could. Ah, revenge—it's a game and nothing more. There's no great danger to your detractors when, in a drunken frenzy, nothing seems enough, and your imagination borders on madness, and you imagine the whole world conquered and punished. But that's just you, as drunk as an artisan, full of impotence and negation, consoling yourself with wine. And it's not enough. And though at first the prince used to drink in large groups, the circle narrowed. Sometimes he drank alone. He had already established a reputation as a dangerous man who had deserted his class and rank, who mocked everything and was capable of anything. It was known that the tsar did not approve of him, remembered his crimes, and frowned openly whenever the conversation turned to him.

6

THAT WAS THE SITUATION when we became friends. We lived for the day, expecting nothing from the future except petty irritations. But life is life. And having become almost the sole proprietor of a large house, Myatlev immediately undertook arranging it to suit him.

In boots and a white lace shirt with an open collar, full of the holy fire of creation, like an inspired architect, he raced here and there in the house. He began with the third floor and refurnished it in the way I have already described. He left the second floor as it was. It consisted of several chambers of varying size. The largest was the main drawing room. It was oval. A huge bronze chandelier hung in the middle. Four darkened mirrors were carefully arranged along the walls between cream-colored columns; comfortable couches of the last century, upholstered in cherry-red French velvet, girdled the room; the luxurious parquet floor shone as though it had been polished yesterday. The place seemed empty, deprived of its piano and armchairs, but now it revealed its expanse, good for fencing and solitude. The small drawing room, which now contained all the card tables, looked like a classroom abandoned forever. I did not ask the prince what had prompted him to rearrange his house this way and no other, but, judging by his excitement and the laughter that accompanied all this moving, I assumed there was a very subtle and almost invisible plan that the new master of the house was following. Finally the time came to execute the first floor. He ordered all the doors nailed shut except those leading to the servants' quarters, and he barred himself forever, he thought, from his father's monumental library-study, first emptying it of the books that interested him. The doors of his father's and his long-dead mother's bedrooms were nailed shut, too, even though everything was left exactly as it had been inside them. Freeing himself in this bizarre manner from his past, he cut the staff by two-thirds, sending the servants he had dismissed back to their villages, which did not make them happy; he left only the chef, the cook, and postilion, the butler, the gardeners, and round-faced Afanasy as valet, majordomo, or adjutant, since he felt that in the person of this country eccentric of his own age he had found a loyal, dependable, and original man.

Having done all this, he continued living a new life. And, apparently as a result of all these innovations, about which malicious gossip had spread quickly, he was visited by his sister, Elizaveta Vasilyevna, a lady-in-waiting to Grand Duchess Elena Pavlovna. She made her way up to the third floor in vicious silence, refusing to remove her fur coat. She also refused to sit down but stood in the doorway of his room, disdainfully peering at the deliberate sparseness of the prince's household goods. Myatlev listened with a gentle smile to her abusive anger, unwilling to acknowledge his guilt, which was terrible—if only because it represented a challenge, since all this transformation and style of behavior were nothing more. He tried unsuccessfully to get a word in edgewise, but she cut him off with a wave of the hand and talked on and on. And he nodded, as though in agreement, but she knew how little agreement there was in the nods of that hothead. She had no intention of being forced to blush for him and see disbelief and condemnation in the eyes of the people around her and listen to their commiseration! More than anything else . . . shameless behavior . . . the tsar's anger . . . self-indulgence . . .

7

WHILE HE HAD BEEN feverishly wasting his youth, women had not been the chief object of his rapt attention. Their image had not dominated his other customary passions. And he believed that the capacity to fall in and out of love had passed early. His memories of first love were funny and remote. While he was in the Corps of Pages he met Mashenka Strekalova at a children's ball at the Sheremetyevs'. His head began spinning at the sound of her capricious little voice. He realized that he would never be able to forget her, and right after their first dance slipped off with her into the empty buffet. They sat down on a bench, and Seryozha Myatlev, leaning over her, saw inside her neckline two pink mounds, two barely visible swellings, something very tender and alive. He kissed her round shoulder, squinting as he kissed into the semidarkness there, watching them rise and fall anxiously and frequently.

"Ah," she said without moving away, "you should talk with *Maman*!"

"About what?" he asked, not understanding. "I love you for the ages."

"All the more reason," she said. "If you are asking for my hand, how can you do it without talking to *Maman*? Whatever she says will be. You please me, too—I won't hide it—but how can we do anything without *Maman*?"

They went back to the dancing, unnoticed by anyone. Later, Myatlev went home. And in the carriage, falling asleep on his tutor's shoulder, he thought that he didn't know what to talk about with Mashenka's mother and how to go about it, and then also thought that the girl wasn't all that pretty, even though *they* were tender and probably very hot and he had wanted to touch them.

And yet this was already a beginning, which he would draw upon later in conversation with world-weary Horse Guards' officers.

Then he seduced a young, pink, priest's daughter on his way to his estate in Kostroma. Actually, she seduced him. She smelled of youth, the river, and onions, and Myatlev remembered it all his life. Thus infused with the experience of love, he developed a skeptical attitude toward women until the Horse Guards' fate forced him to subscribe to convention. In that noisy milieu, everything was done in the open. Don Juans in cuirasses confessed to one another with the fervor of those going into mortal combat or to the scaffold. Story followed story, affair after affair. The barracks hummed with love stories. Beginners felt their heads spin and spirits brighten. Listening to the talk, you might think that all the women of Petersburg, having gone mad, had vowed eternal infidelity to their husbands and rushed into the embrace of the bored officers. There might have been some truth in it. Handsomeness, nobility, and persistence—that is, tolerable looks, money, and gall—made up the symphony of feelings. The ability to be friends with the husband as though nothing were going on—that was the height of refinement and perfection. He wanted to try that, too—dipping his toes into icy water before plunging in, so to speak. A convenient opportunity arose quickly, since one is always nearby and will announce itself as soon as we indicate our inclination.

8

THE WIFE OF BARON Fredericks, a privy councillor and gentleman-in-waiting, Anna Mikhailovna Fredericks, *née* Glebova, had just turned thirty, but she still was the same captivating Aneta, with the features of a young Creole and movements resplendent with charm and grace. She rarely went out, which lent her name a certain mystery, and her silence increased her reputation in the eyes of the people around her. Myatlev had met her before, but the fact that she was a married woman, and her natural restraint, bordering on coldness, did not predispose him to any special feelings for her. However, time passed, and they met at a great ball—I think at Christmas, or maybe earlier—and he danced with her for the first time. Something set fire to him the moment he touched her hand, A subtle, haughty fragrance came from her pink silk and her black curls. Her large olive eyes were on him constantly, but they expressed more indifference than interest. She danced easily, but without the passion and fever of young ladies, despite the fact that Myatlev tried to convey some tiny spark of the ball's exhilaration to her.

"You are rarely about," he said, to establish contact.

She did not reply, but merely smiled condescendingly.

Suddenly he realized that she was unbelievably beautiful, an enchantress, and that something terrible would happen if he couldn't see her frequently from that moment on. He had never felt anything like it before. He tried not looking at her, and in an effort to maintain some balance, laughed in his soul, trying to douse the raging fire, but to no avail. Her deep eyes and the pink silk of her dress were like a stormy sky to him. He could barely breathe; he was terrified. She, apparently, was feeling nothing of the sort, since whenever he dared look at her, he met her steady gaze and the same condescending smile.

"Will you be at the Borinskys' next Thursday?" he asked, holding his breath.

She shrugged, never taking her eyes off him.

A storm raged in Myatlev's heart. He looked for her for a second dance, but he couldn't find her. Finally someone told him she had left. He was in a state of confusion, but on his way home he suddenly felt healthy and calm. He explained away the change as the result of his stony hardness and, irritated, tried to work himself into a frenzy again. He began a letter to her, but the words were too cool. Thursday came! He raced in his carriage and thought, "What a shame, I'm so damn calm! What's the matter with me? No, I love her! I really love her." He went in. She wasn't there. Suddenly she appeared with her husband, a middle-aged, red-haired man, who immediately sat down with another man just like him, either to play cards or to share their impressions of the day. As soon as he saw her, a serious passion exploded within him, without invitation. "Aha!" he gloated. She was merciful. She recognized him. They danced. She no longer looked condescending. On the contrary, something warm flickered in her gaze and in her expression, so that Myatlev was freed of the nightmares that had tortured him all week.

"I thought about you all the time," he confessed.

She did not reply, but looked at him with interest.

"Please stay longer," he begged. "You always disappear."

She disappeared without even waiting for the halfway point in the ball, leaving him once again hollow and utterly confused. And immediately, to his dismay, the fire began going out. He tried to fan it, remembering her shoulders and cheeks and the warmth that emanated from them, eternal, captivating, and damned. He still tried to fill his thoughts with his matchless love, but he spoke more calmly now, seeing in himself the clear outline of an adulterer.

Suddenly he received an invitation from the Frederickses to visit them! The scented envelope was so simple and yet exotic that my prince rushed out two hours early. He dismissed his carriage. Too late, he realized he was early. And, waiting for the moment when it would be proper to appear, he idled away an hour and half not far from the Frederickses' house. And finally he stepped onto the saving shore, where there were completely different mores, rules, and passions. The carpet under his feet felt different, the candles crackled differently, and a strange draft wafted over him while he went up the stairs on wooden legs. The fire that had almost gone out was raging within him again.

He was in love again and was happy. Everything he saw pleased him; he saw the light touch of her hand, her breath, her gaze on everything around him. The marble staircase seemed endless, and unexpected leaves of live fig trees pushed their way through the white balustrade. For some reason the first line of a catchy song kept running through his head. "I picked this forest flower for you." He couldn't remember the rest, and, feeling drunk, he kept repeating that line. He stopped and squinted before the open door to the drawing room. She met him.

"Good day, Prince. We're happy to see you," she said, and he heard her voice for the first time. His legs got back their firmness and spring. He kissed her hand. He thought he saw something soft, dark, and vague move out of the depths of the room and block the light for a moment. Then it carefully moved closer and stopped nearby.

"How do you do," he heard above him. "Here is our glorious prince."

Fredericks himself stood in front of Myatlev in a simple frock coat. Myatlev compared them mentally.

"I'm very pleased," the gentleman-in-waiting said. "Anna Mikhailovna was not mistaken; you really are extremely nice."

The prince was confused and didn't know what this was: a polite insult or a confession.

"No, this is impossible," he thought, quickly looking at the two of them. "It's a mistake."

"Please come in," the gentleman-in-waiting repeated.

The poor prince. What feelings do to a man! An excess is as harmful as a lack of feeling. Just to think that you climb all the way to that dizzying height only to find out that it's not a height but only a foothill, and the important peak is over there and is unattainable.

"I see your mother's features in you," the baron said when they had sat down. "I remember her; she was an incomparable beauty."

"All the Myatlevs are beautiful," Aneta said.

The prince blushed.

"Really," Fredericks said, "you'll have to get used to this, Prince. Anna Mikhailovna is simply enchanted with you, and I see how right she is. All I hear is the prince, the prince."

Myatlev blushed.

"I love her!" he thought stubbornly.

The gentleman-in-waiting was over fifty. His clean-shaven, glowing face exuded health and serenity. He spoke confidently, almost without opening his youthfully red lips. Yes, confidently, but tactfully.

"Now I finally get to meet you. You're much spoken of. You are a mystery, Prince. As for me, I like transparency. I find mystery burdensome. You smile, Prince, and thank God for that. You, I see, are too smart and perhaps—please don't be offended—too lazy to be ambitious. I think I may have guessed correctly—I mean not the idle laziness of the mediocre, but the ability not to bustle, that's what I mean. Your visit, Prince, is a great honor for me."

"Did you like the party Thursday?" Aneta turned to Myatlev. "Wasn't it pleasant?"

"Oh, yes," Prince Sergei replied quickly, "but the second half became rather dull."

"And we had left by then," Fredericks softly reminded him. "Anna Mikhailovna developed a headache. We left."

Myatlev blushed again and noticed a slight sense of disapproval on her part.

"By the way," the gentleman-in-waiting said, "I once drove past your house; it's a wonderful house, even though it's slightly run-down. But it's becoming. I don't like new houses. They seem too self-sufficient to me. They have a challenging exterior; they seem to be bursting with conceit, obviously feeling that they can get away with anything. This always angers me. Wait a minute, I think; what makes you so conceited? From our first meeting you try to convince me of your importance and of the fact that you are in the right and have everything you want. Aren't you afraid of being mistaken? I want to ask them: Aren't you afraid? After all, a mistake is worse than a crime. And besides, I'm repelled by your confusion when you put your foot in it. Yes, I like your house precisely because it's not conceited and is therefore generous. There is a higher nobility in silence and in the ability not to tempt fate by trying to set up some utopia or other. So you agree with me? Well, naturally."

This time she blushed.

"Some sensations," he continued, "demand to be overcome. Isn't that so? Would you like a pipe, Prince? How did you like the fig trees by the staircase? Anna Mikhailovna expended a lot of effort to make that biblical plant grace our old house."

"I picked this forest flower for you," Myatlev sang under his breath.

"I hear you distinguished yourself in the Caucasus—and were gravely wounded," Fredericks went on. "There's a paradox for you: a Russian Horse Guardsman—you weren't in the Guards then?—a Russian officer, according to his historical character a homey creature, generous, given to luxury and extravagance, is lying on the wild shore of an Asiatic river with his belly torn open—forgive the realism, but it was torn open? And didn't you give any thought to the meaning of your mission? No? There, you see. For a youth it's an adventure, for an average man of middle age—a paradox, and for someone thinking in governmental terms—the only reasonable action and not the whim of someone or other. Now Anna Mikhailovna is signaling me to the effect that I'm talking nonsense. I won't talk any more nonsense, but I want to say that history has a path and our business is to help it along."

"Yes," Myatlev said in a half-dreaming state. "A lot of blood and too many justifying documents."

"You see, Prince"—Fredericks smiled—"another paradox, but a real one: life is elevated only through sacrifice."

He sat back calmly in his chair. Aneta was looking at Myatlev with a mysterious smile. The prince was waiting for something, expecting something, as he listened to the even, confident, slow voice of the gentleman-in-waiting. Gradually he stopped following the meaning and caught only separate words, and then his ability to comprehend would be restored for a time, only to dissolve immediately. But this did not worry him. He was worried by something else: he was waiting for something, and it wasn't coming.

". . . or, for instance," the gentleman-in-waiting was saying, "Western Slavs in no way merit our involvement, for we organized our government without them, we grew and suffered without them, and they . . . dependence . . . nothing . . . historical existence . . ."

Myatlev smiled at her, but she didn't alter her tense expression. He had let her know that he was burning up, that everything was over for him; he had tried somehow to convince her of that. Apparently he had succeeded, and apparently she felt that it was in vain, because she didn't do anything about it.

The time was drawing close for an end to the call.

". . . like all people with excessive conceit," Fredericks continued, "who are afraid of failure, that duke was very shy in financial matters. That's what ruined him . . . receipts . . . snowed under . . . wanting . . ."

Nodding in agreement, wrinkling his forehead and drumming his fingers with false meaningfulness on his knee, Myatlev still managed to glance at her quickly and see her as if for the first time. She was no longer the way she had been in the cotillion: without the aloofness, not as dusky, and not as mysterious. There was something homey about her. "So this is what she's like?" Myatlev thought in surprise.

". . . when enlightenment shines for the semibarbarians," the gentleman-in-waiting continued, "the first thing they grab is luxury, like children . . . fire . . . meaning . . . average . . ."

"We'll always be happy to see you here," she said to Myatlev as he rose.

"Yes, yes," Fredericks added, also getting up. "Very."

She saw him out alone, without her gentleman-in-waiting, who had disappeared, unnoticed, overflowing with unexpected insights. They were completely alone on the white marble stairs, and Myatlev turned his tormented face to her, framed in fig leaves, trying to find out what his lot would be from now on.

"Your passion, Prince"—she put her finger to her lips and laughed—"does you no justice. I hope you weren't bored?" While he was kissing her hand, "I hope you weren't bored?"

It was easy for her to speak. She saw a handsome and attractive Horse Guards' officer before her, diffident either from uncertainty or through very subtle playacting, while he felt himself a pilgrim in tatters who had finally reached his goal and understood the futility of all his endeavors.

"Poor prince," she whispered, "come, well, tomorrow. I'll be waiting for you." And she watched as he went down the white steps and the valet handed him his fur coat, and saw how he wanted to turn around and look at her and how he controlled himself to keep from turning.

9

"TOMORROW"—WHAT A SPITEFUL concept, abounding in emptiness! How many hopes it raises in the human race without ever coming through. Voltaire was so right when he said that we don't live, we only hope to live. Why? Why? The emptiness of the word is alluring. Like an empty wine barrel it echoes and resounds with great import until it falls apart and reveals only long-rotten staves. Why? Why? If you must trust, then trust only the present day, this very moment, and not ephemeral fantasies—unless you want to cry bitter tears and repent. Doesn't the past teach us anything?

She said; "Tomorrow." Ah, Prince! You did not approve of my mockery and deemed me too cynical when I tried to warn you about your hopes.

"I feel sweetness, and my head is spinning," you replied. "Everything will be decided tomorrow." And you went on babbling, "I love her! Oh, how I love her!"

However, he slept soundly. In the morning he put on his fur

coat and went out into the park.

I don't know how fair it is to aggrandize with the name "park" that abandoned kingdom of roots, branches, and leaves on the edge of Petersburg. In any case, it was easy enough to get lost in. No one had taken care of that expanse of land in a long time, giving it total freedom to live as it wished. In front of the house, one's imagination was stirred by the cast-iron railings that severely separated the street and the world from the overgrowth. But on the other sides, the quaint wooden fences had aged and turned to dust, and everything had mixed and intertwined, the *allées* were overgrown, and little paths showed here and there, trampled by rare passersby or stray dogs. Back in the days when the old prince was still alive, the roots and leaves had begun their inexorable battle with man and won, and now it was difficult to establish the true boundaries of the park, and actually no one cared enough to do so, and if the prince were now to come out and make his claim on his park, he would have been laughed at. On summer evenings more and more lovers and tramps found shelter in the thick woods, and on holidays noisy workers' families had their simple picnics there, and the hallooing in the park was as loud as it was in any forest.

In winter this former park was more transparent and light, the mysterious culs-de-sac gone, unseen voices stilled; the clouds of birds were calling to one another somewhere in the south, leaving only the heavy crows to caw in the naked branches, and mysterious tracks showed blue in the even snow.

The park and trees brought to mind a brief episode in his life.

Once, at an unbelievably wild Horse Guards' picnic at the height of summer in some forgotten forest, drunk on wine and the constant bustle of his brother officers, Myatlev hid behind some trees, found a quiet corner, fell into the tall, thick grass, and slept. When he opened his eyes, the world that appeared before him seemed unfamiliar. He was surrounded by motley grasses that hid the slightly damp earth from the sky; little clumsy creatures on spindly legs slowly overcame monstrous obstacles; they had tiny antennae, or terrible horns, or lacy wings; and they all had huge, bulging eyes, filled with thousands of years of sadness and fierceness. Some came up to Myatlev, to his face, and froze in surprise, seeing that huge, ugly freak of nature. Flowers, which served as their food, homes, and roads, hung over him; neither winds nor sounds from another world reached them. And suddenly, in the midst of this fantastic world, in its very center, under the spreading leaves of an unknown plant, Myatlev saw a man. Immobile and alone, made from a pine branch, brought here somehow, he stood leaning against a stem of a plant, his arms flung out triumphantly, his little head thrown back exultantly, with a look of happiness and peace on his little wooden face. Myatlev stretched out his hand, touched the marvel in awe, and put him on his palm. The man, dressed in translucent golden pine film, still gazed out happy and exultant from the prince's hand.

Myatlev didn't wait for the picnic to end, and left, taking the marvelous foundling with him. At home, using an old Damascene knife, he whittled a small pedestal for his find. The prince was in the grip of a feverish passion. As though bewitched, he searched his park and traveled to forests, sloshed through swamps, searching, searching, searching. He tore out new pines, firs, birches, and heather by their roots, shook the soil from the roots, and spent hours examining the cleverly crafted legs, arms, heads, and bodies of suffering, dancing, loving, angry, and ailing figures. And when he found something that amazed him, he cut it out with his Damascene knife, cleaned it, scraped off the excess, put it in a leather sack, and brought it home. Soon the marble windowsills were inhabited by this forest tribe eloquent of passion and silence. Naked mermaids stretched out their wooden, dangerous arms; headless soldiers marched off to somewhere; beautiful women suffocated, intertwined forever in the embrace of their lovers; ballerinas pliéed, turned, and bowed; bathers gingerly touched the water with their toes; and there was a Christ bowed by the weight of the cross, and a Christ crucified, but still alive, his muscles taut, and a Christ already sagging. And there were snakes with bull's heads, black and insidious demons, a bird with a human chest, and a witch embracing an unknown and shameless many-armed monster.

It was a festival of nature and human inspiration, and delighted viewers would for a moment become secret conspirators in it, but as they left the prince, they would have their doubts and laugh at him. A few months later he suddenly cooled to the idea, the maid swept the dry, fragrant garbage from the room, and the dusty tribe gradually disappeared, as though off on a search for its lost homeland.

And so he was walking through the park, along the only definite path, relishing the coming rendezvous and secretly suffering, because the tiny drop of poison I had spilled was working.

The road led from the manor's back porch to the hundred-year-old linden, skirted its trunk, and headed deep into the park toward the Nevka River, apparently hoping to cross the park and the river and the whole world, but breaking off abruptly by the only remaining bench, drowning in a snowbank.

Suddenly he saw a slight movement behind the bench. He went over.

A frowning, rosy-cheeked boy in a peasant vest and black felt boots stood before him. The unexpected little guest had a challenging expression and brandished a wooden sword. The sword trembled in the thin, cold hand, and the fingers of the other hand clutched the branch of a rowan tree whose deep red berries glistened iridescently like glass baubles at a fair.

The boy was not one of the servants' children, the prince was sure of that. He had come from afar, beyond the thickets, from another world, sinking in the crumbly snow and using the wooden sword like a staff.

"Where did you come from, boy?" Myatlev asked softly, and turned to call Afanasy to take the boy back to the house, warm him up and give him some tea, and then bring him home.

"How would you like to taste your own blood!" the boy shouted.

"Ah, I see." Myatlev was confused. "What do you need the rowan tree for?"

The boy laughed impudently and threatened him with his

sword. The cold wind became more pronounced. The hand holding the sword turned blue and tensed, but the one holding the branch amazed Myatlev—the pinky was turned out so exquisitely, as though a small angel with an olive branch stood before the prince—and the prince was embarrassed by his question.

"What rowan tree are you talking about?" the boy asked in disgust. "Where did you see a rowan tree, you pathetic lout? Do you want me to tickle your belly with this?" And he shook his sword once more.

"What do you need the rowan tree for?" Myatlev asked. "The branch—"

"To put on your grave," the boy said loudly and challengingly.

"So that's it." The prince was even more confused. "And what's your name, sir?"

"I'm from the noble line of van Schoenhoven," the boy said with a frozen mouth.

"Little boys shouldn't be alone—in an empty park—"

The boy laughed in reply.

The prince headed for home determinedly.

"Coward!" the boy called, shaking his sword. "Hah!" And he limped over in the direction of the thicket, sinking in the snow, leaning on his sword, and soon disappeared from view.

The gray eyes swam before Myatlev for a long time, and he kept imagining how he might have hid the small, cold hand in his, but by evening the boy no longer came to mind and he was ready to rush to his Aneta's side, paying no heed to my warnings. The hour struck, and he rushed off. But even in the entry Myatlev could tell that something had happened; either the fig leaves didn't seem as lush, or the marble of the stairs was crumbling, leaving a fine pinkish dust on everything.

He was told that the baroness was out. How could that be? It was. She left a long time ago, and when she would return, she didn't say. Prince Myatlev? Certainly, Your Excellency. His Excellency the gentleman-in-waiting? He left in the morning and hasn't been back since.

26

You had to see my prince then. He naturally didn't recall my warnings as he raced through Petersburg back to his three-storied fortress.

Oh, if only fate had brought him to my Georgia and he could have breathed in the blue air at sunrise, redolent of snow and peaches, and seen my sister, Maria Amilakhvari—all his future troubles would have gone away and the pain would have ended immediately.

10

THE PRINCE DID NOT love the baroness, I am more than sure of that. It was just a whim. He was inflamed, being turned down, and every man knows what that means. And existing in a semidelirium of drunkenness and despair, he even tried writing to her.

And then, for the devil knows what reason, it became easier for him. He looked out the window, there was a lot of snow and sun out there, and the baroness's insult faded and almost passed. It even became boring to think about the incident and of himself as a participant in it. "What kind of love was that?" he thought, laughing. "If she had appeared here shamelessly, and cried and groveled at my feet, and I had climbed up on the windowsill in fear, like a young lady protecting my innocence, then in that passionate outburst, that madness, we could have talked about love." And then he saw the boy under the century-old linden, and the prince felt good. So much for the baroness, so much for love! As if I hadn't had a feeling about it.

The sun was shining, and the sky was pale blue. The boy was slowly approaching the house. Finally he was so close that we could make out his pink cheeks and the buttons on his jacket. So much for love of the baroness. If it had existed, then why did it fade so fast? The boy was right at the house, standing near the porch and looking around. Myatlev called Afanasy and told him to invite the traveler in. And a second later, dressed in patched livery and thin felt boots, with a ridiculous top hat perched on his head, Afanasy was opening the heavy door in front of the little guest, beckoning him in, grinning, and stamping his feet in the snow.

Finally the boy came into the room. He didn't have his sword. His plump lips barely moved in a lost smile. The prince remembered his strange name.

"Mr. van Schoenhoven?"

And spreading his arms in a welcoming embrace, he walked toward the guest, without having had time to close his dressing gown over his torn lace shirt.

"Ah!" exclaimed the boy, and quickly turned away.

"Really!" the prince thought, "look at the way I'm dressed and at my hung-over face—"

Afanasy disappeared. The prince wanted to raise the boy's spirits and to say matter-of-factly, "What's the matter, you silly child? Would you like to look at some colored pictures?" But the boy began laughing, showing his white teeth, flopped down into a chair, and calmly looked at his host. "Well?"

"So," Myatlev said, smiling awkwardly "would you like some cabbage soup?"

The boy apparently felt completely at home, particularly since Myatlev's bustling gave him the feeling that he was the host and the prince had dropped in on him for no apparent reason.

"*Maman* has no idea where I am," the guest said. "Were you really scared by me that time? Did you think that I could have struck you with the sword? Did you?"

"Mr. van Schoenhoven," said Myatlev, "what prompted you to seek a meeting with me?"

The guest laughed. Twilight was setting in quickly. It grew blue outside the windows. Bells pealed in the distance.

"No reason," the boy said, and clicked his tongue. "They talk about you a lot"—he clicked again—"and I thought, Why don't I go see?"

"What do they say?"

"Different things."

"Who says them?" Myatlev was interested. "How could the life of old men interest little boys?"

"But it is interesting." The boy laughed.

"There's nothing interesting at all." Myatlev was hurt and told Afanasy to show the little prankster out.

But the guest had crawled under the table and refused to come out, and helpless Afanasy hopped around the table like a goat, mumbling and pleading, "We'll show you—right now, I'll— And where's my whip? Grab him—" Then he began begging, "Sir, they're looking for you. Five valets and seven soldiers with lamps and torches and halberds running all around the yard; your mother sent them, sir."

The boy liked the game, and he laughed to see two grown men trying to fish him out from under the table. They finally managed to do just that, and Afanasy, muttering, led the boy out of the room.

"I'll be back," the boy said in farewell, buttoning his jacket with his thin hand. "Don't be afraid of me."

No sooner had the door shut on him than, damn it, from the semidarkness stepped the image of unattainable Aneta; she slipped quietly through the room and stopped beside him, accompanied by a silent crowd of lucky seducers who did not know the meaning of second thoughts, recriminations, fruitless exclamations, and dubious hopes. They stood in a tight semicircle, their skin smooth and shiny, like new chairs in fancy slipcovers. They smiled, indolently and easily, so graced by Mother Nature that they scorned to use the slightest trick to obtain any other treasures from her. And they probably should have been esteemed for this and even excused, remaining as they did arrogantly in the shadows, from which they could see everything so well.

He was not surprised by her sudden appearance. On the contrary, with unusual and businesslike efficiency he launched into a conversation about the most base and common passions, like a clerk discussing paper that was filled with extraneous material: sticks, pieces of straw, fillings, and other chaff that made his pen catch and create splotches. "You came here, so send your handsome boys away; make them leave, and let's talk some boring nonsense—after all, no one has come up with anything new—so that we'll have something to remember tomorrow."

"All right," she said and ordered everyone out. "Are you pleased? However, you have to realize that my life depends on them, no matter how much I try to fight it. I'm a flower. And they are my bees. Now I am with you they are buzzing and flying outside the window! And we call it madness, despair, passion, ruination, and it's none of those, they are merely buzzing there, understanding nothing about it."

11

... bitterness, bordering on revulsion, and exultant worship at the same time. Tastelessness that will drive me mad, and extreme refinement. No, there's something to this! I'm willing to bet that I'm truly in love as I have never been before, but my doubts keep me from being sure.

This was Myatlev's entry in his diary for December 3, 1844.

No, it's not love. I'm afraid to meet her. What do I need with her banal conversations about the baron and other marvels? Yesterday evening there was rain, and there's nothing left of winter. "Do you remember the horns' mournful call?" Where's that from? "... the splatter of rain, half-light, half-darkness?" I don't know where it's from, but I seem to hear the horns playing, and, having heard them, I'm ready to set off ... but is it in vain? ... Mr. van Schoenhoven was scurrying under the windows this morning. I was as happy to see him as a dear relative; I called and coaxed, but he wouldn't come in and disappeared in his jungle.

This was December 6.

December 9

She said that I'm not like the rest. Seems that's bad. No, I am like the rest, but there is a certain discomfort in it that she can accept and I can't. "Why did you redo your house that way, and why don't you ever go out into society?" What of it? . . . You'd think I was consciously throwing a challenge at them, and so on.

December 11

I haven't become so feebleminded that I refuse new joys and pleasures. . . . The direct honesty of the ancients is very touching, but every era has its own way of expressing it. . . . You look at the light nowadays, and see only darkness. . . . What a brilliant insight. . . . Amilakhvari is a genius in that he sees all of this and still undertakes nothing. He complains of laziness, but he nonetheless takes pride in his behavior. Count S. told me in secret that recently the tsar mentioned my father indulgently in a small group but immediately looked glum and added in reference to me, addressing no one in particular, but loud enough for all to hear, "Now there's an example of a bloodline withering away; the fruit fell far from the tree. Only drunkenness and debauchery. We'll be hearing about him yet. I foresee the worst for him." How disgusting! Now all I can do is resign my commission and go to Hell! I'll pack up my books and go off to the Caucasus with Afanasy. . . . Oh, my Aneta!

December 14*

A sad day! Almost twenty years of imprisonment have passed. My marvelous predecessors have turned into feeble invalids or have died, and there is no end in sight to their existence in Siberia. They are afraid of them to this day; they fear them, they despise me, they hate my limping friend, the Hobbler. . . . And meanwhile I'm burning with lust. Burning like a pimply adolescent. God, what skin she has! Are further discoveries possible?

December 16

Virtues are the fruit of our imagination; with their help we simplify our existence. . . . There is a crude charm in the sha-

---

*A reference to the Decembrist uprising in 1825, when a large number of liberal officers demonstrated in Senate Square against Tsar Nicholas I's ascension to the throne.
—Translator.

mans around the Don River and in their obligation not to wash their feet and to sleep on the bare ground. . . . Yesterday I was invited to the Frederickses'. My heart was fluttering, but in a half hour her ordinary tone soothed me. The baron made believe that he didn't give a damn about anything except government doctrines. He maintains that personal interests cannot override government interests. . . . It all depends on the digestion, I think; he sees it thus, and I see it this way.

December 17

The tsar is giving me wolflike looks, and everyone I run into feels duty-bound to let me know I'm a bad boy.

12

OUR GLOWING ENTHUSIASM FOR the written word began in the middle of Catherine's reign. Some ubiquitous soul realized that words on paper were not only good for issuing orders, or reports on one's health, or confessions of love, but were a marvelously self-indulgent way of feeding one's ego, exploring oneself endlessly before an audience of like-minded people. Pain, suffering, joy, unattainable hopes, false exploits, and much more—all poured onto paper in an endless stream and flew out in all directions in multicolored envelopes. Our grandfathers and grandmothers learned to express themselves thus at length, and our mothers and fathers in Alexandrine times brought this skill to such a peak of artistry that letter-writing was no longer a fact of daily life but a literary movement with its own laws and its own Mozarts and Salieris. And so, when this turbulent flood had reached its height, some other soul scooped up a bucket of it and sent it forth in the form of a book, richly bound in calf's leather with gold trim. A family secret splashed into the outside world, making a lot of noise, creating much sorrow, and enriching the crafty entrepreneur. And since in any civilized society a bad example is contagious, a whole crowd of crafty souls published many such books, making public many intimacies.

But that was not all. All this caught the eye of those who worked in the government and who loved other people's secrets. They immediately learned how to filter the essence from these epistolary outpourings and set up a broad-based business that they turned into a type of science. This gave birth to the so-called Black Cabinets, where employees read in secret the naive thoughts of our fathers. There weren't many such inspectors of correspondence, but they managed to get through mountains of letters, neatly and carefully resealing the envelopes without leaving a trace of their work. However, like any secret, this one gradually came to be known, and people flew into a rage and trembled. The letter-writing stopped, a literary movement faded, the divine spark disappeared, and the genre became no more than a practical necessity.

However, hearts still beat wildly, tormented by the need to turn themselves inside out. Where could they turn? And the bacchanalia began: diaries were born. Naturally, people had turned to them in earlier days, provincial young ladies and high-flown lovers had entrusted their passions to paper, and bewigged diplomats described the deaths of kings and their own cleverness. But diaries did not become a true art until quite recently.

The diarists wrote for themselves, burning with the banked fires of passion or antipathy, carefully hiding their creations in trunks, in secret desk drawers and wall safes, in haystacks and in the ground. Nevertheless, no matter how they tried to assure themselves that it all had to die with them, they were flirting with the future, imagining how someone would discover their diary in a thick layer of dust, its modest pages eaten by rust, and read them, and shed tears, enraptured by his ancestor's passionate frankness. And so they bought thick leather albums and affixed to them brass plates engraved with their names and ranks and dates of birth, followed by a dash expressing the modest but confident hope that someone would take the time to have the date of their death engraved also. Of course, my prince and everyone else whom I loved and love were exceptions to the rule. Even though they also practiced the art, they didn't worry excessively about form or exquisite style, nor did they hope for feverish interest from their descendants.

13

December 19

Hobbling, he went up to Petersburg from the sticks. He has not been permitted to live in the capital since the scandal in Paris, so he showed up, like a spy, in a false beard, riding in the post carriage. His limp is even worse. He's boiling over with anger and threatens the tsar with scandalous exposés. His sharp mind endears him to me, but his anger makes him ridiculous, and his unfettered vanity and feistiness make him hard to approach: With my mind I'm meant for great things, not for rotting out in the sticks. . . . No, getting involved in politics under Nicholas is a sure way to be sent to Siberia.

What would that do for anyone?

Really, there is nothing to politics now. I'm bored by my fellowmen and their idle chatter. My present existence is balanced on the backs of three whales: the books of the great skeptics, silent vodka drinking with Amiran Amilakhvari, and thoughts of Aneta: will she come or not? . . . Mr. van Schoenhoven threw snowballs at the window until Afanasy chased him away!

The baroness referred to was writing in her own diary at approximately the same time:

December 1844

The baron is too engrossed in his politics to give any serious attention to anything as trifling as our marriage. He tends to forget that a woman is an element of nature. His irreproachability is convenient, but, strangely, it saddens me. Today at lunch we had a Prince A., Archpriest of Moscow, and General Ch., a distant relative of the poet T. The baron, as usual, spoke of current events and tried to engage the rest in political talk, but not everyone was enthusiastic about it. . . . Men's pretenses are invisible only to themselves. I've realized that watching Myatlev. . . . I would not have believed the stories if I had not myself felt the tsar's feelings toward me. Last time he looked at me so openly and for such a long time, as though trying to memorize me. I told the baron about it. As usual, he made believe he was napping. Zinaida is in love with General P. The process is so stormy that they had to call the doctor, since she was so sick from suffering. The terrible thing is that she was being totally sincere. And it's so easy to burn that way. Is it all necessary?

December

This morning the baron left with the tsar for Tver. When I picture His tall figure and that smile, like a condescending god's, I go mad. I must meet Myatlev and let him know . . . prepare him . . . I hope that he won't faint. I have to remember to order *The Art Review* at Plyushar's. I don't have time for anything.

December

Today L. and Count N. and his wife lunched with me. Count N. said that we have the mightiest army in the world. That was to be expected. Napoleons are impossible nowadays. We cannot have equal rivals. I have a terrible migraine after last night. Myatlev, with his mind and background, could achieve great things, but his indolence, disdain for life, and lack of any social graces will ruin him. The baron is back from Tver, and he's in a brown study. Perhaps my fate was decided *there*?

December

I'm not sorry I was indulgent with Myatlev. He was pretending. I didn't try to unmask him. Yet I can see real passion behind the pretense. . . . Yesterday the tsar asked the baron, as if in passing, why the baron was hiding me. . . . How strange. "What did you tell the tsar?" I asked, watching his confused face. It's nice to see him confused! And a pity. . . . "I said that I was flattered by his interest," he replied. What will happen now? . . . Yesterday I refused to go to the opera, using my migraine as an excuse. The baron was totally confused and went alone.

14

YES, THERE WAS A good reason for my trepidation, and not a haphazard one. While setting her amusing and not very demanding snares in front of Myatlev, the baroness did not forget her main goal and waited for a signal. She kept remembering how, after dancing with her at a ball, the tsar would find her with his eyes in the midst of all the swirling ladies and their escorts and the soft light of his large eyes would reach her and command her not to forget him. This could not remain unnoticed in the convivial and greedy idleness of the court, and soon it was fairly common knowledge. Sensing the danger, I tried in some subtle way to warn my prince that the situation was not unfolding to his benefit. He paid no attention to my hints. They did not cool him off—on the contrary, they spurred him on. But the denouement promised to come soon.

And truly, just as I had thought, the charming but unstable chariot of love, in which the prince and his passion were riding, fell from a steep cliff and smashed to smithereens. Myatlev railed aloud against his failure, not forgetting to mention his rival's name at confession, telling the priest about his hatred for a certain Nicholas.

"Who is this man?"

"My neighbor and a nobleman," Myatlev replied in a whisper.

"Resign yourself and forgive him."

Leaving the church, Myatlev laughed bitterly. The prank reeked of childishness and did nothing to heal his fresh wound.

He walked from the church to cool off in the January frosts, feeling even more humiliated. But even though it was sunny, the wind penetrated his soul, and his topcoat, lined with fur, was almost no help against its icy needles. And, adding to his turbulent feelings, he could make out more and more clearly the squeak of someone's boots behind him, as if a secret spy were following him inexorably. There were very few pedestrians. Myatlev looked back several times, and the squeaking would stop immediately. When he stopped, so did the steps. When he moved on, so did they, neither closer nor farther away than before, and they sounded clear and firm, out of rhythm with his own vague and hurried gait. He hailed a cab, covered his frozen feet with an old, worn quilt, and, as soon as the horse set out, heard the familiar squeak. The horse ran—and the steps got faster. He turned around desperately, and the steps fell back and disappeared.

At home he ordered the doors locked securely. Nobody was to be admitted except for "that lady," me, and the limping man, if he should suddenly appear in Petersburg.

He seemed to have foreseen it; that very man immediately hobbled into his room, tossed his fur coat to Afanasy, and, when the servant was gone, pulled off his false beard, kissed the prince's pale cheek, and snickered.

"I kiss your cheek. Please accept it as a modest gift from an exile. In this kingdom, to put it mildly, you are the only person it does not disgust me to kiss. However, that is not the pleasantest gift that could be given a wonderful loner like you. But I have nothing else. Just my good points, to put it mildly."

He heard out Myatlev's tale of his lost love, and frowned.

"I loved you because you were cold toward the court, and you, to put it mildly, thrust yourself right into the stall. Or were you really experiencing delight and rapture? Did you go to this lady powdered and pomaded? Yes? Did you babble nonsense? For what? Does she have a marvelous bust?" ("She really does," thought Myatlev.) "And you prattled on and on. And that deputy of God on earth, to put it nicely, that pillar of morality and law, our Bear, who fears nothing so much as the curtailment of his personal power; that one, you know how he talks to a woman who, to put it mildly, has caught his eye? 'Come over here, dearie.'" (The Hobbler had caught Nicholas's pose quite well.) "'Well, well, let me see you. Why, you're charming; where have they been hiding you? Ha-ha—not from me, I hope?' 'I'm overjoyed, Your Majesty.' 'Do you think you can hide from me? Well, answer me.' 'Oh, Your Majesty!' 'Well, all right, I can see you're aflame. Why are things held up? Let's go up to my chambers. But please, make believe you're going up to see the paintings.' 'Oh, Your Majesty!' 'Have you ever been in my chambers before? No? Then see how modestly your monarch lives. Come closer, closer, I tell you. What's that you have there, eh?' 'Oh, Your Majesty!'" (Myatlev burst out laughing.) "And so on, to put it nicely. And the marvelous prince sheds tears, imagining this lady being led to the tyrant at bayonet point. Why, they're all tramps and just waiting for the lucky moment to befall them. They need dirt. They're all like that there—a mixture of Mongolian wildness and Byzantine treachery, covered with European clothes. A combination of ignorance and self-confidence. And you—!"

The story of Prince Andrei Vladimirovich Priymkov, or the Hobbler, as Myatlev called him behind his back without any meanness, was edifying.

The scion of one of the ancient houses, master of a large fortune, he was a man neglected by fate and therefore deeply miserable. A fine mind coupled with testiness, a desire for knowledge plus self-reliance, the wild fires of vanity and an unprepossessing appearance intensified by an ancient limp, aplomb, and, simultaneously, the habit of not maintaining a sufficient dignity—what a mad jumble nature had created! He was a brilliant student, but he was unable to please at the crucial moment, and fortune turned away from him in his early youth, breaking his rising career. As you know, in our higher circles you are welcomed for the clothes you wear and shown the door for the quality of your mind. Women had no interest in him; a political career beckoned his fellows. He decided to dedicate himself to science, for politics in combination with independent judgment was fraught with danger. So what did he take up? A marvelous memory, truly extraordinary capabilities, and a fierce grudge against the court that had disdained him brought the young prince to studying the genealogy of the noble families of Russia, to finding their soft underbellies. The description of family trees was a fascinating pastime and, to a certain degree, a safe one.

Finally he published a collection of notes, entitled *Russian Trees*, which was accepted by society with surprise and approval. His minor success turned his head. Winged, he set off for Paris, where his title and scholarly research made him at first a desired guest in the highest circles of French society. He published another book, under a pseudonym, which informed the French public about the most important Russian families, using all kinds of forbidden facts, not without political overtones. The young genius, feeling his oats, was happy that he had managed to communicate suppressed details about Grand Duke Mikhail Romanov, who in the seventeenth century had accepted a constitutional charter under oath when it was offered to him by the elected assembly. And it had existed in Russia for six years! Besides that, he also mentioned Peter the Great's immorality and that of his court—that is, in mentioning the forefathers of his enemies, he didn't forget to mention certain contemporary powers who had something to do with the murder of Paul I on the one hand and on the other with the condemnation of the Decembrists. A terrible scandal broke out. Some were angered by his political revelations, others by his antipatriotism, and still others—as funny as this may sound—by the fact that their families were not included in the scandalous chronicle. He was ordered back to Russia. With secret fear in his heart, the prince returned to Petersburg, where his fate was resolved rather mildly. His contemporaries expected at least Siberian hard labor for the young author, but he was generously allowed to live in the kingdom, in all its regions, except, of course, the northern capital. "His Majesty is not overlooking the readiness with which you returned from Paris," the prince was told. However, while pleased with his light punishment, he knew what had helped him: at exactly the same time, the well-known Golovin had sent a roughly worded refusal to return to Russia from Paris.

Now, living at his estate in Tula, the prince occasionally visited the forbidden capital, wearing his false beard and a wide-brimmed hat, and using a rented carriage. He would come for short periods, always visiting Myatlev, seeing in him a possible confederate with like-minded views, and without any further announcement would rush back, enriched with negative impressions.

"Baron Fredericks? Oh, him." The Hobbler frowned. "He's not from the German Frederickses, but the Kurland ones. He inherited his title from his grandfather—twice removed, to put it nicely. There was some story about it— But he's an ordinary sponger, not a spy—no, just a sponger—he couldn't handle spying. You know my feelings about the present government, and I'd be happy to hear that every other person is a spy, but I try to be fair. You can't be ruled by personal antipathies in science. Though it's not ruled out that we may be spied on right now"—he laughed—"your man, for instance, or someone hanging upside down in the chimney"—he looked out the window, tugging slightly at the shade—"or, to put it simply, that lone dreamer who's freezing under your windows."

A vague figure in a long coat, muffled in a cowl, was walking back and forth along the street, beyond the fence.

Myatlev laughed nervously, remembering the heavy steps that had pursued him. "As for Afanasy, you're completely wrong," he said firmly.

Priymkov's looks were far from perfect. Short, thin, with a concave chest, the face of a despairing monk, small penetrating, all-noticing eyes, and dressed in the latest fashion from Paris, obviously new but already irreparably crumpled, he presented a bizarre and sorry sight. He loved to talk, releasing the poisons that had collected in his soul, gesticulating savagely as he spoke, but he had learned to move slowly to cover up his lameness.

"All right, all right, Afanasy-Rafanasy," he said frowning. "I'm talking about spies in general. Espionage in Russia is not a new phenomenon, but it's unique here. A European spy, if you will, is a clerk in a specific department. That's all. We, however, besides having spies like that—we are part of Europe, after all, damn it!—draw most of our spies from volunteer ranks, spies who are not in it for the money but combine their basic, decent work with denunciations and surveillance, ready to race over to the Fontanka and passionately, to put it mildly, report someone's impropriety to Dubelt himself. For us, spying is not a service, but a form of existence, inculcated from childhood—and not by people, but by the air of the empire. Of course, if they are also given money on top of all that, they don't turn it down. However, most of them, ruining other people's lives, do it without revenge or rancor, from patriotism, and it's patriotism that makes them crawl into other people's chimneys and hang there upside down, singed, but memorizing every word."

"Our Dutch chimneys have a facing of thick ancient tiles," Myatlev laughed. "Sound doesn't travel through it. To hear you talk, one can't live at all."

A seed, dropped by chance, was growing, its pale shoot already showing through the soil, and Myatlev playfully touched the hot, raspberry-colored tiles, convex and carved. He tapped on them with a bashful smile, like a young and inexperienced doctor tapping a beautiful woman's bare chest, and felt a resonance in the chimney's depths, as though it had shuddered, truly like a live young body.

"Well, you really are a wizard," he said to the Hobbler. "I think there really is someone there."

"What? Who?" Priymkov exclaimed. "What do you mean? Ah, then have them light the fires, all the fireplaces. Put in plenty of branches, and pine cones would be good, very good!" He limped over to the window and bent back the shade. "And that one's in his place, too. Damn it!"

Behind the thick skin of the raspberry tiles, somewhere deep in the chimney, something rustled, crackled, and stirred. Priymkov listened closely, frowned, and stared at Myatlev with his piercing eyes.

"Well, you know— You've gone mad, to put it mildly!"

Myatlev wanted to laugh, but couldn't. He swung open the heavy oak door and looked out into the corridor. Tongues of flame flew out of the firechamber, illuminating the dark hall. Afanasy, dressed in red, just like a devil, with a red book in his hands, smiled, his red eyes sparkling. The prince spoke a few dozen hurried words to him, half in self-mockery, begging him: immediately, right away, without delay, think of something, some ridiculous thing, while he and the Hobbler watched from above; but do it immediately, instantly, while the man downstairs was still there and didn't leave them in tormenting uncertainty.

Afanasy took stock of the situation, bowed exquisitely, still smiling, and disappeared in the red smoke. Both princes, having blown out all the candles in the room, stationed themselves at the windows. The early winter twilight had not thickened, and they could see clearly. The unknown man in the cowl continued his slow perambulation along the iron railing, paying no attention to the house, apparently lost in some unpleasant thoughts. He was brought out of his reverie by the sound of the gate. He shuddered and froze—a bizarrely dressed man stood before him, wearing a light black cape, worn felt boots, an ancient, faded top hat, and white summer gloves—and a heavy knobbed cane added to his unbelievability.

The apparition removed his top hat, greeting the cowled stranger. The latter bowed and moved on. They separated, each reaching one end of the fence, turned, and headed for each other. They met at the gate, and the top hat was tipped once more. This was repeated several times until Afanasy (for it was he) said to the man in the cowl,

"How strange, if you will permit me to say so; I've been taking my constitutional here for the past year, and this is the first time I've seen you, sir."

The man in the cowl stopped unwillingly, sniffled, brushed a drop from his red nose and turned his head, but said nothing in reply.

"Perhaps you're a new neighbor?" Afanasy went on, as if this were a perfectly normal conversation. "Here's my house. I'd be happy to see you here. My physician prescribed walking against the thickening of the blood. When you walk at dusk, the blood thins. And it's very good, if you'll allow me to say so, for the liver." He raised his top hat. "The Marquis Troyat—and with whom do I have the honor?"

"Prince Myatlev lives here," the man in the cowl said glumly.

"And what did I say?" Afanasy parried with dignity. "What did I say? Will you believe it, sir, but three years ago my liver was over an inch wider than it was supposed to be. All the doctor's attempts to change it produced no results. The court physician, a German, Dr. Kuntz, ordered me to take walks at sunset. It got better immediately. Oh, yes, with whom do I have the honor?"

The man in the cowl was wearing cracked, cold, leather boots. Clearly he was thoroughly chilled, for he kept stamping his feet, dancing a little jig, and looking at Afanasy with angry despair, then fear, then supplication.

"And after my constitutional, if you'll permit me," Afanasy went on, "I run right into the house, to the stove, and partake of spirits, warming my back and my soul."

"What spirits?" the stranger asked, shaking another drop from his nose.

Afanasy didn't rush it. He took the poor man by the arm, gave him a shove, and led him slowly along the length of the railing.

"Allow me to say that I don't like that vodka," he said confidentially. "Vodka gives you migraine in the morning, swelling, and all that devilish stuff. After a walk, when the frost has gotten to you, you have to take some grog."

"Never heard of it," the stranger said, shuddering in the cold.

"Sir," Afanasy stopped, "wouldn't it be better if we went into the house, where I could give you some grog? I swear you won't be sorry." The stranger quickly pulled his arm away. "However, if you're not in the mood today, we can do it tomorrow. After all, if you'll permit me to say so, you'll be walking here every day, and so will I. Let's just be neighborly about it." The man backed away several paces. "I like you."

"Good-bye," the stranger said hoarsely, "many thanks." And he moved on, almost at a run.

Both princes were waiting impatiently for Afanasy. They demanded a detailed account of the meeting, warmly approved Afanasy's behavior, and laughed at the simpleminded spy.

"Well, well!" the Hobbler exclaimed in delight. "You old dog, you Fonaryasy!"

"Afanasy, if you don't mind, sir," the servant corrected him, bowed ceremoniously, and withdrew.

"So you see, Prince Sergei," the Hobbler said exultantly, "you see the living illustration to my tale. And you are absentminded, to put it mildly."

15

BY THE WAY, AFTER that idiotic duel Myatlev and I settled down in his room in the comfortable chairs upholstered in Dutch chintz, their springs resounding cozily and distantly, in the room where five Venetian windows glowed in the autumn sun and the golden parquet blazed with five silent bonfires into which we had stuck our feet.

We sat like nomads, spread out, arms outflung, eyes half-shut, drinking iced vodka, and the firm, freshly salted pickles cracked with a crunch on our teeth. We were silent, reliving our lives for the hundredth time, fishing from the depths the same shining splinters, now beginning to fade, covered with the weeds of forgetfulness. Once in a while we would exchange a look, and then his sudden bewitching and slightly guilty smile would flash at me, as though we had both been thinking about the same thing and he was embarrassed by his memories.

Oh, if that miracle were only possible! But we enlightened men are not inclined to superstition and do not seem to place any hope in miracles. Yet if you were to dig deeper in our souls, you would certainly find something borrowed from our naive and uneducated ancestors and see hope for a possible miracle glimmering in our cold and calculating consciousness. Thus, knowing full well that my faraway and beloved sister could never become Princess Myatleva, since it would bring her nothing but unhappiness, I secretly imagined that a sudden healing of my prince, the crossing of their earthly paths, a benign attitude of the gods, and God's goodwill would unite their hearts and cleanse their spirits. Actually, if it weren't for Myatlev's eternal and incurable torment and Maria's vow to live a solitary life after the death in Chechne of her beloved Kote Orbeliani, and if he were capable of loving deeply and strongly, and she could allow herself to break her vow—but there are no miracles. Above us an alien, distant land spread across the entire wall, and a long-gone time completed its sad orbit, and the small cluster of doomed, high-cheeked natives was still not thinking of its imminent and inexorable end. And there, in that crowd of the condemned, stood the man with the European face, with a high brow and a gaze whose nobility hid a sense of death and powerlessness before the harshness of nature. The conquistadores with evil faces were crawling up to them from the left side of the canvas, already imagining the belated cries of the wounded, and the moans of the dying, and the dusky, cold bodies. In their dreams they had already divided up the treasures of the natives that would fall into their clutches: heavy cold bars and unkempt Indian women, whom they were already embracing mentally, without any feeling of repugnance, since they had little sense of hygiene themselves. Their dirty, louse-ridden lace collared jackets and their boots with wooden buckles gave them a sense of superiority and courage. Their bearded, unwashed faces seemed to them the epitome of perfection. Slaves in their homeland, trained to depend and beg, often beaten and mocked by the aristocrats, they dreamed of power and rushed eagerly to achieve it here on this foreign, helpless shore. There was only a second left before the moment when their ruthless thirst for violence and power would be satisfied, while the natives, childlike in their trust, extended their dusky arms in welcome, not suspecting that they were doomed and that the gates of Heaven were the only thing that they could count on.

Gentlemen, our pride and our cultivated bloodlines, refined upbringing and exquisite manners, our preference for philosophy and the noble twinkle of our eyes—all this does not guard us from the insatiable microbe of servility, which penetrates our souls by the most amazing paths. Where are the preventive methods against it, and what does salvation promise us? Could it be that mankind, perfecting itself, is incapable of withstanding this absurd organism that is eating away the tribe of man? Look around and at yourself. In our presumptuous passion we fail to notice that the contagion has touched us as well, and here in our golden age, when ships are powered by steam and we are transported by smoking, speeding locomotives instead of capricious and fragile carriages, when the thoughts of mankind are directed to the skies in the hope of giving us wings, in our golden age when literature has already reached its zenith in the lines of both Alexander Pushkin and our present genius, Turgenev, whose works will never be surpassed, could it be that in our golden age, secretly hating our brothers, like our uneducated ancestors, we, too, try to establish ourselves at their expense, and that envy, hatred, and passion are the only things we have? Where is perfection then? In what? In our clothes? In our ability to tip our top hats? Our souls are empty and our eyes cold confronting another life. From early childhood we sharpen our weapons against one another, each of us hoping secretly that he will be the lucky one and that fate will bring him to power over everyone else. And that trifling microbe, eating away at our insides, forces us to be hypocrites and to lie, wheedle, and finesse until we can get close enough to stick the knife into our enemy's soft back and, after dancing on the corpse, to proclaim ourselves the only one. And for that, and that alone, we find the energy to forge fatal weapons, and we study the art of their use with pleasure, and we condone it by assuring ourselves and everyone else that it is only for self-defense. And when we get the opportunity to use it, we use it lightly and exult, seeing ourselves another step closer to our ancient goal. But it doesn't seem like enough, and next to our steel weapon we carry an arsenal of tried-and-true methods: lying, calumny, toadying—all of which are more terrible than the knife. And it's always like that. What is civilization? Why doesn't it ennoble us, cleanse us, heal us? In all ages and times there are born lone geniuses who are not concerned with the thirst for power over others and become the victims of their brothers, who in turn swear to their holiness as they gather to perform the next vile deed. History moves on, civilization flourishes and proudly shows only its facade, behind which, in dark corners, helpless geniuses are still murdered, squeezed, and robbed of the fruits of their tormented, inspired, and brief lives.

16

How would you like to hear that this man, despising all conventions, wormed his way into the family of the highly respected Baron Fredericks, leaving very obvious traces of his evildoing there? Of course, Madame Fredericks should have responded to his advances with more restraint, but this merely deepens his guilt, underlining his stubbornness and lack of moral restraint. And on top of that, he so turned her head that she practically visited that man openly in his house of debauchery.

Why am I writing this? It would seem that I have no business sticking my nose into someone else's private life, but permit me to ask why, in these times, when the majority of loyal subjects is trying to expend every effort to be of some use to the motherland, people like that man, setting themselves up in opposition to the rest, wallow in filth, in doing nothing, in destroying the sacred supports of our life?

[From an anonymous letter to the minister of His Majesty's court.]

17

Myatlev said nothing and stayed at home, reading his Greeks and Romans, and trying not to remember the messy story. Only once, when he was quite alone, did he attempt a few sarcastic remarks on the subject, but he wholly lacked the Hobbler's flair, and his light arrows were carried off by the wind.

Right after the break with the baroness, Myatlev got a half-year's leave, pleading problems with his old wound. The request went through channels and reached the tsar. We awaited his decision with faltering hearts. But luckily everything went smoothly and almost, to tell the truth, too quickly, as though someone derived great pleasure from removing the prince temporarily from the list of the most brilliant representatives of the Guards. We spent a lot of time racking our brains trying to figure out what it could mean, but then we decided that with all the difficult and repressive aspects of the tsar's personality it still could not be ruled out that he might want to be generous once in a while. However, we could also be sure that despite all that, his eagle eye saw far, and his generous heart burned with other feelings as well, and his vital mind remembered everything.

"You are still young," people said to Myatlev, "and the tsar might take this as a provocation."

But the ship had already cast off, and it was impossible not to take the risk.

Spring came. Everything was blooming, burgeoning, celebrating. The unbelievable scent of the soil and fresh vegetation rose to the skies, and one wanted to see the world only from its beautiful side. However, Myatlev began complaining of nightmares and a constant foreboding of disaster.

"I must get away," he said, "somewhere far, find some marvelous corner where there is no one. And live there, gathering herbs."

Oh, where are you, you marvelous little corners where man has never trod and where one can gather herbs?

By the way, these corners were becoming increasingly difficult to find, and the hope of finding one dwindled increasingly, and then, as though to dissipate completely the pathetic shreds of the beckoning mirage, late one evening an unexpected guest arrived at Myatlev's wooden three-story fortress.

Myatlev greeted his guest as became an old, unhappy bachelor greeting a representative of another, happy life, laden with well-being and the goodwill of the powers-that-be, the possessor of clear goals, healthy thoughts, and refined self-confidence.

He was prepared to see the familiar, reddish assemblage of uniform and stars, but Baron Fredericks was wearing a dark jacket, topped by a strange, checkered scarf.

It was all much simpler than could have been imagined, and in ten minutes they were chatting like old friends, and the baron did not refuse tea with a liqueur, and then somehow moved over to vodka, which the host preferred.

"There, you see," the baron said, eyes half-shut in contentment, "what you do to me. I'm not talking about dinner, which is always simple and sober for me, starting with *botvinnia* soup and ending with oranges, and I never have supper at all. You see."

While Myatlev did not take the words as total forgiveness, neither did he stiffen his guard. In any case, the baron's speech could be taken to mean that he did not intend some primitive form of revenge. What revenge could there be now?

After the second glass, Myatlev permitted himself to relax and feel like an equal in their unhurried man-talk. Since his guest was wearing neither frock coat nor uniform, and since he had not begun with reproaches but was quiet and even slightly sad, as though he were at fault in regard to his host, what could there be to worry about? The baroness's capricious shadow did not hover over them. Their conversation skirted her and was ready to flow into the familiar channel of political predictions, when suddenly words that seemed to have no meaning fell from the baron's pale and ordinary lips.

"You see," said the baron, "good sense permits us to be fair and not to have recourse to decisive measures, particularly since decisive measures in such delicate situations usually decide nothing." He laughed. "You and I are both set aside now, like two old chairs abandoned for an armchair. Let's not look at it as a reproach for our imperfections but rather as a paean to our ordinariness. Personally, I'm not hurt." And he peered into the prince's face with half-shut eyes.

And Myatlev realized there was no way to avoid the conversation, that this was the conversation, and that the baron, drinking constantly, would begin a series of revelations and, Heaven forbid, shed a tear or two. And Myatlev took a long drink from his glass, to be prepared for the onslaught, but the baron, strangely enough, began talking about something else, never mentioning the baroness, nor the triangle that had been created, with some fourth person hanging in the air, having no corner of his own. And the more the baron sipped, the farther his monologue moved from the basic passions, and the rosier his fresh, healthy face became, and finally, when it had taken on a completely youthful look, as well as a tipsy one, when the sea is only knee-deep and you want glory for your soul and not your pocketbook, the baron said,

"I always sympathized with you. The sad topics, the ones it's hard to joke about, we turn over to oblivion. As a wise woman said one day, constancy is enduring another person's traits. What? There, you see, you and I can become witnesses to the confirmation of one more truth. But let us not be primitively open. Rather, let us pretend to be madmen so as not to deprive ourselves of the right to speak."

In that free, charming, and unconvincing flood of confessions Myatlev noted a certain camouflage with which the master of the unforgettable Aneta tried to cover his disappointment. "He probably is pretending to be mad, so as to tell me everything and even insult me. But I don't understand," thought Myatlev.

Suddenly, in mid-word, the baron disappeared just as he had appeared.

Memories of this meeting continued to disturb Myatlev for several days, but it all faded as soon as he found out that nothing had come of the liaison between the baroness and the tsar. Either she hadn't pleased him, or else he wasn't the way evil tongues painted him. In any case, the unconvincing complaints of the baron lost their meaning, and his attempts at self-sacrifice seemed even more scrambled and sad.

18

ONCE, ON THE CORNER of Bolshaya Morskaya, Myatlev dismissed his carriage and walked down Nevsky Prospect, planning to drop in at the bookstore.

It was a beautiful noon in the middle of spring, one of those rare noons that are so prized in harsh Petersburg.

The streets were crowded with people in bright-colored clothes, some in summer garb; the excited talk cheered him up. He didn't want to think gloomy thoughts.

The prince's attention was caught by a young woman who stood out from the crowd. She was moving toward him much too quickly, passing the slowly flowing human river. She was wearing a dull black dress. Her hat did not cover her head, and her light hair fell loose to her shoulders. Her immobile gaze was directed somewhere in the distance, as though she were walking blind. She was rather tall, graceful, and her slightly stooped shoulders lent her an air of desperation. Myatlev thought her face was beautiful and full of pain. He turned and watched her, but she disappeared quickly, blending into the crowd.

Suddenly, as also happens in Petersburg, an oblique shadow covered the sun, coming from nowhere, and colors dulled, and large drops of rain drummed on the sidewalks and the street, beating down the dust and scattering pedestrians.

There were exclamations, laughter, colors blended, riders spurred their horses, carriages rattled more noisily, a few umbrellas exploded overhead here and there, but the rain increased, and all the pedestrians ran into archways or stores and cafés, hiding under whatever cover they could find. And the rain fell harder, and whistling streams of water, no longer mere drops, pierced the soil. A storm was brewing, and thunder grumbled in the distance.

Myatlev had run into a pastry shop at the first drops and, through the storefront, watched other people finding shelter. Nevsky Prospect, as far as he could see, was dead. The crazed elements were taking over the street, and only an occasional hackney could be seen, having no place else to go.

And then he suddenly saw the same young woman again. She was coming back, not noticing the streams of water, not hearing the thunder; water surrounded her like four walls; her water-logged black dress clung more tightly to her thin body; her stooped shoulders were more apparent; but now her beautiful head was lowered and she walked slowly, as though the need to hurry had passed, cooled off by the rain.

But was the rain its cause? What misfortunes had bowed the thin graceful body? What cruel secret lay in the depths of her soul?

"Ah," thought Myatlev as calmly as possible, "another victim of trust." But the sad young woman slowly floated past the window, surrounded by rain, and he couldn't look at her without pain.

A piercing cry came from somewhere, either in the café or out on the street. The lively conversation in the pastry shop stopped. A thunderclap burst over them. A white flame licked the window. A heavy carriage, in a solitary struggle with the weather, careened around the corner. Four gray horses beat their hooves on the water.

What power urged Myatlev out of the comfortable pastry shop was unclear, but he ran out onto the street and was immediately soaked to the skin. The coach was thundering on. Myatlev saw the wild eyes of the lead horse, the gaping mouth of the postilion, and he reached out and grabbed the thin body of the young woman and pulled her away, even though she resisted, twisting and hitting, and the rain blustered on, lightning blazed, and the thunderbolts blended into one long roar that smelled of the cold, foam boiled around them, and their every step seemed like a step into a chasm.

"Madame," Myatlev called, trying to reason with her, but he couldn't even hear himself. "Madame!" He shouted at the top of his lungs, but his cry was barely audible, choking in the flood.

The rest of the world appeared in the doorways and windows, staring out with curiosity and detachment. Myatlev got a firmer grip on her.

"Leave me alone!" she shouted.

For a moment he thought that she was winning. They staggered in the rain in a clumsy embrace, and the scales balanced. Then, with a surge of fierceness, and half-dissolved in the rain, he managed to overpower her and drag her into the doorway of a tavern that luckily appeared through the dank, windswept storm. He no longer felt her resistance and didn't hear what she was shouting: threats, entreaties, or words of gratitude. With maniacal persistence he shoved her through the door, pushed aside the people gathered in a knot on the threshold, stepped on their feet, elbowed them aside, not hearing their curses, and kept moving on with his mysterious trophy, deep into the tavern, past the stunned doorman, who suddenly recognized the prince and tried to bow, but didn't have time as the frenzied prince and the soaked, screaming witch rushed past, straight into the owner's quarters, and the door slammed shut behind them with an agonized groan.

A second later a marvelous group had gathered in the fetid living room: the owner himself, Savyely Egorov, who looked like a merrily bouncing ball, insolence and servility in his eyes; his consumptive, frightened wife in unnecessary curlers; his puffy daughter, trying to look younger, resembling her father in shape, in a blue apron and with a tray in her plump arms; a serving girl with a pockmarked face; gendarme Colonel von Müffling, in uniform and completely soused; and some other people, who managed simultaneously to look like the tavernkeeper's closest relatives and accidental passersby.

Savyely Egorov recognized Myatlev from his former debaucheries, and even though the prince seemed beside himself, Egorov still rolled around merrily, circling, shouting out orders in his hoarse voice; and everything began spinning, humming, water in a glass appeared in case someone fainted, and vinegar, and towels, and a warm robe, and a hot-water bottle, and another robe.

"Vodka!" Myatlev shouted, forcing his angry prisoner to sit on the blood-colored couch. "Will you sit down?"

"Please leave," the wife told everyone else.

The girl served a glass of vodka, and Myatlev brought it to the stranger's lips. She was shivering with the cold and her sobs.

"Your Excellency"—Egorov rolled up to Myatlev—"I think it would be better if the young lady was moved to the women's quarters."

"Of course," Myatlev agreed, "but drink this first, madame."

THE STRANGER: Don't touch me.
VON MÜFFLING (Hiccuping): P-pooor thing.
THE WIFE: Everyone out. Please, everyone out.
MYATLEV: Drink this, will you please drink—
THE STRANGER: Get away from me.
VON MÜFFLING: P-poor thing.

Egorov's daughter helped get the people out of the room. The stranger, without wiping her tears, without lowering her face, wept silently, pushing away the glass of vodka. Frenzy overwhelmed the prince again. He nodded to the innkeeper, and the two of them held back the thin creature's head and poured vodka into her mouth.

"No!" she shouted and hit her knee with a small fist. "No, no!" and hit herself again, hard, like a man, and once more, and again, hitting and shouting. "What do you want with me? Ohmygod, you villains, did I ask you to? Don't bother me with your good deeds! How dare you keep me here, ohmygod!"

"Madame, madame," Egorov begged, staring at the prince in horror, "madame, please let me take you—to the room, madame—to my wife's room, madame. You'll be more comfortable getting dry there. Madame—"

"Ohmygod, how terrible!" the stranger cried, hitting her knee.

But Myatlev was so determined now that no entreaty or curse could make him waver. At his command the women hoisted the pale, ruffled, wet, weeping creature by the arms and, surrounding her, took her away to dry and comfort her. She no longer resisted.

"Ohmygod! Ohmygod!" rang in the prince's ears, while he, left alone, tried to collect himself. Really, it was—"Ohmygod!"—if you looked at it objectively, it was forcing some poor woman—what swinery. "Ohmygod!"

Suddenly the door opened and von Müffling burst in. A concentrated confusion floated in his blue, murky eyes.

"Prince," he said with difficulty, "it looks like th-that poor woman needsh he'p—I'm ready—"

"Oh, thank you, thank you so much," Myatlev hurried to say. "Everything will be all right, don't worry, I'm touched, this is very touching of you to offer."

"Rilly?" said von Müffling. "F-f-fine," he said, and walked out without bending his knees.

Myatlev was called upstairs, and he went up the shaky steps into the lacy, canary-colored room of Egorov's wife, where his lady was sitting on a lace couch, wrapped in a quilted robe. Coming in, he was afraid he'd hear her angry screams, see her pale face and her eyes full of terror and contempt, but nothing like that happened. On the contrary, there was a light rosiness in her cheeks, her big gray eyes looked at Myatlev with quiet surprise, and her long light hair, dried and thick, rested loosely on her sharp shoulders.

"I hope you're better?" he asked carefully.

"I'm drunk," she said simply, like an old friend, and laughed, and a transparent, soft warmth cascaded from her eyes.

"Some story," Myatlev said. "You were shivering, completely chilled. I had to take pity on you."

"Why was that?" She laughed, not too kindly.

She had a low, thick gypsy voice. Her movements were no longer hurried. It was as though her calm had never left her, and everything that had occurred had happened to someone else. Only the way she held the edge of the robe—that clenched fist, so like a child's clinging to its mother's skirt—that was the only sign of something wrong; something was seething and could erupt any second, and Egorov's consumptive wife was counting the silver spoons in a corner and had no intention of leaving, and Egorov's daughter, settling her clumsy body on a chair, mouth agape, stared shamelessly at the prince and the lady.

The spoons rattled and made it hard to follow the conversation.

"Mother," she frowned, "that's enough!"

"Why should he pity me?" the stranger asked. "Sit down. You can sit here, next to me, you won't disturb me. I'm completely drunk, ohmygod." And she laughed. "Well, what will we do next? What are your intentions for me? What are your plans? Will he grab me again? Will you grab my arm again, or will I be able to act as I see fit?" And she frowned.

"Please," Myatlev said quickly, "I wanted to help you. Is my desire to help you so suspect?"

"Why should he want to help me? Did I ask him to? I never asked him in my life, ohmygod— I don't know you, kind sir. What was the matter with you—you grabbed my arm in full view of everyone. Do you manhandle everyone like that?"

"No, not everyone," Myatlev replied, like a boy.

"Ah, not everyone! So I must have seemed— So he thought—
Well, sir, forgive me— Ohmygod, they poured vodka in me!
That's all I needed."

Suddenly he realized that she was marvelously beautiful,
devilishly beautiful, particularly here, amid the laces, and these
women, and the silver spoons, under these low ceilings, answer-
ing no one and pretending to be drunk; he had to leave, but she
was so beautiful that he couldn't just bow and walk out.

Egorov's wife kept counting the spoons faster, feverishly.
They rang so loud that their words were drowned out. Like
silver fish they cascaded from one hand to the other, clattering
and sparkling, and then into a bowl, and then into a drawer, and
then into her hand, and from one hand to the other.

"Mother, that's enough."

Von Müffling came in the open door on stiff legs. His light-
blue uniform glowed against the canary walls like a piece of sky
framed by a withered summer.

"I'm completely confoozed," he said, trying to smile. "Worried. D-d-do you need anythin'?"

The stranger looked up at Myatlev in fear. Then she walked
behind the folding screen.

"All r-r-right," von Müffling said in satisfaction. "I'll have
them call a—a—car-rriage." Then he nodded at the screen.
"P-poor thing." And disappeared.

"I'm asking you," she said in a singsong voice from behind the
screen, "to leave with me. If you're so kind and generous, surely
you would do that? Why wouldn't you leave with me?"

"But I'm waiting for you," Myatlev said happily, glad that
everything had resolved itself, and seeing a secret signal in it.

"Interesting, why should he be waiting for me—" she muttered as she dressed. "What a strange man, ohmygod—" And
she coughed.

Slowly and ceremoniously, accompanied only by profound
silence (for the silver waterfall had stopped), they descended
from the stuffy lacy heavens and through the curious crowd

down a living corridor. She'd had to put on the damp dress and was shivering again. Egorov rolled after them with a careful respect.

The rain had stopped a long time ago, but heavy clouds still hung over the city. A sharp cold wind was blowing, and the cheery, colorful crowd was gone, and now there were only the gray-faced people in worn civil-service uniforms with brass buttons who crowned the end of the day. Their movements were mechanical, a scuffling walk; a smell of burned onions hung over the street, spreading over the city, rising to the sky, the smell of burned onions, sour cabbage, and sweat. Their dull eyes blended into one, and in it, in that huge eye, at the very bottom of its huge dull pupil, stirred an ugly happiness that came from anticipating the quotidian bliss promised by the smell of burned onions.

A hired carriage with its doors flung open was waiting at the curb outside the inn. Next to it, weaving, dissolved in a foggy smile, stood von Müffling, as if welcoming guests at his own front door.

"Please," he said, extending his hand to the stranger, and helped her into the carriage, almost falling in the process.

Myatlev thanked him, barely containing his laughter.

Savyely Egorov tapped Myatlev on the shoulder and whispered in his ear, "Your Excellency, don't be angry, but my women tell me that they know your lady. 'We know her,' they said. It seems everyone knows her in the sense that she's well— well, you know what they say about that. Not only my women, but everybody. And I know your kindness." And he laughed. "We know you, Your Excellency."

"P-poor thing," said von Müffling, bowing, and went back into the tavern on his stiff legs.

In the carriage, with no embarrassment, she pressed her shivering body close to Myatlev; she leaned her head, smelling of rain, on his shoulder, and he had no choice but to put his arm around her, which he did.

"Ohmygod, where are we going?"

"You're going to my house," he said firmly. "I'll be improper to the end."

No protest followed; how could she protest? She merely looked up to take a peek at his eyes.

"What a strange man, he didn't even ask my name. What hot hands he has, ohmygod! No, no, don't take them away. What's the matter with you? Don't take them away, I beg you. Is it a long ride? Will there be a fire, and tea, and jam? Ohmygod, it means nothing to him! And we'll dry my dress? What a strange man; he dragged me into a tavern, almost sprained my arm, forced me to drink vodka, set some dirty monsters on me, and now he's hugging me—and now I'm warm, and he's promising me tea as well." She laughed happily. "Enough, this must be a dream! Oh, if only I could protect my chest from the wind—"

Myatlev quickly put his other arm around her.

"What a strange man," she laughed, moving even closer to him. "Won't even ask where I live and do I need to be taken home," she said in a whisper, and added something like "Confidence . . . force . . . torture . . . insolence . . ."

19

APPARENTLY HALF-ASLEEP IN the iron embrace of the over-joyed Myatlev, twenty-two-year-old Alexandrina Zhiltsova muttered on, not worrying where the hired Petersburg coach might be taking her.

Her father, Modest Victorovich Zhiltsov, had been buried alive in the thick prison walls of faraway Zerentuy since the well-known incident on Senate Square in December 1825. Inexorable fate had played him a cruel trick, separating him, an innocent man, from his young wife, two-year-old daughter, and an uneventful, proper life.

On December 13, 1825, a day before the unhappy event, he arrived in Petersburg from distant Kaluga to do some business concerning his estate, which was threatened with all kinds of problems. Being a gregarious and kindly man and having many friends among the Guards officers, with whom he had served until his recent retirement, he immediately set out to visit them. Finding several of them out, he decided to call on them the next day, and on December 14 he got into his sleigh and went visiting. On Senate Square he saw the ranks of the Moscow Regiment, surrounded by curious crowds. Thinking that this was a routine inspection or parade, and seeing several old friends among the officers strolling in front of the square, he jumped out of the sleigh and ran to them. When after some time he finally realized what was going on—cut off from everything as he was in the sticks, he could never have imagined anything of the sort—it was too late. Troops headed by the young emperor himself surrounded the square. Zhiltsov, horrified, managed to get away and back to the hotel safely, with only one thought: to sleep and leave for his estate first thing in the morning. And he did sleep, but he was too slow in leaving the capital. Someone saw him, someone reported him, rumors began, and they came for him. Seeing nothing more than an unfortunate mistake in the situation, Zhiltsov did not argue, hoping for a fast hearing. He was taken to a guardhouse, where he found himself sharing a room with a commissary officer he didn't know, who had also been arrested in connection with the incident. Two days later the officer was summoned to interrogation and returned glowing and excited. It turned out that his case had been resolved happily because, he reported, he told them the honest truth, and those who tried to weasel out of it and justify themselves, well, it was too terrible to contemplate what would happen to them.

"But my honest truth—is complete ignorance," said Zhiltsov, smiling.

"Uh-uh, buddy," the officer laughed. "Everyone who pleads ignorance is being locked up. And you know what that means, don't you?"

And truly, the next day the officer was released, and Zhiltsov was taken for questioning. Of course, his innate nobility and his sense of propriety kept him from any thought of denying that on the infamous day he had been among the rebels, but he wanted to explain how it had happened. He was asked to name his officer friends, and he listed them simpleheartedly and even gladly, since they had all been seen there and silence might have been misconstrued as obstruction.

"Have you yourself ever had occasion to express any disapproval of our present laws?" he was asked.

"Never!" he cried in horror.

They sent him back to the guardhouse, suggesting that he try to remember everything accurately and write it all down, thereby mitigating his lot.

He paced his cell, suffering, muttering, thinking about his young wife, damning the day he decided to go to Petersburg, which had grabbed him, an innocent man, in its clutches; and he started writing, remembering every thought he had ever had about possible reforms that might have helped his fatherland blossom even more. His confession was sent off, and they forgot about him.

He waited tensely many long months for someone to come and declare him completely innocent, and he pictured how he would describe and explain it all to his wife, whom he couldn't reach and who, in all probability, was going out of her mind with worry.

Finally the summer came and in the commandant's quarters in Peter and Paul Fortress he learned to his horror that he had been stripped of his nobility and sentenced to twenty years at hard labor.

For several days after his sentencing, he was not himself; he recognized no one, did not touch his food, talked to himself, and wandered from one corner of his cell to the other, unsleeping.

His young wife, barely making ends meet on their small estate that had been mortgaged and remortgaged, finally learned her husband's fate and had a breakdown so severe that no doctors and no medicines could ever restore her to health.

The responsibilities of bringing up a young girl gave her some strength, and the thought that he had really taken part in a conspiracy without telling her and was now paying for his grievous sins was one that she got used to. Now she lived only for the sake of little Alexandrina, trying to give her a decent education, no matter how tight their financial situation.

Several years flew by, and then a long letter came from him, and not by the official mail but passed through dozens of hands, thereby avoiding the censors. And there she learned the truth about the misfortune that had befallen her husband, and that he had suffered unnecessarily and guiltlessly, and now, though innocent, was doomed to further inhuman suffering. And that, plus the knowledge of her helplessness before the government with its complex procedures and ambiguous intentions—all that was the final straw. A few days later she died. The estate was quickly sold to cover their debts, and Alexandrina was taken in by a distant relative—the only one—in Moscow. There the girl began a new life, remembering her father always, having heard so much about him from her mother, and desperately dreaming of his speedy return.

Her life in Moscow was not bad. She was pitied, and she was permitted to do many things. She was rather shy, but loved serious reading and music. The relative's own nephew and sole heir lived in the house, a nice young boy, a student at the university. Sixteen-year-old Alexandrina fell madly in love with him. He returned her feeling, and everything probably would have gone well if the evil spirits had only left them alone and let the young people mature and prepare for connubial bliss. But the terrible fate that attached itself to the entire Zhiltsov family found its victim even in the hustle and bustle of Moscow. Following an incident at the university, several students, including Alexandrina's love, were sent into the army, and after a month in the Caucasus and a skirmish with the natives, he was mortally wounded. Alexandrina confessed in desperate frankness that she was with child. There was a storm. Her relations with her benefactress were broken, and she was asked to leave the house, since her behavior was seen as an attempt to gain the inheritance.

Proud Alexandrina slammed the door, taking with her a small trunk with her few possessions and her bitter memories. She had no place to go. Losing all hope and a roof over her head at sixteen—what could be worse? She decided to wait for evening and then, when it came, ran to the Moscow River down the well-worn paths taken by many predecessors.

I don't know if this is to be regarded as good luck or not, but someone's strong hand kept her from realizing her tragic plan. The man who saved her was a professor of medicine. He let her have her cry—a young girl's sorrow is not long-lasting—and with the wave of a magic wand, a new world opened before her. The professor was a widower, middle-aged. He lived in a fine apartment on Prechistenka Street with his small daughter. He had a maid and a cook. He invited Alexandrina to live in his house, where she would have her own room and all the rights of a member of the family. In return she would teach his daughter music and French. After standing on the threshold of death, she found his offer so improbable in this harsh world that her very life would be a paltry recompense. But the realization that she had not yet confessed her chief secret forced her to refuse. He didn't let her go. He accepted her refusal, but still talked Alexandrina into spending at least the night in his house, so that she could collect her thoughts, and then she could be on her own. She was in such a state that not to take advantage of such a nondemeaning offer would have been stupid. And she agreed.

They entered his apartment after midnight. His daughter was asleep. The maid, asking no questions, got Alexandrina's room ready. It was warm and cozy, smelling of hot wax and fresh sheets. They dined together. Then, mustering her courage, she told him her secret. "That?" he laughed. "That's all? And what am I for? You won't have time to blink before it's all gone." And she stayed.

A week later she was completely well. A marvelous stroke of

luck had freed her from the last vestige of her former life.

Soon after that, he appeared in her room one night wearing a robe and carrying a candle. She was frightened and tried to struggle, pleaded with him, but he tossed off his robe in silence and lay heavily beside her.

Time passed. She busied herself with the little girl and gradually accustomed herself to her life and the nocturnal visits of her elderly host. The professor was tall, good-looking, with reserved and noble manners. On Sundays they went to church and then walked around the boulevards or headed for Sokolniki Park.

His nocturnal visits, his embraces, his gentle words, pronounced in a hurried whisper, no longer frightened her. She came to regard their cohabitation as the inevitable payment for her rescue. But his passion grew, vague hints became reality, he became irritable, lost his usual calm, and finally, embarrassed and stuttering, confessed that he loved her. Strange, but she felt no fleeting triumph nor even the slight headiness of victory. On the contrary, his passionate confession scared her again, and she mumbled and stuttered, too, trying to explain herself, but deep in her heart everything was calm and steady and indifferent, and her conscience didn't bother her.

She was seventeen when on a fine May day, walking with her charge along a boulevard, she noticed that a handsome young officer was following her. An hour later he approached her and introduced himself. She liked him. They met several times after that on the same boulevard, and one day they agreed to meet alone. He took her to his bachelor apartment, and, as it turned out, she spent a week there without ever coming out. She sent a farewell letter to the professor, and the officer offered her his heart and hand, applied for and got leave, and brought her to his estate outside Moscow.

They lived there for several months, but the idea of marriage came up less and less frequently, and she felt that he had cooled toward her and felt burdened by the relationship, and that was probably why he was drinking heavily and only seemed passionate when he was drunk. And then, regretting nothing, she left him quietly and returned to Moscow.

What happened then? She got a position as governess in a merchant's family, and she lived there, never losing the hope of meeting her unhappy father. But lustful and evil fate arrived on her doorstep one night in the person of the master of the house. The young woman defended herself ardently. The merchant's wife, well acquainted with her husband's predilections, appeared in response to Alexandrina's cry, slapped her face, and ordered her out—immediately—this very minute.

Alexandrina was almost eighteen when this happened. She was attractive, knew how to behave in society, and traces of her experiences had not yet marred her pure face. She gave private lessons and earned money, proud of her independence, even though the money was pitiful and came in irregularly.

The professor of medicine ran into her accidentally. He was much older and shabbier. He almost cried when he saw her, and he begged her to return. But she shuddered at the thought and remained unmoved.

She was renting a small, sad room in a cold, four-story house near Saint Nicholas-on-the-Sands. The room was practically under the roof, which made it hard to keep it warm in winter, and it was unbearably stuffy in summer. But it had one marvelous advantage that had attracted Alexandrina: it was remote from the other apartments and had a separate entrance from the stairs. All kinds of lowlifes lived in the house, drunken, greedy, thieving, and envious, but Alexandrina kept to herself, creeping up to her room at nightfall. She would have been completely happy here, despite all the drawbacks that seemed intentionally created by mankind, if it had not been for the constant pestering of a hotel waiter who lived next door. Almost every night, when he was certain his family was asleep, he would creep to her door, breathing heavily, and try to open it, while the young woman languished in helpless revulsion. Sometimes, reeking of alcohol, he would meet her on the stairs and ask, "I'll come tonight? All right? You'll pity me?" But even that would have been all right; she was learning not to be offended by the advances of men, seeing their withered souls and puny bodies behind their arrogant, broad shoulders. She was afraid of the sneaky, furtive glances from the wife of her tormentor, and her female intuition told her that a storm was brewing.

As she grew older, she realized that she was living exclusively on the hope of seeing her father return and that this hope, which had burned within her since childhood, had now become her flesh and blood. For all those years she had been inventing a story about her marvelous life in her letters to her mythical father, and in his rare replies he had expressed his delight in her good fortune and thanked God for His kindness to an orphan. Until then he had never asked her for anything, but finally, apparently believing in her good fortune and at the end of his rope, he asked her to write a grief-laden plea to the tsar to pardon an old, loyal, and innocent veteran. And he also, for the first time, asked her for money.

Crying over the letter, Alexandrina sent him all the money she had, which wasn't very much, promising to send more, much more, soon, and sat down to write to the tsar. Her letter was a long one, full of despair, and it flew off to Petersburg, joining a huge flock of long, desperate, and vain calls for mercy.

And she redoubled her efforts to earn more money, but money never rushes to those who need it most. She didn't eat enough or sleep enough, got wet in the autumn rain, froze in the cold, but still ended up with almost the same amount of money as before. Despair engulfed her with new intensity, and her shame toward her father tormented her whenever she pictured him waiting in the hope that he might finally share in her fantastic good fortune.

The exhausting battle undermined her health. A light flush, a cough, and a constant chill were bad signs.

The house in which she lived became more and more hostile, apparently stirred up by the waiter's wife. She was whistled at openly when she crossed the dark courtyard and ran up the dirty stairs. And she thought more and more often of the professor of medicine, but strangely, when she thought of him, she didn't picture the nights, the bed, her revulsion at his embraces, but his kind face, his restrained manners, and warmth, and light, and peace. And her mythical father was awaiting her wealth and depending on the mercy of the tsar, and, having forgotten any world but the one of hard labor that he inhabited, he couldn't imagine that in the one where his noble and lucky daughter lived there could be dirty boardinghouses, drunken waiters, consumption, or whistles pursuing her.

On the rare days when she permitted herself the luxury of staying home to remain in bed and warm up, the waiter's wife would show up. She would open the door and, without crossing the threshold, stare long and contemptuously at the feverish Alexandrina. And so she had to keep her door locked during the daytime, too, to keep her room safe from prying eyes. It was leading up to one solution only: running away. But she put it off, trying to conserve her waning energy.

However, if a storm is brewing, thunder will roar, and late one evening, coming home, she smelled the strong odor of pitch on the stairs. It smelled as though all the residents of that damned house had polished their boots with pitch for a holiday. The smell was unbearable on the top landing, and when she lit a match to find the lock, she saw a huge, spreading, greasy splotch on her door. Fear, disgust, and outrage overcame her. The disgusting smell choked her. She ran into her room, shutting the door tight to stave off the terrible smell, but the offensive odor was even stronger in the room, and in the candlelight she discovered the same black spreading sign on the inside of the door and on the white wall over her bed. There were greasy spots of pitch on the pillow and blanket, and the whole floor was spotted by someone's frenzied brush. And that was the limit. Controlling her sobs, she gathered her belongings and left the gloomy dive.

Despair brought her back to Prechistenka Street, to the familiar apartment. The professor was terribly pleased to see her, kissing her hands and weeping. His dead gaze lit up once more, and his stooped shoulders straightened. At that moment everything in the house seemed unchanged, and she breathed freely for the first time in many years, for now she feared nothing. She moved back into her old room, where everything had been kept as she had left it. She lay on her old bed and thought how right she had been to discard her girlish prejudices about feeling demeaned by his touch, how right she had been to return to the man who loved her and suffered without her; and that was why, when the door opened and he appeared in a robe and with a candle, she smiled sadly at him, nodded, and shut her eyes. They didn't sleep all night, and it even seemed to her that she loved that old and kindly lover of hers. He learned of her travails and about her father: he kissed her and cried, and tried to comfort her. She began to think that she had never left him, that this was her home, and that the professor was the only one she could count on now.

However, in the morning she noted marked changes in the apartment, which she had not noticed the evening before. The rooms were all run-down and shabby, the maid had long gone, the furniture was worn, and the cook remained only because of old ties and the fact that she had nowhere else to go. The daughter had grown considerably and was cold toward Alexandrina. It turned out that the professor had been forced to stop lecturing a long time ago, since he had taken to drink after Alexandrina left him, and now he was only called once in a while to certain homes as a private physician, for which he received only modest fees. Her hopes for food, comfort, warmth, and financial help for her father crumbled, but it was too late to back out and too terrifying, for loneliness is worse than poverty. So Alexandrina rolled up her sleeves once more and started giving lessons again.

Their relations grew simpler. He did not hide anymore; he spent the night in her room and left her only in the morning. The news of her disease shook him, and crying—this happened often—he promised to heal her; he would exert himself, they would go to Switzerland, and there, in that paradise, she would feel herself reborn. She believed him because she wanted to get better and because she saw how much he loved her. But a few hours later that same evening, he was drunk with a desperate fury, and that was the case the following evening, and all the ones after that. And drunk, he would come to her room, attacking her, demanding love. She tried soothing him, putting him to sleep, lecturing him, but he was stubborn and persistent. She tried fighting him off, again feeling repelled by his attentions, but he overcame her. In the mornings he cried, caressing her with trembling hands, calling himself a torturer and bastard, and he made more empty promises.

Meanwhile an answer to her letter arrived, signed by Benkendorf himself, informing her with icy cordiality that the tsar, in all his kindness, did not think it possible to pardon a dangerous criminal against the state, since such a pardon could be construed as an unfair act in regard to other criminals serving out their sentences, and therefore she should resign herself and wait for a general amnesty to be declared.

Fighting the unbearable pain brought on by this news, she decided to go to Petersburg and throw herself at Benkendorf's feet. Her decision was firm, but the pathetic professor begged her not to leave him alone. He wept like a child, hugging her knees, kissing her hands, shouting in despair that he, too, had claims on her kindness. Out of compassion, she kept postponing her departure, and then, strangely, her cursed fate suddenly took pity on her, as usual, of course, in a cruel way: on an early spring day it pushed the drunken professor under the wheels of a heavy carriage, freeing him from suffering, and her from his love. But the new shock took its toll. Her disease exploded with a bright flame. There could be no thought of the trip to Petersburg. As a wounded animal hurries to hide in its lair, as a migratory bird, exhausted by the migration, tries with its last ounce of strength to reach last year's nest, so did she, sucked dry by the disease, remember her childhood home, and headed for Kaluga Province, to her father's former village, where, as she knew, her old wet nurse still lived.

Everything really was just the way she had remembered it. And the old nurse was alive and recognized Alexandrina, and was happy to take her into her small cottage, where she lived alone. She fed Alexandrina milk, pitied her, and kept her from sad thoughts. The young woman strolled in the woods and helped the old nurse with the housework. Two months passed this way, and the peace, fresh air, and kindness were taking effect. The terrors and wounds of the past tormented her less and less, when suddenly a young gentleman came to see her, the son of the present owner of the Zhiltsovs' former estate. He was dignified and spoke slowly, but Alexandrina saw clearly that he was agitated. His words struck her very heart, for in them she heard once again the voice of her insatiable fate. He had learned that she was here, and he felt it was his duty to call. Was she planning to stay here long? Did she have any interest in his and his mother's estate? She reassured him that she didn't even think about it. "And it was all so long ago, I don't even remember a thing." "Well, I'm very happy to hear that," he said dispassionately, "but Mama is quite worried by your extended stay in *our* village." He bowed politely and left, but this time Alexandrina didn't need to be warned twice. She knew that the human imagination was very refined and capable of inventing something much more effective than a pitch-smeared door. This was a signal, a clear signal, and, embracing her weeping nurse, she left for Petersburg.

She was so depressed by everything that was happening to her that during her first day in Petersburg she didn't think once about where she was. But the next day, more relaxed, she saw the northern capital around her. And she realized how much time she had wasted in Moscow instead of being allied in battle with the burgeoning life-forces that were here, sustained by the cold but firm support of the royal granite of Petersburg. Those were her thoughts as she prepared herself for her final, desperate confrontation with the omnipotent Count Benkendorf.

As soon as she arrived in Petersburg she submitted a request to the Third Section for permission to call on the count, and while waiting for an answer, went about arranging her life.

She was twenty-one then. She was, as they say, in her bloom, and hope had not left her completely. The disease, developing deep inside, had not touched her beauty, and its light flush only made her more attractive. Her big gray eyes, through some miracle, retained their calm and mystery, and no one could guess what was going on in her tortured, turbulent soul.

She was praying very diligently to God in those days, asking Him to take pity on her and to be her generous guardian. And probably her prayers were heard, because she did not have to spend a long time looking for work. Quite by accident, which amazed her, she found a position in the house of the wealthy widow of some councillor of state, an elderly, idle woman, with no relatives, who needed a companion, confidante, or someone to amuse her. Alexandrina read didactic French novels to her, walked with her, listened to her complaints about life and her boring stories about her marriage, with all the details and fine points that the widow remembered so well. Life flowed on monotonously, without joy and without drama, which made Alexandrina very happy. In general, Petersburg at first glance seemed much more restrained and steady, more dependable, and even more compassionate than bustling, noisy, busy Moscow, with its naked curiosity and fierce, annihilating hardheartedness. It seemed that no one was interested in anything but himself, and this was very convenient and attractive for a wounded person like Alexandrina.

But unfortunately this didn't last long. A person finding himself in close proximity to another person can no longer remain calm and concentrated, but must influence, affect, lecture, and even repress his neighbor.

"You like the summer?" the widow asked after a month or two of their life together. "How strange. You must agree that spring is the best time of the year. What's the matter with you, my dear? How can the two even be compared?" And then: "You drink with these tiny sips, and there's this gurgling sound.

Habit? But it's terrible; I find it upsetting. You must drink like this." And then: "Why don't you braid your hair? Braids are one's best feature." And the next day: "I'm sure that a braid would become you." And a day later: "Do you think I'm wrong? No, a braid is an ornament. Everyone knows that." And again, a day later: "I'm tired of telling you the same thing over and over. And I'm quite hurt that I worry about *you*, what things would be better for you, and you—" And Alexandrina braided her hair. After that, another story began: "He likes you. He's a very good person. Why shouldn't you—what do you mean, you're not interested? In any case, you could be nicer to him." And then: "What's the matter with you, my dear? I'm not insisting on marriage; do as you think best, but it would be improper to refuse him." And finally: "You could at least go for a walk with him; he doesn't bite." "Madame," Alexandrina said softly but firmly, "it is impossible." The widow took offense and said that Alexandrina was unbearable. Alexandrina tried to explain that she had her own habits and desires and that she couldn't wear a braid when she didn't like it, or drink tea in large gulps, burning her unaccustomed throat, and she couldn't wear dresses with that many ruffles, which Madame had insisted on, if she would recall. But the widow announced that she was paying money, and for her money— "And then," she added, "you have a cough."

And Alexandrina heard a distant ringing; it was her small hope shattering on the oak parquet of someone else's house.

Her money was running out. She couldn't find any other job. She tried turning to God again, but He was deaf to her entreaties. And then came word of the untimely death of Count Benkendorf, and that meant darkness was descending. Blow followed blow. There wasn't a glimmer of hope anywhere. But suddenly, in a final mockery, she was told that Benkendorf's successor was ready to see her. Long before the appointed hour, she was in Count Orlov's waiting room. Her anxiety was so strong that she saw everything as in a fog, and moved by touch. Everything that was said to her fell into her consciousness, but she didn't understand it, and she didn't see the man who was talking to her, even though she looked at him with her large gray eyes and even nodded in the appropriate places, and even said something in her rich gypsy voice. When she left and went along the embankment of the Fontanka River, she still thought that the meeting was yet to come, and she repeated the words she was going to say to the count over and over, like a lesson. Finally she came out on the Nevsky. It was a sunny May day. It was crowded. People's clothes were colorful. And suddenly she remembered the entire conversation very clearly and realized that her unhappy father, whom she had never seen, had died in exile in Siberia. The slow, indolent, and cheerful movement that she saw on the street was in such contrast to everything that she felt at that moment that she wanted to scream at them, to stamp her feet, but she merely increased her own speed and almost ran, not knowing where. Thunder. The rain started. A thought as bright as lightning hit her: it was all over, and there was no hurry. She stopped, stood for a while, and then moved slowly in the opposite direction. A wind attacked the street. The light and misleading warmth of spring disappeared. The old, soaked dress made her even colder. But Alexandrina felt nothing, and probably would have walked on indefinitely, but suddenly a heavy coach careened toward her, and she opened her arms to it and found herself in Myatlev's embrace.

20

THE CARRIAGE WAS APPROACHING the house. The wind was even more piercing. "Ohmygod," thought Alexandrina, "if only we never stopped!" "If only we never stopped," thought Myatlev, holding the thin, pliant body close.

The old house greeted them with its gracious lines and churchlike darkness in which wordless marble creatures swayed, entwined together, or grieving, or confessing to one another in the language of gesture, paying no attention to the girl who was staring at them in awe and delight. Myatlev had to employ some force here, too, for his young guest immediately lost herself among the statues, caressing them, hugging them, pressing her cheek, her entire body to them, and in a minute it was impossible to distinguish her from the marble figures, despite her lithe and graceful body and streaming hair—like Eriphila, of whom the poet said, "Welcome this captive into the house. . . . A prisoner should not wear a slave's yoke." He called to her, then tried to catch her, but she slid away easily with a quiet laugh and hid among her naked companions. The house Myatlev had taught to be silent now seemed dead, and these figures alone flashed through a world inhabited by no one but themselves. Oh, world that does not demand suffering, does not thirst for subjugation, does not insist on slavery! Oh, world filled with happiness and trust! Where are you?

Finally he caught up with her just at the moment when the arrow silently pierced the Minotaur's heart and he doubled over in pain, turning on the observer his empty, suffering eye sockets as though to warn him that seduction and delusion are no less dangerous than the deadly wounds inflicted by fate.

"Alexandrina," Myatlev said, trying to lead her away, "hurry, hurry. Stop your playing." She coughed. "There, you see?"

"Where are we going?" she asked, holding back slightly. "Back to the tavern?"

They went up to the second floor. She became docile, as though her light had gone out. Nothing interested her anymore. He led her by the hand, as if she were blind, through the empty, echoing reception hall, the dead living room, and up the stairs that led to his fortress. Suddenly she stopped. Above them on the third-floor landing, courteously tipping his old-fashioned, worn top hat, with an Odyssean smile on his round, dignified face, stood Afanasy, like a god of welcome.

Myatlev was touched by the silent scene, and led his lady into the room and seated her in an armchair. She was still stunned.

Meanwhile, the god in Afanasy's form quickly, but with dignity, prepared the living quarters where Myatlev was planning to install Alexandrina Zhiltsova, whom he now felt close to, thanks either to the spell of her beauty or because he was torn with pity for a victim of implacable fate.

He turned his room and everything in it over to her, passionately hoping that she would stay for a long time and accept a real room for herself, commensurate with her beauty and suffering. He had the library fitted out for himself.

The chef was ordered to outdo himself, and in the bowels of the house, far from the casual eye, almost forgotten passions came to a boil.

While the prince gave his orders, Alexandrina, feeling a little better, combed her hair, drank some hot milk brought by Afanasy, then fell into the bed prepared for her and slept.

Myatlev, keeping out of the way, lay in his library with a volume of Augustine opened at random, trying to understand the meaning of the lines that hopped before his eyes. The incident had been unexpected, like a snowfall, and improbable. At first, it had all seemed like a game, strange and difficult, demanding close attention, with fantastic rules and unknown conditions. However, it soon became apparent that there was no game. Instead, there was a woman with a lovely face screaming with pain and beating herself on the knee with a tiny fist, then that carriage and her trembling body in your hands, the hot young body in your hands, the damp, sticky hair on your shoulder and cheek, and the hot body in your hands— "Protect my chest from the wind." Yes, and her small, hot, firm breasts, and your hand feeling them through the worn, cold, damp dress— What game was this? And "Ohmygod, ohmygod," like a plea for help— What kind of a game? And was it a game at all? But the young woman with the hot, pliant body was asleep, spread out, on the other side of the oak door, five steps away from you, which in itself should be no surprise, but it had to be a surprise for if her young, hot body had been in your arms, her hot pliant body and her hair, smelling of the rain— "Doubts, oh Lord, my mind is full of doubts." However, was he in any condition to go in to her there, in a robe and with a candle, muttering trite Horse Guards' banalities? At first it seemed like a game, a game of rescue, but after that, when her young hot body— And what will she say, seeing you in a robe and with a candle? But if she allowed herself to be embraced, and came to your house, and is lying there, spread out, in your nightshirt, within five feet of you— Ah, ah, ah, why do you go on with your complications! She's not sleeping, but despising you in silence, the way Aneta Fredericks despised you. And of course, now that several hours have passed and she's given up, and you suddenly appear in your robe and with your candle, well then, you know— "The father didn't know that his daughter the princess was carrying Phoebus's child—" And Myatlev let out his breath in a whistle of confusion.

Alexandrina woke up, hearing the whistle. She did not understand right away where she was, but then she remembered. A flickering yellow light came from the half-opened library door. Of course, her position seemed improper, but in whose eyes? And he wanted her to live in this three-storied wooden palace and be healthy and happy, this prince, ohmygod, with the grabby hands and the guilty smile. When he protected her from the wind, like a gray stork shielding a fallen female stork with his nervous wings, didn't she know then how it all was supposed to go? Didn't she know? Didn't that waiter, reeking of cheap brandy, scratch at her door and try to break through the walls with his head? And didn't the professor, offering a helping hand, still take advantage of her youthful nobility? And didn't she, love-stricken, cling to her student? And didn't she know what made the officer on Prechistensky Boulevard so attractive? And when she looked into the library where his bed had been made up, didn't it take a great effort not to laugh, since his impeccable pretense was so transparent? And didn't she know that as soon as she fell into the warm bed he would come in his robe and with a candle? And falling into a deep sleep, she had time for a prayer that it wouldn't happen, that it wouldn't happen now—later, later, but not now—ohmygod, ruin—duty—beauty—inevitability—fever—

What was that fever? The fever of disease or the fever of inevitability, eternal fever, kept alive, as though tended by priests, by her naive student, and the lonely professor of medicine, and the dandy in the green top hat, and the oxlike waiter; eternal fever, despising shame, delightfully pure when it was sent by Heaven, but now debased by disgusting odors and filth, illuminated by the flicker of a guttering candle, giving naked bodies a divine perfection, burning us throughout our brief, happy, disgusting, wretched, and kingly life until there is nothing left of us but a cold blob of wax— What was it?

The whistle was not repeated. A puzzling silence spread across the room. The cold supper stood on a low table. A heavenly warmth came from the Dutch tiles. She leaped out of bed, waving the huge sleeves of his nightshirt; noiseless, like a Valkyrie, she crossed the room and peeked into the library. He was asleep, his hands under his head, the useless book on the floor.

21

July 18, 1846

My Alexandrina's health is improving, and Dr. Schwanenbach is quite pleased now. And I can see for myself that she is blooming. The danger, I think, is past. However, the doctor gave me this news with the usual expression of sadness in his Saxon eyes. Somewhere in the depths of his soul the clever Aesculapius is hiding something. My hints about retirement brought on a storm of controversy *there* and all sorts of hostile exclamations. Must I continue to follow the general rules, having already lived the greater part of my life? That's how we destroy the best of ourselves, the most beautiful impulses of our souls, listening to gossip, obeying the rules and other people's tastes. My godlike sister has organized an entire party of like-minded people and, using her position, is arousing public opinion against me. I'm certain that Alexandrina's turn will come, and then the storm will be terrible. My sister has begun using the formal "you" when speaking to me now.

July 20

Unpleasant news from Mikhailovka. The manor house has rotted and fallen into disrepair in the past four years and needs almost total rebuilding. The smaller house is dilapidated, too. Of course, if it were cleaned up and dried out, Alexandrina and I could manage there for the summer, and by then the big house would be ready, too. And there, perhaps, I could hide from your attacks. . . . I've given orders for the big house to be finished by autumn. The bailiff swears that it will be. That means I shouldn't expect it before next summer. I tell all this to Alexandrina and see terror in her eyes. She's afraid of becoming Princess Myatleva. She *wants* to be with me, but she's afraid of becoming Princess Myatleva. That frightens her. After everything that she's been through, she feels she is unworthy of that empty title, and of me. . . . On the other hand, she's just as afraid that it won't happen. She doesn't want the illusion to crumble! She keeps thinking that my Fate, wheezing, gray, shapeless, stamping its hooves in the dark, implacably demanding victims, that my fate is not only mine, but hers as well, and that it will not allow her to be truly happy.

July 26

She was right; the cough took a turn for the worse, and she's running a low-grade temperature. Stubborn Schwanenbach insists that the summer humidity is at fault and that if we go to Mikhailovka, the country air will have a beneficial effect. I spent the whole day at it, but got nowhere. The question of my retirement is still moot, and time is passing, and the climate in Petersburg is not the best for recovering from an illness. To distract Alexandrina from the gloomy thoughts she has when she thinks I'm not watching and to improve her wardrobe at least a little, I suggested a shopping trip to Gostiny Dvor. She was as delighted as a child. We rushed over there. She was awhirl among the fabrics, ribbons, and laces, picking things out, trying them on, rejecting them. Suddenly she cooled to the whole project. Perhaps the stuffiness of the store make her ill. Then nothing pleased her, and she didn't want to buy anything, and it took great effort to convince her to buy at least something, making stupid jokes about my nightshirts falling apart. After lunch there was a small incident. Idiot Afanasy mentioned the damned ghosts that inhabit our house. Ever since then, I've noticed that in the evenings she listens to the sounds of the house, and just now she ran into the library, swearing that she had seen someone in white appear before her and dissolve. "You shouldn't listen to that idiot," I said. "Ohmygod, I'm not insisting that it happened," she said, trying to smile. "I'm not insisting."

July 28

The bailiff suggested that he bring Alexandrina out to the estate so that she could live there while I got my affairs in order here. She refused to go without me. I was secretly pleased, even though I carried on, blustered, and lied. She understands all that naturally, but forgives me. "Ohmygod, how he loves me!" Amilakhvari was here yesterday. She charmed him immediately, and it could have been no other way; she is truly touching and lovely, and he is always ready to take in a wounded bird, and one like her, well. . . . She asked me, "Does it ever occur to you that I want to please you only so that I can have a comfortable life?" "Think what you're saying, Alexandrina," I said. "God sees, I never think anything like that." "What a strange man," she sang. "He thinks that I can't help but fear poverty and because of that— And who told him so? As though I—I've told you! I told you, I told you all about it." And so on . . . By the way, more on the day before yesterday's business with the ghosts. "I'm not insisting," she said. Then I called in Afanasy. He showed up with some ridiculous scarf wrapped around his throat, a trussed-up Walter Scott, obviously well-fed but with romantic shadows under his eyes. I upbraided him for repeating such silly nonsense and scaring Alexandrina. "But I didn't invent them," he replied with dignity. "They're historical—if you'll permit me to say so— legends." In order to convince me, he brought in a piece of an old sheet, insisting that he had torn it off some ghost who had tried to detain him. "It was completely incorporeal; I couldn't get a grip on it. And it was covered with this thin fabric." All of this has had a detrimental effect on Alexandrina.

"The horns' call, half-light, half-darkness"— an excess of nature or a human creation, as bitter as the creator?

July 30

A disgusting day . . . My godlike sister managed to descend upon us just when Alexandrina was resting after lunch. The poor girl, having heard about the lady-in-waiting, jumped up, pulling herself together feverishly, but my sister made believe she did not notice her and went on into my library. We had the following conversation.

SHE: I know everything. You don't have to bother making excuses.

I: I wasn't thinking of it. I have nothing to excuse. And another thing, Liza, you don't have to storm into my house.

SHE: Aside from the fact that you have upset all of Petersburg with your shenanigans—

I: You should have first—

SHE: —I'm not even mentioning the court; you've sunk so low that you bring back a woman from a tavern—

I: What are you saying? Come to your senses!

SHE: —and that you dragged her in full view—and everyone in Petersburg is talking about it openly. You've compromised yourself—

I: Listen, Liza—

SHE: —so that you will never be able to restore your reputation, but why—

I: Don't insult me—Listen to me—

SHE: —why don't you think about me and the reputation of our family? You've turned the house into a pothouse, and you look like a servant. Even your butler is more *comme il faut* than you—

I: The point is I do not wish anyone to—

SHE: You could at least keep an apartment for assignations,

SHE: and not turn the house into a public spectacle—

I: —interfere in my life! I thought I had made it clear to you and the others—

SHE: —a public spectacle of your indecent relations with God knows whom. One day you will come to your senses, but it will be too late. Too late! You do not have the right—

I: —I plan to behave as I see fit—

SHE: —to make our position in society suffer from your egotism. I will be forced—

I: —damn it!

SHE: —to turn to my friends to have them set you straight and if necessary—

I: Tell your friends—

SHE: —to force you to live a decent and proper life. People shun you. No one calls on you. They all despise you. Is that what you want? I'm terrified to think—

I: Tell your friends—

SHE: —what will happen when on top of all the grief you've caused him, the tsar—

I: Tell your friends—

SHE: —the tsar hears about *this!*

I: Tell your friends—

But she tore out of the library, knowing that Alexandrina would have heard everything and hoping to top it off with the impact of her wrathful countenance. I ran after her, but my worries were superfluous; Alexandrina was facing the window and didn't even stir when our evil Cassandra ostentatiously clacked across the floor directly behind her and just as ostentatiously slammed the door.

I ran after her to shout something exquisitely nasty and memorable, but it turned out that someone was waiting for her in the entry. It was Countess Rumyantseva, Cassandra's friend, the twenty-four-year-old seductress of our heroes. It was inconceivable that that woman should wait downstairs like a maid! What a pathetic female performance!

"Natalya Andreyevna!" I feigned amazement. "What brings you here? And why didn't you come up?"

The countess was very beautiful and, in the semidarkness of the hall, absolutely bewitching. But I knew that she was stupid, and it was written all over her lovely face. She did not reply, but merely touched a curl with her delicate fingers, managing to convey her hostility but nevertheless not averting her eyes. I almost laughed out loud, but I was kept from this ultimate breech of good breeding by something pathetic, almost bovine, that flickered in her amazing, deep eyes.

I forgot that just a minute ago I was fencing with Elizaveta Vasilyevna. I saw only those dark eyes, pleading secretly for compassion.

She turned slowly and followed her friend to the door. I stood and watched her go, as though seeing her for the first time. Petersburg had never seen such perfection in any woman.

August 2

. . . reject anyone who thinks differently. And they try to suppress them with aloofness, contempt, and even force. I see the mark of their fist on Alexandrina's brow. Even blue-uniformed von Müffling permitted himself to condescend to her. Sister mine, you are a fake! Your impeccability is bloodthirsty. . . . Alexandrina can't get over the depression brought on by my sister's visit. Dr. Schwanenbach just looks away. The poor girl lies in bed and, when I come in, smiles and nods conspiratorially, seeing my drawn and desperate, horsey face. . . . And I make her the victim of my indecisiveness. She has confused me, that damned Cassandra! If Alexandrina and I leave for Mikhailovka just now, she'll definitely come up with some nasty trick. Noble Amilakhvari, in his compassion for us, suggested we get away somewhere much further, but she is forbidden to get out of bed for now. . . . And where could we go? Perhaps I will be able to escape you on the other side of the Caucasus. But that's the point—it's "perhaps," but perhaps not. Yesterday I had just helped Alexandrina over to the window so that we could watch the sunset together, when I saw a carriage stop outside the fence. A blue uniform came out and entered the house. A minute later Afanasy informed me that a Lieutenant Katakazi was asking for me. I went down to see him with foreboding, and we spoke in the entry. I made it clear that I had no intention of wasting time on official talk. But that didn't faze him. He told me that the police were worried by information that a Marquis Troyat was living in Petersburg without any visible means of support. I expressed my ignorance. "In particular," said Katakazi, "we have information that he is living in your house." I was ready to give him a curt reply, but remembered the mysterious cowled man whom Afanasy had tried to mystify last winter, and I laughed. "I'm sorry, I'm so sorry," I said. His face didn't flinch, and he left. "What made you so happy?" Alexandrina asked, hearing my laughter. I told her the silly story from last winter, still laughing, but she took it much too seriously and I stopped too late. I finally guessed what those eyes remind me of! They remind me of the eyes of the vanished Mr. van Schoenhoven.

22

THE TENSION THAT HAD settled on the Myatlev household did not abate for a minute, and the fiercer the fever of Alexandrina's illness and the more often she shuddered in the throes of her coughing spells, the more ceaselessly Myatlev raced around the house with a soothing smile on his lips and the more the tension became palpable and tormenting.

First of all, he ordered Afanasy to hire maids for Alexandrina; two wordless creatures, one with red hair, called Aglaya, the other with a black braid, called Stesha, whirled around the house, caught up in the violent vortex, serving, cleaning, combing, bowing, and appearing at the right moment and then disappearing, forcing Afanasy to change his loutish walk to one befitting a majordomo, and bringing to his round face an expression of deep mystery and condescension, particularly when he managed to paw one of the unwary girls in the hallway.

Secondly, hammers and saws went to work in the house, to the horror of Dr. Schwanenbach; from the second floor, where three rooms intended for Alexandrina were being quickly constructed, came the delicious fragrance of fresh wood shavings, leather, and paint—this was Myatlev's attempt to battle public opinion and prove his serious intentions toward Alexandrina—and even though Dr. Schwanenbach tried to convince him that all this was not helping the young woman regain her strength, the madness that had Myatlev in thrall was remorseless.

As a climax to all his conversations with Alexandrina about the heartless fate that pursued her, Myatlev began thinking that he, too, not only accepted the existence of that monster but could feel its presence, even see it feasting and debauching, coming between them, between their love and suffering. How free and easy it lived, how deafeningly it laughed, how brazenly and confidently it mocked the weakness of its victim. It was that mysterious, wheezing, trampling, incorporeal, and disgusting genius born of our passions. "And everyone who is kind to me, all of them suffer from it," Alexandrina said.

This daily duel usually ended in late evening, when the patient, exhausted by the day, fell into a restless sleep; and then Myatlev would sit by the open window, drinking vodka, inhaling the summer night, stunned by battle fatigue.

Did he think the battle was hopeless? I don't know. He wasn't very confiding in those days and laughed off direct questions. In fighting for the life of the person you love, skepticism and prayers are poor helpers. Only fierceness and love are capable of performing miracles, even though these miracles are often short-lived.

Suddenly, despite all Schwanenbach's predictions, the cruel hand gripping Alexandrina's throat relaxed, and the young woman woke up one morning feeling completely cured. She was permitted to get out of bed after a while, and then one fine day in late July, the ancient oval table was set for lunch on the veranda that opened onto the park in the back of the house. The doctor and I were standing near the table when the French doors squeaked and Myatlev brought out Alexandrina. She looked ravishing in a new dress of light-brown silk. A soft light shawl covered her sharp shoulders, restoring their former roundness. I thought I had seen tears in her eyes, but a closer look revealed that I was wrong. She smiled with a child's spontaneity, knowing she was among friends. She was like a little girl joining the adults for lunch for the first time. I hadn't seen Myatlev so festive and calm in a long time. He gave the sign, and the table seemed to come alive. The ringing of crystal, the light, summery burbling of wine, the aroma of soup, the flaky pastry of the tiny piroshki, the red crust of the veal roast, the colorful array of sauces, and the sparkle of the heavy silver dinnerware with the princely monogram—it all blended, ringing, trembling, and exuding happiness. The valet slowly poured the soup.

You would think, What more could there be? What else could you dream of after everything that had befallen them? But trained by life to expect trouble, and in the conviction that immortality was not their lot, the people at the table watched each other with an eagle eye, never missing a single movement, a random sigh that might contain the slightest confirmation of the sad imperfection of their destiny and the briefness of their earthly existence.

Alexandrina brought her thin fingers up to her neckline several times; Myatlev ate with the exaggerated calm of a man expecting to be shot; Dr. Schwanenbach was distracted and once or twice brought an empty spoon to his mouth. Only the words spoken at the table veiled the anxiety of the diners. The saving sounds of speech interrupted and covered up any unwanted sighs, and the meaning of the words served as a screen to hide their doubts.

"And why shouldn't we go to the opera?" Myatlev inquired. "Now it seems all we have to do is amuse ourselves."

"Ohmygod," laughed Alexandrina, knowing his dislike of going out and of public entertainments, "I've never been to the opera in my entire life! But it's summer now—"

"Doctor," said Myatlev, and drank some vodka, "do you give your blessing?"

"Giving blessings is not my profession," Dr. Schwanenbach said, looking away. "The opera is full of bad air. Go for a walk in the park or go out to the island. But what opera is there in the summer?"

"All the better," Alexandrina agreed. "Now that I've met Princess Elizaveta Vasilyevna"—she coughed lightly—"Princess Myatleva. It wouldn't look very good, would it? Right? Not very good at all? If we were to show up at the opera—"

"You're in no danger of going to the opera," I said. "It's summer. Unless, of course, you go to Tsarskoe Selo—"

"No, no," Myatlev said, draining his glass, "what does that have to do with it? Of course, four hours in a stuffy place— That's the problem. It's crammed with foxes in low-cut dresses, bears in epaulettes, bearded rabbits in double-breasted jackets in the balcony— Ah yes, it's summer— Well, perhaps at Tsarskoe Selo. But they're so proper there that they would chase us out. You really don't want to go?"

"I don't," said Alexandrina firmly, without regret.

"Or we could override the doctor's objections." And he drained another glass. "Well, how about Mikhailovka?"

"I think it would be all right," Dr. Schwanenbach said, looking away, "in a week or so."

Myatlev filled another glass and winked at Alexandrina. She smiled sadly at him.

> ...Remember the horns' mournful call,
> The splatter of rain, half-light, half-darkness?

Some bits and pieces, limp words, but they make up a terrible episode in someone's life, and you can't get away from their sound: " . . . half-light, half-darkness?"

The veranda was surrounded by a part of the park that had been transformed by the gardeners into a lush garden with red paths—a green meadow with white benches. The gardeners worked for the sake of Alexandrina, waging a skillful battle with nature. In a white, well-worn frock coat handed down by the prince, carefully ironed, with an impossible scarf at his throat, round-faced and bowlegged, a walnut cane in his hand, Afanasy strolled in the garden at a distance precisely calculated to be far enough away so that he wouldn't intrude on the master's conversation and yet close enough to allow him to respond to any wish the prince might have. His slow, aloof dance corresponded perfectly to the spirit of the table; not the spirit that expressed itself in the hurried, seemingly random sentences, but in the constrained and tense movements, flickering glances, and smiles that vainly attempted to cover sadness.

The more Myatlev attacked the vodka, the sadder Alexandrina's decorous smile became, and the more the helpless doctor kept looking away, and the clearer and more complex became the pattern of Afanasy's dance, his movements faster and more energetic, whipped on by the fever that was rising at the oval table.

"In the long run," said Dr. Schwanenbach to Myatlev, watching the bowlegged valet floating along the red path, "with your determination, energy, and desire, I'm sure that you will get what you want and they will have to apologize to you."

"Hah," laughed Myatlev, "you fool yourself, Dr. Schwanenbach. You fool yourself, imagining that they are capable of renouncing even an iota of their prejudices—no, that's not the word, their privileges—no, their passions—their madness—Hah! their extravagance—" He sipped his vodka. "Do you want to know what turned me away from them? Boredom, Doctor. My brain was drying out from dealing with them, I could feel it—by dealing with them my brain was—that's easy for you; you're an Aesculapius, and you are brimming with professional secrets—you hide behind them as if they were a brick wall. And you say—" He finished his glass and reached for the decanter. "You see them individually, hah! But I know them *en masse*. For you they are the victims of pain and illness, but for me it's one monster—one huge villain. And I've been trying to get away from them for most of my life and fighting as much as I can, and my heart can no longer contain all the pain and all the graves."

It had all happened to him within a year's time. First a bullet brought down his comrade, who lay, a stranger now, cold on the cold stone, spread-eagled, as though flying from a cliff, his lips pursed in offense; brought back to his homeland, he was buried there, but Myatlev had buried him in his heart, fully realizing the results of forcing one's opinions on one's friends. His dead comrade, that short-legged Hussar lieutenant with the huge brow of a genius and impotent despair in his unbelieving, velvety eyes, with the unpleasant, offensive manner of a mean child made irritable by envy who therefore stubbornly despises everything around him and consequently suffers; he, whose huge drops of sweat were mixed with drops of blood as he gave voice to curses, invocations, prayers, and words not inferior to those of Pushkin—he was buried in Myatlev's heart, where many others were already buried who in the past had been hanged, stood up against a wall, or who had rotted in mines or smashed their heads against the doors of casemates. And his heart was overflowing with that death and also with the knowledge that the short-legged Hussar lieutenant had asked for trouble with the stupidity of a shepherd, stumbling and falling instead of buying himself off, not with his death, but with anything else: deception, money, blindness. And so, first there was his death, and then the battle—no, the brief, unplanned skirmish with a handful of maddened natives with shaved heads, forced into a crevasse and convinced that marksmanship, bravery, and hatred of those dead men lying silenced behind the rocks was destiny's highest moment and the greatest meaning of life, even though it was beastly madness, the madness not of despair but of servile self-satisfaction. And so they pressed the obedient triggers of their rusty rifles—them and us, them and us—until Myatlev's bullet landed in the hot stomach of his enemy with the shaved head, and he saw him twist and fall on the stones and heard wild curses in an unfamiliar tongue, and then someone's return bullet, hissing, hit Myatlev, and he fell, feeling that the huge dirty bullet had cleft him in two, torn out his guts, and thrown them all over the crevasse.

Delirious in the hospital bed while the pain remained unbearable, he kept seeing the same thing: a dull road in the mountains and himself moving along it in terrible pain toward his rescuers, but his strength failed him. Only a few steps and a merciful hand would tear the pain out of him—but he was lying on the road, moving his mouth soundlessly— He was lying on the road, and next to him stood a downcast little donkey, hitched to a cart, sadly looking around for grass, but everything was bare. It was hungry, and it refused to budge. And then, desperate, Myatlev with a cry tore out juicy handfuls of Alpine grass from his belly and breast and fed the donkey, and the donkey, chewing slowly, pulled the cart slowly, and Myatlev lay in the cart, tearing the blades of string grass from his body and feeding them to the animal's parched lips.

"No, Dr. Schwanenbach," Myatlev said, "you will never determine the truth, because it is outside the range of your possibilities. Even worse, Doctor," he said sadly, "even you cannot determine the nature of my malady, and no one—You maintain that it is the result of my wound—all right, let's say it is. But you must admit, dear Doctor, that a hip wound cannot give rise to the desire to crawl away into a hole and drink vodka and waste money—" He laughed. "There's an incongruity there, no? Just imagine this: some filthy robber shoots me, and I—and then— No, it's impossible! Heredity? But my father was as strong as a bull, and my godlike sister suffers from absolutely nothing, if you don't count a slavish attachment to etiquette. And you, Dr. Schwanenbach, will never determine the truth, because it is outside the sphere of your concepts about man." And he gestured, as though pulling grass out of his chest.

Afanasy circled at a distance in the green meadow, bending steeply over the trees, as though checking the dependability of the roots. Will they have enough nutritious sap? Have the brown wooly caterpillars and transparent aphids—also nature's children—overdone their feeding and feasting?

"Ohmygod," moaned Alexandrina, "all this stems from the fact that everyone feels he has the right to control my life, to shower me with his beneficence! Or order me about! Or know me—" she began coughing—"ohmygod—smear pitch—grab my arm—"

"Are you all right?" Schwanenbach leaned over her.

"I'm fine!"

"What do you think, Doctor," Myatlev asked Schwanenbach. "What if I have the iron railings replaced with a brick wall twice my height?"

Dr. Schwanenbach's head, liberally doused with toilet water, turned in the direction of the garden, until his chin rested on his shoulder. And Myatlev, trying to look into his eyes, got his hairy pink ear instead, at which he smiled and from which he expected a reply. But, turning a brighter pink, the ear tried angrily to avoid the prince, for Dr. Schwanenbach saw the abyss toward which his patient was tottering, Alexandrina, so young and fair but duped out of life's pleasures and with fear in her heart. He had often heard that fear through his black tube. Besides, in the doctor's kind yet aloof face, in his blue Saxon eyes, alert to her signals, in the tone in which he addressed her, there was something more than simple professional involvement. He, a not very prosperous physician of German origin, began to see himself as the genius who would save this young woman, not only in order to pull her back from the abyss but so that she might share the healing powers of his heart.

And Alexandrina, having cried out in her damned pain, was now concentrating on the piece of soft bread that she was trying to shape into an animal so that she could give it to Myatlev on the palm of her hand. She tried very hard, but kept producing something absolutely hopeless and grotesque, and so it traveled over to him on her hand without legs, torso, or name. "Hah!" he said and kissed her hand, crumpled up the failed masterpiece, and popped it into his mouth with a sip of vodka. And here, probably, another "ohmygod" stirred in the young woman's soul, having no connection, of course, with the lump of bread but with the same old thing: What about tomorrow?

Now Afanasy was hidden by the rose bushes, but his white suit showed through the leaves, and he flickered there, irritating Dr. Schwanenbach and distracting him. "Of course," thought the doctor, "that kind of superficiality and that lightweight approach can be of no help. Indulging one's ever-changing whims is no way to heal someone else's wounds. Sexual attraction is not love. Alcohol is not the medicine for doubts and confusion. The sense of responsibility is not well developed in the wealthy classes; it's replaced by pity and whim."

"Or should I go away?" Myatlev asked. "I mean, should we?" And he brought his lips to Alexandrina's thin hand. "But who would allow us?"

"Of course," thought Schwanenbach, feeling no need to answer idle questions, "of course, with a great deal of money you can allow yourself the luxury of doubting and asking stupid questions or swallowing such a marvelous creature made of bread with such a touching little head and delivered so sweetly on her hand. Of course—"

Redheaded Aglaya jumped from among the rosebushes, hurriedly straightening out the white lace coller of her purple dress, and disappeared among the trees. Afanasy, who appeared after her, continued examining his domain fussily, circling as before.

"If we built that wall," Myatlev said, "it would do a lot of good. Yes, I can imagine a few people—"

Dr. Schwanenbach suggested moving inside. The sun was setting slowly, and the doctor was worried about Alexandrina; but just at that moment the valet announced that Her Excellency the princess was here and wished to see His Excellency. Myatlev made a face and started for the house, but the lady-in-waiting was already at the French doors. She moved on impetuously and opened the doors, disregarding her brother's warning signals. Dr. Schwanenbach jumped up, spilling his glass, and Alexandrina turned slowly. Afanasy froze picturesquely in the far part of the garden. The princess was smiling happily. She came over to Alexandrina and kissed her cold forehead.

"Well," she said in a homey tone, "I managed to get away from Tsarskoe Selo to see you, my dears," and sat down in the chair the valet had brought. "It's unbearable in the city. I kept thinking about you, Alexandrine, how you should be taking care of yourself in your condition. But I see that everything is fine here?" Her eyes moved over the silent men. "Serge," she said in an official tone, "I bring you news of the satisfactory resolution of your affairs: you are permitted to retire. The tsar was so kind as to take an interest in your life. I had to tell him about many of your virtues, most of which you have no idea of at all. Alexandrine, you look marvelous. I'm glad. You know, your estate in Kiev Province can be bought back. Serge should look into it."

"I don't understand," her brother muttered. "This I do not understand at all."

Alexandrina looked at Myatlev. My prince was vainly trying to clear away the haze of vodka. Afanasy was slowly approaching.

"I think it's time to move indoors," said the doctor, never taking his eyes off him.

"No," Myatlev replied stubbornly. "We'll stay here. Here on the veranda. It's better here. But I don't understand."

"You are from the Kiev Zhiltsovs, are you not?" the princess went on. "I know. I checked."

"From the Kaluga ones," said Alexandrina and coughed.

"No, no, from the Kiev line. You were a young girl, and you've forgotten. The Kiev ones." She turned to her brother. "You know, it's the Zhiltsovs who— Doctor, do you remember Panin? No, not this one; the one from Berlin, Nikita Petrovich? This Zhiltsov, the father of our Alexandrine, was married to the sister of the wife of that Berlin one—that is, the mother of Alexandrine. Your mother, Alexandrine, was the sister—"

Alexandrina shook her head.

"No," said Myatlev, "nonsense. It didn't happen. But here's what I would like to understand. You once came to see me, and you dragged along Natalie Rumyantseva, and she looked at me with her bovine, condemning eyes." Elizaveta Vasilyevna waved her brother away. "Was *that* an expression of *your* circle's opinion of me? Or did she perhaps know nothing and just happen to run into you right in front of my door?"

"Serge," his sister insisted, "you have had too much wine. You will ruin yourself and Alexandrine."

"Hah," said Myatlev, "finally! I suspected as much. I under-stand everything. I understand what all this means. Ah, my dear sister. Ah, my dear, dear, sister."

"He really is drunk," the lady-in-waiting said to Alexan-drina, laughing. "Yes, I forgot to tell you what happened *chez nous*. Here's what happened." The princess had a rather pleasant face, although it was marred by a slight yellowish cast to her skin, and even more so by her bulging eyes. Those eyes gave her an untamable look that did not correspond to her nature but did eventually, with the passing of time, have an effect on her personality, so that strident notes crept into the princess's tone. Myatlev simply could not abide those bulging eyes, particularly when she was angry. Lack of intelligence always accentuates physical imperfections, and the good princess was a classic illustration of that simple proposition. As for Dr. Schwanenbach, he considered her a banal hysteric, and therefore did not know how to alleviate her suffering. "Here's what happened," she said. "Madame Yurko, whom you know, was trying to get into the good graces of the handsome Mario—you know, the one from the Italian troupe—and her carriage was often observed waiting on Moika Street—that's where he lived—and *he* was observed blatantly leaving her house . . . it soon became known, and the tsar—lately he's been quite intoler-ant of any form of immorality—had the tenor deported, yes, yes, he's already gone . . . but there's more . . . Madame Yurko is miserable, she is not accepted at court . . . heavy . . . disgusting . . . narrow-minded . . . coldness . . ."

"I find myself between two worlds; one is alien, and the other inaccessible," quoted Myatlev and caressed Alexandrina with a nervous hand.

"As a physician, I insist on the necessity for moving indoors," Schwanenbach announced and bowed to the prince.

Alexandrina, erect and silent, her face pale, and one fist pressed to her chest, stood and took the doctor's arm.

"Why don't you take Alexandrine to Carlsbad?" the lady-in-waiting asked her brother.

"We'll go to Mikhailovka," Myatlev said, his gaze following Alexandrina.

"What nonsense!" His sister was surprised. "I'm sure that she would be better off in Carlsbad."

"Hah!" said Myatlev, "Well, well, well—I understand everything. Well, well, well. You shouldn't have come, you know."

"You are a fool, Serge, I haven't told you everything," she said cruelly. "And you are drunk. You have been abandoned by everyone. You irritate and scare off everyone."

"And I'll make sure that you won't—be able to come—here—I understand everything."

She headed for the door.

"Wait," Myatlev called. "Listen, Elizaveta. You know, Liza, I want— Do you know, that I've—ordered them to erect a brick wall around the house—twice my height— Well? And with no gate or crack in it—hah, can you imagine?"

She rose into the air like a soap bubble and disappeared, and Myatlev collapsed in his chair, bereft of strength and reason, and dully tried to coordinate the toe of his patent-leather shoe with the red garden path.

There, where the path ended and the rosebushes grew tall, mysterious new movements began, flickerings, waving arms, silent motion, living tableaux, in which white tunics intertwined with purple robes for the glory of love, and silent choirs penetrated the very soul, and there was no fate, no struggle, no evil presentiment—only the eternally setting sun and mutual desire.

Myatlev was awakened by the door squeaking; and the blurred picture took on clarity, and he could easily deduce that Afanasy had persisted in his determined intentions vis-à-vis the redheaded Aglaya, and from the open window of the third floor, heralding his return to earth, he could hear Alexandrina's cough, and Dr. Schwanenbach, on the veranda, said, staring at the touching pastoral in the garden:

"You must leave with Alexandrina as soon as possible. Not a moment can be lost."

"And you?" Myatlev asked. "Won't you be going with us?"

"A week may be too late," said Schwanenbach.

"In a week Alexandrina's rooms will be ready, while the floors in Mikhailovka are rotten—I know," Myatlev explained. "You don't think it will hurt her?"

After that unintelligible conversation, having seen the doctor out and splashed cold water on himself, Myatlev, sobered, rushed to Alexandrina's side, but found her asleep.

"Beauty" is an affected and simpering word. What could "she was beautiful" possibly mean other than that everything about her corresponded to certain norms? Yes, she was beautiful, and her nose was flawless, and the smooth roundness of her brow cheered the eye, and the huge gray eyes held dark crystal facets that played and sparkled provocatively in their depths, and the slightly mocking, juicy lips pronounced round, warm words, those lips whose touch brought on sweet excitement, and her hair, tumbling down onto her thin, nervous shoulders, so unlike the fashion favored by her happier girl friends—all, all added up to beauty. But if in those huge gray eyes where dark crystal facets played there had not been the desperation of a dying doe, and if her slightly mocking, juicy lips never gasped out "Ohmygod!" and if her every touch did not seem like the last, and if her fist did not press against her chest and then in sudden madness beat her sharp knee like a small hammer on a soundless anvil, trying to hammer out a more tolerable hope—would she be beautiful, this migratory bird, sowing love, confusion, and despair all around her?

She was asleep, rolled up into a ball. Aglaya's thin, distant laugh rang outside the door. Someone sighed deeply behind Myatlev. He turned. Dr. Schwanenbach threw up his hands, signaling him not to make any noise.

"We must have a talk," he said in a whisper, and headed into the library without an invitation. "I didn't leave, I was downstairs. We must talk. You see, the girl's condition is worsening—you know that." Myatlev was jarred by his unceremoniousness, but the doctor's official position was an excuse. "Now you have your leave, and nothing must keep you from your trip. (He really did have his nerve!) You must not waste time (What gall!), or everything might end catastrophically. And then—and then— However, if you can't or won't—I mean, I would like—I must inform you—I must—" Something was keeping the doctor from finishing his thought—either what he saw out the window or the reluctance to listen he saw on the prince's face. "I would like what I am going to say (Myatlev was getting angry)— What I'm going to— You see, the girl needs quiet, complete quiet." He wrung his hands like a tenor who can't reach the high note. Suddenly he asked, "I hope you sleep in your own room?"

"Eh? What?"

"You see," the doctor continued desperately, "I could save her, I could save her—but that requires total renunciation— I could save her if I had—she wants it, we've talked about it— She's struggling with a sense of duty and gratitude and her desire to survive— (When had they had time to talk?) And she—I've seen it—she trusts me— But you must help her renounce—"

"Listen," laughed Myatlev, "what's the matter with you? I love her and I'll do whatever's necessary."

"That's it," Dr. Schwanenbach said, nodding sadly. "Understand me correctly. Of course, I'm no rival for you in rank or capital, but understand me correctly, your help must consist in the fact that you must (Again, must!)— You see, we're not talking about charity here, charity is nonsense, even a lowly sacrifice is worth more than charity, but in this case— If you want, if you truly want—if you're worried and want the poor girl to—" The action outside the window had apparently intrigued the doctor, for his forehead was pressed against the glass, and he twisted and plaited his fingers feverishly, as though they had become boneless.

They had lain close to each other, on one of the nights before there had been Dr. Schwanenbach or the cough or the vague anxiety, and the fever of illness was mistaken for the fever of love, and she had held his shoulder with her small, slightly damp hand, and her mocking, juicy, tired lips were whispering rounded, warm, hurried words: "Ohmygod, if he only could imagine how much an old woman like me loves him, yes, and didn't laugh— And didn't laugh, and didn't keep me from talking— And this hot, enormous body, if it only knew, ohmygod, if it only knew how hard I pray for this night never to end— I'm not ashamed, I'm not, that's how happy I am, that I'm not ashamed, not ashamed— I'm old, old, and I've seduced such a young, unhappy, tender, wonderful, imaginative man— And more than that, he's patient, and strange, and indulgent, and generous, and trusting like a bunny, like a hedgehog, like a tiny sparrow, and noble like an old shaggy bear, and flawless, like the air, ohmygod—"

"I love her and I'll do whatever's necessary," Myatlev said, losing patience. "Well? What needs to be done?"

"That's it, that's it," the doctor intoned, "that's it. She desperately wants to live, and for that . . . and therefore . . . freedom . . . danger . . . confession . . . great cost . . ."

And another night: "I so much want to get well, I keep trying, but I have no more strength. Just tell that doctor, order him to cure me, and tell him that I don't believe in that tube he keeps jabbing in my chest and back. Let him do the impossible! It was so hard getting to you—" "It was I who got to you," Myatlev had said, "through the rain, and grabbed your arm, and forced vodka on you, it was I—"

"Are you listening to me?" Schwanenbach inquired. "So, if you aren't offended, if you don't find it— Personally, I'm sure, but as for you, I can't— You see, there's also your position in society. Please understand me correctly, in certain ways it interferes with your plans, I can see that. Oh, I understand everything." A pale smile in profile. "But she needs peace and quiet— If a river is troubled, ice cannot form on it. Her Excellency the Princess Elizaveta Vasilyevna is above reproach, but you can't depend—"

"How happy I am" thought Myatlev, looking at the doctor, "and how miserable he must be with his fat German wife, bloated with boredom and potatoes."

And yet another night: "I'm willing to choose between life and death. It's not hard. But there, deep inside me, there's something that isn't willing, do you understand? Do you? Do you?"

"How much do we need?" The doctor spoke, as through a fog, staring at Myatlev. "It isn't a problem for me at forty. And then, of course, I hope you know my value." Calm and reason had returned to him. "Fresh air, healthful, simple food, total quiet, no memories, total quiet, and a small dose of concern, and total quiet—total quiet—"

"What a strange man," thought Myatlev, imitating Alexandrina. "What was that all about?" And he went to see the doctor out, mechanically studying his firm German neck and nape, supported by an impeccable collar.

Interlude

THEY HAD TEA, AS usual, at five in the evening beside the warm fireplace in the small drawing room, under the portrait of the Empress Catherine. The painting was not a run-of-the-mill one, since the central part of the canvas was taken up by an architectural view with a colonnade, buildings disappearing in the distance, arches, and so on; in the left bottom corner of this landscape was a portrait of Catherine in profile against a dark background of green drapes, strangely suspended in midair, with no apparent relationship to the colonnade next to it. The empress was seated, her right arm leaning on the back of the armchair, dressed in a gray-blue dress and a red jacket with elbow-length sleeves; a headdress was barely visible over her hair; the yellow fabric of the chair showed behind her and under her elbow; a smile played on her thin lips, frankly nongovernmental in intent.

Alexandra Fyodorovna, already a grandmother, poured the tea.

The family had grown, and it was hard for all of them to fit around the customary smallish square table, but they could all reach the toast and porcelain sugar bowl and no one complained.

A picture by an unknown artist makes this gathering look unnatural, since Grandfather is shown with his back to the viewer, and Sasha, the elder son, is away from the table, as if he had not been invited or had already finished, even though Grandfather liked a closed, disciplined circle. The artist had wanted to present a panoramic view of a family at tea, but he somehow overdid it, and each figure is endowed with excessive ceremony and tension. But nevertheless, the feeling of intimacy and conversation has not been altogether lost, and if you concentrated you would certainly get the impression that you, too, quite naturally, were part of that normal, habitual family tea party.

Grandfather was in a good mood. His grandsons were crawling around his legs on the worn carpet and wrestling and screeching and grabbing Grandfather's trousers, and instinct had unerringly prompted the little beasts to know that they would not be scolded. Everyone else around the table knew it, too, but were still a bit on guard, having had many years of experience.

Considering his fifty and some years, Grandfather looked quite young and fresh, and knew it, and was proud of it, and demanded that all his sons, especially Sasha, as the eldest and his heir, rise at dawn, jump up without dawdling, and walk and walk and walk, and sleep on a hard bed, and not cringe away from ice water. Ice water burns you, and your circulation improves, and that's the most important thing; and also, you don't have to worry about catching cold hunting or on bivouac; you can sleep in a swamp, get soaked in an autumn rain, and feel fine. Besides that, it is also very healthful to sleep with open windows, even in winter, not open wide but enough to let in fresh air. That was his most holy rule, and everyone around him was amazed at his condition, his strength, his stamina, his clear head, and at the way a lifetime of good health influenced morality, sense of duty, and everything, everything else.

Recently Grandfather had developed a potbelly, and even though there was nothing inherently bad about it, he massaged it fiercely, and cinched himself in, and did not like any reference to the subject.

On his left, as usual, sat his second son, Kostya, his secret favorite. Kostya watched his health; though he was not tall, he was handsome, and what his father liked best about him was his sharp mind and inner strength. Of course, like his father, he was sometimes hotheaded, and that was too bad; but in secret his father adored the son, even loving his Napoleonic profile, and he mentally compared Sasha to Kostya and was sorry that his elder son was gentler and more tender than was advisable for his future, and more inclined to avoid an argument, but where it came from—from conviction or from weakness—he did not know. Sasha's respect for his father was irreproachable, but what lay behind it—filial love or self-control and a sense of duty?

Grandfather did not like hot tea, but he would not pour it into the saucer to cool it. Instead he would invite one of his grandsons to blow into the cup, and they tried to outdo each other in front of him. This time Little Sasha, son of Big Sasha,* was blowing into the cup, drolly standing on tiptoe and puffing out his cheeks. Drops spilled on the tablecloth, and Grandmother, Alexandra Fyodorovna, laughing, tried to move the cup away, but Grandfather wouldn't let her. "Sashka," he said, "don't blow so hard, you little silly. You'll splatter my whole jacket that way." And Sannie, Kostya's wife, with the charming spontaneity of a young woman who is still permitted to do anything she wants, was openly urging Sasha to blow harder. She was nineteen, and she had no children of her own yet, and she was brimming with generosity of spirit toward her nephews and seemed to understand and relate to them much better than the others, who were older. And seeing how happy they were when she gathered them in a circle and played with them made her almost as happy. When Aunt Sannie took the children away, tumultuous shouts, loud singing, and peals of laughter were to be expected. Grandfather liked that. He was pleased with his daughter-in-law, particularly since she was very beautiful. Of course, his face clouded once in a while because of her manners, which were not terribly refined considering her social position, and because of her abominable French.

This interval for tea from five to six was the only time when the family could come together without outsiders and laugh about nonsensical things and not worry too much about the impression they might make, especially since they never talked business. Grandfather's unbuttoned jacket, Alexandra Fyodorovna's and Aunt Sannie's everyday caps, the boys' crumpled

*Big Sasha became Alexander II on his father's death in 1855. He liberated the serfs in 1861 and was assassinated in 1881. His son, Little Sasha, then became Alexander III.

pants—all this was possible at evening tea, and while it was not condoned, it certainly wasn't condemned.

Grandfather sipped from his cup and then put it down—so exquisitely, so casually, and at the same time so masterfully—the way only he knew how—that each time all present noted it in silent admiration. While not one of them could be faulted for lack of refinement and good breeding, what Grandfather did with the cup, and the way he sat in a chair, and turned his head, and bowed, and smiled, and frowned, and did absolutely everything—every gesture that he allowed himself held more refinement, and exquisiteness, and flawlessness than the rest of them put together could manage. And they knew that Grandfather's ability was due to an entire system that he had developed and mastered; and they knew very well how proud of it he was and how his large, slightly bulging blue eyes watched all of them closely, noting regrettable lapses and mistakes, and he was indulgent only toward Aunt Sannie, as though her beauty made him question the rules of his life. But of course, all this applied to any time of day or night, and only at evening tea, from five to six, did he allow his big blue eyes to temper their innate sharpness.

He had not come to this accidentally. From that infamous day, from the very minute, when he had unexpectedly to shoulder the heavy burden of responsibility, he had realized that all the people subordinate to him and even all the people dependent on him, that people in general—humanity—judged and would judge him first and foremost not by what he did for them and not by what he said to them, and not by the level of his kindness or cruelty, or fairness or misconduct, but only by the way he presented himself to them—himself and his intimate circle. Whether this came to him through a sudden impulse or through profound understanding is not for us to decide; but he knew that God's wishes lay at the basis of all his actions and that all the people around him had to appear at least in some small way as though made in his image, and putting off death was one way.

Grandfather had been ill the last few years, but he hid it

carefully, and only those closest to him were in on the secret. However, even the most severe attacks of illness could not keep Grandfather from presenting himself to people the way they were used to seeing him, and the way they wanted to see him. And Kostya, looking at his father, was thinking how this man, unless he was alone, always tried, no matter what happened to him, to appear strong, young, and almost immortal. And then he remembered their entrance into Vienna, and even he, Kostya, who had seen everything and was accustomed to it, was dazzled seeing his father in the brilliance of his uniform, his manly beauty, the majesty of his gigantic figure, erect, haughty, towering above all the princes, aides-de-camp, and chamberlains surrounding him; and he could not tear his eyes away from him, and he thought that he was seeing a demigod, and he wanted to shout, and grovel, and praise him with the rest. Then, a short time later, as he was passing through the rooms assigned to the family, he suddenly saw his father again: he was sitting, stooped over, with a drawn, embittered face, unrecognizable, diminished by half, as if he had fallen from the heights into a gulf of despair and was no longer a demigod but a pathetic, suffering, middle-aged man. His physician was fussing over him, and Kostya slipped away, knowing how carefully his father hid his secret.

Yes, Kostya understood, and it had come to him in childhood, that even unwitting spying on his part would be seen as treachery, and that pretended ignorance was better than his father's eyes turned on him, fixed in a gaze both steely and minatory. That's why he and all the other members of this happy family never, under any circumstances, would dare to judge the actions of its mighty head. Of course, even feeble doubts about his rightness, expressed aloud, were incompatible with their innate concepts of his power and privileges. All this could exist only in the depths of their souls, at the very bottom, so deeply that no unconscious movement—a trembling hand, a flickering eyelash, a dilated pupil—nor an intonation, nor a gait could ever give them away, "Yes," thought Kostya, "he is so mighty and so accustomed to it that he can no longer see the small unpleasantnesses and minor mishaps or imperfections that occur around him, for if he were to see them, then it would mean admitting that his life and his wisdom are full of all kinds of flaws. And yet, while he goes on believing in his personal infallibility, so much around him is falling into ruin and going downhill— But how can I tell him about it without becoming his enemy?"

And so they sat around the customary table in postures that seemed freely chosen, apparently relaxed, but were so only to the point of not appearing to be impertinent. Blood, breeding, responsibility, position, experience—all this held their nerves in check, cemented their spines, lent inscrutability to their eyes and majesty to their poses.

For instance, they all knew that Catherine had adopted the habit—and kept it all her life—of holding her head high in public, which made her seem taller. And this artistry, in which she was incomparable, was rooted by tradition in their family. However, their great-grandmother was not held up as an example, and the portrait of her in the small drawing room was the only one that was tolerated. The rest were in the cellars, and the portraits of all her lovers had been destroyed.

The toast crunched in their teeth. Little Sasha, stretching his neck, blew as hard as he could into his grandfather's cup, but he either splashed the tea or missed the cup altogether.

"Silly," said his grandfather, "don't twist your head about and don't hurry. Here, try again. Like that. Some more. There— there, everyone see how Sasha is blowing into Grandfather's cup."

Little Sasha was crimson with effort and praise. Grandfather took a sip and put down the cup.

"Well, there," he said, "you got what you wanted. I can't manage without you."

Aunt Sannie clapped her hands. Big Sasha kissed his son's sweaty brow. The boy reached for the cup again.

"No, no, that was enough," Grandfather said. "Thank you, you were wonderful."

A storm raged outside. The fireplace radiated warmth. Peace and goodwill reigned at the table.

"How's Marie?" asked Grandfather. "She must be exhausted. These headaches women have are enough to drive them mad. If I had my way"—he laughed and kissed the languid white hand of Alexandra Fyodorovna—"I would force all women to wash with cold water in the morning and sleep on hard beds."

"How horrible!" Grandmother cried. "No, thank you, you just forget about us. You would be the first to spurn a monster like that with weather-beaten skin."

"Marie is suffering not so much from her headache but from the fact that she cannot be with us," said Big Sasha. "She hopes that you, *Maman*, will visit her," and he kissed his mother's hand respectfully.

"It would be amusing to see *Maman* climb into a tub of ice water in the mornings," Aunt Sannie suddenly said.

There was a minute's silence. Grandmother blushed. Kostya looked at his father in confusion.

"Sannie," Grandfather said softly, "is that possible? Would we permit *Maman* to be insulted?" And he, too, kissed his wife's hand, with even greater respect than his son.

Despite his younger daughter-in-law's tactlessness, Grandfather was not angry with her. She had not been very delicately brought up, of course, but her youth, purity, and astounding beauty compensated for her lack of manners. She had so much merry grace and good-natured freedom that it was impossible to be angry. His son Kostya was in love with her, she adored her husband, and Grandfather knew how to evaluate purity of feelings, and his big blue eyes took pleasure in noting it in anyone, particularly in people dear to him.

He loved his daughters-in-law. He was happy that God had granted his sons true love. Yes, he had been in charge of the choosing and he himself had approved the brides for his sons, but his actions were guided by Providence and he did not make mistakes in his choices, and advantage was coupled with love. He loved his daughters-in-law, and he did not like having tea this evening without Marie, the elder one. He sipped his tea and pictured her face, lovely rather than beautiful, illuminated by the docile but penetrating light of her huge, attentive eyes; he pictured her fine mouth with lips compressed, proof of her self-control, and her light, ironic smile, such a contrast with the expression in her eyes. He loved her as he could love a lovely woman chosen by his elder son, even though there had been some secret participation on his part, and he respected his daughter-in-law and valued every rare word she spoke.

"Your *Maman* is not well," Grandfather said to his youngest grandson, Vladimir, "and you're being so naughty. Well? Do you understand what I'm telling you?"

"I understand," said little Vladimir, and began pinching his grandfather's leg.

"Ah, what a naughty boy," said Grandmother Alexandra Fyodorovna. "But how can we punish such a beauty? It's impossible."

"You love him?" Grandfather asked, still looking at the child. "What for?"

"How could I not love him," said Grandmother. "He's such a sweet boy, and he loves his poor *Maman*, and you, and me—"

"Oh, is that so?" Grandfather was surprised. "And I thought that he was merely a naughty boy."

"He's just dumb," said Little Sasha.

"I love everybody," Vladimir said. "Sasha, too."

"He's at an age," thought Grandfather, "when his love is still worth a lot, even though it is short-lived."

When the hour for tea approached, the whole large family congregated in the small drawing room; none of them, probably, could have explained the feelings they shared but never pondered. Their social position was so high, and therefore their life was so different from the lives of those around them, that each of them was aware of being subject to the laws of some higher idea, compared with which all one's own little preferences were meaningless and pathetic. From early childhood they had accepted a heavy burden, a harsh regimen regulating even their dreams, and fantastic rituals that determined everything: their fate and clothes, food and recreation, their married life and the books they read, their choice of friends and the expression of their feelings. Even their deaths did not go beyond the bounds of what was appropriate to their family and were not merely a passing away but a tragic, ritualized ceremony. From early childhood they had been slaves to unbreakable rules and unbelievable conditions, which ruthlessly ruled out everything unplanned, and they gladly bade farewell to spontaneity and to those weaknesses that still tactlessly showed up from time to time due to human nature.

Occasionally performing great deeds, they tried in most cases to make even the minutiae of life seem like great deeds, and therefore their lunches, walks, and prayers took on a higher meaning and demanded as much effort as deeds that were truly great. The clock would strike and they would have to be at a parade, the theater, a reception, a walk, without regard to what they felt like doing. And woe to him who would be so mad as to prefer his personal interests to his duty or who would question the wisdom of such an existence. Only from five to six in the evening were they allowed to be themselves—to the extent permitted by their ingrained concept of their high destiny and their freedom from outside eyes. And that is why they gathered with a pleasure they did not understand within the tranquil walls of the small drawing room, which breathed peace and quiet.

Alexandra Fyodorovna noticed her husband's gaze upon her, full of concern and warmth, and tried to smile secretly in return. But her smile was not hidden from Big Sasha, and he once more—"Ah, *Maman!*"—pressed his lips to her hand. However, the concern in her husband's eyes was not random, for a light shadow of anxiety did not leave his wife's face even in these peaceful hours. He explained it as the result of overtiredness and the spiritual distress due to awareness of encroaching age, and he tried to cheer her up. And Alexandra Fyodorovna, smiling at him, thought that if he knew the real cause of her sorrow, then neither his gentlemanliness, nor his love for her, nor the laws of propriety, nor anything else in the world would keep the storm from breaking.

The problem was that their daughter Maria, her father's favorite, had been given in marriage at seventeen to a handsome young man of very noble birth, a gambler and a wastrel, who, in order to enjoy more freedom himself, had tried to inculcate a more liberal view of morality in his wife. Now, having lost her point of reference, she was having an affair with Count Grigori Stroganov, a deserving and serious man. But from the family's point of view, she had acknowledged her misalliance by falling in love with him, and instead of the light, easy, nonbinding relation they might have enjoyed, she had embarked on a life fraught with danger. And that life could at any moment become the property of gossip-hungry society and thus threaten to reach her father, who had a high enough idea of his position to stop at nothing in his wrath.

Grandfather nodded toward Catherine's portrait and said for no apparent reason, "By the way, when the foulard in which she wrapped her hair at bedtime was cleaned, it gave off sparks."

Alexandra Fyodorovna thought that Catherine was quite talented in that area, but in those days, and even now, her talent would elicit more delight than hostility or reproach. And poor Maria is waiting for the storm and there is no hope for her—

"Sparks showered not only from her foulard," said Aunt Sannie matter-of-factly, "but even from her sheets."

"Perhaps," said Grandfather dryly, and took a sip.

Of course, the charming and incomparable daughter-in-law should be more sensitive and not pour salt on old family wounds with the sweet and offensive simplicity of a child, but she was a newcomer and she could be initiated into their common problems only gradually.

Not that, in this family made up of living and healthy people, they neglected the passions of the heart, or refused the pleasures of love, or rejected any opportunity for satisfaction. Indeed, with the facility of past masters, they wove intricate knots, leaving it up to their descendants to undo them, admired their own ability along these lines and lamented their blunders. But the decorum that they maintained through all of this, and the light, exquisite secrecy with which they covered up their lust—all this was part of their unchanging ritual, too, which no one dared violate. And therefore, while giving Catherine's imperial achievements their due, they could not remember without horror and shame the erotic storm, blatant and almost legalized, that roared over Russia and their house for thirty years in violation of this ritual. And that was why they all—and Grandfather particularly—, wherever possible erased the lustful traces of the overly beloved, brazen, and great empress who had shamed them forever.

Not only Maria's position worried Alexandra Fyodorovna, who poured cup after cup of not very strong and not very hot tea. A few days ago, the old Princess Volkonskaya, the former lady-in-waiting to the late empress, now living out her days in her apartments, had interceded for Prince Myatlev, known to all for his brazenness and many scandalous escapades. She had asked Alexandra Fyodorovna to influence her husband and soften him, and Alexandra Fyodorovna, full of good intentions, could not, as usual, refuse the old woman, but having promised, realized that she had taken on an impracticable task.

It was impracticable because, even though her husband did adore her and she was aware of it every second, since he instantly gratified her every wish with great generosity and magic and love, it only applied to the fantastic carnival in which she lived and was not supposed to extend beyond its limits; and, besides that, anything that might even hint at his having been mistaken in his opinion angered and alienated him. And then he would say in a kind of frenzy, "You know that is not within my power! You are judging this from the point of view of your weak female heart, while I must consider the interests of the state, and isn't everything around us proof of my rightness?" Therefore, loving peace and quiet in her large family, she silently regretted the thoughtlessness of her promise.

But even if things had been different and if he were to extend his adoration of her to everything that existed outside her realm and give in to her request, she still would not be able to plead the cause of that prince, because she had seen him once and could not approve his conduct, and found him simply unpleasant—dry, slightly stooped, bespectacled, with a gaze that was not exactly insolent but unfriendly, with a strange manner of slipping off, melting away, not staying until the end, hanging on the fringes, getting into messes but refusing to answer for his actions.

"What huge expanses," Aunt Sannie was thinking just then, "all those Petersburgs, Moscows, Gatchinas, and—Revels, and Siberia, and he knows all and sees all," and she looked at her father-in-law. She liked his indulging her; in truth, since her recent wedding day she had seen only his indulgence.

"By the way," said Big Sasha, "what is there in the story of that French physician everyone is talking about? Did he really eat human flesh? There's something monstrous in that."

"These scientists are all eccentric," laughed Kostya. "He was in America among the wild tribes, lived with them, and tried to adopt their life. When they were devouring their enemies, the Frenchman tried to join in the feast, but I think he poisoned himself."

"Why did he have to do that terrible thing?" asked Alexandra Fyodorovna, exchanging a look with her husband.

"That's more than eccentric," Grandfather said grimly. "He should be put on a chain. I have nothing against scientific experimentation—you can't do without it—but this was sheer madness. There are limits. These French are always up to something of the sort and inciting people. The government should have some say in these ridiculous flights of fancy. How disgusting."

"Are there really savages like that"—Alexandra Fyodorovna was still shocked—"that are capable—well, that could—"

"Plenty of them," Kostya said.

"That allows us to keep our own perfections in mind," laughed Aunt Sannie.

"We are only as perfect as God wishes us to be," said Grandfather rather touchily. "And to know that one does not have to compare oneself with savages. You say the Frenchman poisoned himself?" he asked Kostya. "Serves him right."

"I can imagine how he regretted it," said Aunt Sannie. "I can't even believe—"

"Enough about that," said Grandfather, and everyone stopped talking.

The wall clock dully chimed half-past five, and the startled old cuckoo, leaping out of its mother-of-pearl house, tried to sing the anthem, but got something in its throat, shut its yellow beak, and retreated to its apartments. Everyone laughed at the trick, which was demonstrated every evening. Something must have broken down in the complex mechanism, and although once they were going to have it fixed, Grandfather had changed his mind; the children and then the grandchildren enjoyed it every time that strange, rumpled bird with the falsetto voice and weird behavior appeared. Then they got used to it, as one does to a distant relative who has moved into the house, with a myriad bizarre habits, but who is kind and indispensable, and they called it Madame Kookoo.

"The late Catherine had something quite masculine in her features," said Alexandra Fyodorovna, waving the cuckoo away. "Don't you think so? Probably that's why she wore so much rouge and teased up her hair so much."

"She was in a difficult position," said Kostya. "She was a woman and an autocrat. And she had to combine the two. Right, Papa?"

"I suppose so," his father agreed, "but it seems to me that there was less of the woman in her. She was alone, and she brightened her loneliness in a rather interesting way—"

"How charming!" laughed Aunt Sannie, and her nephews, tired of playing, laughed with her.

"Precisely," Grandfather replied. "It wasn't a slip of the tongue; what do you take me for? Here is a real woman," he said, kissing his wife's hand, "she is your mother and grandmother, and you all grow under her spread wings, and she is my wife, and my life depends on her a hundredfold, she is kind, she unites us all, and she is an angel. Aren't you convinced of that yet?"

"Papa," said Big Sasha, "I am delighted by you, and your love for *Maman* is the most worthy example of love."

Grandfather was not being cunning, speaking his high-flown phrases. He loved Alexandra Fyodorovna and felt for her—that fragile, thoughtless, and graceful creature—the passionate and indisputable adoration of a powerful personality for a weak one. With fanatical persistence he created a cult about her, which had become extensive in scope and indispensable for him, for his entire family, and for the many who inhabited those vast expanses that Aunt Sannie had just been contemplating.

But adoring his wife, transforming her existence into a grand festival of riches, exquisite luxury, and cloudless skies, he still saw other women, and honored them with his attention, and was attracted to them. At the same time, while respecting them as an ideal, and giving them due honor with all the outward magnificence of a courtier, he never deluded himself on their score.

There were quite a few of them in his life, and because he remembered everything and was sharp-eyed, nothing in their behavior could escape him. He enriched his experience with their help easily and quickly, without defiling his domestic sanctuary. He knew what multilayered projects were ripening behind their charming simplicity, what an unquenchable desire to rule burgeoned in their weak souls and freighted their tiny fingers, what blatant calculation hid in their marvelous eyes, dewy with tears of helplessness and reverence, and what improbable sacrifices they made to self-love—that deity of their nature. He knew the unique perfidy of which they were capable, and, naturally, he knew what he was doing when he wrote to his brother Constantine in Warsaw back in the days of the Polish Uprising to advise him how to escape the clutches of the beautiful Polish women, who with their innate seductiveness lured Russian officers away, destroying morale in the army. He was always amazed by their lack of moderation, but things that offended him in others delighted him in members of his family, for the family was also a ritual for him among the many other rituals he had been brought up on.

This was family, and the others elicited an easy disregard in him when he ran into them, and he forgot them when they were away.

Nowadays he permitted himself to indulge one once in a while in order to watch them light up and lose their reason—like Baroness Fredericks, for instance, that proud and unapproachable Aneta, who had stooped so low, they said, as to visit Prince Myatlev in his home, and how quickly she forgot about her prince, once she saw the beckoning signals from Grandfather, and how she rushed to him, losing her appeal like feathers. He amused himself.

In the past there had been even better stories, and there were some that he enjoyed telling in private circles, not afraid to depict himself in a bad light, since the distant past, as he saw it, had been forgiven, and the ideas and laws of Grandfather were immutable.

And today he suddenly remembered a silly situation that he found himself in some twenty years ago, and he wanted to share it, and he said to the people around him, "Once a marvelous incident occurred—about twenty years ago, *Maman* knows about it—it is funny and instructive, and I want to tell it to you. It's about that musician," he said to Alexandra Fyodorovna. "You remember, of course." And he kissed his wife's hand.

Once in that long-ago January, walking as usual along the embankment (he used to get up at dawn, took care of business, had breakfast, heard the early reports, and exactly at nine went out for his walk), he saw a young girl coming toward him on the bridge by the Winter Canal. She was modestly but nicely dressed, and held a big music case in her hands.

He gave her a careful look, noting her good points, and walked on, and he probably would have forgotten her if they hadn't met the following morning at the same spot.

He was interested, particularly since the young thing was extremely pretty and carried herself very modestly and properly. She, in turn, had noticed the handsome young officer from the Izmailovsky Regiment, and therefore on the third or fourth day when he smiled in greeting, she answered with a friendly smile. An exchange of friendly nods followed, and then more or less frank conversation. That went on for a month. He was vastly amused that she had no idea who he was and behaved as though they were equals.

Avoiding saying much about himself, he learned the stranger's entire simple biography. She was the daughter of a former teacher of German who had retired because of total deafness; she gave music lessons; her mother was a housewife and did almost everything herself because they could afford only one servant. Finally he learned that she lived on Gorokhovaya Street, in the house of a former provisions merchant where they rented a four-bedroom apartment.

From casual conversation about this and that, they moved on to more intimate topics, and he carefully introduced the notion that he would like to get to know the young music teacher better.

He was not refused. The girl agreed easily to the idea of her new friend visiting and meeting her parents, who, she said, would be pleased and flattered to meet him.

They set a date and time for his first visit, and that day, after dinner, he announced at home that he was going for a walk.

There was no talk of bodyguards in those days; he walked freely wherever and whenever he wanted, and what subsequently came to be considered solicitude and necessary and vital watchfulness would in those days have been regarded as nothing less than insolent and unforgivable spying.

And so, the collar of his overcoat turned up, he strode through the darkened streets, anticipating the coming meeting. On the corner of Gorokhovaya, practiced Don Juan that he was, he looked around in all directions and headed toward the house. At the entrance, he inquired whether he had reached the right place and then, passing the courtyard, went up the narrow wooden stairs. Contrary to all expectations, the stairs were lighted. Of course, the illumination consisted of a melting candle stub in a dull lantern, but for Gorokhovaya Street in those days that was luxurious.

Carefully going up the dirty and slippery steps, he heard the sounds of the piano from a distance and sniffed a strange odor— a mixture of burned oil and cheap cologne. To cap all these bizarre things, a similar lantern glowed over the door he wanted. His amazement was growing. But what could he do? Not retreat like a mere mortal. He lowered his collar and bravely yanked the iron bell handle that dangled on top of the peeling wallpaper. The door flew open, an aggressive cloud of vapors overwhelmed him, and he saw a servant's coppery face.

"Who do you want?" she asked hostilely.

He gave the father's name.

"Not home! Come another time!" And she tried to slam the door, but he wouldn't let her.

"And the young lady?"

"I told you, no one's here. God, you're sticky!"

"But how can that be? I was told—I'm expected—"

She was wearing a cotton dress with a greasy apron pinned over it.

The stench of onion was becoming unbearable.

"They're expecting someone, but not you!" she shouted. "We don't have time for regular guests today."

"So they are at home?" he asked.

"They're home, they're home," she said in a horrible whisper, "but I'm not supposed to let anyone in. They're expecting the emperor himself!"

"Who?"

"The emperor. So you and your officer's uniform get going while I'm still asking you politely—understand?"

"I understand," he said docilely, "but please tell me, who was it that said that the emperor was coming?"

"The young lady. And we have everything ready, too: *zakuski*, and dinner—and we even bought fruit!"

"And your young lady took care of all of this?"

"Of course—by herself."

"Well, then, tell your young lady that she's a fool!" he said, turned up his collar, and hurried off.

The cook shouted obscenities after him, the piano music mocked him, and he was already leaving the courtyard.

"And you didn't give her what-for?" Kostya asked, laughing.

"Lord," said his father, enjoying the effect of his story, "a simple filthy peasant woman. That's what made it so piquant."

"Oh, please," asked Aunt Sannie, "do tell us more about your courting."

"Sannie," said the shocked Alexandra Fyodorovna, "wouldn't you like *some more tea*?"

Grandfather looked at his watch. The big hand was approaching six. Soon, soon the rumpled Madame Kookoo would appear to say her final hoarse good-byes.

"Oh, please," Sannie repeated, but stopped immediately, because her father-in-law's face no longer conveyed the desire to amuse them with stories from his own life. It became sterner, and the barely visible line in his brow darkened and deepened. His eyes looked past them, somewhere out the window where the January snowstorm was doing the devil knew what. He wasn't with them anymore, and that's why all of them, even the grandsons, quieted down considerably, tensed, preparing themselves to bid farewell forever to this cozy, familiar drawing room.

"You haven't forgotten that I will be expecting you at exactly half-past six?" the father said to his elder son, and Big Sasha respectfully bowed his head.

And then, to the mutterings of pealing Madame Kookoo, he again kissed his wife's hand, nodded curtly to the rest of them, and left the room first.

He walked down the hall, head held high, his right hand inside his jacket, his left behind his back, duty and majesty incarnate, and the tall sentries with burning eyes froze to attention at their posts.

23

Sometimes her illness left Alexandrina completely, and everything seemed to be bathed in light, and then the old monster with the yellowed teeth, forgotten by Myatlev but still alive, would emit such marvelous, youthful melodies under her slight fingers, shudder so gently under her caress, groan so deliciously from a surfeit of pleasure and sensuality that everyone reached by its sounds felt better, and stronger, and richer, and happier. And then all kinds of sacramental thoughts arose about immortality and eternity, propitious conjunctions of the heavenly bodies, a fair price for life, and a happy end to suffering.

On such days Myatlev threw off his evil forebodings and Afanasy donned his silly top hat and bowed ceremoniously at every step, certain that he was bringing great pleasure to one and all in doing so, and pursued the warm, slippery Aglaya with greater impetus while maintaining his expression of solid respectability. And Lady-in-Waiting Elizaveta Vasilyevna, strewing her studied kindnesses, would say to her brother hopefully, "You're tired, my dear brother, you are tired. Just think what a burden you have taken on. What pain you must be feeling, and you're burning yourself up in your generous solicitude!" And Dr. Schwanenbach, sitting opposite Alexandrina, never taking his Saxon blue eyes from her inspired, lovely face, studied and memorized her features with professional acuity, and trembled at every smile she bestowed upon him.

But these short-lived moments were replaced by new attacks and fever. Alexandrina would be felled by chills, her thin body drowning in blankets and bedwarmers, and the princess would say to her brother, shrugging her shoulders, "Why don't you and Alexandrine go to Carlsbad? Well, what could they do about it now, even if they did take it the wrong way? Now, when they have given up on you. Now, when you have besmirched yourself with all of this." And Alexandrina from her pillows, blankets, and hot-water bottles, her eyes on the lady-in-waiting, would mutter through her coughing about greasy, black pitch, and being forced. Myatlev sank into sorrow and confusion, listening to his sister's lectures and watching Schwanenbach, exuding toilet water, lean over Alexandrina and press his cheek to her chest, his nostrils dilated and holding his breath.

And then, particularly at night, visions of the past floated before the patient's dulled eyes, and the white household ghost flitted around the room with the brazenness of a bat, and the maids, sleepy blue circles under their eyes, would chase it away and fluff up her pillows and run around the house, agilely sidestepping the amorous embraces of the imperturbable valet. And Dr. Schwanenbach would come, always fresh and tense, and listen to her chest again; and his experienced hand would slide slowly down her damp face from forehead to chin.

That's how it was the night when she suddenly pushed the doctor away and sat up in bed, her bare feet dangling over the side. "What are you grabbing me for, ohmygod!" She cried, and her tight little fist struck her knee. "Don't grab my hand! Don't you dare—don't you dare— I will not permit it!" And she cried even more. "You have no right—no right— And you— And you!" she shouted at Myatlev. "How strange they are, ohmygod—they don't even ask me— Don't you dare! They don't even ask me, ohmygod! But I'm grateful to you, grateful! I'm thanking you, do you hear me? Grateful— I'm choking on gratitude —overwhelmed by it, ohmygod—" She was choking on her tears. "Lying in wait to grab my hand! They'll work up to the pitch— It won't cost them a thing— How dare you! Who gave you the right—to be charitable—without even asking, ohmygod—god—god—god—"

"What did I do wrong?" thought Myatlev sadly. "My poor Alexandrina."

And he watched Dr. Schwanenbach, like the kind hound in a fairy tale, approach her, avoiding her fist, pressing his lips to her ear, quickly whispering something, his nostrils dilating as he nuzzled her in the shoulder, neck, chest, and put her to sleep, giving her hope, that blue-eyed Saxon, the liar, the—

Then she fell asleep. By morning her fever was down. She smiled guiltily at Myatlev, and kissed him with dry lips, and waved to him with her thin hand because it was time for him to leave.

He had been invited by his old regimental commander to join in celebrating his daughter's name-day. There Myatlev found himself surrounded by his former comrades, whom he had almost completely forgotten. Resonant, sparkling, well-mannered, pedigreed, well-spoken, they greeted Myatlev with sincere joy and affection, and conversation flowed like a river. However, their voices soon thundered off in the distance, and their useless questions hung in the air, motionless, having shed any sense they once had. They were soon bored by his other-worldliness and the guilty smile on his long, immobile face, and his sober, unfestive suit, even though it was British and well-tailored; and, as though suddenly enlightened, they remembered that he was a piece cut from the loaf, and living in a cloud of conspicuous mystery, sewn with white thread, as they say, an object of criticism and controversy, the one that Aneta Fredericks left (meaningful winks: For what reasons does a woman leave a man?), who then, in a fit of panic, had conquered the heart of a blahblahblah who now blahblahblah and he blahblahblah (deep sighs and shaking of heads). And his mystery no longer interested them, since its elements were nothing compared to their own mysteries and their amusements. He had nothing left to do but drink with them and blink, hoping that they would forget about him soon. And when they turned to one another again, the living to the living, he disappeared, unnoticed.

He traveled home slowly in his comfortable open carriage. Petersburg's summer emptiness made it seem like a small town. Probably the wine made Myatlev long for winter, steam, crowds, and frost. Where are you, winter's evening dark, shattered by the golden, unsteady spots of the streetlamps? The pale, stuffy dust swirled around the wheels of his carriage and settled on his face and shoulders. Not one familiar face. Nor the sound of a familiar voice. Not a word of sympathy. But even this Petersburg was not dead. Its sleepy, withered corpse, it turns out, was still breathing and twitching; you had only to look closely, and a sober von Müffling in blue uniform stood leaning on a parapet, recognized Myatlev, and gave a low bow. And the owner himself was standing in front of Savyely Egorov's tavern with his entire family, following the prince's carriage with a disapproving glance. And Lieutenant Katakazi in civilian clothes was strolling by the bookstore, pretending not to know Myatlev. And one other man in a blue suit and striped trousers, with an insolent red mustache, walked by, giving Katakazi an imperceptible nod—this passion for light blue!—and another one in blue stepped off the curb, looking for a cab. But that was von Müffling again! How did he get ahead of Myatlev and pop up on the Angiskaya Embankment? Behind him he heard the footsteps of a running man. Myatlev turned and saw Katakazi pursuing him, wiping his brow and tripping on the cobblestones. The carriage sped on, and Katakazi began falling behind. Myatlev stuck his tongue out at him and turned away, but then felt he had behaved badly. The horse was at a gallop. "Don't!" shouted Myatlev, grabbing his heart, but the coachman had lost control. Petersburg was far behind them, the sun had set, but the crazy horse, shedding flecks of foam, flew on and on, dragging the lightweight carriage. The whole business was taking on an unpleasant cast. Myatlev had just decided to jump out when out of nowhere von Müffling appeared and stopped the horse with one hand. A silence ensued. "An iron hand," the gendarme boasted, "be thankful." He rubbed the horse's nose. "Aren't you ashamed of yourself, you silly?" "Thank you," said Myatlev, "you are always rescuing me. I'd like to know where we are." Von Müffling climbed up on the coachbox and, cursing, said in the driver's voice:

"We're home, sir."

Myatlev opened his eyes. The carriage was in front of the house.

Afanasy was running toward him with an anguished look on

his face. His stupid scarf was falling off. His arms were doing God knows what. The prince froze.

"What happened?!" he called in a reedy voice.

"Your Excellency, Excellency," the valet cried, sobbing and shaking, "Mademoiselle Alexandrina—Your Excellency—"

"The doctor!" ordered Myatlev, and ran to Alexandrina.

A high-pitched wail fell on him, surrounding him, filling his ears, waxing and waning, hanging from the ceilings, seeping out of the walls, rising from the floor, swirling like fog, rising to a screech, ebbing away, barely perceptible, then increasing in volume, roaring, tearing his heart, keening, cursing, praying. The two maids, Stesha and Aglaya, scurried after Myatlev, not bothering to wipe away their tears. The door was wide open, the blanket on the bed thrown back, and the bed was empty.

"Silence!" roared Myatlev, and the wailing stopped. "Silence! Where's Alexandrina? Stop sobbing! Where's Alexandrina?"

He ran into the library, the maids, the valet, and Afanasy on his tracks. The library was empty. The quiet sobs were turning into a wail again.

"Silence!"

"Your Excellency," Afanasy managed to get out, "if you permit, we should be down at the river— We should, Excellency, be at the Nevka—we should, Your Excellency—" And he kept on repeating it while all of them, headed by the maddened prince, crossed the park on a straight path, trampling the grass, tearing out rosebushes, their eyes bulging, their faces pale, whipped by the branches, covered with cobwebs, out of breath, "to the Nevka, if I may say so—to the river, Your Excellency— as she was leaving, that's what she said— There was nowhere else for her to go, she said, Your Excellency—the Nevka, the Nevka—the Nevka—"

"It can't be," thought Myatlev, "it can't be! It would be too unfair—"

There was already a crowd at the riverbank, surrounding a woman's still body. Both maids began crying again, but Myatlev shut them up.

"Ohmygod," thought the prince in horror, "ohmygod!"

Suddenly Afanasy touched his hand.

"Your Excellency, it's someone else!"

Myatlev looked and couldn't believe it; before him, arms flung out on the grass, lay a drowned woman in peasant dress, her face broad and peaceful, as though asleep.

It was someone else, someone else, unknown to everyone there and to everyone living far away, in other cities, in another world, who had dropped her unneeded body into the swift and murky waters, either on someone's orders or wantonly, and now lay on the grass with a calm face among the living, who didn't feel they were strangers.

"It can't be," thought Myatlev in relief, returning through the park, "it can't be. It would have been unfair."

"Your Excellency," said Afanasy, still sobbing. "Mademoiselle Alexandrina is gone, gone, completely gone away, left the house— She ran down the stairs so fast—and ran out—Your Excellency, she ran through the park. Right along this very path, if I may—"

"What are you babbling about!" the prince said angrily, but increased his pace.

"She kept talking to herself about where to go— 'Where could I go?' And ran through the park— And the river is there, Your Excellency."

Myatlev hurried even more. Afanasy minced along next to him, peering into his face. Nearing the house, they ran again, and the stairs clattered and creaked underfoot. Their small unit bounded into the third floor, but Alexandrina was not there.

"Maybe she went into town, damn it?" asked Myatlev without hope.

"No, no, Excellency, she went straight through the park—and the river is there— She was crying hard, complaining, if I may say so, and then she ran away—"

"But you saw, you blockhead, whom they pulled out of the river!"

"I saw, Your Excellency—a strange lady—from the peasant class, if I may— But Mademoiselle Alexandrina ran toward the river, too—right through the park—"

No one noticed Dr. Schwanenbach come in, but the mocking scent of toilet water announced his presence, and Myatlev had Afanasy repeat his sad tale.

The doctor listened with great concentration, his head cocked and his Saxon blue eyes half-shut.

"And," he asked courageously, "did you see her reach the river? Right up to the river? Or did you see her run through the park? They're very different things," he said, and smiled a tight, controlled smile.

"Dr. Schwanenbach," Myatlev said in agitation, "time isn't standing still. We're losing precious minutes."

The maids began bawling again.

"If she was simply going through the park," the doctor continued confidently, "that does not give us the basis for assuming she had tragic intentions"—he was carefully looking out the window as he spoke, as though expecting Alexandrina to show up any minute—"even if, let's say, you"—here he addressed Afanasy—"saw her on the bank, that still doesn't mean anything because, exhausted by her illness, she may have simply wanted to go for a walk. I think—"

"And the tears? And her words? And the running away?" Myatlev asked grimly.

The doctor shrugged.

"She left for good, Your Excellency," Afanasy said, "she cried and said, if I may, that she had nowhere else to go—she was running toward the Nevka— I said, if I may, 'Where are you going? Why are you doing this, mam'selle?' And she said, 'Leave me alone, ohmygod!' "

"There you see!" cried Myatlev. "And you, you fool, you couldn't hold her by the arm, keep her here? There, you see how it happened, Dr. Schwanenbach? Now do you see?"

And he and the doctor headed for the river once more hot on the track of the poor young woman, but the shore was quiet, the river murky and deserted, and their bizarre figures seemed like wild sculptures in the early twilight.

Then, continuing their prodigious battle with the dark forces of nature, Myatlev and Dr. Schwanenbach got into the carriage and, facing away from each other, raced around town to all the police precincts until fate took pity on them (but what cruel pity it was!). They found out that a few hours before a young drowned woman had been brought to the morgue of Maria Hospital, her body taken from "Yes, yes, the Nevka—a young woman of noble mien— Yes, yes, long fair hair— Yes, thin and beautiful—"

The carriage, careening madly and covered with dust, raced to Maria Hospital, where the elderly caretaker took the two men to the refrigerated room. It is difficult to describe the state in which Myatlev crossed the threshold of that gloomy room. He walked in, took a step, and stopped in total prostration. He tried to see what was lying on the wooden bed in the corner, but he couldn't force his eyes open. Suddenly he heard Dr. Schwanenbach say in relief, "I knew it, I just knew it. This could not have been Alexandrina," Myatlev almost wept, and through the film of tears he saw a half-covered body on the bed.

"There," said Dr. Schwanenbach, when they were back in the carriage, "you should have listened to me. Alexandrina's psychological state was not that bad yet, for her to— A young organism, you know—" And he stared at the prince.

"Yes, of course," Myatlev said, stung by the Saxon's calm. "But what happened to her?"

"Guessing is not my profession," the doctor said. "I'm helpless here. But I think that the worst is over." He smiled with dignity. "You, however, should not have procrastinated back then, when things were still going well for you. Yes, you see— And now what?"

"But Alexandrina," Myatlev sobbed, "she ran to the river— she ran to the Nevka—through the park—she was crying—"

"Probably," said Dr. Schwanenbach with professional calm, "I'm not denying that. In all probability, her body is caught on something underwater. But we are helpless, Your Excellency."

24

SEVERAL MONTHS PASSED. WINTER began. The rivers froze. My prince, after all that had happened, sought solace wherever he could; he tried reliving his former escapades and follies in the company of his old comrades, but he soon moved on, for one cannot step into a flowing stream where one first entered it. Nevertheless, he had time to add to his sad record of wrongdoing with more than one infamous affair, once again disappointing and upsetting his family and friends and even the tsar himself. Then, not finding relief in that, he set out for his Mikhailovka, where he discovered chaos and disrepair, called the lazy bailiff on the carpet, even though he himself was just as lazy and helpless, wandered alone in the snowy woods, grew bored in the company of provincial and unbearable neighbors, suddenly developed a passion for writing stories, some based on his life but mostly invented ones, achieved a certain success at it, felt better and calmer, and returned to Petersburg.

Again he was greeted with monstrous refinement by Afanasy, who had resurrected his old top hat for the occasion, and by a subdued, redheaded Aglaya, who gave him a frightened smile, straightening the same purple dress. And the same objects and walls reminded him not only of past hurts but of his lost happiness. Everything seemed in balance, settled down, quiet. But this was only on the surface. It all seemed in balance, settled, and smoothed out, when actually nothing had been settled at all but had simply evolved, the better to encircle and torture and test him once more.

And therefore, overcoming his aversion to long trips, he rushed desperately to the passport office to get permission to travel abroad, hoping to go to England and then to the New World, where there were other shores, other customs, less dangerous than those of our swamps. But he was unlucky again, for his decision coincided with that damned Golovin's second refusal to return to Russia, and therefore the reply to Myatlev's request was cold and unambiguous.

Finally he remembered my blessed warm country, blue in dawn and pink at sunset, and the image of Maria Amilakhvari stirred in his consciousness like a cure for spiritual wounds, but his strength had left him and he shrugged off the trip, letting life do what it would with him.

Without any inner tremors but with a light sadness, Myatlev strolled through the second-floor rooms. They were covered with a layer of dust and had lost the fragrance of fresh leather, wood, and paint. They were marvelous rooms, so recently created out of his love of life, but now they merely reminded him of well-made canvases: carefully and accurately depicting every detail, but uninhabitable.

The cold rooms gave off an air, without awakening any memories, since Alexandrina's foot had never stepped on these marvelously refinished floors and her hands had never touched the many lovely objects lying about.

Having wandered through the rooms and having failed to find in them any resonance of his feelings, Myatlev ordered those doors hammered shut, too, so as not to return to the past.

The past, however, no matter how it retreats, still lives within us, for it is our hard-won experience that gives us a consciousness of our unique meaning as well as of our amazing nothingness and that makes us human. And this past chooses to appear to us in various guises, to remind us of itself with a light touch and keep us from being completely involved in our present successes and present sufferings.

So all Myatlev had to do was return to Petersburg, to his hearth and home, rid himself of his terrible memories, seal the second-floor doors, and pick up his cold books with their descriptions of other people's tragedies and passions, for Afanasy to inform him that Madame Schwanenbach was begging to see him on urgent business.

Suspecting nothing, he instructed Afanasy to bring up the doctor's wife, bracing himself to receive the fat, smug German woman. He was thus astounded to see a rather young, fashionably and tastefully dressed woman, trailed by a clutch of boys as blue-eyed as she, with thick napes and powerful necks, who bowed to the prince with decorous dignity.

After all possible apologies and necessary greetings, after all kinds of sympathy extended in respect of last summer's tragedy, which Myatlev barely heard, she said:

"The point is, Your Excellency, that Dr. Schwanenbach has abandoned us. Yes, oh yes. No, this didn't happen recently, and I wouldn't burden you with this—so many things can happen between husband and wife— Oh, yes, he's gone for good. And not now, but back then, when, just after the sad story, when you yourself, Your Excellency, quit Petersburg. I understood how it must have been unbearable for you after all that. I did not have the honor to know that woman, but Dr. Schwanenbach always kept me informed of his cases so thoroughly that I felt I did know her and sympathized sincerely with her, and you, and Dr. Schwanenbach, for he was quite nervous and was emotionally prostrate during that woman's illness. And when it happened, and I found out about it from Dr. Schwanenbach, knowing his attachment to that woman, I expected him to suffer, even to cry, and finally even to freeze up emotionally, as can happen, but I was totally unprepared for what did happen—and that is, Dr. Schwanenbach remained completely calm, as though nothing had happened at all, slightly distracted, which was not like him, and very businesslike. I thought that he had become somewhat mixed up in his mind, and the boys and I took pains to calm him down, because if he had only cried, this would not have happened to him, but he never cried, and I suppose the tension affected his brain. That was what I thought, Your Excellency, and I did not leave his side, for strong people in despair are capable of any act. And so, Your Excellency, he somehow managed to slip away from us and disappear."

"The poor doctor," thought Myatlev, "how great was his

despair if he could have killed himself and leave such sons and such a marvelous wife."

"Yes, there was something feverish about him the last few days," he said sympathetically. "I remember—I remember how heated he would get, and how strangely he spoke, and I remember just the way he was— Yes, I remember, now I understand why he would look away when he talked to me, and how nervous he was, and when he listened to *her* he would lean over her as though he had already noted something about himself there—"

"So, Your Excellency," Madame Schwanenbach continued, not paying too much attention to what the prince was saying, "he disappeared. I was desperate; my boys were falling asleep on their feet searching for him or at least his body, for a strong person is capable of almost anything in that condition; but all our investigations were in vain and there was no limit to our sorrow, when suddenly, Your Excellency, petrified with grief, I realized that along with Dr. Schwanenbach certain things that he could not do without were also gone. They were things that one does not take along if he is planning suicide. Not simply a handkerchief that you could carry off in your pocket without realizing, and not a snuffbox, or a coin purse— Well, boys, why don't you list the things we found missing."

"An English razor with all the saving accoutrements," said the first boy in a low voice.

"It was a rare and excellent razor, given to Dr. Schwanenbach by his older brother, which he prized highly," Madame Schwanenbach clarified. "Go on."

"Several pairs of good Dutch underwear," the second boy reported.

"You see?" said Madame Schwanenbach. "Four pair!"

"Two large medical dictionaries weighing eight pounds each," said the third.

"There you see? Sixteen pounds of paper! A little too much for a drowning victim, no?" And her blue Saxon eyes narrowed.

"And the plaid," said the first boy.

"Yes, the plaid," added Madame Schwanenbach. "It was his favorite plaid." And she laughed bitterly. "It would have been strange if he had left without it. Now do you see? Well, and finally, he took exactly half of our money. When I saw all that, I realized that Dr. Schwanenbach was alive. But what can it all mean, Your Excellency?"

Really, what could it mean? And what business was it of his, this disappearance of Dr. Schwanenbach, a vague, confusing man, already forgotten, a man who had allowed himself various hints and insinuations, a man with a powerful neck, pushed up by an impeccable collar, exuding a nauseating toilet water, ill-bred and unimportant? Really, what could it mean? Perhaps it meant that Dr. Schwanenbach, without even thinking about death, had simply slipped away from some difficulties in his life to some secret happiness that he had been hiding successfully? There are plenty of men who escape from the very paradises they themselves create. What does she want? Or perhaps that refined Saxon was horrified one day seeing himself in his three blue-eyed heirs, pedantic and pointedly well-behaved? Poor Alexandrina! How he would listen with fluttering heart to her piano playing, and how he would press his ear to her chest when she had no intention at all of coughing or choking, and how he would come first thing in the morning and immediately touch her, feeling her with his short, strong fingers, exposing her shoulders, chest, throwing back the blankets with a proprietary air! Poor Alexandrina!

"Your Excellency," Madame Schwanenbach inquired in a businesslike way, "have you ever seen the body of that woman? Or has it never been discovered? You stopped trying—you were no longer interested— I understand it could have caught on something, but it could have been found, perhaps, before the river froze. Yes, I understand that the ice is thick now, of course. But if with your connections you tried to have the body found— You know, Your Excellency, it's occurred to me that it could have been this way . . . saved . . . argument . . . documents . . . tobacco . . ."

Poor Alexandrina. He would promise Madame Schwanenbach everything that was within his power. But what would it achieve? He understood her state, shared her grief, but what would it achieve? If she was taken care of and wasn't threatened by the poorhouse, what did she care about the mad Saxon who ran into the unknown under cover of his own plaid? Poor Alexandrina.

At first Myatlev tried to keep his word, tried to get in touch with the proper people, but nothing seemed to work, he put it off, procrastinated, Mrs. Schwanenbach didn't remind him, the whole idea seemed pointless, began irritating him, and he dropped it.

25

... but he wasn't satisfied with that. He picked up a questionable woman on the street, promised to make her Princess Myatleva—how demeaned titles have become!—as is his wont took advantage of her, and then turned away.

The poor creature drowned herself, and he, as though nothing had happened, continues his evil ways, laughing at public opinion.

Prince Priymkov, known for his antigovernment views, sneaks into Petersburg despite the ban on visiting the capital, and stays—where do you think? Right there, at that man's house.

In the evening that man's servant parades on the street in the most prejudicial manner—a ridiculous hat, felt boots, and a dickey, frightening decent people.

[From an anonymous letter to the minister of His Majesty's court]

26

One afternoon, when the cold day was declining into twilight—and twilight in winter Petersburg is brief and dove-gray—the familiar figure in the long overcoat and cowl appeared outside the iron railing.

The figure appeared, as it had the last time, suddenly, as a reminder to the idle that a concerned society cares about and keeps an eye on them. Behaving quite decorously, the man in the cowl took his slow constitutional until Myatlev, burning with curiosity, pushed the reluctant Afanasy out for a walk in the frosty air.

"Your Excellency." said Afanasy, pulling on his felt boots and settling his top hat on his head, "if I may, I'm not against going for a walk, but those people don't like jokes, Excellency."

And carefully placing one crooked foot in front of the other, the so-called Marquis Troyat set off to meet his so-called neighbor. However, this time the cowled man behaved much more naturally, without any fear, took the bull by the horns, not even waiting for a hint from Afanasy, and complained of the cold and wind. Afanasy, overjoyed at the chance to avoid the chilly and tiring walk, hurried to invite him in. And Myatlev watched the charming pair go up to the porch.

The valet fed his guest tea and rum, but, try as he might, he couldn't get the guest to accept another glass. The stranger introduced himself as Sverbeyev and said he was a tradesman. Afanasy took him to be forty or forty-five. He had a wrinkled, weather-beaten face, small, sad eyes, and an equally sad, drooping mustache. They had a simple and meaningless conversation—about prices and the weather—and Afanasy, as he reported to Myatlev in the morning, was about to yawn, when the guest quite casually alluded to the incident of last summer and then, while taking his leave, expressed surprise at the prince's way of life.

"What surprised him about it?" Myatlev asked.

"Here's what, Your Excellency," Afanasy said. " 'How is it that this prince of yours, if I may, lives such a solitary life? He probably has solitary friends, too? You mean, he just reads and reads and reads?' 'Yes' I said, 'imagine that.' 'And no one comes to visit him—from the provinces, for instance? Or from somewhere else?' 'No' I said, 'no one.' 'So he just reads and reads?' And then he said, 'Well, he's a prince; he can just read if he wants to.' And when he was leaving, he asked, 'Maybe someone from Tula Province comes to visit him?' 'Why from Tula Province?' I asked. 'Just an example,' he said."

The powerful specter of the impotent Hobbler soared above Petersburg. It was he who was forcing the sad Mr. Sverbeyev to take his icy constitutionals, exceeding all known limits for human tolerance of the cold. Next he brought Lieutenant Katakazi back to the three-story wooden house with its shady reputation, where the lieutenant was not admitted past the entry—which did violence to his ambition. And it was the specter who spun the thin thread, invisible but strong, between the Hobbler's estate in Tula and the staff of detectives, and used it, pulled it taut, to discover the moods and feeble impulses of the outcast prince.

What prompted that flawless apparatus to such strict surveillance? Were questionable sounds coming from its own wheels, which had been greased with such mind-boggling calculation and effort? After all, the wave that had once splashed up on Senate Square had ebbed a long time ago, and Herzen* was living abroad in exile. And hordes of dull, unwashed students had turned, with the revulsion of truly loyal citizens, from anything that might confuse them or arouse them, and sang foolish songs about gluttony and merrymaking with bought women, which in no way threatened the government. There was really nothing left that was worth suppressing, and in that very

*Alexander Herzen (1812–70), a leading revolutionary thinker and writer.—Translator.

atmosphere of general prosperity lay the reason why the mighty specter of the impotent Hobbler seemed even more threatening than the secret conspiracies of the past.

And my prince? What did he care about the complexities of his time? And—let alone the complexities—about those contrivances that served only to keep the sluggish, steady flow of life protected from disturbing sights, words, and deeds? And what could he have done? He knew there was nothing he could do, and so he did not ask for a pedestal. And he compared himself with a sad smile to the students, for if they sang hymns to gluttony, then so did he, even though his table was set much more elaborately. And if, unwilling to let their flesh die, they embraced their unwashed women, then so did he, even though his ladies were somewhat more refined and did not reek of bedbugs and dampness. And so he entered his age of consent without thinking of great possibilities, as though he did not even suspect their existence. And when he listened to the verbose and monstrous opinions of Andrei Vladimirovich, only an unexpected smile would light up his long face, because agreeing with the Hobbler meant counting oneself as one of the empty talkers, and there was no point in substantiating his skepticism.

Rail, belch out curses, brag of your imprudence, but the apparatus will drone on, grinding up you and your fantasies, and a force unknown to you will beckon you and other lucky men just where it wants you to go. It has already trampled insolent poets and all the young officers who believed in themselves, and poor Alexandrina, despite her struggles and no matter how she struck her knee with her fist, and Dr. Schwanenbach, and many, many others.

Well, all right. But still is it really our destiny to imitate the worm, the one that comes out after rain, pink and fat? That's the question. The soul, like the body, should be firm and inflexible. Ah, prince, have you gotten too soft?

And that is the way it was until once again hurried, tiny, sneaky footsteps scampered to the house from the wilds of the park. Whose, do you think? They quickly crossed the meadow, trampled the rosebushes, stopped for a second, and then cascaded, as if from a horn of plenty, across the veranda, around the house, and up the porch steps.

"A visitor," Afanasy whispered, his version of a smile on his face. And he flung open the doors.

"Good Lord," said Myatlev, "it's you?"

"Some good lord," laughed Mr. van Schoenhoven, turning red. "Who did you think?"

The boy had grown noticeably during their long separation. He was still wearing the same jacket, now older and shorter, and the same black felt boots and the raspberry-colored hat. And the thin, much longer arms were held tightly to his side, as though he were a little soldier about to report his successful arrival. The dark chestnut hair pushed confidently from under the hat, and the big gray eyes, amazingly familiar, studied the prince openly.

"And you're still wearing the same robe," said the boy, "as though you had never taken it off." He sat down in a chair, waving his legs. "*Maman* and I had time to go to Italy this summer," he announced. "We were in Rome and Genoa, and bathed in the sea. And then we settled on our estate, thinking to pass the entire winter there, but my tears"—he laughed—"and *Maman*, who hates the country, but she decided to stay there to teach Kaleria, that's my aunt, a long-nosed bird, a lesson, but my tears, and pale visage, and suffering—" He laughed again, showing his even white teeth with their child's notched edges. "Hey, hitch up the horses, and hurry it up, and bring the suitcases, and bake some pies! Wolves chased us," he announced, bugging out his eyes, "aren't you scared? Really, really, four mangy wolves, and I fed them a lot of bread and bones. Scary, isn't it? Oooh, *Maman* was mad at me during the entire trip, but I had only one idea: to get home, and I would lead them through the park to you. Are you glad?" And he blushed again.

"Have you been back long?" Myatlev said, happy to see Mr. van Schoenhoven again. "I'm so glad you came to see me. Three days ago? You should have come right away, right away. As soon as you arrived.

"That's easy enough to say," laughed Mr. van Schoenhoven,

"right away. I have to prepare, sir, weigh all the possibilities, take everything into account—right away. Madame Jacqueline, my governess, suddenly had a fever, manna from Heaven—a big fever—influenza— I had to look in the trunks—where did this damn jacket get to? 'What are you looking for?' 'Ah, *Maman,* I had a ribbon here—' " He suddenly broke off. "Of course, I should have let you know I was coming, and not just rush in like this, but what can one do, Prince?"

"And now, Mr. van Schoenhoven," said Myatlev, "take off your jacket and get comfortable. I hope you won't object to some conversation. I'll have tea served—"

"Eh, what nonsense," the boy said angrily, "you are always up to some formality or other. What's bothering you about my clothes? I'm just fine the way I am. However, if this shocks you, fine." And Mr. van Schoenhoven pulled off his raspberry hat and tossed it across the room. "Is that better?" And his dark chestnut hair fell to his shoulders.

Myatlev laughed and ordered tea, and, while he was ordering, kept looking over at Mr. van Schoenhoven out of the corner of his eye, trying to recollect whom this thin little creature reminded him of.

"I would have been pleased to have gotten a letter from you," he said. "Why didn't you write?"

"What would I have written about?" laughed the boy. "I'm coming home, meet me? Yes? I can imagine *Maman*'s reaction if she knew I was writing to *you*. What do you mean, why? Because I don't write to anyone, and suddenly I—" said Mr. van Schoenhoven, getting his sleeve in the jam. "There," he said, saddened, and cleaned off his sleeve with his napkin, "there's all kinds of talk about you as it is, and suddenly I write to you—"

"Mr. van Schoenhoven," said Myatlev, looking angry, "if associating with me is regarded as reprehensible, then you should not—"

"Maybe it's only flattery," the boy muttered, embarrassed. "Maybe it's not reprehensible at all—how would you know?" And he got stuck in the jam again and got embarrassed again.

"Take off that jacket, for God's sake!" Myatlev wailed. "Why suffer?"

Mr. van Schoenhoven, without raising his red face, quickly and obediently took off his jacket, tossing it somewhere, and remained dressed in a replica of a Hussar's uniform, which became him greatly. He stared into his cup.

"Bah!" thought Myatlev. "What is it? What is it?"

Really, something had happened, something had changed inexplicably in Mr. van Schoenhoven's face, in the way he leaned hunched over his cup, narrowing his thin shoulders, and the way his dark chestnut hair fell forward, covering his red face, when he brought the cup to his lips. "You know," Myatlev said, understanding nothing, "I thought about you, I really did. I even have an entry in my diary about it. You see how I missed you—"

"Eh, eh," the boy said, "drop the consoling talk, sir. I'm no child."

Of course, Mr. van Schoenhoven had grown up considerably. It was obvious immediately. Not only in size, but in his carriage and gestures and manner of speaking—all so common in boys at the age when they begin to see themselves as little men and try to hide their ingenuousness under a casual air. It all added up to the fact that Mr. van Schoenhoven had passed a certain barrier and that now, freed of childhood's fetters, throwing them off like the raspberry hat, he could join the mainstream of life, tripping, falling, and rising again. Of course, Mr. van Schoenhoven had grown visibly, but that was not it, it wasn't what was bothering Myatlev, stealthily watching the boy. Something had happened that demanded an explanation, but what, he couldn't imagine. It kept slipping away, ran off, melted in his hands and consciousness, like the first undependable snowfall. And Myatlev kept trying to unravel the ball, listening to Mr. van Schoenhoven's story about yesterday's matinee at someone's house, where he danced for the first time, and how he was stuck at the very first dance with a fat and dull fourteen-year-old-boy and how it was all rather interesting and fun at first—even "taking his breath away"—but then Mr. van Schoenhoven became "bored, bored, bored," for all the girls were artificial and unbearable, and the boys "stupid and lazy and asked stupid questions." Then they had tea with fresh rolls and fresh butter—"very tasty"—and there was a lot of candy and a grab bag, but Mr. van Schoenhoven was "terribly tired" of it all and he made "unbearable Kaleria" take him home.

"If only you had been there!" Mr. van Schoenhoven sighed.

He set aside his empty cup and leaned back in the chair, the picture of satiety and content. Yes, but whom did he remind Myatlev of as he did this, his thin hands pushing back the unruly hair falling on his narrow shoulders, opening as wide as possible gray eyes that glimmered with a soft light? No, he does not belong to us; he comes from a foreign land, an Aeolian son, now concentrating on the clumsy masterpiece on the wall in front of him, or making believe; yesterday he had danced at a children's ball where the girls were unbearable and artificial—all of them?

"Yes, of course, one was worse than the other," he maintained, "as though you didn't know. You of all people. They were all little Kalerias—or little *mamans*."

"And you didn't like a single one of the girls? You're a bluebeard, Mr. van Schoenhoven!"

"When spring comes," said the boy, barely suppressing his laughter, "let's go down to the big Neva River together to watch the ice break up."

Yes, that would make a marvelous outing, if, of course, Kaleria or Madame Jacqueline didn't interfere, but could it really be possible that Mr. van Schoenhoven didn't like a single girl there? He remembered when he was—eh—?

"Thirteen, sir, thirteen."

Yes, when he was thirteen he was no Bluebeard, and he liked giving girls presents—well, like flowers—and he defended them from the advances of fat and obnoxious boys, and—

Here Mr. van Schoenhoven clapped his hands and burst out laughing. What a silly that Myatlev was! How could anyone be that silly? To whom could he possibly give flowers? Mr. van Schoenhoven giving flowers? Ridiculous! What nonsense!

He leaped up from his chair, rolling with laughter, wiping away tears, doubling over, grabbing the table, the windowsill, his stomach—a well-built boy in a Hussar uniform, such a marvelous laugher, inventor, and prankster, who danced—just think of it!—with a fat fourteen-year-old lout who stepped on his feet and permitted himself to say ridiculous things.

Finally Mr. van Schoenhoven had laughed his fill and stopped by the window. Now his exquisite silhouette showed dark against the white, frosty glass. And Myatlev was beginning to understand, beginning to guess everything, but he would not allow himself to speak first; it might sound crude, and crudity in these situations was a crime. He had to be patient until this mystification worked itself out.

"Madame Jacqueline is exhausted," said Mr. van Schoenhoven quietly, without turning around, "*Maman* scolds me, Kaleria has prepared poisoned arrows for me. Madame Jacqueline won't be sick for a long time again; she's as healthy as a horse." A deep sigh came from the window. "You promise to take me to see the ice in spring?" Myatlev promised. "If you like, I'll write you a letter—well, something, if you want—if you won't think it's silly— Ah, what nonsense—"

"Please do," Myatlev said softly, feeling the denouement coming on and trying not to frighten the subdued Mr. van Schoenhoven. "I'd be very happy if you did. I'm lonely all by myself, and I'll reply. But why letters? Why can't you just drop over for tea?"

"Prince," Mr. van Schoenhoven said with difficulty, "I want to reveal a terrible secret to you. But you must swear not to laugh or despise me. Cross yourself—like that."

The boy turned to Myatlev. Now he was facing him, his arms along his seams, trying not to avert his eyes. The prince nodded.

"And what is your real name, then?"

"Lavinia. Do you forgive me?"

And it was a small girl who bade the prince farewell, and not so small at that, a graceful reed, a budding young lady. Now every gesture, every movement revealed it, and how could Myatlev not have seen it from the first? Everything, absolutely everything gave her away; and only when the dark chestnut hair was tucked away under the raspberry cap did the vague image of Mr. van Schoenhoven reappear, but only for a second, melting away instantly. Lavinia—the wife of Aeneas! Lavinia Bravura—the daughter of a man of Polish extraction. She had been born after his death and adopted by General Tuchkov, who had died quite recently of an apoplectic stroke. His young widow tried to get permission to revert to her first surname, but that was impossible and fraught with unpleasantness. So she remained a Tuchkova, but she would say, "We Bravuras," thus giving her first love his due.

"*Maman* never speaks of the general," Lavinia explained as they parted. "It's as though he had never existed." And she laughed. "The poor general— But my father's portraits are all over the house, and Aunt Kaleria is worried that it will lead to trouble—"

Mr. van Schoenhoven? Just like that? Well, it's just a picture— Well, there's a picture in her room, a picture of a Madame van Schoenhoven— A Dutch lady. And when she was little she had wanted to be like that woman. Yes, very beautiful, with a white apron, can you picture it? And in a tall head-dress— And with a very serene gaze, Madame van Schoenhoven had achieved the highest— What? Well, she doesn't know what the highest is, but it must exist, no? When you reach it, you find out— No-o-o, *Maman* is far from reaching it—it's time to go, and let Myatlev's funny man see her out.

She was glad that the prince would see her to the porch himself.

They left the room and went slowly down the stairs. The house was still and seemed almost uninhabited. Just the old planks of the house creaking and a barely discernible muttering of conversation coming from deep downstairs.

On the second floor they passed the roughly sealed door to the rooms of poor Alexandrina.

"Aren't you afraid alone in the house?" Lavinia whispered, as though the invisible shade of the dead woman had touched her shoulder.

The sounds of life downstairs increased. The muttering was more distinct. Aglaya, deftly sidestepping the marble statues, brought a samovar into Afanasy's room. She bowed embarrassedly to Myatlev and went inside. The sun's rays poured in through the small windows of the entry.

"Enough," said Lavinia. "I'll do the rest myself. Do you forgive me?"

And she fearlessly started out through the park, bathed in the winter sun, sinking into the snow, raising her thin hands, leaving Myatlev amazed and delighted.

Returning through the vestibule, Myatlev peeked past the half-open door into Afanasy's room. The valet was sitting at the table in his shirtsleeves, a tea saucer in his outspread fingers and the same old Walter Scott in the other hand. A bright red neckerchief, not of sparkling freshness, evinced both his overwhelming tastelessness and his undisguised desire to turn the heads of his colleagues, who saw him almost as an aristocrat—if not by birth, then certainly in his habits.

The samovar towered over him on the table, and on his left, sprawled in a chair the master had discarded, lay Mr. Sverbeyev himself, dipping his long mustache into a saucer of tea.

"What an unpleasant face," thought Myatlev of Sverbeyev, as he turned away. "A real phenomenon."

And yet he had to laugh at the idyllic picture they presented and approve the actions of his crafty valet. The mustachioed bird was in their hands and burning its wings on the samovar. Suspecting nothing, it was hoping to please its high-placed patrons.

Gradually the spy's face dulled and was replaced in his consciousness by the image of the Hobbler, who was tied invisibly to the spy. Myatlev suddenly realized that his exiled friend was the only one who could understand him and evaluate the situation. He wrote him an expansive letter, which included lines like this:

. . . what can you do, dear Andrei Vladimirovich? The brilliance and freedom of the Alexandrine generation is not for you and me. It is now remembered as a fairy tale, a delightful idyll. We know of it only by hearsay. Our lot is to freeze. I no longer see the point of living, not merely existing, but living with inspiration and hope. There was a person I wanted to serve, a poor lovely woman (you know), but she, too, became the victim of the force inexorably suppressing us.

Now, thanks to you, and perhaps to several of my past "misadventures," I'm suspected and surrounded like a bear in his lair, and believe me, I don't even feel like protesting. What is there to protest about? The same spy whom you once discovered upside down in my chimney now visits my home as Afanasy's close friend and drinks tea with him. Just imagine for a minute that it is not I who am master of this house—I, who have given up on right and wrong—but my father with his principles, with his sense of honor and of duty to an enlightened government. He would take up a cudgel and throw the spy out, and would also beat the spy's boss for daring to dream up such a farce. But in those days this sort of thing would never have happened. The spies were more noble in those days, too, not the ones we have today—all light-blue, multitudinous, semiliterate, and of doubtful origins. And I'm not speaking of the likes of the Sverbeyevs, that lowest order of spyhood, who are prepared to freeze and hang upside down in chimneys.

What's left? I loved a woman—she died. I did not succeed as an officer; it's not for me. I'm repelled by the idea of serving society, for I don't believe in it, and, in general, I'm not drawn by official temptations. And because of this they point their fingers at me and shower me with reproaches, and now they've put a spy on me. You think your exposés are very significant. God bless you if they are, but I don't see any point in it.

Perhaps I should marry and become a good landowner? So you believe in that path? And whom should I marry? I just don't see the right woman. I mentioned it to my sister, and she tried to stick me with her high-born, pampered beauty with the cow eyes. You should see that monster!

I thought of getting away—I'd been thinking about it a long

time—and went to the country, but it was even worse. In the capital we have at least learned—again through our own weaknesses—to hide our helplessness under tinsel and glitter, the appearance of civilization, but there everything is exposed and therefore revolting.

There are rumors of reforms, but how is that possible if every third person is a policeman in disguise?

I had another attack yesterday; I was walking around the Praskovya Palace when I felt its onset. It apparently lasted longer than usual, because when everything was over I was already on Bolshoi Prospect. An empty cab was moving alongside me, and the driver was watching me in horror. I got in and went home. On the way he told me that I'd been trying to force money on a passerby, who refused to take it even though I begged him and followed him until I ended up on Bolshoi Prospect. All I remembered was that I had run into General Balmashev—you must certainly know him through your studies—and that he had for some reason handed me his English microscope and refused to accept any money for it.

They say there's a Dr. Morinari in Moscow who can cure similar cases.

Finishing the letter, Myatlev was lost in thought. Then he heard noises: either choral singing or bitter weeping, together with the sound of slamming doors. He went out of the room. Several colored lanterns blinked on the stairs and landings, barely dissipating the gloom.

Down below, where the marble people suffered in their immobility, extending their arms to one another in hopeless entreaty, someone's restless shadow raced about, stumbling and falling and getting up, accompanied by mutterings and groans. And it wasn't Afanasy, or the gardener, or the postilion, or the chef, or the porter, or one of the taciturn lackeys. It was the two-legged shadow of an unknown person, and it spun and ran moaning, in some strange sorrow, lost in the marble labyrinth.

"Damn it all!" thought Myatlev, slowly coming down the stairs. His step was heavy and perplexed, for his soul was still filled with the bitterness of the letter he had just written; it had not had time to dissipate. His perplexity had arisen as soon as the figure in the raspberry cap disappeared behind the first trees, and it had increased the minute he put down his pen. "What, I'm still alive?" That was his first thought as he came out on the stairs. "And this is my house? And this is my fortress? This was what Alexandrina scorned? The countless Numidian regiments were here already, crawling in all the corners, sharpening their poisoned arrows, lying in wait, reeking of sweat and sheep fat, each one wearing a dried lizard instead of a cross around his wrinkled, sweaty neck—"

Redheaded Aglaya appeared from the dusk, her white apron billowing over her stomach.

"What's this?" thought the prince, stunned by the size of her belly. "That's something new."

Her belly really was quite large, and swollen, and growing like a blister, so that Aglaya's thin arms barely encircled it, but she gave Myatlev an insolent look.

"What's that?" he asked stupidly. "What have you there? What's the matter?"

"The usual thing," she replied disrespectfully.

"But that's a belly," he muttered. "Look how big it is! How did you do that?"

"The usual thing," she repeated, and suddenly began mumbling, "Your Excellency, what will happen now? What else can I do now, Your Excellency? Please influence him!"

In Alexandrina's former rooms, beyond the door, something fell and rolled. Evidently the spirit of that poor suffering creature was moaning there, disgusted by the inequities it had discovered and unable to find a resting place. Myatlev shouted for Afanasy, but he was already by his side, in his formal livery with the torn galloon, barefoot, a look of despair on his stupid, round face. Sverbeyev was behind him. He bowed tavern-style, formally and drunkenly, and left the house without shutting the door behind him.

"I," said Afanasy, "dare to relate that I said to her more than once, 'What are you thinking of? I have His Excellency on my hands, I'm not a free man.' And her? What did you say to that, hah? Nothing— 'No, don't you worry, come here,' she said. She kept trying to confuse me. Her brazen eyes would entrap me and inflame me! And I would say, 'Come to your senses, I don't love you—' "

"Charming," thought Myatlev.

Afanasy's bare feet padded on the parquet, the torn galoon dangled like a pendulum, his index finger poked threateningly at Aglaya's belly; and his stupid, despairing gaze was directed there, too.

"I told her, 'Where are you leading me, where? You, if I may dare report, don't realize the consequences— I don't love you! I love another!' But her damn eyes didn't listen to the voice of reason; they didn't pay attention!"

The anxiety left Myatlev. A futile boredom and a sense of the uselessness of life hung over him like a cloud. Discrete words reached him; their vague meanings still reached his brain, but they were harmless. He wanted to escape from the house and not return until morning, but Aglaya began moaning louder, and an irritating new note crept into Afanasy's argument.

"Lord have mercy," he insisted, "don't you remember, Excellency, how she chased me in the rosebushes that very day when your sister, Her Excellency, came to the veranda during lunch and that doctor, the German, argued with you— Oh, how she chased me, Your Excellency, shamelessly and without conscience, and yet I kept whispering to her, 'Come to your senses, leave me alone, you crazy woman; I love another!' "

"Oh-oy-oy!" cried Aglaya, pushing Myatlev with her heavy belly.

"Silence!" shouted the prince, like a sergeant, and stamped his foot.

Then, despite my suggestions and pleading, Myatlev, in some kind of semimadness, chose the worst possible way out: he decided to have that incongruous pair married and thereby, he felt, restore justice. (The desire to restore justice is always noble but not always just. Force is a poor substitute for more lawful impulses, and, as they say, hurry is the sister of failure and

144

impetuosity the sister of blindness. What justice could there be?)

He made this decision in the heat of passion. Then he immediately changed his mind and wanted to release them from it. But once again something clicked inside him, and poor Afanasy's fate was sealed.

Red-haired Aglaya was triumphant, and the valet's desperation reached such a point that he dropped his usual aplomb and threw himself at Myatlev's feet.

The prince knew his decision was abhorrent, but he could not take it back a second time. You should have seen him, in his flawless frock coat, accompanying the miserable couple to church. His face was pale and reflected his ill-concealed suffering. *Why*, prince? How could you? How could you set yourself up as the stern judge? "And who are the judges?" asked the poet.

"Ohmygod!" whispered Afanasy at the altar, wringing his hands.

The newlyweds settled in the majordomo's familiar room. A short time later Aglaya delivered herself of a spindly infant. The prince, still suffering from guilt, hoped to be the godfather, but the child died without ever opening its eyes.

Life went on. Afanasy was taciturn, formal, pointedly helpful—a silent walking reproach. Aglaya blossomed, her wide hips quivering and her insolent eyes steady on the prince when she talked to him. Sverbeyev continued to drop over for family tea, and behind the closed door they moved chairs, rustled, clattered, jangled, and boisterous echoes raced along the house and settled in Alexandrina's rooms.

Myatlev had noticed that the usual noises of his half-empty house had been supplemented by new, unknown ones, coming from somewhere. Sometimes during the day, or in deepest night, he would suddenly hear an inexplicable creak, a groan, a distant, dying scream. He would jump out of bed, run from his room, and listen, but the strange noises would stop, only to return the next day, at the most unexpected moments. It was as though the household ghosts people talked about were rushing through the rooms, cursing, tearing up loose boards as they passed, and

145

rattling the rafters. Or perhaps a band of robbers lived in the attic expanses.

Finally, losing his temper, Myatlev, accompanied by Afanasy and armed with a lantern and pistol, toured the unused parts of the house and the attic, layered with viscous dust, but he found nothing suspicious. Yet as soon as they had given up, somewhere over their heads or perhaps off to one side, something screeched like a rusty nail torn from its place, mocking them, and voices muttered. And then it was still.

Winter was coming; rain fell mixed with snow, and the skies lowered, and none of this induced serenity of spirit, and now there was this bacchanalia of evil sounds; and Myatlev envisioned blue skies, and yellow sands, and a cliff overgrown with forest, and Maria Amilakhvari on a huge balcony warmed by the sun, which is unknown in Petersburg in October. "I must get away!" he exclaimed to himself once more, like an old swan flapping his wings. "Run away! Hide!"

And I, an old fool, supported the prince's desire, for I saw that his seclusion and vague dissatisfaction would lead to no good.

27

USUALLY IN MOMENTS OF melancholy, when words repelled him, when oranges reeked of onion, dust motes wounded his bronchial tubes, and the touch of silk hurt, he would gulp down several glasses of vodka in order to forestall the onslaught of dizziness. In those moments the surrounding world would stop existing: gardens died, streets emptied, and his compatriots dissolved into a blurred impression.

But this time everything had changed, and Providence had prompted Myatlev to leave his fortress, cross the moat, pass the gates, trick the guards, and throw himself into the Sodom of Petersburg.

At first he felt the strange, uncomfortable sensation of not belonging to the environment, but this did not upset him, as it should have; instead, it even excited him, and his smiling, bespectacled face began to attract attention. Suddenly he felt that he had entered the water, and the water wasn't cold—it was, in fact, just right: it was easy, pleasant, and quiet. Then he stopped a coach and named the first address that came to mind.

He drove along, and nothing hinted at the coming storm; but secret forces were doing their work, blinding and exciting him. Suddenly he dismissed the coach, as though he had seen someone walking in the distance, someone who was the whole point of the day, the trip, and the break in his routine; he ran ahead; it felt as though he were waving his arms, his toes barely touching the sidewalk, his neck thrust forward, peering and sniffing. Finally he saw a woman get out of a carriage and head for a front door. He ran as fast as he could. She turned slowly, painfully. Her beautiful, haughty face quivered; her deep, dark eyes flew open. She saw Prince Myatlev coming toward her and had time to notice that the street was practically empty, that the prince was almost handsome, despite his slightly sunken cheeks and his spectacles, that his single-breasted navy-blue suit made him look pale, and his gray hat was set too far back on his head, but that in his gait as he approached there was a certain desperate charm, that he had the eyes of a wise man and the smile of an adulterer. And what were all those stories about him? And that woman who threw herself into the Neva—what did it all mean?

He tipped his hat clumsily. She nodded clumsily to him. He wasn't smiling.

"Natalie?" he said simply. "It was as though I knew I would meet you."

Countess Rumyantseva looked down the street. It was empty.

"I hope that doesn't upset you too much," she said with bemused dignity.

"Why did I always think her stupid?" he thought. "She's charming, honest to God—"

Ill fortune continued weaving its web in feverish haste,

causing the countess to smile helplessly and utter a few meaningless phrases, to which he replied, attaching no great meaning to them, either, but studying her almost frankly and more and more amazed by her perfection.

They came to some forty minutes later.

She looked around. The street was empty.

"But was I condemning you?" she asked, continuing the conversation. "It just seemed that way to you. On the contrary, I—I always—you have so much mystery and appeal, Prince—" She blushed, but continued her confessions. "They don't love you, but I almost do—"

The unhurried coachman fed his horses some oats.

MYATLEV: For some reason, I had thought that you—
NATALYA: Loneliness is playing cruel tricks on you.
MYATLEV: I suppose— Wait—I would like to— Are you leaving? I would like to continue our conversation.
NATALYA: What? What do you have in mind?
MYATLEV: You see, Natalie, it's—
NATALYA: No, no, Prince— It's impossible, you see that.
MYATLEV: We could, for instance—
NATALYA: You seem troubled by something.
MYATLEV: You're troubling me—I don't understand; you're so young, so beautiful—we've known each other a long time—we'll get in the carriage—I don't understand—
NATALYA: We'll get in the carriage, and then?
MYATLEV: Well, we'll drive around town—
NATALYA: Ah, I see.
MYATLEV: No, you don't. Why do you keep looking around? We'll go for a drive— Or, if you want—

The horses had finished their oats.

She looked around. The street was empty.

"It's so difficult with you," she said in agitation. "You keep saying something, demanding something—I no longer understand you."

"Listen, Natalie," he said completely calm, coming so close that they were almost touching, "well, all right, let's do it this way—"

Just then two strange men tumbled noisily out of the front door. One was quite young, of medium height, slender, with wild, curly hair, wearing the long baggy jacket which was just coming into fashion; he had moist lips, shiny eyes, and a thick bamboo cane under his arm.

The other was older, a lieutenant in the uniform of the Preobrazhensky Regiment, tall, rather corpulent, with bow-shaped lips and bulging, watery eyes; the huge red rose in his left fist was drooping and half its petals were gone.

"Here they are!" called the one in civilian garb.

"Ah," said Natalya, "here are the charlatans—springing up from the earth— My nephews," she said to Myatlev.

"Mikhail Berg the Third," the lieutenant introduced himself with a mournful mien. "A second cousin—"

"And this is Koko Tetenborn," Natalya said.

"Yes, Tetenborn," the curly-haired one laughed, "precisely, and also a nephew. But I'm Tetenborn the Second, first of all, and secondly, I'm a third cousin, as opposed to Lieutenant Misha—he's Berg the Third, but a second cousin. That's the difference. And besides that, he's a courageous mercenary, while I, despising the sword and lance, am a titular councillor, and there is no greater expert in the postal department—"

"Calm down, Koko," Natalya said. "Do you like them?" she asked Myatlev. "Aren't they sweet?"

The prince's excitement did not lessen as he listened to the young men's chatter. He still kept his eyes fixed on Natalya, devouring and adoring her, and the two youths, so very different, seemed good-natured, and were only a little arrogant, and appeared to be absolutely charming.

"You have marvelous nephews," he said.

And everything was good: the early summer's day, empty, quiet Sergiyevskaya Street, and the gray dappled horses and the coach, and the two impossible nephews, and, finally, Natalya herself, of whom for some reason he had thought badly and degradingly, and who, it turned out, was not only beautiful but full of the most amazing virtues you couldn't even name right off the bat.

"We were sitting there," shouted Koko Tetenborn, "and they, you see, were right here under the windows. Well, we were watching you from up there," he admitted. "What can you talk about for two hours? Hah? What about? Your *maman* asked us, 'What is Natalie talking to the prince about for so long, at such length, and so gracefully and so nervously?' 'What do you mean what about? There's plenty to talk about.' Time passes and conversation flows—right? But the most amazing thing is how you managed your meeting so cleverly! The minute you stepped out of the carriage, the prince was here—"

Natalya blushed slightly.

"Why don't we go to some second-rate tavern, where there is dirt, and smoke, and drunken faces, and miasmas?" Lieutenant Berg suggested dourly.

"Fool," Natalya laughed. "What a monster—"

"My brother calls that a cleansing," Koko explained. "I myself prefer to cleanse myself in a decent place, in some proper, clean, patriarchal, hospitable home, on a good couch, with champagne, and my auntie next to me—right, Natalie? And your *maman* shouldn't know where we were—"

"It really would be a good idea to crash into a tavern," thought Myatlev, "or anywhere else. Just so that we don't part."

Natalya's eyes were shining feverishly. Excitement had over-taken them all.

"Yes, yes," she said, giving Myatlev her arm, "let's go, let's go somewhere, even to a tavern—even to a dirty one—"

"How charming they are!" thought Myatlev, looking at his new friends. "We have to go, we must hurry, there isn't a moment to waste!"

At some secret signal they all headed for the carriage. They scurried to sit down, panted, laughed, stepped all over one another's feet. Myatlev tried to sit next to Natalya, but when the horses set off, it turned out that she was on the back seat, squeezed in on both sides by her nephews, and Myatlev sat on the front seat, all alone.

"Let's go, let's go!" Koko shouted, kissing his aunt's hand.

She stared intently at Myatlev. Her dark, deep, lovely eyes frightened him—just barely, the tiniest, most insignificant bit.

Myatlev didn't even notice that he had ordered the coachman to drive to his house. And the people sitting opposite him showed neither disagreement nor surprise, as though they had all decided on the three-story wooden fortress as their destination.

"Auntie," shouted Koko Tetenborn, still showering her with kisses, "you are such a bad girl! How cleverly you arranged all this! with such inspiration. What do you say, Berg?"

But Lieutenant Berg sat in gloomy silence, leaning on his aunt. His closely cropped blond head rocked on her rounded shoulder. The worn rose rubbed forgotten against the carriage door, shedding its last petals.

"We love our aunt very much," continued Tetenborn, "we simply adore her. She is our goddess, Prince. And not only because she is beautiful—there are plenty of beautiful women, goddamn them!—but because she is wise, and softhearted, and not willful, and a sweetie, and a sneaky darling, and our little queenie—"

The horses raced along at full speed, the carriage rolling slightly, and Lieutenant Misha's light head kept slipping off the shoulder of the magnificent young woman. He was asleep. Meanwhile, Koko was becoming more and more exuberant and reckless, shouting all kinds of nonsense, laughing, kissing Natalya's hands and soft elbows, running his lips over her shoulder, winking at Myatlev; and Myatlev responded in kind, though at another time he would have jumped out of the carriage while it was moving, not even bothering to hide his distaste. But here he put up with all of it, and all because of Natalya, her deep, dark, eternal eyes still staring at him intently.

Providence went on weaving its foolish web, and they were jolted so severely at one pothole that they thought the end had come, that the carriage would fly into the Neva: but everything turned out all right, the wheels went on spinning, the hoofbeats continued, and Natalya was sitting next to Myatlev, Lieutenant Berg was slowly picking himself up from the floor, and Koko

Tetenborn was grinning wildly and still blathering as though nothing had happened.

"Hold me up," Natalya asked in a whisper. "Otherwise I'll fall."

And Myatlev had no choice but to hold her tighter.

"Auntie," shouted Koko, "tell the truth; did you ask the driver to jolt us? Well, well, how sneaky! My brother and I won't forgive you for that, particularly since he bumped his nose on the floor. Look out, Prince Sergei Vasilyevich, that she doesn't drop you on your nose, too. Hold her tight!" And he laughed. "What a pleasure it is to squeeze a woman in your arms, I swear. Oh, what bliss!"

The countess was warm, slender, and firm, and Myatlev held her even tighter.

"Ca-are-ful—" she whispered, but didn't move away.

"I, for one, adore impromptu gatherings," Tetenborn said. "Now, if we had planned all this ahead of time, nothing would have come of it, I swear to God. You plan and plan, and then everything goes the other way, and goes wrong, and the places are wrong, and the people are dull and disgusting—right, queenie?"

"How could they be brothers?" thought Myatlev. "They're so different—"

But his fleeting doubts vanished, for the carriage had stopped and they moved into Myatlev's house in a raucous brigade.

They encountered a hilarious scene in the entry: the staff, running out to see the cause of the noise, were frozen picturesquely among the marble statues, so long unaccustomed to the presence of riotous hordes within the dying house. Redheaded Aglaya, like Diana, stood with her arms spread, leaning against Mars, eloquent of unbridled passion; Afanasy peered out from Apollo's shoulder, like a wounded Gaul trying to hide behind his hand; and the rest—whether valets or depressed gods, whether alive or sculpted—could be glimpsed here and there.

"How charming!" thought Myatlev, without stopping. And then he dragged Natalya up the stairs, hoping that the amazing nephews would lose their way and disappear, especially since he noticed that Koko Tetenborn was already draped all over Aglaya, making believe he thought her a statue, and his brother had vanished.

"Hurry, hurry, Natalie!" Myatlev said, out of breath, as they rushed past the first landing. "Hurry, hurry—" And they flew even higher, not seeing Lieutenant Misha Berg pursuing them up the stairs with huge, leaping bounds.

Myatlev seated the countess and went off to call Afanasy; then Aglaya began babbling downstairs, and he rushed back to Natalya. The countess continued to stare at him; she was sitting on a wide settee, once more surrounded by her happy, red-faced nephews. Lieutenant Berg still clutched the dilapidated red rose, almost petalless by now.

"How merry it is here!" shouted Koko. "Sergei Vasilyevich, now we know!"

"Is there any hope of champagne?" asked Berg.

The table and some dusty Saxon porcelain emerged from somewhere; green champagne bottles arrived; overripe fruits filled the room with their aroma; the crystal glasses clinked delicately. A decanter of vodka stood before Myatlev, and without waiting for the general toasts, he greedily gulped down a glass.

Natalya never took her eyes from him. He smiled at her over the heads of her nephews, as though trying to say, "We're separated once more. This is intolerable." She shrugged, as if to say, "What can I do? You see for yourself—" "Yes," he replied with a lifted eyebrow, "would you like me to kill them?" "Be brave," he read in her eyes.

Lieutenant Berg whispered something to her, and she laughed.

Afanasy stood in the doorway.

"Go away, go away," Koko Tetenborn ordered. "We'll call."

The majordomo departed huffily. Myatlev followed to tell him something but forgot what it was as soon as he stood up. When he returned to the room, he was astounded by the silence.

153

Koko Tetenborn was swilling champagne and crying. The countess and the lieutenant were gone. The table was a mess: squashed fruit, empty bottles.

"When did we have time to do all that?" Myatlev thought in horror. But it was twilight and the candles were lit. He had some vodka.

"Hello, I'm your aunt," laughed Koko, and sighed.

"Really," Myatlev said in irritation, "where *is* your aunt?"

Koko indicated the library door with his eyes. Myatlev was there in two bounds. Natalya, pale and stern, was sitting in an armchair. Lieutenant Berg was on his knees before her. She was patting his head.

"Poor little nephew," she said with difficulty. "Well, get up, get up, they're calling us." And she stared at the prince.

"Is there any way to get rid of them?" he asked with his eyes. She spread her hands.

The table was cleared and reset, but the dust was still thickly layered on the china.

"Lieutenant," Tetenborn said suddenly and coldly, "I trust you haven't forgotten what you owe me?"

The formality of his tone made Myatlev shudder. "They're not brothers at all!" he thought, and felt his head clearing.

"Are you happy I came to you?" the countess asked quickly, and Myatlev saw that she was drunk. But he was indeed happy that she had forgotten her nephews and was addressing him. She was indescribably beautiful. She smiled at Myatlev, and everything swam before his eyes. Her huge pupils were fixed on him, and the light of a thousand candles glowed within them. She extended her hand, and he kissed it. She was now sitting next to him. Somewhere far away, barely discernible, the nephews were arguing. Afanasy stood in the doorway, weaving strangely. An expression of anxiety was firmly etched on his stupid, round, loyal face.

"Natalie," said Myatlev, not releasing her hand, "why did I think so badly of you?"

She sighed.

"Where did you find those nephews of yours?"

> NATALYA: Ah, by accident yesterday at someone's house.
> They amused me greatly— We played— You know,
> there's this game—
>
> MYATLEV: I know—
>
> NATALYA: Well, we were playing, just playing, and got
> carried away— And we're continuing today—
>
> MYATLEV: What was it they couldn't share?
>
> NATALYA: Me.
>
> MYATLEV: And now they're dividing you up?
>
> NATALYA: How could I possibly have imagined that I would
> be sitting with you in your own house, you—
>
> MYATLEV: Let's get rid of them—
>
> NATALYA: Don't rush things— We have time, yes? I see a
> madness in your eyes— Do you want me to drown
> myself, too? No, no, prince, that won't—
>
> MYATLEV: Heaven forbid!
>
> NATALYA: We still have time— But I want to know if
> you're listening. I want to know who you and I will—
> Are you listening?

Myatlev had not noticed the nephews leave. He was so
intrigued by that fact that he forgot about Natalya for a second.
His head was spinning, and the candle's flame was double.
Suddenly he heard Tetenborn's voice quite clearly.

"Why can't you simply calm down and stop harping on it, as
though it were premeditated evil," said Koko from somewhere.
"After all, it's not for you to judge my morality."

"You're getting off the subject again," Lieutenant Berg replied morosely. "We had decided—"

"Not up to you, not for you to judge— There are enough
judges without you, thanks."

"But we had agreed—"

"And you want me to withdraw my rights just like that?"

"The hell with rights!" Lieutenant Berg yelled. "Are you in
your right mind? We had agreed—"

Myatlev shook his head. The nephews were back in their

places, as though nobody had drunk anything, and were carrying on a lively conversation.

"Gentlemen," said Myatlev, "are you bored? I'm not feeling very well, and I don't know how to amuse you."

They paid no attention to his words and didn't even turn in his direction. Meanwhile, Natalya had disappeared. Myatlev stared at the objects shimmering and swaying before him. Then he suddenly spied her in an armchair in the library. She called him over with a slight nod. The nephews were still arguing.

"Natalie," he said, embracing her, "now you won't get away from me."

"Shh," she whispered, "this is no time for jokes."

"What about them?"

"They'll leave, they'll leave— Silence— They're gone."

And truly, silence reigned outside the door, if you didn't count the distant creaking of the slowly deteriorating walls and stairs. The dampness of the light Petersburg night came in through the open window. The extinguished candles still gave off the elusive smell of burned wax.

Time passed. The tired lovers slept without dreams or pangs of conscience. Morning was approaching. Some rooster, suffering from insomnia and unable to wait for the appointed hour, screamed out his unanswered prayer.

Natalya was gone, leaving one orphaned and flirtatiously curled hair on the pillow. The pillow was cold. Afanasy was in the doorway; he reported the following:

It hadn't been the walls falling apart, but a heated battle between the two nephews. At first, not daring to disturb the peace of the lovers, they had raced around the house searching for objects with which they could shorten their already short lives. They ransacked the entire house, luring Afanasy and the trusting Aglaya to search with them, even though they didn't quite understand what it was the young men sought, and the nephews found laughable everything they offered. Finally the nephews, still berating each other, discovered two ancient swords hanging on the walls of the ballroom on the second floor, relics

156

of the ancient past. To the shouts of Agalya and the entreaties of Afanasy, they began fighting, and soon Lieutenant Berg received a wound in the chest; bleeding profusely, he was taken by Afanasy to his room, laid on the bed, and ministered to by Aglaya. Then Afanasy rushed to aid Koko Tetenborn, who was also wounded. Koko was bandaged and went home without even inquiring about the fate of his recent comrade. Returning, Afanasy discovered that the wounded lieutenant was pawing his darling wife and, hugging her to his bleeding wounds, was determined to have his way with her. Afanasy lost all self-control and knocked the lieutenant unconscious by applying a three-legged stool to his head, dragged him out into the street, away from the house, and leaned him against someone else's fence. That nice man, Mr. Sverbeyev, who just happened to be around at that early hour, became concerned on the family's account and dragged the lieutenant even farther away, somewhere. Aglaya, covered with bruises and blood, also tried to tell Myatlev about the assault on her, but Myatlev waved her away and told Afanasy to continue. Afanasy had gone upstairs to warn His Excellency about the bloodshed when he saw Her Excellency the countess leaving the library, all sleepy-like and unkempt, and in a hurry to leave but unable to locate the door. He had to run out in the street and get a carriage and send Her Excellency home; she seemed quite unhappy and swore at him. Why was she unhappy? Because she did not wish to sleep in the prince's house, where the Baroness Fredericks herself used to sleep. Then it really was morning, and he, Afanasy, decided to report to His Excellency to inform him of what had happened in the night.

It was all so bizarre, not to say fantastic, that Myatlev wanted proof that it wasn't a dream, that the nephews had really fought one another, and that Natalya had been indulgent. On Saturday night he therefore accepted an invitation to a house where his almost forgotten companions were still relishing the same old monotonous pleasures. He hoped to find Countess Rumyantseva there, and perhaps obtain a confirmation of the incident from her. She was indeed there, surrounded by her female friends, of whom the most senior and experienced was Cassandra. Myatlev thought that his entrance was accompanied by a break in the music and by everyone turning to look at him. "Aha," he thought with hostility, "what an entrance!" He felt as though they had undressed him and dunked him in ice water. But he found several acquaintances among the men and joined their group. The conversation immediately switched to the events of the night before. Had the prince heard that Lieutenant Berg was cruelly beaten by someone at someone's house? They say that Natalie Rumyantseva was mixed up in the horrible story. Myatlev was at great pains to maintain his self-possession. He smiled and nodded, and tried simultaneously to convey to Natalya his burning desire to see her, ask, tell, confirm— But her gaze wandered and never rested on him. Finally his patience wore out, and he slipped out of the ballroom. He turned once more in the doorway. The deep, dark eyes of Countess Rumyantseva, filled with oppressive, bovine sadness, were fixed on him.

A few days later a short letter arrived. Among its numerous reproaches and exclamations several lines managed to reach his mind:

> . . . now I am shamed. My love for you has become public knowledge. My honor is besmirched, and you alone can rescue me. Rescue me! . . . I hope that I won't be forced to turn for defense elsewhere. Reply to my pleas.

Myatlev could hear Cassandra in the letter. He bustled about and rushed off to Mikhailovka, far away from Petersburg. The prospect of rescuing Countess Rumyantseva in the very unoriginal manner that she hinted at did not attract him. He took Afanasy and Aglaya with him, was gracious to them, considerate, and friendly—all in an attempt to justify himself and soothe his conscience. But during the entire trip the couple did not utter a single word, and no matter how Myatlev tried to bring them closer, they remained cold and alienated.

As soon as they had gotten there and settled in, breathing pine and fresh hay warmed by the late summer sun, scents almost forgotten back home, a letter came from Petersburg ordering Prince Myatlev to return to the capital. Count Alexei Fyodorovich Orlov, commander of the gendarmes, as the Hobbler had dubbed him, and an old friend of Myatlev's father, urged him not to tarry.

Myatlev did not tarry, since it was easy to gather up his belongings, and an invitation from the omnipotent assistant to the tsar could not be refused. And they returned to their hearth.

"I don't know how to address you now," the graying count smiled. "Once you were simply Seryozha to me. And now you're not so young. But you do remind me of your father, a little. Personally I would never have dared disturb your trip. We live in a world of rumors. There are more about you than anyone else. Therefore, they should be discounted. But when there are too many it gets confusing. You still live in the same place? Think how well they built houses in the old days. Look at that, a wooden house, and it's still standing—and won't collapse. I've been to the house. But I don't know, by today's standards of comfort, isn't it too old? Who was it who drowned there, one of the servants? They even say it was a lady. Your father always kept the house full. You love solitude. Yes, and now they say that those two puppies were beating each other to death with ancient swords. The tsar, naturally, found out about it. He has his own opinion of you; however, it may be rather exaggerated or even distorted."

Count Alexei Fyodorovich chatted standing up. Nature had endowed him with great height. He had gotten flabby with old age, but he took care of himself, following the example of Tsar Nicholas. Nature had further exerted herself and framed his broad face with a luxurious gray mane, giving him a certain resemblance to a lion, but she had not forgotten to pinch his nose slightly, so that it resembled the muzzle of a fox, which was part of his character, as it is of any man who has risen high above the rest; his great and multifaceted experience had lent his eyes the glow of wisdom; and all this, coupled with a large mouth, on which a smile hovered, made him impressive.

"Our responsibilities do not include observing the private concupiscence of the inhabitants of the empire," the old lion said. "However, the tsar wanted me to get to the bottom of this business and to have a talk with you. His Imperial Highness did not wish to talk with you in person. All the better, I tell you, all the better. I was worried at first, in view of the possibility . . . wondering how it could all end . . . without condemning your proclivities in any way, I want you to understand the degree of responsibility that lies on the tsar's shoulders for the well-being of all his subjects . . . as far as he is able . . . somehow . . . the situation . . . more . . . less . . . ."

And the count stopped, stunned. Prince Myatlev, smiling guiltily, staring off to one side, was holding out some crumpled notes and offering them to the count.

"What's the matter with you!" Orlov said withdrawing in disgust. "Are you mad?" He wanted to call his aide, but the extreme pallor of Myatlev's face restrained him and he offered the prince a chair.

"You insult me greatly," Myatlev mumbled, half prostrated and sitting down. "Please, I beg you—"

The old lion was confused, but suddenly and abruptly it was over as it had begun, and Myatlev's face took on its old look, and he rose.

"So, therefore," said Orlov, still horrified, pretending to riffle his papers, but watching Myatlev look around like a cornered wolf. "So, my dear Prince," the chief of the gendarmes repeated, returning to the conversation, "I don't dare detain you any longer, and I hope that in the future you will endeavor to keep your affairs *en ordre*."

Leaving Count Orlov's office, Myatlev swore never again to give them cause to put him in such a humiliating position—little imagining that cruel fate would bring him up against Count Orlov many times and in much more painful circumstances.

A few days passed, and everything seemed to have relaxed, when a new letter arrived from Natalya Rumyantseva, a white, scented envelope—the white, fluffy cloud that is a harbinger of gray storm clouds. Myatlev couldn't see the rainclouds yet, but he felt the dampness in the air, and his soul trembled like a leaf.

The letter contained lines like: "Prince, you betrayed me. Didn't you pledge your love to me? Didn't you promise to protect me? I'm deserted by you, thrown to the whims of fate. . . . I fear the worst. Please reply."

At first the prince's punctiliousness and noble feelings remained untouched by this desperate signal. But the story did not end there.

28

[From Moscow to Petersburg, from Lavinia to Myatlev]

The person writing to you is one you have probably long forgotten, but one who has not forgotten you and never will. We are living in Moscow now, and God only knows how much longer we'll spend here. We live in the Arbat section in Starokonyushenny Lane, in the house of Mr. Ladimirovsky.

When he sees me he begins smiling and asking about my life in Petersburg, but doesn't listen to my answers. Or he takes my hand and says, "What a hand, just like a grown-up young lady's. Actually, you are a young lady now." *Maman* gets nervous when she sees this. In general, whenever she observes men paying attention to me, she gets pleasant palpitations, but in this case she worries and has even asked Mr. Ladimirovsky not to kiss my hand. They're all fishy characters.

I turned fifteen in January, and now it appears that as far as *Maman* is concerned I'm bridal material. This didn't offend me as much as it surprised me. She said to me, "You talk to men as though you have done something wrong, and you should talk to them as though they owed you something." I sit before my mirror and remember Petersburg and you, and I say to her inside the mirror, "Why so glum, you silly fool, Mr. van Schoenhoven? Hold on, you fool." This always helps.

The most terrible thing is that my Aunt Kaleria follows me around and accompanies me everywhere, even to the pension and back. There was a ball at Shrovetide in Blagorodny. It was rather merry, with a lottery and charades, but as we were getting ready *Maman* was very worried that I was too thin and inexpressive.

Good Lord, I'm chattering away. It took a lot of effort to make up my mind to write to you, and now that I've started I can't stop. But I'm writing to you, my older friend, just describing my life, that's all.

Mr. van Schoenhoven
[From Petersburg to Moscow, from Myatlev to Lavinia]

Mr. van Schoenhoven, what has happened to you?! Where are your sword and shield? And you're fifteen at that!

One fine Tuesday, before I had time to breakfast, Afanasy brought me your letter, which made me very happy, and it seemed that a light had come on in the impenetrable darkness.

I think of you often, particularly in difficult moments. I kept hoping that you would show up and dissipate the gloom. What force has banished you to Moscow? How much longer will you be suffering in our first capital?

As for Mr. Ladimirovsky, here is my suggestion: give him ironic glances. This will confuse him greatly, and he will drop his obnoxiousness.

Your *maman*, apparently, is like all *mamans*; they dream only of marrying off their daughters successfully, especially if they have only one daughter.

In one of my sad moments I tried sitting at the mirror, as you suggested, and scolded the person I saw inside it for his acutely depressing helplessness. But what did I see? Someone who was practically an old man sat before me, staring at me in an estranged manner. I tried convincing and admonishing him, but he laughed wryly and turned away.

You're another thing altogether. Your vis-à-vis is young,

slender, beautiful; it's a pleasure to look at her and flattering to admonish her. But with me?

Nothing's changed in Petersburg, if one doesn't count your absence. The park is completely overgrown. The Neva is murky. My house is rotted through and through. Society is off at their dachas and villages. Ships go up the Neva as far as Tsarskoe Selo. I've committed a mass of idiotic acts—well, like any normal man—but I have to pay for their consequences, and not pay myself, but society.

29

But the story did not end with the deceived countess's plaintive cry, and one fine day Natalya Rumyantseva demanded a meeting. As sometimes happens—either the day was truly fine, or Myatlev's conscience softened, or the subtle hints about possible ways of resolving any difficulties in the countess's life took their toll—he suddenly felt a surge of energy, fervent repentance warmed his stony soul, and he wanted, as they say, to put his dependable hand on her frail, trusting shoulder.

Natalya was more alluring than ever. Her control pleased him. In general, he was susceptible to delight that day. Her face, paler than usual, seemed flawless. At first she gave him a look of light curiosity, and he smiled with understanding in reply; but she seemed to forget him immediately, and he was overwhelmed with confusion.

"I hope," he said condescendingly, like an older friend, "that you have not so lost your wits that you are contemplating giving up your independence in exchange for the life exemplified by your female friends, who pretend to be happy."

She said nothing in reply and did not even turn in his direction, which increased his discomfort. When he squinted, he could see her profile, and there was something about it that might have made him completely irresponsible. "It wouldn't hurt for her to be more natural," he thought. "After everything that's happened, she could turn off some of her coquetry." But the thought didn't comfort him, for beside him walked a woman burning, as he guessed, with longing and with a fantastic belief in her future.

They were slowly following the fence of the Summer Garden, and the breeze coming from the Neva was ineffectual in cooling their agitated souls.

"Besides," he continued, completely lost, "what do you think? That society can genuinely appreciate your predilections? Do you really think so? You hope so?"

He thought that she laughed curtly. He wanted to look into her deep, dark eyes and kiss her soft, hot lips. Her profile, as usual, was haughty. And then he remembered her notes, her party conversations, his own conclusions; and what he had just said to her seemed ridiculous. Power is what one obtains in exchange for independence, and he was just babbling.

They stopped at the parapet. The Neva flowed indolently below them. A wooden ship hurried past, and tiny officers and ladies waved from the deck with their parasols, caps, and gloves to no one in particular. The embankment was empty except for a peasant carrying a barrel on his back. His face was covered with sweat, and even at a distance they could smell the nauseating odor of fish, coming either from him or the barrel.

"Well?" said the woman standing beside Myatlev.

He encircled her waist. She pressed closer to him, having first looked around. The embankment was empty.

"Do you still think that I will bring you unhappiness?"

She turned to him. Her deep, dark eyes swayed before him. He heard her shallow breathing, and her small, persistent hand was touching the back of his neck with a light, nervous caress.

When passion begins howling around us, our eyes become moist, a blue mist films our pupils, and the tip of our tongue beats feverishly against our teeth, like an animal preparing to pounce, and our body leans forward, and our neck becomes longer and tense.

164

It's a joke: that two-legged creature, racked by disease, laws, and humiliation, pursued by terror and doubt, heavily powdered in order to hide the clayey color of its face, curled and pomaded; that creature that is the personification of confidence and even brazenness, shod in huge Wellington boots or squeezed into crinolines, and all to hide the thin, crooked legs that help it run God knows where; that creature, highest among the creatures that move, that allows itself the pleasure of sinning so that it can suffer and repent at length, secretly proud of itself and contemptuous of its fellow creatures but publicly bursting with love for them and with contempt for itself, its history as a lover discreditable and its perfidiousness notorious—how that creature becomes inflamed when about its head howls the passion for possession, power, control, or to be charitable, or to elicit pity.

The peasant dropped his barrel. Natalya jumped. Myatlev quickly removed his arm. A pearly, headless fish fell out of the barrel.

"Your letters, Natalie," said Myatlev, "have depressed me. Really, Natalie, what were you thinking of when you wrote me those letters? Do I look like a bridegroom? Please— Perhaps that Koko or *your* Lieutenant Berg—please— Why did you ever think of me in those terms?"

They heard hoofbeats. An old, peeling coach slowly went past. On the back seat, stretched out languidly, lay Lieutenant Katakazi in his light-blue uniform. He was asleep.

"He's asleep," said Myatlev, watching the coach go past.

"Couldn't you hail me a cab?" the countess asked coldly. Her face was extremely pale, and she seemed even more irresistible than ever.

"We can go to my place," said Myatlev. "Do you have a migraine?"

"I can take care of myself," she hissed. "I wanted to hear words of comfort and friendship from you, and instead— I came to cry on your shoulder about my misfortune, and you reject me as though I were a blackmailer."

The wooden ship was coming back. All aquiver, it raced on

the broad expanse of the Neva. The fortunate passengers stood on its decks, and among them Myatlev saw himself and Countess Rumyantseva. She was wearing a pink dress, and he was clad in an impeccable suit of Chinese tussah, and a broad smile never left the lips of the former Horse Guards officer.

She got into a carriage quickly, her face still pale and haughty, but there was something pathetic in her eyes, and there was something in her face that Myatlev felt was incompatible with his idea of her beauty.

For the next few days he stayed in his crumbling fortress, but Countess Rumyantseva's love was so boundlessly great and so demanding that he would awaken at night, picturing her alone and magnificent. And thus, when she came to him, disregarding all propriety and disdaining any roundabout approach, came to him despite the locks, chain bridges, guards, and hungry lions, he wasn't even surprised.

"I'm in a great rush," she said, appearing on the doorstep of his abode. "I've brought you an invitation to dinner; *Maman* would be very happy to see you." She spoke lightly, as if in a fairy tale, and her confidence showed in her light and easy movements. "I did not trust a servant and brought the invitation myself. It's better that way. Are you pleased?"

The pink envelope slipped onto the table, seemed to fly across it on its own, and she disappeared, giving him one of her most significant smiles.

When I teased him, he flared up.

"It was all to keep in my good graces—she likes me," he announced, not believing his own words. "It's terrible for her to go back to those Tetenborns and Bergs, and she likes me— I dined with them, and everything was very nice. What more is there?"

She gave him a charming small canvas on which the artist had painted a crafty, luxuriant Cupid sharpening an arrow that would serve admirably for a real murder. Then her caring, clever hands placed an exquisite silver candlestick on his table, a sad remnant of the long-destroyed Orlov service.* "Oh, what madness!" He shuddered, but said nothing. Then, as cleverly as she could, she took away his unattractive ring—his memento of old Raspevin, who had been born on Senate Square and died on the Valerik River. Myatlev tried to hold onto his honor, but Natalya, brimming with love, assured him that she had no designs on the family heirlooms.

"All the more," she whispered with conviction, "since this was a gift from a woman."

He told her the story of Raspevin. She shed a tear of pity for the old man but did not return the ring.

"No, no, Prince," she said, shaking her finger at him, "it's touching but not convincing. You won't get it back."

And there were many passionate kisses, and niggling, sharp little kisses, and embraces, and touches, and all kinds of hints. Afanasy and Aglaya hovered with long faces, trying to please her. The house creaked more loudly. Mr. Sverbeyev, in an unbuttoned shirt, all sweaty from tea and concentration, met her downstairs. It was he who led her among the marble figures, patiently explaining their qualities, and when she decided to have them all moved back into the darkness so that the entry would be larger and more elegant, he laughed with her, watching the silent servants strain to fulfill her commands.

When Myatlev tried to defend the wordless marble folk, she immediately countermanded his efforts.

"No, no, *mon cher*, they will all fit over there, but here we must have space."

"Space," agreed Mr. Sverbeyev.

"You're used to it and don't see how bad it looks," she went on. "Look, isn't this better?"

"She feels sorry for you," seconded the noble spy.

And Myatlev merely spread his hands in dismay and received his allotment of passionate kisses, each of which followed some

*A three-thousand-piece table service ordered by Catherine the Great in 1770 for Prince Grigori Orlov.—Translator.

167

such minor demonstration of her love.

And so the beautiful conquistadora, having tasted Myatlev's blood, kept penetrating deeper into his territory, and he retreated with the band of his bronze-faced brothers, and their arrows were helpless before her musket.

"Is this love or pretense?" Myatlev thought, drinking his vodka. "Love or pretense?"

Whirling through the disintegrating house, Natalya, like a crazed doe, kept bumping into the gigantic canvas where her persistent ancestors were crowding out the natives in the name of future perfection, and, every time, the image of the sad European among the brown bodies halted her brigandage. Finally she could stand it no longer, and Myatlev, weakened by vodka, revealed the name of the famous political criminal who had been resurrected on canvas through the efforts of the clever dauber.

"Goodness, what nonsense," she said in amazement, seeing no significance in the name. "Is it a joke? Is he alive? Are you in contact with criminals?"

"You see, Natalie," he said seriously, "this man was executed long ago, but I want to keep his portrait. I would be very obliged if you did not—"

"I heard about it," she said. "It was the year I was born. Is he alive?"

"He was executed."

"Oh, yes, you said so."

He kept examining her face, not understanding what there was about it that could elicit a sad sense of imperfection. Its lines were so flawless, every detail in proportion, that it was hard to explain his sudden irritation. At first, he thought that it was caused by her excessive pallor, but at the same time, if the face had not been hers, it would have been supernatural. Finally he managed to unearth in that marvel of nature a tiny flaw that had been escaping his fogged vision for several days; once it became visible, Myatlev had no more trouble recognizing it. The countess's lower jaw was a tiny bit larger than necessary and slightly weighed down the exquisite face; and it was not the deep, dark eyes that gave her the royal hauteur that so impressed Myatlev, but that insignificant detail neglected by nature.

"Why would you want to keep a memento of that?" she laughed, nodding toward the portrait. "It won't help him." And Myatlev saw that the flaw in her face was much more significant than he had thought at first.

"I could go to Moscow and get lost there," he thought. "Any Moscow traffic policeman is happier than I am."

"Everyone is at their dachas, and only you are here in the broiling heat," she said. "Come visit us, come visit us, come visit us."

"The only time to live in Petersburg, Natalie, is when the rest of the city is at their dachas."

"Then we'll be here together; I won't let you go to pieces," she said without a trace of embarrassment. "I want you to be happy." At which point, he felt duty-bound to kiss that confident young woman who meant nothing to him. She accepted it as her due.

"I want you to be overjoyed—we are going to have a charming baby," she said, using the English word.

Myatlev's heart contracted, and his breathing stopped for a minute. The idea that the guilty party in this joyous situation might be some Lieutenant Berg or Koko Tetenborn would be monstrous, and he thought in despair, "Ohmygod!," but he spoke calmly, even playfully—even, he supposed, with a smile.

"Natalie, you jest, I'm not suited for the role you have chosen for me." And he took a sip of vodka.

Her dark bay stallions raced off with her carriage without touching the ground, carrying away their mistress, who was too haughty to allow herself to weep and too beautiful to believe that she could be unloved or rejected.

"A woman with a heavy jaw cannot but be a despot," he wrote in his diary, and decided to leave for Moscow without delay to see the famous Dr. Morinari. His true goal was to quiet his conscience, for he did not believe that medicine could relieve him of the consequences of that severe wound he had suffered near the Valerik River.

30

AFTER THAT, FOR SOME ten days Petersburg was quiet and silent. The Countess Rumyantseva, that playful woman, gave no sign of life; she was either reconciled to his firmness or preparing some fresh intrigue. Whatever the reason, Myatlev, feeling refreshed and younger because of having some purpose at last, straightened out his papers, ordered the carriage, impatiently gestured at its door for Afanasy, got in himself, and they headed south toward Moscow, leaving the Northern Palmyra in proud solitude.

While they were en route, Lavinia mustered her courage and wrote a reply to the prince, the tip of her tongue peeking out of the corner of her mouth in the strain of her efforts. Her letter, if we disregard the necessary conventional phrases of the genre, also contained such lines as:

Your letter was like a bomb. Unbearable Kaleria, of course, had snuck into my room, saw it, read it, and ran to *Maman*. I demanded that they return it, but they wouldn't hear of it. "Ah, ah, who is he? How dare he? Since when? You're disgracing yourself! What foolishness! I'll complain to the tsar!"

I locked myself in my room. They raged outside. And after all was said and done they put me on a long, heavy chain so that I wouldn't dare think of living my own life.

Don't let it worry you. Please write to me. Write in care of my friend, Ekaterina Balashova, at their house in Krivokolenny Lane.

Now let's forget the unpleasant things. I laughed so much when I read how you sit before the mirror. How can you call yourself an old man? And why did the one inside the mirror turn away from you? I was so sorry that my system doesn't work for you.

We will be in Moscow until Christmas. That's what *Maman* says. She has business here that she won't tell me about. Can you imagine, spending the entire summer in hot and dusty Moscow for something that probably isn't very important if you don't count the cherry jam that I skim. I still have the impression that *Maman* has decided to design my future and is working on it behind my back. I'm scared to think about it. Of course, I can't argue with her, but if she does come up with something, I'll either drown myself or take poison. Actually, I won't do that at all, I'll simply run off with some Hussar.

You must laugh as you read my letters. It was probably better when I was Mr. van Schoenhoven. You can't imagine how I'd like to show up at your house again in my jacket and sword and see your reaction. But what can be done? You can't go back.

I can imagine how ugly I will seem to you if we ever meet again. I can't stand looking at myself! Your letter was such a surprise. Now *Maman* keeps telling me horror stories about you.

We had a doctor who prescribed bathing and lying in the sun for me. We went to Fili for that. When we drove through the woods we saw a wolf, as gaunt as I am. He ran off.

But of all the people I know, you are the wisest and most pleasant. And when I see Mr. Ladimirovsky, there is no comparison possible. That's what a bad upbringing can do. *Maman* maintains that I have bad tendencies, too, since I dared to correspond with you. Do you think it's bad? Don't you derive a little pleasure from getting my letters?

Mr. van Schoenhoven

P.S. If you should get to Moscow and happen to walk past our house and hear barking coming from the yard, don't be afraid; that's me in the middle of the yard on a chain, barking from loneliness and despair.

31

Breathing was easier in Moscow than in Petersburg; the court fluids seeped into the first capital slowly and in diluted form. However, violence was being wreaked here, too, for Mr. van Schoenhoven, his old friend, was chained up. And while Myatlev hadn't yet received that desperate and funny letter, the closer the carriage got to Moscow, the more clearly he saw the obvious methods they used to stop plucky individuals from being plucky. Poor Lavinia!

And he pictured the crude house of Mr. Ladimirovsky and the dirty green fence that enclosed the dusty yard where Mr. van Schoenhoven sat crying, an iron collar around his thin neck.

The picture did not horrify him; it made him laugh as he entered Arbat Boulevard, smelling the cherry scum from afar and hearing the clink of the chains.

In those days Moscow was half-empty, but early autumn was in the air and the first careful caravans, bells jangling, were converging on the capital from estates near and far. It was the best time to live among your fellowmen without rubbing elbows with them, the best time to complain to God without worrying that you'd be turned in, and the best time to free those who were in chains.

While Afanasy was killing flies in the hotel by Okhotny Ryad, Myatlev turned into Starokonyushenny Lane, happy that such a mischievous idea had come to him in Petersburg and was now leading him around.

He tried not to think about Dr. Morinari, who was expecting him. Instead he assumed, as he had so many times before, that his disease would not pounce on him again, and even if it did, it still wasn't such a problem and basically not dangerous, so there was really no point in getting involved with doctors, inhaling carbolic acid, and explaining his private wounds at length, instead of enjoying his trip and the opportunity to give his imagination free rein.

Mr. Ladimirovsky's house towered over a coquettish cast-iron fence and did not in the least resemble the pathetic structure the prince's feverish imagination had created. It was a roomy three-story house, built with taste and love, with a false colonnade in the most refined traditions of the Russian Empire style, with huge windows on the second floor open to the sunlight and with a festive entry opening on a shady garden where the famous Moscow lindens grew, surrounded by the gigantic sprays of aromatic tobacco. Strolling along the well-kept English garden paths was a young woman in a pink dress and matching hat with an inordinately wide brim—a pink cloud in a green shade.

Now he would ask for Madame Tuchkova—he thought that was the name. And Mr. van Schoenhoven, appearing in the doorway, would open her eyes wide. The young woman approached the fence and opened her eyes wide.

"Is it you?" she demanded, and Myatlev had no choice but to turn into the garden.

What an amazing sight—this young lady in the pink dress with the big gray eyes, clutching two little fists to her chest as she had in the past. Ohmygod! Could she be the daughter of that poor woman? Her sister? Not yet a lady but no longer Mr. van Schoenhoven. And the Empire building, and the fence, and the clean windows and the space behind them, and the English paths—was all this a sham? Do you remember how you came to visit me in a rather shabby jacket, which, as I now understand, belonged to one of the servant boys? And how we had tea? And do you remember how you used to go away all by yourself in the deep snow, waving your sword; and your tracks were even, like a chain, like an arrow—a sign of luck—yes, yes. And here I am at thirty-three still unlucky and have come here especially to complain to you, my old friend; and besides, I had imagined that I would take you by the hand and we would go, say, to the zoo or for a carousel ride, but you've grown up so much that it would

173

be ludicrous to take your hand and go to the zoo. Of course, you're so thin—almost as thin as you said you were—and your cheeks are sunken, but the Moscow climate seems to suit you; look how you've matured, how elegant you are, how meaningfully your collarbones are placed, and there is something in your face that keeps one from taking your hand and going to the zoo; and the real young men—and I mean real young men—will have to notice you, and complicated days await you. And I'm still enthralled by my thwarted hopes and still think everything is worthless, except, perhaps, what I can't have. But do you remember? Do you? And I thought you were in the middle of a pathetic yard on a chain, and here you have an English garden and such loveliness around you, and I probably needn't have rushed—

"Is it really you?" laughed Lavinia, blushing. "What a surprise!"

And yet there is no happiness in your smile, but disbelief; and of course, I can imagine how strange my appearance must seem, for being your protector is no longer quite possible; see how grown-up you are; I can't take you to the zoo—

"And you came to see me? What a silly prank," she drawled.

"What a prank," laughed Myatlev, sobering up from his own tactlessness. "However, if you must know, I really came here on business, and, walking by, I saw you over the fence. It's always a pleasure to see an old friend." She kept looking over at the house, and he realized that he had to leave before unbearable Kaleria fell out of a storm cloud brandishing lightning and thunder.

"What a pity," she said sincerely, "we're having a picnic tomorrow. And here comes someone now. We're leaving —we've been invited—however, you don't know them— Will you come again?" she asked politely.

"Depends on my business, Mr. van Schoenhoven, depends on business."

"A-a-a-ah," she said, and took a step back.

Three roomy coaches stopped on the street, each with four

horses. The coachmen wore raspberry top hats, each man more impeccable than the last, and stared from their boxes at Mr. Ladimirovsky's house.

"Well," she said, taking another backward step, "here they all come."

It sounded like a signal to retreat, but strangely he didn't want to. He felt a brazen curiosity mixed with shame and bitterness and vain regrets for the stupid Petersburg fantasies that had prompted him to take the trip.

And the door of the house flew open, and into the green haze of the lindens came a line of unfamiliar men and women who proceeded down a neat, yoke-shaped path; and Myatlev found himself in the middle of this yoke, and everyone naturally turned in his direction. Realizing that flight was demeaning and pointless, he prepared himself for the worst, but there was no storm. Instead, Madame Tuchkova, an alluring Polish lady barely older than Myatlev, and perhaps even younger, nodded benignly and simply walked over with a wonderful smile. The bright-colored, elegant line broke up, and they all encircled the prince as well. Among the guests he recognized Lieutenant Misha Berg and Koko Tetenborn, dressed to the nines in civilian clothes. They bowed coolly, as though they had not been introduced. He wanted to laugh, remembering their silly duel, when he saw that Lavinia, standing apart from the rest, was on tiptoe looking intently in his direction. The presence of these worldly cavaliers seemed suspicious to him, and sure enough, just then the lieutenant walked over to the bright-red Lavinia and handed her her parasol.

"Just imagine, *Maman*," Lavinia said breathlessly, "Prince Sergei Vasilyevich was here on business and saw me through the fence."

"Have you been in Moscow long?" Madame Tuchkova inquired, not listening to her daughter. "We would be happy to see you tomorrow at our picnic. Unfortunately, we're about to leave right now."

The guests, having seen their fill of the notorious man, slowly settled into the coaches. Lieutenant Berg and Koko Tetenborn led Lavinia away. She, it seemed to Myatlev, tried to look back. Madame Tuchkova and the prince were left alone.

"How strange," she said, "in Petersburg we're neighbors, and chance has never brought us together, and yet here in this giant anthill you managed to run into Lavinia." And she looked at Myatlev as if to say, "Don't lie, Prince, I know everything." "How do you find her? Hasn't she matured? The one on the left, there, that's Mikhail Berg. A month ago he fell at my feet. But I don't think people die of that, and Lavinia should wait another year or two. I'm a widow, and I have to be careful." And showing her marvelous teeth, she laughed.

The widow was in her prime, so that the late general must have loathed giving up life.

"And who is that Berg?" asked Myatlev. "What—do you know him well?"

"Oh, Prince"—she laughed again—"in my hands everyone becomes proper." And, leaning over to him, she added in a flirtatious whisper, "Of course, there's no comparing him to you, and if you weren't about to marry the charming Countess Rumyantseva, who knows, prince, who knows—"

"I have the impression that you are somehow connecting my letters to your little girl and my presence in Moscow," said the prince distractedly, "and I—"

"Please don't!" she said, astounded, arching her brows. "I never even thought such a thing. As for my saying that if it were not for your upcoming marriage— Couldn't you tell I was being insincere?" And that quiet, confident laugh came once more. "Actually, I'm lying, I'm pretending, don't judge me harshly. Do you want me to make a clean breast of it? I read your letter to Lavinia, and in that letter, I, and no one else, caught what no one else possibly could—the barely audible tone of your loneliness and your disposition toward my daughter. Wait—someone else might not have seen it, but I, Prince, believe me, I did. Wait—it's because, where my daughter is concerned, I can hear grass grow and fish converse. I'm a witch, Prince." And she

176

laughed, pleased with the effect of her statement. "Don't shake your head, don't deny it. I'm not interested in your opinion; I care only for what I myself hear. I could even agree with you out of politeness, but that would mean nothing if I still heard this and not that—"

The jolly caravan had long disappeared from view, but Myatlev was still there. Finally he found the strength to return to the hotel and, waking up puffy-faced Afanasy, ordered him to take care of dinner.

After eating, when the vodka was beginning to soothe his jangling nerves, the prince said to his sleepy servant, "She's a charming creature, pretending to be a philosopher, but she is full of superstitions and, if you will, vices. I seemed improper to her—that is, she tried to portray me thus—but you see, sir, I had thought that her daughter was chained up and that I could rescue her."

"Do you think so?" Afanasy inquired lazily.

"Do you think otherwise? Doesn't it seem to you that her activities are directed not to turning her daughter into a diamond, and thus giving her her true worth, but simply to calling her a diamond and setting her in her own crown?"

"Do you think so?" asked Afanasy, all ears.

"I was placed in a foolish position, sir. I was under suspicion, and I have no argument in my defense. Well, that lady is quite clever. And I have to clear my name in my own eyes. But that is impossible, and tomorrow we will quit this inhospitable city."

"Your Excellency," said Afanasy, taking advantage of the prince's good mood, "why did you, if I may ask, marry me off? Why, Your Excellency?"

"Precisely," replied Myatlev. "But do you dislike your wife so much?"

"She's stupid," the majordomo replied. "I beat her, Your Excellency, and she kisses my hands, bears it all, and forgives me."

"Madame Tuchkova," the prince went on, waving him off, "is overly concerned with the flesh, which induces her very personal view of humanity. She assumes I must feel the same way and that therefore, while having an affair with Countess Rumyantseva, I cannot deny myself the pleasure of varying and enriching her grudging embraces with those of a little girl with pointy collarbones— do you hear that, sir? That's what my openness and my trustfulness have led to. And now everyone knows I am marrying the countess—except me. And if she heard about it up there, in Petersburg, her fever would reach such a height you could fall from it and break your neck."

"Dog fat is very helpful in those cases," Afanasy noted.

Talking cooled Myatlev off. He realized that he wanted to go to the picnic to settle accounts with Madame Tuchkova and prove to her that Lavinia meant nothing to him, and the next morning he was aware that this desire had strengthened and that even the likelihood of appearing ludicrous and persistent would not keep him from pursuing it. Of course, his active, unbearable conscience reminded him in the carriage of his presumed reason for coming to Moscow, and the rejected doctor's spirit rose before him; but the weather was good, Countess Rumyantseva almost forgotten, and it pleased him to feel like an adventurer. And he thought how pathetic were those who thought of themselves as connoisseurs of talent but did not appreciate the great gift of injecting a drop of exciting illusion into the sleepy blood of humanity.

That idea excited him and so raised his self-esteem that for the first time in many years he thought well of himself and even vowed to end his seclusion and to walk on the earth, convinced suddenly that its climate and mores were fatal only to those who rejected them.

Somewhere beyond Vsekhsvyatsky, when the sun had quit the zenith and the river water had taken on a lavender hue, Myatlev came upon yesterday's company in a marvelous spot near an abandoned mill. The feasting was coming to an end, and some of the guests were wandering in the meadow; the young people were playing a circle game called hoop-la; the servants were dashing about near the huge carpet, covered with an equally huge white tablecloth; and the multicolored silk cushions on which the guests had recently lain were scattered about.

No one was surprised—or they pretended not to be surprised—by Myatlev's appearance, and only Madame Tuchkova, raising the hem of the light-blue dress that hugged her almost youthful waist, moved toward him along the yellowing September grass.

"How mistaken I was," she said, gazing into his face with obvious interest. "I thought that you wouldn't come, that you would be held up by business."

"I've come for only a second," he lied. "I thought that you wanted to tell me something yesterday and didn't get the chance." He was looking around; Lavinia was nowhere to be seen. "But I see that you are in the very swing of things, and I will slip away quietly, so as not to interrupt—"

"Lavinia is at her grandmother's, she did not wish to join us," Madame Tuchkova explained, smiling blindingly. "Too bad you're in a hurry—"

"Do you let her do whatever she wishes?" Myatlev asked irritably.

"Oh, yes," she said. "She's almost sixteen, and she has her own interests."

The servants had set the tablecloth with more plates, drinks, and crystal. Madame Tuchkova made an inviting gesture, strictly out of politeness. Myatlev kept looking but couldn't see Lieutenant Berg or his curly-headed friend.

"Lieutenant Berg and his friend also ignored us," Madame Tuchkova laughed. "They went to the races; they think we're too old for them. So, you are leaving us?"

"I'm leaving for Petersburg today," said Myatlev. "I'm very sorry."

"I'm very sorry," she echoed. "Good-bye."

What appeared to be an empty dialogue contained much hidden meaning for its participants, but it was interrupted by the jangle of a silver tray, dropped by a careless valet.

"Well," said Madame Tuchkova in relief, "there, you see?" And she waved.

Feeling all eyes on him, Myatlev hurried over to his waiting phaeton and instructed the driver to take him to Moscow, to Starokonyushenny Lane, and hurry. The driver was happy to race along. Myatlev was bursting with indignation, with no apparent reason for it beyond the fact that nature produces flawless people and then the false principles ruling their environment make them evil. Once there had been a tiny, charming creature with blue eyes and angelic curls, full of love and kindness, but time and environment had taken care of it and turned it into Madame Tuchkova. Vice in a marvelous container! A pinch of poison in a golden flask. In the struggle between nature and society, nature had yet to win. It always lost, and as loser it got to supervise the person's exterior while the victor got the soul and altered it to suit its own needs. Thus Myatlev reasoned, in a frenzy, even though he had nothing to base his theory on except a certain disappointment in himself because of his own rashness. As for Madame Tuchkova, she—and he acknowledged this with sadness—was not only attractive but had enough insight and irony to interest him.

So, tortured by doubt, repentance, pangs of conscience and vulgar anger, he reached Starokonyushenny Lane at twilight, dismissed the carriage, and headed for Mr. Ladimirovsky's house. It was dark, and the garden was empty. But beyond the windows of the second floor, open wide to the night, there were voices, and a multitude of candle flames fought with the enveloping darkness.

Myatlev was so tense and overwrought that he would probably not have been too embarrassed to climb up in the old lindens to hear better and watch what was going on and thus free himself once and for all of his doubts and torments. But the lindens grew at a great distance from the windows, and so he paced back and forth in front of the house, stopping now and then, like Mr. Sverbeyev, and envying the spy's ability to hang in a chimney by the hour.

He did not hear Lavinia's voice, but he already understood that he had been tricked, as though Madame Tuchkova's blue eyes and tone of voice had not been proof enough and he had to rush over here to convince himself.

"She said 'So what.'" Misha Berg's voice spoke. "What did she mean?"

"It means," laughed curly-haired Koko Tetenborn, "that Lavinochka, the queenie, considers what happened to her a mere trifle."

BERG: Too bad that I don't have a saber; I'd run you through with pleasure.

TETENBORN: You'd think you weren't the one who was just recently pried loose from the embraces of a red-headed maid and thrown wounded into the bushes, into the dirt and stench. I'm amazed that they managed to get you out!

BERG: If you are my friend, help me fool Kaleria. Let's get the key from her.

TETENBORN: Robbery is not my profession. I leave that to you. Personally, I prefer going out into the garden and taking Lavinia out through the window.

BERG: You can't expect her to go with you. I beg you to work with me. Don't destroy our friendship.

TETENBORN: Friendship, blendship, battleship, bullship—

BERG: After all, there's nothing to keep me from hitting you with an ordinary chair.

TETENBORN: That's not gentlemanly.

BERG: Gentlemanly, not gentlemanly— Do you want to lose *this* girl too?

TETENBORN: Phooey, stop shouting. You're giving me neurasthenia. I don't want the girl I love with all my heart to be the object of your scheming.

BERG: You love her? You so-and-so. He loves her.

TETENBORN: Put down that chair. Put down that chair. Put that chair down or else—put it down!

BERG: You know that with one word from me they'll stop indulging you in the department.

TETENBORN: No one kept you from flopping on your knees before Rumyantseva. Now don't get in my way, damn it!

BERG: Monster! Her *Maman* had a talk with me. Everything is decided.

TETENBORN: You are a rogue, but I have honorable inten-

181

tions; and if I didn't wallow at her feet, it's because I controlled myself, not because I'm calculating. Put that chair down!

The racket coming from the window made it clear that the battle was joined, and in earnest. Imagining how it might end, Myatlev slowly moved along the house. Suddenly he was hailed from a dark corner window.

"Is it really you?" Lavinia drawled, invisible in the dark. "And if I hadn't been locked up but had gone to the picnic, our paths wouldn't have crossed?"

"I was at the picnic," Myatlev reported, listening to the sounds of battle.

"What a silly prank," she laughed. "Now *that* I can't believe."

The warfare had stopped, and the voices rang out once more.

"Who chained you up?" Myatlev asked.

"Here's something strange," she said. "They locked me up because of you, and those marvelous, generous, noble souls were planning to rescue me. Why don't *you* save me? Kaleria is closeted in her room, I was reading, and they are killing each other. Everything is so mixed up, isn't it? I can't see your face; you're probably laughing at me."

"How could they chain you up, you so strong and brave, such a proud Mr. van Schoenhoven?" asked Myatlev, suspecting that there was a grain of truth in his joke. "Where's your sword?"

"Don't be silly," Lavinia laughed, "I didn't think of arguing. What for? This is all just a whim of *Maman*'s. Do you think she really intends to marry me off to that Berg? Don't be silly. That's what they want; they've gotten it into their heads—"

Koko Tetenborn flew out the front door. Paying no attention to Myatlev, he called to Lavinia, "Don't cry, queenie. I killed him." And he disappeared down the lane.

"He's a liar!" shouted Misha Berg, leaning out of a lighted window. "I've been listening to you exchange chatter with the prince." He was sticking out as far as his waist, risking defenestration. Then he stepped back into the room and the many candles illuminated him. His jacket was crumpled, one sleeve torn off, and there was a dark smear on his cheek—either blood or dirt.

"He's covered with blood," said Myatlev.

"There, you see!" She laughed. "How could *Maman* entrust me to them? Never in your life. Were you really at the picnic? Honestly? How wonderful!" And after a silence, she said, "You, for instance, can't be locked up, and I can. That's terrible."

Just then they heard the rattle of wheels, hoofbeats, and the carriages stopped outside the fence. Lavinia disappeared immediately, and Myatlev, trying to be inconspicuous, slipped out onto a sidestreet.

His life, particularly his distant youth, had been filled with incidents like this, when, pressing his elbows to his sides, he had run off to save his neck, laughing at himself and his pursuers in the morning and thereby developing a capacity for sound sleep, a hearty appetite, and a sense of self-mockery. Like a character in a *drame bourgeois*, like a courtier in a knightly romance, he had wept copiously, and burned his hands on rope ladders, and hurt his heels falling from fortress walls. But age, apparently, no longer permits you to laugh at yourself, and blows up trifles like this to universal tragedy.

What was the point of this senseless journey between Petersburg and Moscow? The desire to hide from the terrible countess, or the hope of somehow easing the lot of Mr. van Schoenhoven?

Now there were two van Schoenhovens entrenched in his mind, rather than just one: the one from the past, and Lavinia. The former seemed like an old friend lost in the sea of life, and the latter, a slender-throated young lady who had already had a taste of Vanity Fair. He could only mourn the loss.

His only Moscow find, if you didn't count Koko Tetenborn's licentious behavior and the bashed-in head of Misha Berg, which was no longer a phenomenon at all, was the incomparable Madame Tuchkova, that lithe Polish woman with chestnut curls, a cold heart, and ardent lips, a goose pretending to be a snake. Those curious creatures tend always to make you imagine some happy little spider who had generously been admitted to their embraces but who nonetheless escapes its intended fate. She was a find who would require a good deal of thinking about if he were to keep from losing faith in his ability to handle what was coming.

Riding back to Petersburg, Myatlev, to his own surprise, felt no bitterness, despair, disillusionment, or other debilitating emotion, except for a light regret for some unidentified loss that had accompanied him like a sister since childhood.

It is no secret that he sometimes irritated me with his gloom and his depressions, but that's what makes a close friend close—the fact that he communes with the soul of his tormented friend and does not judge him from the outside. "Remember the horns' . . ." But he used to pronounce those dreary words with a smile. What a mystery!

32

DURING HIS BRIEF ABSENCE Petersburg had been transformed. Myatlev's house was filled with multicolored envelopes containing invitations, greetings, and other nonsense. It seemed that the hard, calculating heart of the Northern Palmyra had finally melted and everyone wanted to see the prince, as though he were no longer the pariah he had been but a full-fledged and adored member of society.

Among the other scribblings, which left him cold, flashed Lavinia's letter with its faint call for help, but it flashed and faded, like a small sail headed for foreign shores.

In losing, we find. Oh, would that were so! And yet the ground was still under his feet, and the candles burned once more, and the aphorisms of the great inspired hope, and the house crumbled so slowly that he did not have to hurry. However, the effect of these good omens lasted only a short while, while his memories of the ridiculous trip were still fresh enough to make Petersburg look like the Promised Land in comparison. At first, calm as could be, Natalya returned. Her animated, festive, and exalted face was irresistible. "I want you to be happy!" "You're happy with me, aren't you?" "Now you can devote yourself to your nonsense, and I will take care of the rest." "We will read aloud in the evenings, and we won't need anyone else." "I want you to forget your past; you'll feel better immediately."

And he met her halfway, as though she were the only living creature in the shabby, dilapidated world, this woman who was fighting so appealingly for the right to be alone with his long face and his spectacles, so touchingly naive, so candid, and so honest. And everything began swirling about his head once more. All caution, all foreboding were flung aside. Her wonderful face retreated and came closer as she told him the news of the city, not hiding her pleasure at seeing him. Her small chin delicately cut the air, and he no longer noticed its former regrettable flaws. A cherry velvet mantle, trimmed with black lace, clasped her perfect bosom, and the benign warmth that emanated from her could be felt far off. "Your past is making you ill and estranged. I want to free you from it, do you hear me?" "Do you believe that you will be happy with me?" "Are you glad that you will have a little prince?" "To tell the truth, I was a little worried, but I've been told that I have nothing to fear, because, I've been told, everything is well arranged." And she blushed, touching her hip. "I don't have to worry because I'm created for motherhood—can you imagine?"

While she was saying all this and caressing her hip and nervously moving bric-a-brac from one spot to another, he sat in silence and watched her, trying to understand what was happening and trying to picture his coming bliss clearly. Suddenly he remembered Madame Tuchkova, and, nodding to Natalya in agreement, he began comparing them. Madame Tuchkova gained points for experience but lost them for lack of spontaneity, won again thanks to her disdain of illusions, whereas the countess's susceptibility to them made her seem pitiful. In general, neither of the women could be led around by the nose or twisted around one's finger. Experience allowed the elder to anticipate events, while youth gave the other tenacity and drive. In the prince's view, the concept of "predatory temptress" did not insult either of them because as far as he was concerned it simply implied a unity with nature and nothing more. It masked their earthly passions even as it determined their actions—which often delight and astound us. It was the source of their untamed quality, their blind instinct and their need for motherhood and a nest—ideally the warmest and richest one possible—their fear of the future, and their regret for the mistakes of the past. And who of the stronger sex, unless already prejudiced, would object to this? Who would even think of condemning his female friends for their feeble attempts to mask their passions, which he in any event could not resist, with a thin veil of good breeding? However, despite these thoughts and even while feeling somewhat indulgent toward women, Myatlev remained himself, knowing that at the decisive moment he would not forego the pleasure of being firm.

"Natalie," he said as casually as possible, "you surprise me somewhat, my dear. I value your friendship, and I'm in awe of your beauty, but I cannot share your illusions."

"If I didn't see how much you love me, I might think that you hate me," she said with a charming smile. "Instead of hurrying to do what must be done in these instances, you carry on with some nonsense, as though I couldn't see how much you love me and want to be with me, and how grateful you are to me for everything, everything . . . It gives you pleasure . . . Think how happy you will be . . . One might think that you didn't care at all, that the fate of your son . . . at length . . . come up with these ideas . . . happy omens . . . take care of things . . . "

Afanasy announced that Her Excellency Elizaveta Vasilyevna had arrived, and Cassandra floated in, doling out kisses. Then she seated herself so that her brother and future sister-in-law were facing her, and she beamed at them. Then she cried.

"Well, there," she said through her tears, "I congratulate you from the bottom of my heart, both you, Natalie, and you, Serge. Now there is nothing more for me to do. Love will take care of the rest. I thought that I could be of some use, but I see that I'm too late. You've managed without me. Though I simply can't understand where you plan to live. Would you please get this house in shape at least for my sake? If you, my dear brother, would stop thinking of yourself for just a second, and give some thought to Natalie and the coming child—" And she cried some more.

Myatlev, totally confused, rang for Afanasy, but as if to add the final note to the surrounding madness, Mr. Sverbeyev appeared with his sad mustache to explain that Aglaya, fending off her husband's blows, had just accidentally knocked him downstairs, and the noble majordomo was lying in his room with pains in his back and neck. In reporting this, the spy addressed only Countess Rumyantseva, ignoring the prince and his sister. At any other time he would have been thrown out, but this was not the moment for expounding the rules of politeness, and Myatlev ordered him to bring some water and vinegar for his sister.

No sooner had the spy gone than Elizaveta Vasilyevna continued her teary monologue:

"Where do you dig up such freaks? You could at least dress him properly! Nothing should be allowed to cause talk and criticism about you now. Thank God that you are going to be united, and the honor of our family— I've begun to be afraid of the tsar and any questions about you he might ask. What could I have told him? The cup of his irritation needed just one more drop, no more than that, let me tell you. And thank God I no longer have to hide my face." She turned to her friend. "With his spiritual wealth, talents, and inner virtues, he was becoming known in society as a dangerous and evil man!"

"What are you talking about?" Myatlev wanted to shout, but he couldn't.

Mr. Sverbeyev brought the water and vinegar, which did not interest the lady-in-waiting at all.

"You should buy a new house," she went on, addressing Myatlev. "Closer to all of us, hire new servants, and set up a new order. In any case, if these ruins are so dear to you, you could at least call in an architect and have him fix them up, make them more presentable."

"Presentable," echoed Mr. Sverbeyev.

Myatlev made a threatening gesture in his direction, indicating that the spy should withdraw, but Mr. Sverbeyev stood his ground.

"Go, go," Natalya said contemptuously.

Myatlev wanted them to leave immediately so that he could be alone and lose himself in his diary and write down the curious observations that had occurred to him while they chattered about their projects. But the lady-in-waiting continued:

"I don't understand why you can't just straighten out. Nothing is holding you back but your own whims. You should be thinking of Natalie now. Everything is perfectly clear to everyone, and there is no need to pretend. And if you would finally deign to appreciate the degree of your guilt toward society and would hurry up and clear yourself somehow, enter government service, display your capabilities, you would compel them to speak of you differently, as a person who is of real use and value to the tsar, and you would come to be recognized not as a villain who challenges everyone but as a person who cares about the welfare of the reigning house. Then, I assure you, everything would be forgotten, my dear brother, and you would be among us once more. Don't you . . . condition . . . joys . . . indications . . . generosity . . . loneliness . . . "

It was late evening when it finally occurred to them to leave. As usual, Natalya gave him a farewell gift. This time it was a small canvas, *The Annunciation* by Guercino.

"What are you doing?" he wanted to say. "You are binding me hand and foot. You invite me to succumb to your charms, taking advantage of the fact that I'm a man of few words and that you are so lovely, and noble, and in the right. But even though you are clever enough to pretend not to understand me, I

188

can still see you are not sufficiently clever to abandon your overconfidence. And that will ruin you. It will hurt when I escape. As God is my witness, I do not want to hurt you."

The ceremony was set for the last Sunday in October.

33

"A fugitive was grabbed by some people who were looking for someone else. When they saw they had captured the wrong man, they took pity on him and let him run off into the woods. However, his hiding place became known to his real pursuers, and they came after him. Then the fugitive turned to his original captors and cried to them in desperation, 'Kill me! It was you who took pity on me, and you must get the reward.' So, dying, he repaid their pity and compassion."

I can't resist copying down these words from Appian, who so prophetically divined our fate, even though we live eighteen centuries later. I read them with a shiver, but I can't imagine behaving any other way. As I run into the dewy grass of the forest, I can hear the pursuing voices and the barking behind me, always gaining on me.

If people lived forever, then the experience of one life would be enough to keep you from making mistakes in another life. But each new generation learns anew and dies because of its ignorance.

What could I offer to counterpoise the chorus of two babbling ladies whose voices besieged me like two catapults? What besides silence? And yet they thought that I had ripened enough to share their plans and enthusiasms. Thank God, I'm too lazy to move now, but at the critical moment I will jump out the window, like a moth, and fly off, maybe to the paradise that Amiran Amilakhvari buzzes about in my ear.

The Hobbler wrote me a letter. I can only conclude from it that that wise black crow who hovers over tsars can't fly high enough to see that his own exposés are just more of the usual muddle. In killing the Bear, he is trying to prove that he himself is the true Bear and the other is a liar and usurper. That is really the basis of his battle for justice!

He's become completely monomaniacal on the subject; he'd be better off writing novels. With his education, talent, and ability to portray character, novel writing would be ideal. He's bitter because all his attempts to attract me to his intrigues and inflame me with his passions have come to naught. He can't understand that I become so nauseated the moment I come in contact with politics that I give away money right and left, and that money is only good to somebody else.

I looked at myself in the mirror; I'm still rather handsome, and there's something about my eyes. . . .

34

ENSNARED IN THE SILKEN nets set by the ladies, Myatlev almost lost the ability to resist and began obeying blindly. This must have resulted from a prolonged siege of his disease, involving a loss of freedom that only a miracle could end. I prayed to God to save my friend from weakness and blindness, and apparently my prayers were so fervent and desperate that Providence provided an opportunity for a happy resolution.

Having agreed to enlist, "to clear his name in society," he set off to introduce himself to Count Nesselrode. The meeting was brief, the elderly count courtierlike and cordial; clearly, the complex and Byzantine machinations of Elizaveta Vasilyevna had reached him in sufficiently convincing form so that the old bootlicker took his cue from them to appear cordial on his own behalf. An excellent diplomat where trifles were concerned, despite his advanced age, he used all his tried-and-true charms; but he made little impression on Myatlev, who was not used to government service and watched the refined maneuvers of that high-placed personage with the implacability of an ancient shepherd.

In the past they had met socially, but if this was basis enough for the count to picture the prince as a wayward goose, it certainly wasn't enough to enable Myatlev to judge the count's behavior, for his memory of people who were not close to him was monstrously inefficient.

The count felt it his duty to stress the fact that Myatlev's appearance in his office was not a simple accident and not the result of pressure, but the logical outcome of the prince's prolonged meditation on his place in society, and a sign of the wisdom that comes with maturity, and so on.

"I'm skeptical of young men who choose this work at their fathers' insistence and not from the promptings of their hearts," he said. "But I am happy to see in you a man sufficiently ripened to make an independent decision."

Myatlev went back home, not in the least charmed by the aged flatterer's cordiality. On the contrary, his recent doubts flared up again, but there was nothing he could do, and the azure net drew tighter and tighter.

And so, with its marks on his body and with clouded vision, he walked down Gorokhovaya Street, having sent his carriage home. Suddenly a familiar name looked down at him from a light-blue sign: SALON SVERBEYEV AND CO. LADIES' AND GENTLEMEN'S CLOTHES FROM THE FINEST ENGLISH MODELS. Actually, the word "English" had been written over the still-visible "French." This sight was so unexpected and blinding that Myatlev stopped. His cloudy brain came alive, feverishly selecting and putting together random scraps of memory. Something distant and threatening, improper and vague, indecent and ridiculous came to him, and he remembered. This made him laugh—the surname of his familiar haunter of chimneys was so out of place on a sign displaying red scissors, yellow thread, and a green needle.

The bell rang matter-of-factly, and a portly female of about forty, wrapped in a bright shawl, with a sniffling cold, appeared before Myatlev, looking him over with professional suspicion.

She saw a man in a not-very-new black redingote and a tall gray hat that had not been spared either wind or rain. However, the collar and white tie peeping out were impeccable. His spectacles glittered, and this made her gloomy. He was leaning on a black umbrella and looking around, as though he had the wrong address.

"Please come in," she simpered, "the owner will be right with you."

He realized that he ought to turn and leave, but his curiosity got the better of him and he asked how long this place had existed.

"Company!" the woman called out in a thin, sweet voice.

Myatlev was beginning to feel quite ill, what with the sound of that voice and the fact that he hadn't been asked to take his coat off, and that he had been to see Count Nesselrode, and that they had, as they say, hit it off, and it was all because of Cassandra and Natalya and his own carelessness; and now he had climbed into this den on his own, to talk with this female with a head cold, instead of laughing at all of it and himself, walking stiffly out and slamming the door disrespectfully, and then, freed at least, sending Count Nesselrode and his ministry to Hell—for there is no such thing as a ministry in nature, just a building stuffed with clerks in dark-green uniforms—and then sending Natalya, who was pretending to be in love with him, to Hell, and then sending himself to Hell for pretending that a decent man could be made happy by getting his share of the state feedbag.

He was ready to act on his angry intentions when Mr. Sverbeyev himself came out from behind a curtain, out of the dark, and bowed to him. His long, ungainly body seemed to break as he bowed; there was an audible creaking and cracking; the sad mustache swept the floor, leaving—as Myatlev could clearly see—two thin tracks on the dusty floorboards.

"Your Excellency!" he exclaimed with joy. "I never thought, never suspected that you would— Please, let me take your redingote. Well, well. So you need something from me?" He turned to the female with the cold. "Why are you standing there, as though nailed to the floor? When people find out that Prince Myatlev himself was here, I'll have to beat off customers with a stick. Go make tea—what are you standing around for?"

"How do you manage to combine spying and tailoring?" Myatlev wanted to ask, but didn't.

"I have fashion plates here," Sverbeyev went on, gasping. "Do they please you? What a day for me, your coming here!" And he shouted at the gloomy woman, "What a day, I said! Remember what day this is!" And he turned back to Myatlev. "I get merchants, well, and civil servants, and well, people from various walks of life, but you, Your Excellency, as I see it, fate sent you here to me."

As he spoke, Mr. Sverbeyev bustled about, hopping, spreading the pungent odor of tobacco, onion, and incense, and his clinging red fingers palpated the prince's jacket, as though taking its measure, or perhaps actually measuring it, determining its length, width, and the length of his pantaloons and his hip size and waist size, stopping to deprecate his puny chest and immediately planning to add horsehair and cotton padding to make the chest more manly, and then figuring the distance from cuff to shoulder, and from shoulder to shoulder, and from waist to footstraps, and from the straps to the most private place—

"Why are you a spy?" Myatlev wanted to ask, but didn't.

The cloth curtain moved, and a man came out, dressed in the most unprepossessing manner. He was wearing a dark-green uniform jacket, unbuttoned and sleeveless, no pantaloons at all, merely the prescribed black underwear, and no shoes. His broad, smoothly shaven face exuded health, his fleshy lips were smiling, and his small, wise eyes stared intently.

"I heard 'Prince Myatlev' and couldn't resist coming out of my hiding place," he said with a certain dignity. "I have heard much about you," he said, and bowed. "Kolesnikov, Adrian Semyonovich, collegiate secretary of the horse-breeding department, pleased to meet you. Perhaps you have read some of my works in the journals? I can't boast of great fame, but I do have some admirers among my readers."

Neither Sverbeyev nor the woman with the cold seemed surprised by the appearance of the half-dressed scribbler, and while he went on about his exploits and acquaintances, taking advantage of Myatlev's confusion, they stood motionless, not uttering a word.

The scribbler's bare feet must have been cold, and like a dragoon's steed, he hopped from foot to foot while he went on addressing the astounded prince.

"There are all kinds of rumors abroad about you, Prince—one more fantastic than the other—but personally, I discount them. For me, personally, you are still the friend of our sad genius, isn't that right? I'm amazed that you still haven't taken the time to write your memoirs, though in these less than propitious days they could hardly be published, could they? Let's sit down," he said, indicating a chair with an easy and attractive gesture Myatlev found hard to resist. "Of course, anything discordant or inauspicious can easily be dealt with by invoking reasons of state in such a way as to permit no argument. For example, drinking coffee in the morning could be forbidden, citing reasons of state, and you would not drink it and would even convince yourself that it was truly necessary not to. By the way, a certain guardian of public morals has suggested banishing all novels from Russia so that no one can read novels! It's under consideration. What do you think of that?"

All this while, Mr. Sverbeyev's hands went on working, determining something only he could understand about the prince's clothes. And he would lean back, squint, visualize, while waves of inspiration and passion swept over his morose face.

"He's not a liar," thought Myatlev sympathetically, looking at Mr. Kolesnikov's bare feet. "But how naive he is! And everything is so clear to him, and so simple, that it would be a sin to insult him."

"Personally, I would like to see your memoirs. If you like, I can suggest a few journals. For example, take *The Contemporary*. Nekrasov is carrying on the work there, even though he's hanging by a hair—"

"What work?"

Kolesnikov laughed conspiratorially. His toes turned red, then curled up and turned blue. On the other side of the curtain, someone was moving and arranging dishes.

"What *work*?" Kolesnikov said happily. "Well, just look. We've been worried by certain events in Europe. What a pleasant delusion it is to think that those European events were the result of reading books and of an interest in the sciences, and that therefore we must do away with science and with reading so as to avoid similar cataclysms here."

"Do you think so?" Myatlev asked distractedly.

"That's what those who call themselves patriots think. But the true patriots are trying to counteract such vile opinions and actions." And then he whispered, "Ignorance is being turned into a system . . . While events in Europe—"

"What events?" Myatlev asked. "What are you referring to?"

Here Kolesnikov laughed aloud and banged the floor with his heels. The dishes on the other side of the curtain rattled louder. The two of them were alone in the seedy salon.

"You like to joke, Prince," said Kolesnikov, looking around. "What do you call the fact that Europe, no longer tolerating arbitrary rule, has risen up? I'm referring to revolution, Prince."

"You want that here?" said Myatlev, not quite following the drift of the scribbler's thoughts.

"One might think you were defending arbitrary rule," Kolesnikov said huffily, rubbing his toes with his hands.

"I don't understand much of all this," Myatlev confessed, smiling. "Aren't you personally satisfied with the way things are?"

"I beg you, Prince," said Kolesnikov, and his feet thumped the floor, as though they were doing the talking. "What I think isn't at issue here; the government is that same government which in its day gave rise to Pugachev* and many others."

"Personally, I'm afraid of Pugachevs," said Myatlev to the scribbler's feet.

"Prince," exclaimed Kolesnikov with distrust, "are you an

*Peasant leader of a large-scale rebellion in 1773–75.—Translator.

obscurantist? We're being suffocated by ignorance, groaning under the knout, losing our human dignity, arbitrary rule abounds, and you can say that—or do you approve of it?"

"No, I don't approve of it," Myatlev said firmly, "but I don't know what to do, how to make it better. I don't know what needs to be done. I'm not sure—"

"It's better to fight on the side of a few good men against many base ones, than vice versa," shouted Kolesnikov.

"That's Antisthenes," laughed Myatlev. "You know his work?"

"I know a few other things besides." Kolesnikov sighed bitterly and wriggled his stiffened toes.

"Governments fall because they can't distinguish the good men from the bad," said Myatlev, and he thought, "Good Lord, I really don't want to wear black underwear and a dark-green uniform and pretend that I'm being useful to society."

Mr. Sverbeyev brought out a bolt of dark-green fabric, deftly tossed it onto a chair, unrolled it, threw the free end over the prince's shoulder as though it were a toga, and then leaned back to see if it made him look too pale.

"I beg your pardon," Kolesnikov said abruptly, blushing deeply. "I can't understand how I—" He wriggled his bare toes, staring at them in amazement. "How could I? How humiliating!" He jumped up and hobbled over to the curtain just as the woman was coming out. "Pardon, Prince, please forgive me." And then from behind the curtain: "This damn outfit has to be ready by tomorrow morning. Oh, God. But if you should change your mind, don't hesitate to call on me. I'll be happy to introduce you to the right editors, at your convenience. Oh, God, the uniform is almost ready, that was just a last fitting—and I think I caught a cold going barefoot. So that's how you feel? That we can't tell if a man is good or bad? Then we must follow the example of Oldenburgsky, who refuses to recognize a friend of mine, and do you know why? Just listen. He met my friend . . . wearing a black tie instead of a white one, as specified in the rules. And do you know what? . . . unjustly accused of free thinking . . . Just think . . ."

196

"I'm not interested in that," thought Myatlev.

Mr. Kolesnikov's round, ruddy face peered out from the curtain, like a mask, and hoarse phrases tumbled out of his round mouth. Mr. Sverbeyev ran in and out, as though he were a spectator of the play they were putting on.

"Or, for instance," the mask whispered, "how about the right of directors to dismiss a clerk for undependability or for mistakes that can't be proved. What is that?"

"Really, what is *this*?" thought Myatlev. "You can't even go out of the house without running into trouble. Perhaps I should just order an English telescope and spend my time studying the skies. And if I point it at Petersburg, I'll look only at the contours of the belfries. And if I should espy two citizens in conversation, at least I won't hear their voices and I'll not know what they're talking about. Isn't it better to have tea with Mr. van Schoenhoven at home than to hang around for no reason in the house of a spy? Where are you, Mr. van Schoenhoven?"

"What is this?" Kolesnikov went on. "You can't ignore the danger of losing one's life simply because of somebody's slander or because of someone's bad mood. No, no, Your Excellency, if your friend who perished so tragically were still alive, he would bombard us with such poems that we would begin to see and understand that we are on the edge of a precipice. Your friend, Prince Myatlev, your friend was a true genius."

The face of that friend, with its big eyes and short mustache, flashed before Myatlev's eyes and disappeared, without making anything clearer.

The bell over the door jangled. A more youthful Myatlev, full of daring intentions, strode away under the October rain, hearing a foreign voice muttering after him, "Your Excellency, Your Excellency—the samovar is ready— Excellency—"

35

Oh, what a wonderfully daring man and what an unimaginably good boy I am! How wonderful to know I'm an individual! What blessings my decisiveness augurs!

First of all, I'm still alive and well, thank God. It is not for me to emulate Mr. Kolesnikov, who is blind, and hoarse, and mad. He's a fine match for my Hobbler. I can just see them working together, breaking all the dishes, deciding whom to blacklist and whom to put on some white list. How they would subvert and destroy, while secretly worrying about their own interests. Secondly, didn't the uniform seem strange on me, dark green or even dark blue, and didn't it make me feel like an alien from another planet? Let the tsar and his intimate servants dream up laws that determine the required color for underwear, thereby countering European infections. To each his own. Thirdly, do I look like the blissful husband of a woman with a heavy jaw? What dizziness enveloped me in that miasma! What a lucky accident whistled up this fresh breeze!

I had Afanasy get me some of the famous liberal journals. I can't deny the authors their talent and the publishers a certain liberalism, but the word "liberalism" is not so dangerous a word as it is an empty one. I can even understand Pugachevs, lusting for power, more than I can these gentlemen suffering for the people. I'm convinced that they really suffer because of their personal problems or as a result of personal inadequacies and failures. If they would deign to study history a bit, they would discover to their astonishment that there have always been, in all periods, perfumed and refined loners who proclaimed their unity with the people until such time as their disillusionment set in, until their legs were broken or their faces punched. I've known a few of them myself, and while giving their noble impulses and saintly blindness their due, I see that they deluded themselves, thinking that their tears were needed by those they wept over.

And besides, if you're going to weep, then why not weep over me, putting on a uniform I've suddenly become worthy of? How sad that my simple yearning to live according to my desires brings nothing but aggravation and sorrow to so many perfect and irreproachable creatures?

The most terrible thing is that I can no longer return to the past! I can't bring Alexandrina back to life and, because life is short, be kind to her. I can't bring old man Raspevin back and reward him for the purity of his loyalty to empty hopes. I can't bring back *that poet* without exposing him to another duel. . . . Nothing can be done. And I can't invite Mr. van Schoenhoven for a cup of tea or go off with him to watch the ice break up along the Neva. I can't, I can't.

The spy has reappeared in my house, casual as ever, and has naturally settled down for tea in the family circle. He bowed to me in surprise, as though he had never expected to see me again.

Almost everyone is saying aloud that our country is on the brink of catastrophe, that thievery and bribery have reached their apogee, and if it is announced tomorrow that the tsar is missing, it will mean that he has been stolen and will be returned in exchange for a ransom—the award of an order or a medal.

Suddenly, like snow on your head, a letter from Aneta Fredericks. "Why have you forgotten me? Or do you attribute a deeper meaning to what transpired between us? I had always thought better of your mind, dear Seryozha. And then you should have guessed, not loving me seriously, that I make a better friend than lover. I keep hearing things about you, and I feel sorry for you. You should drop by; after all, nothing at all happened, just hazy trifles."

October 13

I don't have the energy to have it out with Countess Rumyantseva. I wrote her a brief note to the effect that her hopes are groundless. I was afraid that a lengthy siege would follow, with curses, migraines, and harangues. However, she displayed the utmost nobility, which is very strange considering her condition and her views, and replied with a refined couplet, delivered in a business envelope. She threw in a bitter phrase about my egotism, but I can take it. "The law demands that leftovers be thrown to the hounds." Someday, if we meet again, not as antagonists but simply as old acquaintances, I'll probably tell her that vehement protestations of love, like vehement protestations of patriotic feelings, are suspect.

The leaves are falling. . . . Desolation in nature is depressing. That's probably why there are more beggars in Petersburg now, and their unwashed hordes are crowding all the parapets, so that it's almost impossible to get by.

> Do you remember the horns' mournful call,
> The splatter of rain, half-light, half-darkness.

If I had two lives, I could devote one to vain regrets and bitterness. But I have only one.

Amiran Amilakhvari has one marvelous trait: not sharing many of my opinions or my way of life, and so on, he does not nag, or insist, or disdain, or blaspheme; he merely pretends—not in the sense of sham, but out of respect for foreign mores—to share them all. The freedom-loving spirit that was inculcated in him from childhood in his paradisal Georgia forbids him to be a judge of other men. There must be—there is—something in his native land that cannot be learned but can only be absorbed in one's mother's milk. Despite his flawless French and true aristocracy, he is a charming child of the mountains, and no Petersburg could ever spoil his blood. You have to hear him speak lovingly of his native land, which he left as a child, about his sister, whom he sees every three or four years, his parents, and Georgian cuisine, hear how he sings in his guttural language, see how he clutches his saber to keep from dropping everything here and rushing back home to be cured. "Perhaps, on the other side of the Caucasus."

What marvelous silence! Blockhead Afanasy has come to his senses, stuck on his stupid tie, and stands before me with reproach in his eyes. Actually, even though I am to blame, I'm getting tired of his condemning face. I tolerate him because he is a great original and also out of habit, but he shouldn't take advantage of it. The spy, it seems, has moved into the house. He despises me and, judging from everything, nonetheless expects me to wear the uniform he is sewing for me. Yesterday, at his insistence, I gave him a lecture about my painting, not, of course, mentioning the name of poor Muravyev.* However, the bastard must sense something or know something; he keeps thinking about something, wheezing meaningfully, and snorting. . . . Keeping in mind that any reference to the incident on Senate Square is a sharp knife for the tsar, then it's possible that secret name will come to the ears of those who are interested in it.

I'm curious as to how my mad ladies will sound retreat and stop the wedding. What feelings will fill their souls; what curses will be showered on me?

October 15

Could they be right when they condemn me for indifference toward public office? Cassandra, for instance, who insists that government service will not "demean" me? Or don't I know how it looks?

"You are conspicuous for a tendency in your opinions that is storing up great future unpleasantness for you," she said.

What could that mean? Could the desire to be independent really sadden all normal-thinking people? Poor Cassandra, she is so involved in the court's way of thinking that she pictures the entire planet as an anteroom for ladies-in-waiting, where any deviation from the imperial way of thinking is a sin.

Not a word from Natalya. What bliss!

October 17

Lieutenant Katakazi has fallen on my head out of nowhere. Meticulous, scented with French perfume, he looks like a well-clipped poodle. One had to observe him as he tossed his soaked redingote to the valet and see how magisterially he dealt with his hat, how his beady eyes attacked me as he waited for me to insult him—as I once did in the past, not letting him beyond my doorstep. However, this time my feisty devil willed me to be kind to this pathetic authenticator of other people's suspicions. Then he pretended that he had expected no other reception, although a light blush exploded on his cheeks and his inordinately smooth gait revealed the storm raging within him.

Our conversation was portentous.

*Sergei Muravyev-Apostol, the European in the crowd of Indians, was one of the five Decembrist leaders who were hanged.—Translator.

201

KATAKAZI: Please forgive me, Prince, for disturbing you, but as you can imagine, I'm not here because of any desire on my part.

I: I'm pleased to see you in my home, Lieutenant.

KATAKAZI: I'm flattered, but I reserve the right to doubt that a meeting with me could bring you pleasure.

I: You are wrong. I'm truly happy to have an opportunity to make up for my recent insensitivity, and I'm ready to hear you out.

KATAKAZI (*triumphantly*): Prince, I must return to our old topic of the Marquis Troyat living in your house.

I: Oh, God, you and that marquis!

KATAKAZI: You see, there is an unsolved case [*Laughs.*] and I can't close the file until I clear it up. So, does he live here or not?

I: Believe me, he is a wholly mythical figure.

KATAKAZI: Are you saying that you invented him?

I: Exactly. I'm surprised that a joke like that could cause so much trouble in your department.

KATAKAZI: Permit me to doubt you. All the data point to the exact opposite.

I: What data? Lieutenant, you are joking. I know everyone in my household. Well, perhaps he's disguised as one of the servants.

KATAKAZI: Why not?

I: Then I pass.

KATAKAZI (*whispering*): The Marquis Troyat, as we have learned in the Third Section, is an exile from France, an advocate of republican ideas, living secretly in your house for a purpose we can only guess at.

I (*becoming curious*): Why in my house?

KATAKAZI: Well, that's very simple. On the recommendation of your friend Andrei Vladimirovich Priymkov. [*Laughs.*]

I: What nonsense. What does Priymkov have to do with it? There is no Marquis Troyat.

KATAKAZI (*sighs*): All right, but you do know Prince Priymkov, I hope?

I: Listen, Lieutenant, doesn't it strike you that I should have you thrown out? Aren't you worried by that kind of ending to our conversation?

KATAKAZI (*with a charming smile*): No, Prince, I'm not. I wouldn't come if that were a possibility. I'm not here to chat with you, and not at my own prompting but, as I already had the honor of informing you, at the behest of others, to ask you a series of questions, and you, Prince, would not be so tactless. [*Laughs.*] You do know Prince Priymkov?

I: Yes, I do.

KATAKAZI: We have information that despite the ban on visiting Petersburg, he secretly comes to visit you.

I (*confused*): Well, how can I put it. I heard that he was in Petersburg once, but—I can't remember who it was who told me.

KATAKAZI: That's not important. He was here, and he was in your house.

I: Well, you know—

KATAKAZI: You've forgotten. He was in your house because in your seclusion you need to talk to someone, and except for him there are no people around you worthy of that—in your opinion.

I: That's a fantasy and has nothing to do with this imagined marquis. Particularly since I have many friends.

KATAKAZI: It's not fantasy, but a chain of logical deductions.

I: (*stubbornly*): It's nonsense.

KATAKAZI: A word that is meaningless in an argument.

I: We are dragging out this conversation.

KATAKAZI: Look at my side of it—the files of the Third Section indicate that the Marquis Troyat visited you two years ago, in January of 1846. This has been corroborated. I don't insist that he is living here now, but if it says he was here, then he was. [*Laughs.*] See my side of it—I have to close this case, and I can't. Now, when France has confronted us with such dread events, and all of Europe is boiling and in rebellion, the case of the Marquis Troyat is taking on new dimensions. Look at my side of it—

I: I would be happy to help you in any way, but this is such nonsense—

KATAKAZI: We are not maintaining that you share his opinions, Heaven forbid; just that he dropped in for an hour, made a mistake in the address, said nothing, had a cup of coffee, disappeared—anything, just so that I can close the case.

I: But this is madness.

KATAKAZI: All you have to do is confirm that he was here. We'll close the case, and that's it.

I: You're mocking me.

KATAKAZI: Is this a joking matter? I beg you to see my side of it. It won't cost you a thing, but it'll take a mountain off my shoulders.

I: If this empty formality can help you—

KATAKAZI (*animatedly*): Precisely. I've been having problems over this at work for several years.

I: Damn it, here then: he passed by, stayed for a half hour while his wheel was fixed—

KATAKAZI: Wonderful, Prince, but not his wheel, since this took place in winter, in January, if you recall.

I: All right, the runner on his sleigh, the whip, the yoke, the bells—you can't ride without bells? A French bell! They reshod the lead horse, put a compress on the coachman, bled the marquis—

KATAKAZI: You laugh, but I've had a mountain taken off my shoulders. Now we can close the damn case, and that's it. By the way, Prince, it wouldn't hurt—this is just friendly advice—if the next time this mysterious marquis shows up, you could send your man to tell us; we would be very grateful, and you would spare yourself excessive bother. [*Very obnoxiously*] Personally, I try to avoid having people develop any prejudiced opinions of me.

I: You are permitting yourself to lecture me.

KATAKAZI: Forgive me, it never even occurred to me. I'm grateful, so grateful to you—you've helped me out. You've saved me. [*Stands up to leave*] What can I do, Prince? In my position I have no choice. I can't allow myself the luxury of thinking only about my soul, Your Excellency. For you, perhaps, this is all nonsense, but for me the service is, as they say, my mother, and my uniform is my father. Please forgive the interruption. [*In the doorway*] By the way, simple curiosity: your friend Mr. Kolesnikov—what do you think of his work?

I: I don't seem to recall anyone like that.

KATAKAZI: Kolesnikov? Please—the writer, he's published in the journals—

I: No, no, I can't recall—

KATAKAZI: Strange. He knows you.

I (*remembering Sverbeyev's salon and the two freezing feet*): Ah, of course—but we're not really acquainted. A chance meeting— Why Lieutenant, do you—I haven't read his work I must admit—were you implying—I don't read contemporary journals. He seemed a rather curious creature to me.

KATAKAZI (*animatedly*): Precisely! Absolutely curious. In one of his articles an opinion slipped through—oh-oh— there was a detail—well, a hint that some arbitrary power was forcing its way into art with the intention of eradicating it.

I: You would know better than I. If you know him—I don't read articles.

KATAKAZI: I was just— Don't ever start talking to him; he'll talk you to death. [*Laughs.*] Aplomb. And bad manners. Don't you think?

And he began moving away from me, vanishing into the distance, disappearing. When I came to, he was no longer in the room or in the house. I realized that I had had one of my attacks. I had begun to laugh at them, thinking I had gotten over them because of not having had one in a long time. What a situation! Where can I seek help? And suppose that Dr. Morinari could have healed me with a wave of the hand! Oh, belated regrets!

October 19

Nothing occurs without some consequences. That ridiculous scene with the lieutenant had a sequel. Today I received a letter.

Your Excellency!

I feel it is my duty to thank you for your amazing nobility and generosity, with which I came into contact when I was at your home on an official visit two days ago. I admit that for a brief moment I was indignant at the thought that you were trying to bribe an official. I repeat, it was only for a brief moment, because you offered me the money with such sincerity and friendliness that to suspect you would have been base, and to refuse the money would have meant offending you and your good intentions.

I am amazed by your intuitiveness; how could you have known that my family and I are in terrible straits?

From this moment on, I consider myself your debtor, both financially and spiritually, and I pray to God that He will grant me a chance to prove it to you at the soonest possible opportunity.

> Always prepared to be at your service,
> Your Excellency's humble servant,
> Lieutenant Timofey Katakazi.

So that was how our conversation had ended! In a fit of idiocy I must have thrust my wallet on him, and he didn't dare refuse me. But I'm afraid that he accepted the money as a bribe in exchange for my peace and quiet. What a business! As I remember, there were three hundred rubles in there! Isn't that too much for one lousy Katakazi?

October 21

What a letter I have just received from Moscow—short, haughty, mocking! I am "dear sir," and my tactfulness turns out to be nothing more than cowardice; I did not behave as a van Schoenhoven should, and there is no forgiveness!

I'm bolder in letters, note. This is probably my final letter. I'm writing because I still can't get over your visit to Moscow. I can't hide the fact that I was so pleased that I became a block of wood. I suppose that if I were in your place and you in mine, your behavior would have angered me greatly! What insolence— to greet someone so coldly! I know that you will never want to see me again. I realized that as soon as I saw you near our house—I could see that you were saddened by meeting me. My *maman* looks at me with surprise and follows me around with a halberd. And she adds: "We Bravuras were always noted for our extreme control in expressing emotion." I'm ashamed to think that you might have thought that *Maman* wished me ill.

After your shameful flight, we all had a pleasant dinner, bandaged Lieutenant Berg's head, and sent him off to the Caucasus in the active army. He hopes quickly to vanquish all the natives and return with a Saint Vladimir or Saint Anna Cross. So everything is fine with me. I hear that things are going well for you, too, and that soon you will be living in wedded bliss, and thank God for that.

Yes, there is no forgiveness for me. Lavinia Bravura will have nothing to do with me, and for good reason. Amiran, having read her letter, said: "Is she in love with you? These girls of fifteen spend all their time falling in love. She writes about Misha Berg, but he can only be pitied, because this thin daughter of a witch is too mocking to be a happy bride."

That Mr. van Schoenhoven, who no longer exists! However, something like sadness gnaws at me at the thought that Lieutenant Berg, shooting holes into some natives in revenge for the trouncings he has gotten from Koko, will return and take Mr. van Schoenhoven down the aisle! . . . There was no Mr. van Schoenhoven, and there isn't now.

"Who is Mr. van Schoenhoven?" I asked Afanasy.

"Who knows?" the sluggard replied.

"You brought him in here yourself."

"If I may say so, I brought everyone in here," the monster replied.

That means that there really is no Mr. van Schoenhoven.

October 23

Poor Natalya. What can a woman in her situation do? Really, it's a difficult situation. My terror of being coerced made me see something terrible in the countess herself, but she's just an ordinary female with a rather heavy jaw, which probably means absolutely nothing. The desire to marry me was a whim; the fervor and stubbornness with which she tried to achieve her goal was just faithful service to her nature. It's time to get used to that and not despise them for it, for if you look at yourself objectively, you don't present the prettiest picture, either, particularly when you are striking a pose or not even trying to restrain your instincts or make an effort to suit the times, but persist in your unbridled behavior and gulp noisily at the sight of a delicious morsel, and stretch out your neck like a gander, and shuffle your feet in the attempt to get at something. . . . And yet the measure of everyone's worth exactly equals the worth of what he wants. The ancients are right again.

Reading the ancients means conversing with them, and these conversations cleanse you. So I converse with them. And I don't want to converse with my contemporaries. Why not? Probably because the ancients talk about you, too, while my contemporaries always talk about themselves.

The only one whom I can talk to or maintain a glorious silence with, without feeling uncomfortable, is still Amiran. Whenever he appears in my house, that loving marvel in whom glow coals that are always ready to burst into flame at the moment of need, I want to throw on my cape and fall into the moonless night, turn into a small shadow protected by his big one, sneak through the park, fly across the Neva, catch up with some carriage, hook onto the back of it, and race off into the unknown—or else, pass the carriage in giant strides, my cape rustling against the door, frightening some Evdokiya Spiridonovna or Matryona Evlampiyevna who is sleeping in there unburdened by empty sorrows and looking forward to getting back to her estate, where sweet biscuits from the city and hats from Dupré's await her. . . . I want. . . .

But instead we went to a ball where Amilakhvari hoped to dissipate my melancholy and make me "resemble a human being" and where I expected to see what had happened during my prolonged absence from society.

But there was nothing to dissipate, since lately I've been filled with unswerving determination and willpower, and nothing had happened during my absence; and what could really have happened in such a stable world? Naturally, Natalya was there, but pretended not to see me, which I noted with great relief, since I had no desire to enter into diplomatic negotiations. It was, and it is over. . . . She was beautiful and sad, but seemed almost a stranger to me. Madame Nesselrode bowed very sweetly to me, from which I deduced that my government service, my wedding, and my future no longer trouble these people and that I am already regarded as having been forgiven and am beloved.

Without disillusioning them, I hurried away from the dancing and spent my time between the buffet and the card tables until I was certain that the world was quite all right.

They have left me alone, if only for a while, at least until they find out the depth of my fall. Then the storm will break. . . . And meanwhile, I'm left to my own devices.

And how can they know what's going on inside me and what I need, if I, master of my body, cannot determine that myself?

36

IT WAS THE HEIGHT of the ball. The chandeliers were aflame. The orchestra was wailing. It seemed that in this huge, brightly lit box something wild, not confined to one specific shape but with many faces, was laughing, smiling, groaning, sweating, not knowing how to stop, its whole brief life, without past or future, marked only by this uncontrollable jostling and shuddering in an enclosed space, where even Natalya's former haughtiness disappeared without a trace as she pursued the scattered particles of her self, her head thrown back, her insolent mouth slightly open, her eyes clouded with pleasure; the separate, identical, happy faces of the Horse Guards Apollos; and a multitude of unspoiled, long-necked, gray-eyed little van Schoenhovens, nervously hanging onto gold-braided shoulders, eyes rolled back, flying into the brilliant void with the delight of discovery. And new explosions from the orchestra, now on the brink of catastrophe somewhere up above, trying as hard as possible to convince the crowd that this is what it's all about, that this is life, that this is happiness, as it always has been and will be unto the ages. And when the rumor spread that the tsar

209

was about to appear, then everything swirled even more, so that he could once again see each of them in their splendor of loyalty and talent and thus drown out the hysterical cries of barefoot Mr. Kolesnikov in his dark-green uniform, who was not allowed to attend such revels and for that reason somewhat resembled Pugachev.

In the buffet Myatlev ran into Colonel von Müffling just coming out. His sandy eyebrows and mustache glowed in the tobacco smoke.

"One would think that all of Russia was dancing here tonight," he said, winking. He seemed happy to run into Myatlev and have an excuse for another drink. "If Mr. Priymkov and his ideas were brought here, he would probably be torn to pieces, eh? One would think that our whole lives were one brilliant holiday, eh?"

He swayed gently before Myatlev, never taking his pale-blue eyes from him. His uniform gave off a pacifying glow, and Myatlev felt he was the luckiest man in the kingdom, and even Natalya regained her position as the crown of creation, and he decided to get to her and tell her that there could be no greater happiness for him than to marry her, and that she should believe him despite his condition, and tomorrow—and that she should tear up his last letter containing his refusal and other nonsense.

But von Müffling was standing in front of him, and that saved Myatlev from a false move. As for the colonel, Myatlev really did enjoy talking to him, for he seemed to be the only one alive in that sea of symbols, and besides, they had something to talk about, to remember, meaning poor Alexandrina, and von Müffling said:

"You have a kind heart, you're a fine fellow— She was such a creature that I cried, I swear to God, I cried when you were rescuing her—then I couldn't keep from crying—and when I found out that she ran off on you—"

"You're confused," Myatlev said. "She committed suicide. Consumption."

"Precisely," von Müffling said. "Poor little thing."

"Colonel," said Myatlev, "your Lieutenant Katakazi seems overly interested in me. What is this?

"Katakazi? Who's that?"

"Your Katakazi," Myatlev said angrily. "Your lieutenant. He bursts in on me with hints, threats, and suspicions—"

"With suspicions?" Von Müffling was surprised. "What could you be suspected of? Who is this Katakazi? Where? Ah, just send him to Hell. Don't be shy—don't be shy— Who knows what's going on— You know, every man thinks he's— Wait, maybe he's just in love?"

"With whom?"

"With your drowned woman—" The colonel shook himself. "I'm confused," he said soberly. "Different points in time and various situations have gotten mixed up in my mind, layering one another. It happens—" And he went into the card room.

Someone said that the tsar was about to arrive. It was time to leave, to avoid running into him. Myatlev feared the tsar as an unloved stepchild fears its stepfather, as a rabbit fears a wolf in January, a maid her new master, and a tramp a policeman. He feared his own powerlessness, for he knew he would hate himself if he were to appear powerless before *him,* and that there could be no other way. And later he berated himself for going to that ball; the minute he leaves his house, misfortune attacks him.

37

October 25

This morning I had Afanasy restore the entry to its original arrangement. Here, in my own house, I can do what I want. That will have to content me. "Public policy is contrary to our happiness, but love is the reward for disappointment." If Philostratos is right, then why worry? Afanasy got the servants together, and they grunted and groaned down there, making the house shake like a small hunting tent.

A man from the Rumyantsevs' brought one more souvenir. The big package wrapped in gold straw paper was opened right in the entry, Afanasy and Mr. Sverbeyev working almost nonstop for quite a while. Particularly Afanasy, since the spy tried to get away with supervising the effort. The majordomo listens to him more than he does to me, peering into his eyes, servilely awaiting approval. They withdrew a smaller package, and a marvelous porcelain snuffbox in a gold frame from that. The top had a picture of two sad parrots, turned away from each other, on a reddish branch. The snuffbox was an eighteenth-century piece and rather valuable, but I noticed only the pathetic hint in it, which kept me from enjoying its artistry. I wonder which one of the parrots I'm supposed to be?

I wanted to drop by Aneta's to get things off my chest, but I couldn't manage . . .

A strange event, and I'm involved in it! I was told how it happened. That sympathetic little Kolesnikov, who sang his own praises with a child's sincerity and was firmly convinced of his own righteousness, was seated in the bosom of his family, at the head of his table, and, probably proclaiming his principles and spreading nonsense on the wind, as he did everywhere, at the same time glancing lovingly at his brand-new uniform—the right to wear which he had won with sweat and tears and daily humiliations—prattling on about this and that, modestly lowering his eyes and kicking his bare feet under the table, and suddenly someone is at the door, and Lieutenant Katakazi shows up with the local police and orders him to dress, on orders from General Dubelt. He didn't even have time to say that Mr. Nekrasov in *The Contemporary* was carrying on the work and that Mr. Krayevsky in *Fatherland Notes* was the victim of censorship, when he was ordered to dress. "Wait a minute," he muttered, still not understanding. But Lieutenant Katakazi did not wait but instead was implacable; he had the right to be so because he was wearing a dark-blue uniform for which he had to pay his dues. A flurry of activity, panic, and tears ensued, since not one member of the family could have imagined such a turn of events, and he himself was completely prostrated, for how could he, possessor of a dark-green uniform, rank, position, and salary, earned the hard way through loyal suffering, how could he be forced to go down to the police station and be accused, and by whom? Why, by someone who was just like himself, only dressed in a blue uniform! "What is this," he must have thought, "does a blue uniform say more about a man's qualities than a green one?" "This is terrible—a misunderstanding, friends," he said, his lips white. "I'm well-known—this is a misunderstanding—" And even as he dressed he still couldn't understand that a dark-green uniform is not handed out so that one can preen in it before his subordinates and decide the fate of those under him, but so that one should never forget that he is wearing a dark-green uniform and his worth is just that and no more, and that he cannot combine dark-green success with an insolent point of view. In other words: if you like riding in a sled, you should like pulling it uphill, too; and if say, you are against sleds, then there's no point in getting into one and speeding along, enjoying the delicious ride.

And so they took him away, and I don't know anything about his subsequent fate.

I must have looked terrible when I came in, because Afanasy jumped up and froze in the shadows. I immediately went to his room and threw open the door. The spy, as usual, was sitting by the samovar, gulping tea from a saucer. This time his mug seemed even more repulsive than usual. "And where are your dark-green uniforms," I wanted to shout, "and the red scissors with which you pretend and pretend, and where is all the rest of your fake stuff, and what the hell are you doing relaxing in my house! What're you doing here, goddamn you! Get out! I don't want a trace of you left! Afanasy, you swine, bring my riding crop!" I wanted to shout, but couldn't.

But apparently he managed to read all that in my face, because he set aside his saucer, jumped up, and bowed low— insolently, I thought.

I turned to leave and slam the door, but he stopped me and

begged me to stay, so I waited. Then he unwrapped a small package on the table and took out a spanking new dark-green uniform that he had made especially for me. I was stunned, but got control of myself and said to Afanasy, "Pay this man immediately, and then throw out those rags so that I never see them. I'm very sorry, but I no longer need them. I don't need that."

"You should try it on, Your Excellency," the spy said, almost weeping. "You'll never have a better made anywhere."

I left, cursing my weakness and at the same time experiencing a strange feeling of the unreality of what had transpired. I suddenly stopped believing that I had ever been in his salon, where that bony spy had thrown the cloth, smelling of wax, over my shoulder.

38

[From Lavinia to Myatlev, from Moscow]

Dear Sergei Vasilyevich, I would not dare to disturb your peace if it were not for the terrible rumors of your tragedy. All of Moscow talks about the horrible fire. Was there nothing left to save? Are you at least safe and sound? I feel very bitter for you and for myself, as well; now the house where Mr. van Schoenhoven strutted and where he was received so warmly is no more. And how could this misfortune happen? Was it done with evil aforethought? It is said that many do not like you.

I'm also taking this opportunity to tell you that I'm fine. We spent Christmas *en famille,* with Mr. Ladimirovsky, whom I've told you about. He's a nice man, and once he shaved off his beard, he seems quite youthful. We are quite good friends now, and there is nothing left of my childish dislike for him. He's teaching me fencing and pistol-shooting, and I can hit a champagne bottle at thirty paces.

We were all very happy for you when we heard you were planning to marry Countess Rumyantseva. That's marvelous. However, our joy was premature, now that you've had this terrible fire. . . . This is hardly the time for a wedding.

Be brave, dear Prince, everything will work out.

Recently I remembered how once, when we were spending the summer in the country, I, bored with everyone, killed Kaleria and headed for an uninhabited island. There was this sandy island with a few pines, and I built myself a cabin and tried to move in. But they found me and tried to convince me that a marriageable young lady must think about other things. But while I was sitting in my cabin, I thought of you and how good it would be for you to move in, too. We could talk about whatever we felt like, without anywhere to hurry to. What if you suddenly decide to do it? Then I'll be happy to show you everything: how to find the island and what to use to build the cabin.

Ah, Prince, it's all so complicated. Sometimes I want to scream, but my good upbringing won't let me. Forgive me, as an old friend, for boring you. It's amazing what one will do. You don't have to exert yourself to answer my letter—I won't be hurt.

39

SLOWLY AND IMPERCEPTIBLY, A storm was gathering in the damp Petersburg sky. Its principal target was the wooden three-story fortress of Sergei Myatlev, who was finally free of visitors, spies, and pangs of conscience; who had finally forgotten the ill-fated dark-green Kolesnikov, the slender-throated Mr. van Schoenhoven, Countess Rumyantseva, and his recent troubles. Everything seemed stable; even red-haired Aglaya, who had seemed groggy from the stupid majordomo's handling, suddenly blossomed, straightening her rounded shoulders, thrust out her lustful bosom, giggled, bumped into Myatlev in hallways, on the stairs, among the marble statues, reminding the young recluse that life went on and that it was time to revive. And all this, it turned out, was a warning of the gathering storm, but one had to have more than man's ordinary perception and sensitivity to sense its coming. Only later, when it rolls in and strikes, do we clutch our hearts, bug out our eyes, and rebuke ourselves for our former lack of seriousness, but earlier, when it's gathering strength, ripening like an apple, we carelessly grin and take the sudden stormy freshness in the air as a good sign.

October passed, and then November; snow followed the rain; the forests were hard hit; the ice clattered on the Neva; the sad aspens trembled in the barren park; a distant wolf's howl could be heard at night; the wooden three-story fortress, not having been burned down by anyone, creaked and swayed more noticeably; and the almost useless streetlamps were lit early in the evening.

First came the long-suffering lady-in-waiting, Elizaveta Vasilyevna, burdened by grief and chagrin, having long since lost any resemblance to his sister, forgetting words, confusing her accusations. One had only to see her tragic face to lose one's last regrets, if there were any left. Nature could not have invented a worse intercessor for Countess Rumyantseva.

"Listen," Myatlev said coldly, formally stressing the line between past and present, letting her know that his cup had overflowed and that from now on they could be on the most formal terms only, "listen, the suffering of that young lady, too clever for her years, does not interest me. I trust that you are well and have avoided influenza? You see, her irresolute impulses are too frank, and furthermore, there is a completely mediocre collection of titled stopgaps who could—"

THE PRINCESS: What? Who?

MYATLEV: Well, who could help out the countess in her natural need to burden herself with a family.

THE PRINCESS: You insult the woman who loves you and carries your child beneath her heart.

MYATLEV: I'm very sorry, but you must agree—

THE PRINCESS: Ah, you dare to assume that the child—

MYATLEV: I'm talking about something else.

THE PRINCESS: Count Nesselrode is thoroughly confused. All right, take Prince Amiran—now here's a man who is calm and fair, and he has so much sympathy for you—

let him say if you're not outraging my opinion and the opinion of society; let him say, as your friend and confidant— [Turns to me.] I respect you so, and your word— Tell this man, for God's sake, this man infected with stubbornness, that his behavior— No, now don't be shy, you tell him—don't try to be delicate, I'm asking you to tell him—

I: All right, I will tell him, dear Elizaveta Vasilyevna. But what can I say? I think that if my friend— Countess Rumyantseva is a charming woman, she has so many fine qualities that it's absolutely amazing. That's indisputable. But what I think—

THE PRINCESS: No, no, don't be delicate; say what you think; that's how it should be among us.

I: Yes, yes, well— Many men would have been happy to offer their hearts and hands to the countess; I'm keeping that in mind. She's charming and marvelous. She is one of those women who in the name of love can—but, my dear Elizaveta Vasilyevna—

THE PRINCESS: My dear man, tell me straight out—that is, tell him, tell him that— You have the right—

I: Of course.

THE PRINCESS: You have the right because I do not know of any woman whom you have hurt; you are irreproachable; and you have the right to tell him—

I: Of course. Has even one of the women I've known ever complained about me? Who says so? No one. No one could say that. That's why I feel it is my duty to tell you—

THE PRINCESS: Tell him, not me.

I: I've already told him everything. I want to tell *you* that he is my friend and that goes without saying—of course, I may be flattering myself, but you are so generous in evaluating my relations with women, and you judge me so highly, that I always think of my friend in the most noble way, even though, dear Elizaveta Vasilyevna, this in no way contradicts what you were saying, and your chagrin rends my heart—

THE PRINCESS: I don't quite understand—that is, I do

217

understand you, but I would like— I asked you to tell him—we can't— It's impossible— I have no more strength—

MYATLEV: Perhaps you should abdicate your high plenipotentiary powers, renounce the unbearable burden, and speak for yourself.

THE PRINCESS: I don't understand you.

MYATLEV: Well, send me to Hell!

THE PRINCESS: What about our name? Your unassuming manner and your passion for scandal are well known. What about our name? What do you suggest—just what do you suggest I do when I see our name being ruined and besmirched? What do you command me to do?

I: Elizaveta Vasilyevna, my dear, no more arguing! It's using a scythe on a rock. You won't come to any decision now. Why do all this? You'll just exchange mutual insults, hurt each other, and then tomorrow we'll cry about it.

But my words had no effect. She left with tears in her eyes, which she had never permitted herself in earlier battles. A rock turns to sand, to say nothing of a woman's heart.

"Damn it!" he said, when she had left. "A real female. Did you see? You saw her fight for her ideals? I'm glad that you saw it, and maybe that'll teach you something, because you always adore them, whether they deserve it or not, and I see your innocent, clear eyes filled with adoration; you just melt when you see any of them, and you pray that they'll swindle you a little, thereby ennobling your woman-loving heart."

I tried to remind him how delicately and with what virtuosity I had carried on the conversation, but he waved me off. "Who of us is capable of competing with their innate passion for overlooking the truth for the sake of some present gain? As for me, I pass. Everything aches in me after these attempts, Amiran. Amiran! It's as though I've been carrying logs; my shoulders ache, my back and arms; and instead of your angels worthy of adoration, I see Titans with a clumsy gait, with rough hands and heavy jaws; and now I look at you and I get mad and envy your ability to be generous and patient with them. And they idolize you, as though they were all your wives; and each of them has secrets and smiles and little jokes for you, which you probably like very much. And, for instance, if I say about one of them that she's conceited, that doesn't put you on your guard; no, you say, 'Of course, but what marvelous skin!' Or I say, 'There's a fury with a heavy jaw and all the earmarks of a hysteric,' and you reply, 'What else is there for her? What can she do if I'm slipping away from her? It's better that I should convince her that she is Eve—that'll cheer her up.' "

I disagreed here, saying that he was idealizing me, even though I do employ superhuman efforts to avoid tears, but that's innate in me; I just picture her naked, that fury, and my knees buckle, my breath stops, and my eyes see a divine sight. He laughed and asked, "And then?"

"And then," I said, "then she leaves, and I see her leave, and try to picture her naked, and I see that a goddess is leaving."

He laughed again and said, "Damn it, for me it's either kill or be killed. Well, all right, I was trying to catch you, but you got away, you Caucasian!" And he added after a pause, "I think that someone's going through my diary." I expressed incredulity, but he went on heatedly, "I swear to God, I always shut it, and now I find it open—for the third time—and always at October thirteenth, and it's December now. And my house is falling apart."

Yes, the house was falling apart. The ghosts were really raging now. In the attic, under the blue dust, we found bent rusty nails that had fallen out, disintegrating beams, and wood dust that the eternal-seeming oaken rafters had dissolved into. The light creaking of the stairs was now replaced by groans, mutterings, wheezes, and imprecations, and, without actually studying the matter, Myatlev realized that he could tell just by the sound what was happening above the ground floor. It was often an amusing pastime, since the stairs reacted to each person differently, and the sounds revealed not only who was moving but his mood as well, so that Myatlev knew how to greet whoever was coming up and whether to greet him at all or to hide in the library. Yes, the house was falling apart, and much faster than could have been expected. It was like an old man who had lost control of his body and mind: speaking in non sequiturs, unconsciously moving his legs, his face wrinkled up in a childish smile behind which hides a secret past that he himself no longer remembers, some delicious fog. Now all it needed was one good lightning bolt for the three-story old man with the innocent smile to keel over and disintegrate, burying under its rubble ancient destinies, once-blazing passions, unfinished diaries, snatches of words that had lost both meaning and value, and doubtful hopes.

And then the thunder struck, and the storm began.

"You're mad!" wrote the Hobbler hysterically from distant Tula, that subverter who had not torn himself away in ages, either because he had lost his false beard or else had finally unearthed the deepest secrets of the world's most powerful men and was about to reveal them. "You're mad, to put it mildly! With your talent for writing, for observation and irony, you have enmeshed yourself in petty intrigues, adultery, scandal, impregnated some woman, in imitation of your own lackey, that Fonaryasy with the stupid face, who cannot be redeemed by Sir Walter Scott or your cast-off cravats. Russia is choking on Scottism, and you're prancing at balls, dancing attendance on the Nesselrodes."

And no sooner had Myatlev burst out laughing over this howl from the pretender to the title of the tsar's greatest rival, when old Fonaryasy himself appeared to report that some men had come to escort the prince to His Excellency Count Orlov this very evening, right this minute, immediately. The count wished to see him at the Winter Palace for some reason, and there was a court carriage waiting downstairs.

"Ah, yes," thought Myatlev in the carriage, "I haven't been at the palace in over two years. I wonder how things are going there?" And he said under his breath, astounding the constable, " 'I picked this forest flower for you . . .' "

Of course, he could not have suspected what was going to happen nor that he would shortly be leaving the palace in a new capacity. He could not have known, and so he asked the officer accompanying him:

"What's the rush?"

"What, sir?"

"What could have happened there? Do you know why I'm needed?"

The officer did not reply.

The old graying wolf met him with a small cordial roar.

"Well," he said, carefully examining Myatlev and, with a slight nudge, leading him off somewhere, "His Majesty has decided—just imagine, Sergei Vasilyevich—to take a personal hand in your happiness; he's taken it on himself. Not many are so fortunate! Just think how wonderfully this will reflect on you and your descendants! I still can't get over how merciful and generous he is to you. Of course, we ourselves are such dullards and fools that without a fatherly nudge we can't imagine where we are going and why. I have experienced it myself many a time when giving in to some weakness, I would feel that sure and gentle touch and everything would be back in place. Not many, Sergei Vasilyevich, have been honored this way, but those lucky few who have—well, just look at them, at what their lives are now. And I won't repeat how I was charmed and captivated when he first expressed a willingness—I mean, his interest in your fate. For the tsar does all this for us, for our own good. Does he worry about himself? Until we learn to think governmentally and globally, he must do it for us; it is his cross, his duty, his burden; while we cavort and wallow in egotism, thinking ourselves citizens of the empire, he goes without sleep so as to hold us up by the elbows, so that we don't fall down in a frenzy and break our necks. Does he think of himself?"

"What? Why?" thought Myatlev, and a weightless fear, like a small, tattered sparrow, stirred in his breast.

"I think," continued Count Orlov, leading Myatlev further and further downstairs, through corridors and empty ballrooms,

"I think it's marvelous and stupendous that this doesn't require any extreme measures, now that His Majesty himself is participating in it. Well, don't be tense; relax, my dear man. No one's died of happiness yet."

A few candelabra shone. The palace was quiet and rather everyday. The sentinels, like stone statues, were at their posts for the umpteenth century.

"Her Majesty the Tsaritsa Alexandra Fyodorovna was so moved and pleased by all this that she had planned to be here, too, to congratulate you and express her predisposition toward you and her concern, but a sudden illness—"

"Aha," thought Myatlev, losing courage, "I'm being drawn into their secrets again. I can't. I can't take it, Your Excellency," he wanted to say. "Why don't you just give it to me straight— tell me what's happening?" But he couldn't utter a word, and some strangled sound fell from his lips.

"Well, of course," the count said animatedly, as though he had read Myatlev's thought, "I never doubted it. I'm sure that things will be completely different from now on, you'll see. And then, just between us, we're at an age now when the past must seem silly and excessive—isn't that so?"

"I'm afraid of him," thought Myatlev about the emperor, "but I'll be firm, and I won't let myself be humiliated in any way. Let him just try—" However, he knew that his determination would disappear without a trace the moment he saw the tsar.

In the study, which was not very brightly, in fact dimly, lit, someone in a semimilitary jacket, casting a huge shadow, left the fireplace and moved to meet him, arms outspread.

"Finally," he exclaimed in a pleasant, ringing voice. "Here's our hero."

"I am afraid of him," Myatlev had time to think, "and of course, I'll do as he wills."

From the interior of the study, from the reddish dusk, came a sigh, deep and fleeting, like a whispered "Ah!"

Myatlev's whole life abandoned him, sad and stumbling, like an unfaithful woman left unguarded, and burned up in the fireplace.

And so they met. Aneta Fredericks's seducer was closer and friendlier to him than ever. Time had marked the handsome face, and the bags under his eyes were more prominent, the cheeks sagged, but the lips smiled. How strange!

He stood, half facing Myatlev, his right arm behind his back, and the five steps between them seemed a chasm. A mortal would not be able to cross it. From *his* side of it, he examined the prince closely, not understanding how women could get interested in these puny, four-eyed men with sadness in their eyes and a hidden insolence in their movements, admittedly not very dangerous, but very inconvenient, undependable, always thinking of themselves. What could women see beyond that appearance, not being given to deep meditation? He was like an eagle who had been distracted from his gazing beyond the clouds and come upon a sparrow and thought, "Should it be allowed to live at all?" Wasn't he tired of himself, this sneaky, insolent, wingless, cowardly nonentity? However, there must be something to him if Baroness Fredericks could be indulgent to his chirping and if he not only distinguished himself on the battlefield but was seriously wounded. He had survived and was now standing before him in an impeccable frock coat, lithe, flashing his idiotic spectacles, as though they were the one thing about himself he was most proud of. "Well," thought Nicholas, "this insolent good-for-nothing is one of my children, whatever else he is, a malcontent who disdained serving in the Horse Guards, but still he's one of my children, so clumsily trying to hide his fear and frailty, yes, yes, he's not brave at all, he's a coward, guilty before me of many sins, he remembers them all." So he thought, mustering a magisterial mood appropriate to the moment, and searching for the chords of royal magnanimity in his soul so that he could pluck them. "That rascal," he thought, still staring at Myatlev, "how did he manage to get around the countess and get her pregnant—him, one of my children, the subject of evil talk, a disgusting creature on spindly legs, a drooling nonentity, a cowardly adulterer—"

"Here he is!"

The "he" sounded vicious coming from him. But there was nothing to do, for Myatlev understood nothing of what was happening. "How small and insignificant I am," thought Myatlev, not taking his eyes off the tsar. He was not depressed by the fact that all his past confrontations with the tsar had ended in defeat. Could it be any other way? But what did this meeting bode, lit as it was by the weak glow of the few candelabra, which seemed to have been chosen to cast a mysterious light on the occasion? What power had brought them together: this former Horse Guards' officer with the high brow, sunken cheeks, and a delicate independence hiding somewhere in the corners of his eyes, and the aging giant with marble skin, confidence, his hands behind his back, who knew that he could do anything and that anything he did was vital to Myatlev and all his innumerable subjects, happy and unhappy. If they were happy, as he saw it, it was thanks only to him and his efforts and generosity, and if they were unhappy, then it was their own fault. Why did they have to meet and stand on the borders of that chasm in the presence of the respectful and suddenly much smaller Count Orlov?

A weak guess flashed through Myatlev's mind, but, illuminating nothing, it went out immediately. "Impossible!" he thought in terror, looking into the face of Tsar Nicholas, into that impenetrable face. "It can't be!"

"Listen," said the sovereign, "you're so indecisive. You're unequaled at dreaming up disgusting pranks." He turned to Orlov. "Burying General Rot! To do such a thing! A living general! And he thought the whole thing up himself. I remember." And he forced himself to smile.

"I suppose he's right to bring up that pathetic story," thought Myatlev. "Since we meet so rarely—you could even say never—he must remind me of everything that's been bothering him all these years so that he needn't ever mention it again, spew out all the bile; and it's probably a good thing that he's doing it, otherwise I would always be his enemy and I would never be left alone. Now he'll have it all out, and then he'll never bother with me again." He thought this as he stared into the red shadows where another gentle sigh was heard.

There, in the reddish dark, alone and disregarded, stood an unfamiliar woman, her strengthless arms dangling at her sides, her face, as flat as a mask, expressing nothing, two gaping holes instead of eyes and a dark crack for a mouth—that was all that Myatlev could see. And yet it was a woman, and she was breathing and sighing; the sighs, like sobs, came from her part of the room.

"Just think," the sovereign said gently, "he buried a live general. What a mind. Thank God that the general didn't have a stroke. What am I to do with you? Hah? You'll say that it happened a long time ago? I suppose it did. You've started wearing spectacles now."

And suddenly Myatlev caught himself being pleased by the fact that the tsar remembered him so accurately and that he bore no grudge.

"I'm very sorry, Your Majesty," he announced, with some courage. "I know that I've caused you grief, but if you were to permit me to return there, I would try to make amends."

"Where?" Nicholas did not understand, but suddenly laughed. "Ah, I see. If only I could return *there*, too." And he thought, "There are men who become speechless when faced with a rounded female belly. Instead of being happy, they turn tail and run. Even though later he'll grovel at her feet, weeping joyous tears, the way she groveled at mine, begging me to save her and defend her. From him? Some villain she found, the fool! Basically they're all intolerable when their bellies swell up and their faces become blotchy. How she carried on about indulgence and generosity and so on, meaning, naturally, herself and her belly. But I have to be indulgent to this terrified seducer, not to her, and generous to him; that stupid woman—"

225

"Ah, I wish he'd get it over with!" thought Myatlev. "I can't change anything, anyway, and he's not free to behave any other way. Hurry it up. That heavy, heavy coach, dragged by wild horses, will still fly on its own secret way, and nothing will change if the passengers are embattled. No one can change a thing. And if our earthly life is nothing more than a brief suffering, then its meaning must lie in not trying to avoid the suffering but in trying to make it commensurate with one's abilities. So hurry it up, hurry—" And he looked over once more at the unknown woman. He got a better look at her this time. She seemed very tall and beautiful, and she was young, and therefore, even with her head thrown back and her round chin thrust out, she did not seem haughty, only young and in the throes of an impulsive, troubling passion. He couldn't help but delight in her. "No, there's nothing we can do. We can only love and be grateful if chance brings us together once in a while with such magnificent creations of nature, and die twice over from happiness if we are able not only to love but be loved in return. That is something we can do, and that is what we should devote our energies to and not laugh off success, for it is very rare and there is not enough to go around."

"Well, all right," said Nicholas. "Let's forget that. I see that you understand everything. You did cause me a lot of grief, but today we will forget it all." And with his big hand he took Myatlev's small one and pressed it lightly, and they stood like that for a moment, united over the chasm.

"How kind he is today," thought the prince, softening. "I'm going to cry soon."

The tsar's hand was soft, warm, and moderately powerful, so that its touch was not offensive but rather fatherly. From his hand emanated the warmth and kindness of a kind and strong mentor; he held Myatlev by the hand like a sympathetic and wise teacher or an old and loyal tutor holding his small, senseless, and penitent favorite, who had imagined until this moment that all his previous life, a brief span of false independence and false freedom, was truly independent and free, and only now did he understand his error and feel happy to renounce it.

The tall woman with the marvelous features moved toward them, and a brief "Ah!" splashed out of the shadows.

Sigh, despair, wring your hands, shed tears, rid yourself of the last remnants of your aloofness. Apparently, I love you, I have convinced myself of it; no, you convinced me with your beauty, anxiety, light-mindedness. Apparently, I love you—there is no escaping you. Apparently, I was destined for an early death, and you were sent to save me, to prolong my life—that's how wonderful and miraculous your appearance is. You sow joy and hope all around you, and the variegated seeds of goodness, clarity, and pleasure spill from your hands.

Myatlev tried to calm down, but Nicholas's hot palm made that impossible; it was burning him. Hurry it up! When we are powerless, we are like these clammy pinkish garden snails that have lost their shells; we can only hide our despair under a mask of respectability, or frenzied pleasure, or false indifference. Physically, the effect is quite simple: the body stops obeying this will; and as for the mind, it is obsessed with the idea of fairness, which I myself seek, but I couldn't see my way clear; thank God that my destiny is now in capable hands. How kind he is! How kind he is, and I'm not worth his little finger.

"Come here." Nicholas summoned the woman triumphantly, and she stepped toward them.

"Hurry it up!" thought Myatlev, realizing that his fate was being sealed. "Everything is behind me now. Apparently, I do love her."

She stepped forward with a loud sigh, either of yearning or relief, her skirts rustling, her arms helplessly outstretched, as if she simply did not know what to do with them, or with such long, clumsy, disobedient hands, which were ready to push ahead of her body before it was proper and grab the unfortunate neck of that bespectacled madman standing riveted by fear, grab him the way they used to on those nights when it seemed that everything depended on it, when she would run one hand over his stiff neck and caress his strong, hot back with the other, and all without shame or doubt, forever, for the ages, until morning came, bringing sober light and shame and fear of what had happened.

Yet she took a step and stretched out her hand, and the tsar moved toward her and extended his while he still held the prince firmly with his other hand. Earlier he had grasped him like a teacher, but now he was leading him like a sovereign, and Myatlev followed obediently, like Afanasy. He knew that for the rest of his life he would break out in a cold sweat remembering this moment, for the terrible remains in our memory, whereas joy, once we've had our fill of it, becomes habitual and hence disappears from our consciousness. That's why remembering a long period of freedom does not cheer us for very long, but the memory of one moment in chains upsets us to the end.

That pink, slimy snail without its shell moved ahead slowly, trying to impose a calm and peaceful expression on its face. Yet something within its docile body remained untouched; something howled inside, rustled, squeaked, tried to burst forth; and someone's unfamiliar, high-pitched, foreign voice tried to cry out words that had never before been uttered: "Merciful God, this can't be happening! It can't. I told her that I don't love her; she knows that, she knows! I told her, but she didn't care. I told her. Come to your senses! But she didn't care. I told her— Ohmygod!"

And then Nicholas took her hand and placed it in Myatlev's, and her tiny hand clutched Myatlev's with a shiver.

"I hope," the sovereign said, leaning toward the prince, "you're not about to accuse me of cruelty. Do I worry about myself? Everything I do is for you, for your own good. Until you learn to think governmentally and globally, I must do it for you. It is my cross, my duty, my burden. While you cavort and abandon yourselves to pleasure and egotism, and consider yourselves citizens of the empire, I go without sleep to hold you up by the elbows so that you don't fall and break your necks. Do I worry about myself?" He smiled the way only he knew how—

abruptly and harshly. "This is an act of justice and kindness, not only in regard to her, but to you as well. I'm not forcing you; I'm only prompting you to recognize what's right under your nose but which you can't see."

Suddenly Myatlev saw that this had all happened a long time ago, that in its very improbability lay its predestined outcome; and he saw himself in a dark-green uniform, in which he could no longer fantasize, or fly, but merely move—and learn to be grateful for it. He saw that the dark, majestic study contained the entire universe, consisting of the four of them, of whom two would always play out Lucian, imploring God to grant the most diametrically opposed prayers, promising the very same sacrifices, while the other two would exist only to accept their ludicrous sacrifices casually.

And he looked at the woman once more and half shut his eyes, for she was beautiful and fantastic in the light of the fireplace, which drowned in her deep, dark eyes only to reappear transformed into a barely discernible, new glow, full of charm and mystery, taking his breath away.

"Well, children," said the sovereign in a pure, clear voice, the way only he knew how, "enough hiding. I unite you and bless you." And first he made the sign of the cross over the woman and kissed her brow, and then he turned to Myatlev and made the sign of the cross and bent down and brought his warm lips to that cold, damp brow.

Natalya was weeping. Count Orlov nodded from his corner with friendly indifference.

"What happiness," thought Myatlev. "It's all over now, and now there's nothing to hide, or pretend, or lie about."

As they were leaving, the sovereign willed that the young couple should ride in one coach. A scurrying aide-de-camp saw them to the carriage; he was in a rush to be somewhere, but managed to express his sincere envy, for the tsar did not extend this honor to many—such kindness, attention, and love—

They rode in silence, and Natalya, full of patience, did not disturb Myatlev, while he tore out juicy clumps of Alpine grass from his breast and belly in the desperate hope that the little donkey would take pity on him and drag the wagon to the saving bend in the road.

40

[From Lavinia to Myatlev, from Moscow]

Dear Sergei Vasilyevich, I must congratulate you. From the bottom of my heart! Please don't be annoyed at having to stop and read my letters, but people dear to me don't get married every day, and I must tell you how I feel. Yes, they say that the tsar himself united you. All Moscow is talking about it, and everyone feels that such a singular honor has to affect your future life and that everything will be the best possible. *Maman* and I and Alexander Vladimirovich were just talking about it and came to the conclusion that nothing better could happen: your mind and rank, a beautiful wife, and the tsar's blessing! I congratulate you wholeheartedly once more.... There, you see—your house burned down, but look how God has consoled you.

And my fatal hour, as they say, approaches, too. Soon I will be doing my duty. Be happy for me.

Mr. Ladimirovsky is now wonderful and has obtained a house in Petersburg. He is invited to court festivities, and when everything here is done, I naturally will be there, too. I get goose bumps. *Maman* is worried about my looks. Naturally she's a beauty and knows how to do everything, but I still have to learn and work at it.

Once more, congratulations from the bottom of my heart!

41

SEVERAL MONTHS PASSED OF half-sleep, half-delirium, half-despair, half-indifference, half-contemplation; several long, woolly, quiet, heavenly, perfect months, free of painful thoughts on the meaning of life, decorated like a Christmas tree with bright, ephemeral pleasures created by a sated and luxuriant imagination.

It seemed that the world stood still, stopped spinning, and its rusty axis finally needed replacement, and one found surcease from the constant spinning motion, the wind, the fruitless attempts to escape something, to get away, to slip off; and there was time to devote to the modest perfection of personal feelings, which had been in a chaotic state until then; and there was time to prolong one's life as each new day became an eternity, tightly packed like a traveling bag with minor details for which there had never been time.

It seemed that the world stood still and life was like a golden buggy left behind the shed while the winged steeds were put out to pasture. The past no longer existed. The future was unnecessary.

With no regrets, the handful of ancient thinkers and writers set off down rocky roads in squeaky wagons, or riding donkeys, or on foot, with a cohort of bronze soldiers, great military leaders and travelers, beautiful hetaeras, wives, robbers, highwaymen, surrounded by herds of monsters and wild dogs, with baskets of bread and wine-grapes, hand in hand with their gods, never abandoning their endless, witty discourses.

Only the three-story wooden palace was left, besieged by carpenters and workmen who appeared at the wave of beautiful Natalya's white hand. And Myatlev moved into the Rumyantsev house and proceeded to astound and shock the inhabitants by his unusual aloof presence.

The people in the house were preparing for the birth of young Myatlev, and the dark-green uniform, brought over by Mr. Sverbeyev in the nick of time, marked the culmination of the madness engendered by providence.

The dangerously ballooning belly reigned everywhere, and everything altered and accommodated itself to the new conditions. The princess's languid gestures hid storms of anxiety and intimations of dark changes. Her interest in art had disappeared.

Her silent husband with his long, surprised face greeted guests and behaved politely, trying to no avail to remember their faces and names. "Ohmygod" hovered in the air like dust.

42

[From Lavinia to Myatlev, from Saint Petersburg]

Dear Sergei Vasilyevich, what have we learned! It seems your house did not burn down at all! What luck! As soon as we arrived I decided to go down to look at the ruins, but instead, everything was as it used to be. I can imagine how upset you were receiving my stupid letter, but all of Moscow was saying it was so—how could I not believe it?

Please forgive my persistence, but I'm so happy, so happy, that none of this horror had happened.

Here we are in Petersburg. I was pleased to return; everything is familiar, friendly, and the same; only I have changed. Madame van Schoenhoven smiles down from the wall, my books are covered with dust, and the ceilings seem a bit lower. My trousseau is being made, and the house is topsy-turvy. . . . I never imagined the trouble this ceremony creates. . . . And Mr. Ladimirovsky and I continue to fence and shoot at bottles, which I am quite good at.

Here's what I've heard: Misha Berg received a golden weapon for his distinction in the Caucasus, though I don't think it will have a salutary effect on him. As for Koko—remember him?—he hasn't received anything golden as he's working in the commissary and doesn't have an opportunity to kill anyone, but while traveling around Georgia, he fell in love with some princess, whom Berg had also loved, and they went at it again. As I heard it, Koko won once more, but they didn't give him a golden weapon for that, either.

Do you know this: "Remember the horns' mournful call, the

splatter of rain, half-light, half-darkness"? Could that be about me? So that you and I will always remember it and never fear it . . .

43

MR. LADIMIROVSKY WAS HAVING tea in the Tuchkov living room. He no longer had a beard. Fortune had smiled on him. The rank of councillor of state opened seductive vistas before him. He bought a house in Petersburg with a garden and an Empire stable; he was given a high post in the postal department; his snow-white Orlov trotters showed up on Znamenskaya Street, thrilling the connoisseurs; his smile was disarming as soon as he stepped over the threshold of the old house, despite the fact that the thin beauty who lived there continued to speak to him sharply; vast estates in Chernigov and Orlov provinces spread behind him; he was broad-shouldered, kind-hearted, had little hair, a ready smile, and was as persistent as a wild boar in April. "We Bravuras," Madame Tuchkova would say, referring to qualities known only to her. "We Ladimirovskys," Mr. Ladimirovsky would say, comfortably ensconced in his chair, conscious of the extensive family at the back of his head.

The question that had been ripening for a long time was settled quite simply. Lavinia had no objection to the huge hand and hot heart of Mr. Ladimirovsky. With melancholy obedience she left it up to her mother to decide her fate, for she did not know how to combat the domestic tyranny of Madame Tuchkova, which was both refined and implacable.

"I promise you, Lavinia," he once said, "that I will rescue you from the dependence that chafes you so."

"I didn't ask for that," she said, laughing and appreciating his sensitivity.

"We Ladimirovskys," he said, "never shone at court, but our

233

line is an ancient one, and that means something, you'll see."

His promises meant almost nothing to her—she could scarcely believe in success and popularity—but she did hope that behind his broad back she could hide from her mother's sleepless eye, from the soft, hot, silky, and inexorable hand that held Mr. van Schoenhoven so tightly; and, hating herself, she agreed with Mr. Ladimirovsky, and he promised her freedom so charmingly, as though laughing at himself and blushing slightly, and it was a pleasure to listen to him—long live freedom! And in her marvelous mind, filled with fantasies, she pictured the unthinkable: a fog and everything drowning in it—*Maman*'s tyranny— down with tyranny!—the frightened, wrinkled face of Kaleria, the terrified trembling of Madame Jacqueline, the indecent suggestions of Misha Berg—down with suggestions! Was it really possible?

"After all," said Mr. Ladimirovsky in a conspiratorial tone, "I'm only thirty. Your mother was twenty-seven years younger than her general, and here there's only a fourteen-year difference. And I've known and loved you for a long time."

His frock coat gave off penetrating Parisian scents, and his neat, broad hands lay on his powerful knees like a silent guarantee of future success.

"*Maman* will take you in tow, too," Lavinia laughed. "One fine morning you'll wake up to find Kaleria armed with a stick under your bed and the janitor Mefody in your clothes closet. Would you like that? Well, then, all right." But then out of the fog that she had invented came a memory of a very recent episode she thought was forgotten, but no, here it was, clear as day: under her window at twilight, two silhouettes teasing and depressing her, unnaturally close to each other, and the nervous voices of Myatlev and, probably, Countess Rumyantseva—that is, Princess Myatleva. And Lavinia, forgetting all propriety, had called into the next room, "*Maman*, take a look —this can't be!"

"I know about your recent childhood friendship with Prince Myatlev," said Mr. Ladimirovsky. "They speak ill of him, but in this case I see an example of rare nobility and constancy. You corresponded?"

"Oh, that was long ago," she said desperately, "and it's not true—that is, it had no meaning."

"If a woman crosses out her past with sadness, it means she still dwells on it." Mr. Ladimirovsky had remembered a recently read aphorism. "You won't regret a thing," he sighed. "I'm a very strong man." And he kissed her small hand.

At night she would force herself to cry, but there were no tears. But then she dreamed of happy Myatlev on a white steed. He was calling her. She would have gone—he seemed so happy—but rolled up into a ball across the doorstep lay a huge Kaleria, and there was no getting over her.

Two forces were contending within her. Sometimes her memories had the upper hand; sometimes reality did. First the silly prince who had betrayed her under the spell of Rumyantseva's charms looked at her coolly; then Mr. Ladimirovsky's strong shoulders blocked out everything else, and freedom beckoned—long live freedom!—but if that were so, then why, why, when the bell rang did she think that it was Myatlev in a snowy fur coat bowing to Mr. van Schoenhoven? Why?

But Lavinia overcame these feelings and hurried to meet the inevitable. What was the prince? A child's toy, and nothing more. Anachoretes who led his mistress to the pond, his long face full of woe, like a long flute sounding one note in the autumn twilight.

"You must not use Prince Myatlev's name in connection with me," she told Mr. Ladimirovsky. "That was just child's play."

He kissed her hand gratefully, thinking that if a child dismisses childhood, it means that it is still in it.

Finally it all came to pass. Everything flowed smoothly, not deviating from Madame Tuchkova's schedule. Of course, just before it was time to get into the carriage to go to church, a tiny devil almost made Lavinia do something. She got away for a minute from the women who were dressing her, ran into the empty dining room, and looked out the window. Prince Myatlev was outside, looking up tensely into the dark windows.

"Aha! About time!" she thought without surprise, weakening, losing her breath. But it was just some man in a torn coat, hatless. "What a silly prank," she sighed with relief, unable to imagine how she would ever face Myatlev, not as Mr. van Schoenhoven but as—this—well, woman. "What would we talk about?" she thought in horror, and returned to the mirror.

And so everything flowed according to Madame Tuchkova's schedule. Of course, when they were greeting the wedding guests, their appearance and the circumstances reminded her of another scene from the past, and for an entire moment she was trapped in that past. As she sat, bored to death, in a certain house where she had paid a call with her mother after their return from Moscow, Myatlev and the young princess had arrived, the young princess so lovely she took your breath away. That strange man, a complete stranger, couldn't see Mr. van Schoenhoven through his stupid spectacles, and Madame Tuchkova began recounting some insignificant story so loudly and unnaturally, with such a feverish air, that Lavinia wanted to stroke her hand and say, "*Maman*, what's the matter? Calm yourself. It's all nonsense. Better take a look at how marvelous she is—that lady. Don't be silly; how could you worry?" At that very moment the prince abandoned his wife and the other ladies and went into the next room where the men were smoking; but there, in that other room, he accidentally sat so that he was in her field of vision. His unclear, wavering face, framed by a tobacco cloud, swayed in melancholy, almost in despair. Ah, what was he doing there, so wonderful, among all those dull people, one just like the other? "*Maman*," she whispered, "isn't this terrible?" And Madame Tuchkova, indulging her weakness, took her away before tea was served.

"With all her fantasies," Madame Tuchkova was saying to

her newly hatched son-in-law, "she is practical enough to appreciate the staunch loyalty of Pushkin's Tatiana."*

"However," thought Mr. Ladimirovsky with a sad smile, "I'm not a general unfortunately, and so I am, alas, not impervious to pain, and I obviously have no battle scars."

And so, everything flowed according to Madame Tuchkova's schedule. But the freedom that had beckoned faded and died the moment Lavinia entered her new house, for freedom is almost palpable when you dream about it, but as soon as it appears, there are enough modifying circumstances to keep you from losing your head over it. And Mr. Ladimirovsky's lonely aunt, Evdokiya Yuryevna Speshnyova, moved in so that Lavinia would have no cause to feel abandoned. She was a small, frail woman, suffering from her own inadequacies, capable of lying for your own good, smiling in the blinding Ladimirovsky manner, generously and good-naturedly. She was almost fifty, but her childless state enabled her to pass for forty, which she treasured as she might. Bored by her solitude, she jumped at the role of managing the house, so that from the beginning Lavinia did not have to waste time on trifles. Evdokiya Yuryevna was not a mean woman, but she never missed an opportunity to express in one way or another her amazement that such a young woman, from a not at all wonderful family, had been lucky enough to marry into the Chernigov and Orlov money, and be invited to court thanks to Sashenka Ladimirovsky, and his ancient family and high position, for they, the Tuchkovs, with their Polish blood, would never have seen any of it on their own. They're strict with Poles nowadays. And here you are, all settled. Be happy, I wish you the best, the best. And in the evenings, when she laid out cards, it always came down to the fact that the happiness that had befallen Lavinia was due strictly to their

*Heroine of *Eugene Onegin.* As a young girl she declared her love for Onegin and was rebuffed. When Onegin sees her years later at a ball—glamorous, beautiful—he falls in love, but she is married to an old general and, while loving Onegin, rejects him and remains true to her husband.—Translator.

family. She had found good fortune, but what about Sashenka? Sashenka was a man on the rise, all by himself.

And on the morning of the day when they were to set off on their wedding trip, about which Lavinia had thought with great hope, for true freedom begins the moment you get beyond the tollgates, it turned out that Evdokiya Yuryevna was going to accompany the newlyweds, because you will be too distracted, and all the valuables need watching, and Lord give me the strength to do it for you. I'm not doing it for myself, but for you. What do I need a trip for? My time has passed, you dear child, and of course, with my aches I would be better off without all this bustle, isn't that so? But when I look at you and see how young you are— How will you manage everything alone? All those valuables? That's why I say bah, pardon, to my personal complaints, so that at least your life will not be hampered by these awesome cares—

So Lavinia had to choose between Evdokiya Yuryevna and Kaleria and Madame Jacqueline. The choice kept being put off.

"You're complaining?" Madame Tuchkova asked in surprise, for some reason using the formal "you" with her daughter. "Now, I trust, you'll be able to appreciate my concern for you."

But the choice was never made, and it was time to leave. True, when everything was ready and the coachman had gotten up on his box, she looked at the open gates, angry that even at such a moment the lazy prince couldn't pass by to bid her farewell forever.

"I hope you're happy so far?" Mr. Ladimirovsky asked, leaning over her with a rapturous smile.

"Utterly!" she replied in a doomed voice.

The carriage set off.

"If I weren't so unattractive," Lavinia thought just then, "he wouldn't have had to unite his life with Countess Rumyantseva's."

44

[From Myatlev to Lavinia, from Saint Petersburg]

Young lady, what are you thinking of with your nonsense about an uninhabited island? How could we live there together? What would your *maman* think? I swear it would be misunderstood. Drop the idea.

45

FINALLY DONNING HIS UNIFORM, Myatlev presented himself to Count Nesselrode and was introduced to his new job and his direct superior, his old acquaintance Baron Fredericks, head of the American Department.

The baron greeted Myatlev warmly and immediately saddled him with a problem. A certain academician, Councillor of State Gamel, was pestering the Ministry of Education for permission to go to New York and to England to study their achievements in utilizing electricity. Norov, the minister, had written a report covering the whole matter, including the tsar's stipulation: "Agreed, but he must secretly swear never to try human flesh as food in America, and you must obtain an affidavit to that effect signed by him and must show it to me."

"There you see," said Baron Fredericks, "how age and the storms of life turn us into creatures who think governmentally." His pink cheeks took on a deeper hue. "I'm glad that you have seen to everything so quickly and that now we have only to obtain the necessary affidavit from Mr. Gamel." The baron was crimson as a maiden by now and was trying not to look at the document. "There are higher considerations, and if the consumption of human flesh runs counter to them, then, naturally, Academician Gamel must keep that in mind, no?" He was deep purple and continued to turn away. He read disbelief and depression in Myatlev's eyes, but he pretended to be agitated by the excitement of the work. "In any case, this is very clever, isn't it? In any case, you must, in the government's interest, obtain the affidavit. I'm very happy that fate has brought us together again. You've changed considerably. Baroness Fredericks will be happy to see you in our home—you haven't forgotten her? . . . with a wife . . . the past . . . unbelievable . . . enterprising . . . the tsar . . ." Suddenly he whispered mysteriously, "When you are worrying about the welfare of the fatherland, you come to know yourself."

And so a brief period passed during which Myatlev served the fatherland in this manner, while correspondence dragged on between departments as to the possibility of sending Academician Gamel abroad, and Mr. Gamel considered the text of his affidavit, torn between duty and curiosity, at night seeing visions of smoking human filets, losing himself in conjecture and trying to make sense of the mysterious interdiction. Finally Myatlev, nearly mad with tension, received the following letter: "I, the undersigned, in keeping with the secret prohibition made known to me by his Imperial Majesty's Minister of National Education, herewith declare that during my intended stay in America I will never consume human flesh. [Signed] Josif Christianovich Gamel, Member of the Academy of Sciences, Councillor of State."

However, the fortuitous resolution of the correspondence and the gratitude of his superiors did not ensure domestic happiness. The tsar's recent meddling came to seem nothing more than a pointless anecdote when the flu that had attacked Natalya and had begun with chills and headaches spread and deepened, and in four days killed the poor princess and her child. The Rumyantsev house turned away from Myatlev as if he had been the cause of the tragedy, and the widower, still in shock, understanding nothing, threw off his uniform at my insistence, got in his carriage, and went off to Mikhailovka to come to his senses. It was all like a dream.

46

TIME PASSED. HIS WOUNDS healed, as if there had never been that heavy, endless time during which invisible forces had tried to bend his inflexible bones to give them a new, more acceptable shape. That attempt had been in vain, and the prince returned to Petersburg. The three-story fortress remained untouched; the workers had been dispatched quickly. The fortress creaked and fell apart faster than ever, but the smells of childhood hit the Prodigal Son even harder. As though cured of a fatal disease, at first Myatlev went from room to room, his face taut with surprise that he was alive again, that he could think and even make plans, shuddering each time he came across one of the many presents with which Natalya had tried to win his heart by hinting at her interest in art. And all those small canvases by famous Western masters, and the Chinese fans created with mind-boggling work, and the porcelain snuff boxes decorated with meaningful, specially selected themes—all these were a silent reproach that he ordered removed from his sight. Now the past did not torture him—dreams are not remembered very long—and only a few incidents from those days remained imprinted on his consciousness as on a daguerreotype.

Once Myatlev had been strolling with Natalya along a quiet street in the September twilight, discussing their relationship in half-whispers, and, by a caprice of fate, they had stopped in front of a silent white house with an iron fence. Suddenly a little figure appeared in the open window and, pointing at them, shouted deperately, "*Maman*, take a look, this can't be!"

Myatlev shivered, for he was sure the cry was meant for him. He led Natalya away quickly, but he did not forget the incident.

Sometime later they were on their way to an evening tea, a quiet tea in someone's house where there would be a small gathering of already forgotten faces, as inexpressive as his life. Natalya was quite heavy by then, and she breathed with difficulty as she sat beside him in the carriage. He remembered that it had been evening, a few lampposts; the rest was lost in a haze, the insignificant rest. They were welcomed as though they had been coming there for tea for many years, and Natalya, joining the ladies, immediately entered their perpetual and never-ending restructuring of everything under the sun. They all gave Myatlev one second's attention and then turned to one another. In the next room the men were playing cards and smoking their pipes, and, to look at them, you would think that the world had reached its final level of development and everything had stopped and was suspended in absolute perfection.

And so, bowing to the ladies and planning to hide in the next room, Myatlev suddenly noticed a young thing who had just come in and seated herself a bit to one side of the lively circle of her sisters. She looked sixteen or seventeen. She was wearing a pale-blue dress with white lace. Her pointy, helpless collarbones showed above the rather high neckline, and he could see two pointy elbows, even though she tried to hug them to her sides. Two small, natural curls, dark chestnut in color, freely caressed her cheeks. A folded fan moved convulsively in her hand. Her gray eyes were open wide and unmoving, fixed on Myatlev with an empty party coquetry, and her lips were compressed in an uneasy blend of confusion and mockery. She might have seemed attractive if it weren't for the vestiges of a funny childish grandeur in her face and body. She was looking at Myatlev so shamelessly that he preferred not to tarry. She reminded him of Lavinia, but she wasn't Lavinia. He joined the men and sat at a card table. He didn't think at all about the seat he chose, but he had only to look up to see the door to the other room and the young thing framed in it. "That's all I need," he thought.

The young thing continued examining Myatlev. And although the distance between them almost obliterated any resem-

242

blance to Mr. van Schoenhoven, he couldn't resist looking at her, anyway. He even imagined that she nodded to him, although he knew that was an optical illusion caused by the flickering candles. Then he tried to become engrossed in the game, staring at his cards, but they were soon called into tea. They all went into the room with the ladies. The young thing was gone. Natalya was very cool. When they got home, she broke her silence:

"So! It seems you know Tuchkova?"

"Who?" Myatlev almost shouted.

She said, either laughing or crying, "Well, you certainly put on a good act!"

"That's all I need," he thought. "Was that really Lavinia?"

"If it's the same Tuchkova, then—"

"The same! The same!" shouted Natalya.

"—I knew her when she was eight years old."

"What does the girl have to do with it?" Natalya yelled, more irritated than ever. "I'm talking about the mother. You had an affair with her!"

"Please," Myatlev said, "are you all right? What affair?"

Natalya left him an estate in Smolensk Province; he returned it to the parents of the ill-fated princess and thereby seemed to slight her gift, which incensed society for a long time. Then he turned to his ancient friends, but they were aloof and indifferent to his tribulations and peripatetic life, and the marble statues in the entry turned their backs on him. He wrote a polite but firm letter to Nesselrode, resigning from the service, ordered Afanasy to take the uniform away, and, watching it go, thought, "How I might have been forced to live if I didn't have an income! Would the civil service have been my only means of support?" But his attempt to delve into the mysteries of our society—a subject that had engrossed many of his contemporaries for many years— ended there. Instead, armed with a pen and a ream of fresh paper, he undertook the writing of his memoirs in the library. The work captivated him, and memories so engulfed him that his surroundings faded and disappeared, leaving room for inspiration. The image of the Hussar lieutenant killed in the Caucasus came alive and visited him, slightly more ennobled than he had been in real life, but that's understandable, for time forgives much in villains, and that certainly holds for geniuses. Line after line covered the pages, and piercing notes rose from their mighty chorus, endowing his memories of the distant past with the flavor of actuality, tragedy, and inevitability. Take his first sentence, for instance: "He appeared at my house, so intoxicated by his unbridled hopes for success that his short body looked gigantic, and to this day I can't rid myself of the impression that he had to bend down to get through the door." Some anger sounded here and set the tone for the entire work, and Myatlev was unable to get away from this opening motif but plunged deeper and deeper into the dark, the night, into mystery and melancholy. He made it appear that people who were jealous of the poet and were mired in their petty passions had thirsted for his death in order to be free of his accusing gaze. Whether the tsar was to blame in this, as some maintained, or whether it was the fault of the society in which the tsar had been brought up, or whether the poet was so singular a phenomenon in our crude, sad world that he himself kept bumping into sharp corners, only time would tell, but he was evidently so thin-skinned and sensitive that a pinprick seemed like a stab to him.

> Truly, he felt trapped in any room. He could not stand the presence of walls. They cramped him as did his uniform, and he kept playing with the collar, as though trying to tear it off. Music aroused him, too, not in the vulgar meaning we give the word, but by causing him a degree of pain that embarrassed him, which he would never reveal for all the world's wealth. When I sat down at the piano at his request, his face would change in an instant and he would start to wheeze, cough, giggle, in order to hide the rising tears, and then he would tease me, turning away so that I would not see him weep.

However, something in nature itself could be blamed for his premeditated murder, something that had focused its hostility on the lieutenant and tied into one last fatal knot the many strands of hatred people felt for him. There must have been some reason why he was so embarrassed by his suffering, which seemed groundless; why he was so irritable; and why he tried to get away—"Perhaps beyond the Caucasus"—although he saw with supernatural insight that there was no salvation there.

> It seemed that he had consciously doomed himself to one brief, cruel experience: to combat everyone and prove with his own death that any attempt to fight against the mob of his insignificant brothers and sisters was in vain . . . reduced once again to a struggle between the mob and the individual. Does that mean that the mob was to blame?

When he pictured the tsar, he could not escape that evil attraction—just like the pathetic scribbler, Mr. Kolesnikov, the antagonist of tsars and the happy possessor of a dark-green uniform, who had said, "Your friend was a true genius," by which he probably meant that "your friend" fought against injustice. But it was Kolesnikov's blunder, for which he paid, to assume that the murdered Hussar lieutenant was also a victim; and Myatlev tried to develop the notion that the tsar was a victim, too, taking everything into account, and was certainly not responsible for the poet's ill-starred fate. But his own impressions and personal hurts led him down a path he had not foreseen. He wanted to be as fair as history and ended up as unfair as a historian.

> The latent bad instincts of the tsar appeared in childhood with irrepressible impact. Whatever happened to him—whether he fell, made a mistake, or felt that his desires were not being gratified and that he had been insulted—he would curse, chop up his toys with an ax, and beat his friends with a stick, even though he loved them. . . . Later all his actions revealed his conviction that he could not be measured against anyone in the land, that he was a god, and that he could do anything.

Thus, moving back and forth between memories of "your friend" and lists of Nicholas I's base qualities, he came to the vulgar conclusion, without realizing it himself, that the tsar was responsible for the death of the genius. But he couldn't bring it all together. Finally, on rereading his argument, he realized he was not so much writing about his murdered friend as settling accounts with the tsar. While he did not feel guilty about this, he did stop work on the project without ever putting finis to it. The secret of the lieutenant's death hung in the air. At the end, he confessed bitterly:

> An analysis of this tragedy is beyond me. I'm too insignificant to keep personal injuries out of it. I feel a terrible heaviness, but I cannot account for its origins. It's quite possible that the main culprit is our life and not the caprices of our ruler. But I'm not a genius; when I hurt, I scream and curse. . . . "And he who lives and he who died are equally its victims."

Oddly, this unfinished work was destined to float to the top of the stagnant pool and land in the plump, middle-aged, trembling paws of Mr. Kolesnikov himself. That gentleman, having lived through the horrors of a week's confinement and distinctly unambiguous threats, was allowed to continue his valiant career, and his uniform sweated and strained in the bowels of the horse-breeding department. And then fate decided to bring him in contact with Myatlev once again, this time in Kunzel's Konditorei on Kamennoostrovsky Prospect. The scribbler had changed greatly since their last memorable meeting; he had aged, gotten fat, moved more slowly, and had adopted a more high-flown manner of speech. But this did not conceal his sincere pleasure at running into his old friend.

A few minutes later they were in the prince's carriage. Myatlev had merely mentioned his literary endeavors, and the professional demanded a look at his young friend's work. In his heart of hearts, Myatlev had hoped that the pages would produce some effect on his visitor, but the effect was much more than he had hoped for. The pages shook in Mr. Kolesnikov's hands. His face first tensed and turned red, then glowed, then

246

fell, and a deathly pallor spread over it, which turned gradually to an unhealthy yellow. He wheezed and choked, and something inside him burbled and boiled so that it seemed as if excess steam were pouring out of a hole in the back of his head, making his thin hair rustle. His shoes rubbed against one another as though trying to jump off his gouty feet; he was either in the throes of some strident pleasure or of despair—it was impossible to tell which. Finally he put down the last page and looked up slowly. There was a grimace of disgust on his face, his eyes were filled with fear, and his thick, biscuitlike lips flapped soundlessly.

"If I had known *what* you were going to slip me," he squeezed out, "I never would have come. What is this?"

"What is what?"

"Why are you trying to tempt me, sir? Do you take me for a fool?"

"He's mad," thought Myatlev. "His eyes are crazy."

"Do you think this shows courage?" continued Kolesnikov. "No, kind sir, no, Your Excellency, these are all lies. Your friend was a genius at writing poetry, but he was also an evil genius, and that's what destroyed him. According to you, society, led by His Majesty, conspired to ruin your friend's life. What nonsense. My God!"

"You misunderstood me," Myatlev interrupted. "I was only trying to—"

"I've had enough of all this gloom and inevitability!" The scribbler's face was gray; the last gusts of steam hit the ceiling; and his body sank into the chair. "When you think that the tsar neither sleeps nor rests— I can't believe that you are one of those evil people, of whom there are now so many, who refuse to separate the private lives of sovereigns from their political lives and pick on their weaknesses in order to blacken their political accomplishments! I can't believe it, sir."

"That's enough," laughed Myatlev. "Don't attribute the devil knows what to me." And he thought, "Where are you, Mr. van Schoenhoven?"

"No, no," insisted Kolesnikov, "don't you discredit the tsar. In my day," he added softly, "I had a fling at it, too, but I was blind. We're all ready to fly at each other's throats as it is, and you just confirm the mood of the robbers and blackguards with your meditations."

And his soul continued spewing forth words soaked in fear, almost disjointed, while his cumbersome body jumped out of the chair; and he stood wringing his hands in entreaty before Myatlev, behaving as though it were not the prince whom he was addressing but Leonty Vasilyevich Dubelt himself, the fortunate police general, a wonderful and wise man, a fount of charm, tall, elegant, with a thin, tired face, gray eyes, a gentle handshake, and the stamp of suffering in his gaze, in his drooping gray mustache, in his bitter, miserable smile. "My kind friend, don't rush to conclusions. It's very easy to criticize. There are hundreds of critics and subversives, but so few creators. It's hard. Loyalty is not a weakness, my kind friend, as it may seem to some ignoramuses; loyalty is the desire to get the best for your fatherland. These people tend to latch onto every failure and misfortune and blow them up out of all proportion, when these errors should be quietly, calmly, and, in keeping with the course of history, gradually reduced to nothing. I beg of you, my kind friend, listen to my words. Don't imitate the subversives, don't add to the evil in our long-suffering fatherland. It's hard."

"Why, you're the politician!" Myatlev said. "I'm not interested in that at all. God knows that all I wanted to do was to understand the contradictions between the poet and the world."

"No, no, and once more no!" shouted Kolesnikov, looking around. "What contradictions? Look where you're headed. And that's the problem, that we judge tsars from our own petty anthills, and we don't see their suffering. No and no! You should record instead how your friend rejected the general peace and quiet in order to please his own egotism, for which he paid, and you—"

"Egotism?" said Myatlev, and took a step toward the collegiate secretary.

"Kind friend," Kolesnikov said, the wind out of his sails, "I used to think the same way, believe me. But believe me, life is more complicated than it seems. You cannot set one against another; that will lead to nothing but chaos. The state will suffer, and then you will, too. Were you really planning to submit that to a *journal*?" He pointed to the scattered pages. "Come to your senses. I don't believe it."

"He took away Aneta, he tortured Alexandrina, he forced me to marry Natalya," thought Myatlev. "I won't give him the next one."

"You misunderstood me," he said, smiling. "I am not involved in politics. It's too hectic. I prefer sensuous pleasures. From here on, I will try to shift smoothly to talking of love." Kolesnikov looked at him suspiciously. "Picture a young thing—" Myatlev laughed. "By the way," he asked sarcastically, "is Mr. Nekrasov still carrying on the work?"

The scribbler choked, said nothing for a long time, and then whispered, "He's a real card fanatic. I am deeply disappointed in him."

Providence suddenly took pity on him. Its thin voice began to whisper promises of wonderful changes in Myatlev's ear, and the prince kept seeing more and more clearly the pointy collarbones and unbearable gray eyes of the former Mr. van Schoenhoven. He was sometimes brought up short by the fact that this vision took up more of his time than his attempts to analyze the late tribulations of the pathetic poet. Yes, yes, indeed; something had happened that interfered with his thinking of the slender daughter of Madame Tuchkova with his former tender condescension.

What do you think, Mr. Kolesnikov? How could this have happened? But Mr. Kolesnikov, torn by horrible premonitions, had long since disappeared, and Lavinia was still on Myatlev's mind. The prince's anxiety was inspired, and Misha Berg's seductions no longer worried him. Where are you, Mr. van Schoenhoven?

47

[From Lavinia to Myatlev, from the village of K., en route]

Dear Sergei Vasilyevich, I presume to disturb you once again only because I have heard of a new tragedy in your life. I am nurturing a small hope that this, too, was an erroneous rumor, like the one about your house burning down, and that the beautiful Princess Myatleva is alive and well. I pray that it is so, and I'm sure that the blessing of the tsar could not turn into misfortune. [Here Myatlev shrugged, not quite getting the young lady's meaning.] All my problems are insignificant and my joys quotidian compared to yours. You are a man who is worthy of much and all of it most wonderful. [Here Myatlev blushed and emitted a low whistle.]

Now, just a few words about me, even if I'm embarrassed to burden you, though as long as I'm writing I might as well. . . . I'm fine, except for the illness that struck suddenly, breaking off our wedding trip outside Moscow. We're stuck here. The fever went down a long time ago, but the doctor has ordered me not to budge. We're living country-style and studying the art, to be applied once I'm well, of doing everything, becoming rich and famous, charming everyone, leaving them with a good impression, befriending everyone, speaking pleasantries to everyone, missing nothing, and dying with dignity, and so on. . . . Our absurd honeymoon incident is dragging on, and, can you imagine, we haven't fenced or shot bottles once. Evdokiya Yuryevna is a charming woman, and God prompted her to travel with us, and when Alexander Vladimirovich is forced by pressing affairs to leave us, she keeps me from falling into despair. She's a marvelous storyteller, and thanks to her my information on many subjects has been broadened and deepened. [Here Myatlev burst out laughing, which made the shocked Afanasy try to peek over his shoulder to read the letter.] I had hoped that a new life would begin on the other side of the tollgates, but we must have passed through the wrong ones; I don't see any particular changes in my lot.

Dear Prince, as for the uninhabited island that so worried you, believe me, your anxiety is for nothing; *Maman* cannot be shocked by such fantasies, and even if it were to happen and we found ourselves in such a place, who could possibly care? Two adult and well-brought-up people move to a desert island—why worry about them? Your terror, dear Prince, is also unnecessary since I hear all the uninhabited islands have been grabbed up of late, and the situation is the same beyond the nearest tollgates.

48

WHERE ARE YOU, MR. van Schoenhoven? That question made his head spin more than any of his former Horse Guards' revels.

It was August in the middle of the century, and the prince raced around Petersburg in his well-traveled carriage as though he had vowed to take its measure from one end to the other. A lone sad crow cawed unintelligibly over Saint Isaac's Cathedral.

Everything in the decaying house had been abandoned: the literary exercises, the preaching of the ancients, Afanasy beating his Aglaya, and Aglaya trying to seduce the prince. Truly, the house and his whole life were coming apart at the seams since there was no reason, no passion, no hot blood, or health to hold them together.

"And really," thought the prince with pathos, in a daze, "what am I? Feeble attempts at suffering—that's my lot. Where is the goal that spurs everyone on—even the insignificant Mr. Kolesnikov? What storms have I overcome? For whose sake made any sacrifices?" And then he laughed at his unusual rhetoric. Where are you, Mr. van Schoenhoven? Only those pointy collarbones seemed like the truth to him, a truth that had fled, melted away, and been conquered by another—by a clever and inevitable man. "You appear confident, but your eyes give you away," a well-wisher once said to the prince, and even though the comment was not particularly profound, Myatlev wanted to think about it, for a man of his inclinations always must know everything bitter about himself, bitterness being the best cure for self-delusion. Ah, did he have time to delude himself?

But wasn't the almost forgotten Baron Fredericks right in his own way, happy in the knowledge of his dependence on others? And wasn't Mr. Sverbeyev right, freezing in the cold and hanging upside down in the chimney for goals that had been revealed to him one day? And boxy Dr. Schwanenbach, ending his life in a burst of love's inspiration, when he could finally believe in it? And the pathetic red-haired Aglaya, taming her monstrous Fonaryasy? And Fonaryasy himself, leafing through the prince's diaries furiously, on orders from Sverbeyev, in the name, apparently, of some promised heavenly delights? And the tsar, who hanged those five because, as he said, he was directed by the will of the people? Weren't they all right in their own way?

As for the uninhabited island, dear Mr. van Schoenhoven, it really is funny—fearing your *maman*'s opinion, since you are no longer a little girl and have probably weighed all the possibilities. I'm slowly coming to the conclusion that you are absolutely right to be fantasizing on this subject, but I'm afraid that the project will not be warmly approved by the kind Mr. Ladimirovsky.

A few days later he found himself writing Lermontov's familiar line: "And the years pass, all the best years." But he couldn't remember if he wrote it in his diary or in his daily letter to Mr. van Schoenhoven.

Then, driven to distraction by his depression, introspection, and his whim of going off to a desert island with a young seductress, he himself began fantasizing, and he came up with the marvelous Horse Guards' idea of bursting into the orphaned home of Madame Tuchkova and, holding a pistol to her ardent breast, compelling her participation in a rather ticklish business, a quite piquant one, that at first glance would not seem quite proper— All in good time.

And so he raced around the city making plans, to the accompaniment of the pounding wheels, rubbing his hands in satisfaction and clicking his tongue, imagining how happy I would be at the chance to prove myself his equal in the noble intrigue he was devising.

Refusing to help him was beyond me, and the enterprise seemed exciting, even though I cooled his fervor a bit, and proposed some changes, and tempered his premature triumph. Our ossified hearts began beating wildly, as though our youth had not abandoned us after all.

How we announced ourselves at the home of Madame Tuchkova, I don't remember, as God is my witness. In any case, contrary to our expectations, we were received immediately and quite pleasantly, and in our black suits, looking simultaneously like deposed Danish princes and London clerks, we proceeded through the rooms of that wretched house to find ourselves before Madame Tuchkova.

I had expected a fury, and instead I saw a charming woman whose eyes were both clever and pleasant, and whose smile had been brought to perfection.

"Oho," thought I, "if this is the mother, I can imagine the daughter!" I had seen Mr. van Schoenhoven as a child, and not since then. It was quite possible, I thought, that she might have turned into a beauty, even though the prince had had ample opportunity to find many beauties. Apparently, the pointy collarbones had made enough of an impression on him to keep him from noticing the rest. "How will we manage before these all-seeing eyes," I thought, "or is our reputation already worthless?" And Myatlev himself seemed to realize that his hotheaded plan was no more than an empty fantasy and that something markedly unpleasant was about to occur. She said, "Please, gentlemen," with such a marvelous intonation that I had to shut my eyes for a moment to relish it. But there was no thunderclap. We were sitting immobile and tense, as if at a funeral. Nothing but desperate determination showed on the prince's pale face. "Please tell me," I thought, "how long one can pretend to be made of stone?" Meanwhile, the flame that came from her licked at our knees.

"Your face is familiar," she murmured nonchalantly, looking at the prince calmly, not in the tactless manner of provincial women.

"Apparently, we have met before," the prince concurred graciously.

She was pretending that they were not acquainted. How strange, I thought. And she did not ask how the gentlemen had learned about the little masterpiece she was being forced to sell.

"Extreme circumstances, gentlemen," she said with a laugh, and led the way.

What extreme circumstances could there be with a son-in-law like that, I wondered, trying to stay in step with Myatlev. There, that must be Mr. van Schoenhoven's room, Myatlev guessed, trying to remember all the doors just in case. Madame Tuchkova gracefully preceded us, lightly hoisting the heavy candelabrum, her slippers barely touching the floor.

"My daughter, gentlemen," she added nonchalantly, "loves this particular work. And even though she no longer lives with me, I must take that into account." A strange blue haze enveloped this charming witch, and the haze grew thicker as we approached our goal. "Strange things are happening, gentlemen," she said, not waiting for a reply. "Works by the old masters are suddenly in disrepute, or undesirable, or something of the sort, or perhaps it's related to our present point of view, which was unknown to the old masters, since if they had been aware of it, they certainly wouldn't have continued painting their favorite subjects." I thought that she laughed. "Does that frighten you, gentlemen?" But we went on, silent and stubborn, maintaining what dignity we could, striding like sentinels a few paces behind her, not finding much evidence of a great love of art on the part of the owners of this house. "Have you perhaps encountered my daughter in society, gentlemen? She's appeared several times and made quite an impression. The last time was at Easter. She wore a light-blue gown of silk tulle, with straw camellias and leaves on the ruffles, can you imagine it?" I heard her giggle once more. "His Majesty showed an interest in her. Her husband didn't know whether to laugh or cry. Have you met her?"

We sighed bitterly and finally came into the room, or rather, storeroom, since the place was stuffed with refuse that may have been cherished still but was clearly no longer necessary. In a dark corner, illuminated by the yellow and unsteady light of the candle, a dusty nobleman nodded from his canvas. Prince Sapega, that rebellious Pole whom Madame Tuchkova was hoping to get rid of, stared at us, yellow-faced and aloof, without much kindness. Why is she rushing, thought Myatlev, unless Mr. Sverbeyev has been here, too, copying the portrait so as to inform against her in the right places?

"Do you know Mr. Sverbeyev?" he asked casually. When it turned out that he was none other than a tailor and secret agent, or an agent and secret tailor—what miracles do not occur?—she permitted herself to laugh mockingly, which she did with a kindly grace. The storm is coming, I thought, as I seriously examined the Pole. And of course, neither Myatlev nor I had any idea what lines were ripening in the magnificent head of Madame Tuchkova, how letter by letter the heavy words were forming, how stuffy—how gloomy—even the dust didn't stir:

Hear me out. That rich monster, that seducer of many women, appeared in my home and I could tell from his expression that he was truly mad about you and would move heaven and earth to change your life. Giving his mind, education, and title their due, I am determined to shield your happiness from any attack. I'm doing it as subtly as possible, but God only knows how it will turn out. . . . If he dares to write to you, in God's name, don't answer, even in the coldest terms. That will be enough incentive for him.

"Prince Sapega," the witch said, "fell in love with a charming young woman, the wife of one of his courtiers. He fell in love.

He wanted her desperately. However, she was steadfast, and through the efforts of her husband and mother it seems his dishonorable intentions were circumvented."

"She was steadfast, but the efforts of her husband and mother were required?" Myatlev asked softly, flicking melted wax from the candle.

Madame Tuchkova pretended not to hear.

"And so," she went on, "he decided one night—just imagine!—to take advantage of the absence of his love object and her father, and he crept into the bedchamber of the mother and, threatening her with a pistol, demanded that she consent to his marrying her daughter."

"Did he climb in the window?" Myatlev asked distractedly, and looked at the window. It was low. He could easily stretch out and reach the sill . . . *A crowd teemed under the window. Laughter. The terrified Madame Tuchkova crossed herself at the sight of him as if he were the Devil. The middle-aged demon in spectacles and black cape, and carrying a bizarre dueling pistol, crashed into her house. The crowd was in a frenzy. . . .* "Just so that I don't drop my specs," he thought fervently.

"He climbed in the window. It was summer; the windows were open," she said, and blanched.

The jaundiced, heavyset Pole looked haughtily at Myatlev, not trying to deny his guilt in the tragedy.

"And then? Did he fail?" asked Myatlev indifferently.

"No, no," she exclaimed. "He abducted the daughter, but they poisoned her in time, and she died in his arms."

"Charming family," laughed Myatlev, prodding me in the ribs, and he said challengingly, "I'll take this portrait. The puny children of our own age have something to learn from this prince, don't you agree?"

"I will send it to you."

"No," said Myatlev with childlike stubbornness, "I will take it with me. Your daughter won't be too upset?"

"Who?" she asked in terror.

"Your daughter."

256

"What does she have to do with it?"

"You said your daughter loved this painting."

"What does my daughter have to do with it?" she asked more calmly, and confessed that keeping a portrait painted by a Pole and of a Pole well known for his anti-Russian sentiment meant bringing displeasure and perhaps wrath upon her house.

In the letter to her daughter, which she was still composing in her heart, she wrote new lines:

> I sold him the portrait of Prince Sapega, so beloved by you. He didn't think twice, even though, as you might guess, he needed it like a fifth leg. He was thinking of you, and his eyes were filled with the desire—I could see it—to destroy you, as he has so many other women. I doubt that it will end with this. You should have seen that emaciated old man, that horsey face with its spectacles, aged prematurely by debauchery and caprice. What those foolish women were thinking of, I can't imagine. He was accompanied by a quiet, fierce-looking Georgian. What luck that you are away! They would have carried you off with the painting. And of course, your darling spouse would have been unable to do anything. I could tell that they were armed. They stank of wine, like highwaymen.

"Gentlemen," she said, "would you care for some wine?" Oh, she truly disapproved of Prince Sapega's temperament. How dared he do that!

> Incomparable *Maman*, I trust that the danger of my abduction has passed and that you saw the highwaymen out as graciously and firmly as only you can. My dear Alexander in a fury of righteousness wanted to go to Petersburg to help you, particularly since you hinted rather unflatteringly that he would be of no use in defending his honor, but on second thought decided that you, as usual, may have exaggerated a bit. The point is the gentleman you wrote about does not resemble an old man; he is elegant, slender, and sensitive. And could the outward appearance of any man threatening our family peace matter in the least? Aren't you too cruel, to frighten me like that? I'm not only

257

not corresponding with him, but I don't even remember his name—that's how uninterested I am in him, and he in me, I'm quite sure. . . . We are each going our separate ways. You made me very happy, giving my hand to Alexander. God sees how happy and secure I am here.

Madame Tuchkova received this letter quite a few days after our visit. Myatlev received a letter at about the same time.

[From Lavinia to Myatlev, from the village of K.]

Dear Sergei Vasilyevich! Thank God that autumn is here and Petersburg is closer. There's no trace of my illness, and I'm waiting for my incomparable Mr. Ladimirovsky to give the orders to leave. I bribed his auntie to find out when, but my diplomacy failed—nothing came of it. I still haven't lost the hope of returning to Petersburg in time for the first snow and making tracks across your park to your house. Perhaps you might even want to see me and ask me something with your sweet smile. I had forbidden myself to write to you, and then I thought, Why not? Really, why not? Whom else can I talk to? After all, I thought, he would have let me know if it bothered him, and here in the country, when it rains, it's impossible not to write to you, dear Sergei Vasilyevich!

"Gentlemen," she said, "would you care for some wine?" We refused.

"My daughter married recently," she said, seeing us out. "It was very touching to see the newlyweds after the ceremony. Their love is boundless. They looked at each other with the most passionate and elevated expressions on their faces." Here I definitely heard a laugh, but Madame Tuchkova's face was serious. Myatlev walked along silently with the portrait of Sapega under his arm. There was no triumph in his gait. The witch's banality was monstrous. "You should have seen them, gentlemen, holding hands, entwining their fingers, and this in front of everyone—everyone talked about it later—they all thought it delightful. Do you have daughters, gentlemen? I hope you'll remember Prince Sapega's story." This was a frontal assault. I was interested in seeing which side would give in first. Who would first drop the pretense and attack, with furious screams of hatred, making the walls and corridors shake, the useless portrait shattered to pieces against the wall, the masks of gentility falling from their faces, jaws outthrust and fists waving. "Now my daughter is far away, gentlemen, and I'm all alone. That's the lot of all mothers." She suddenly laughed, not the way a triumphant witch should laugh, but with great and natural sadness. "Have you met my daughter in society, gentlemen? I think I've asked you that. If you had met her, you would have remembered her. She has a charming face, and when Princess Myatleva was alive, many people couldn't decide which was the more beautiful." Myatlev stalked like a crane, lifting his feet high and not looking at the gabbling witch flying around him. There was no storm. I dreamed of one thing only: to get out of this nest unharmed, before the iron bird sank her claws into my back.

And if ever, my incomparable *Maman*, you should think that I am dissatisfied with your choice, put that down to my stupidity and innate ungratefulness. I was always like that, wasn't I? I'll try to control myself, but only God knows what lies ahead for us, isn't that so?

I did not see Madame Tuchkova's face when she read the letter, and I'm sorry, but those lines contained all kinds of delicate hints of events to come. The contemporary woman, free of sentimentality and filled with every kind of practical knowledge, would not have missed it. However, I can't see how, in that case, Madame Tuchkova didn't manage to keep events from developing along a path she had not herself determined.

49

The operation would have been a resounding success had I not inopportunely swallowed a poker that kept me from behaving naturally. And yet we did establish the most important things: first of all, that there is no point in my counting on her silent complicity—she's ready to tear my throat out, she remembers me, she dreads me. She hopes that Mr. Ladimirovsky's appearance will settle things because he has prospects and I don't. Secondly, things are not as wonderful for Lavinia as one might suppose from a cursory reading of her letters. I'm afraid that this was an ordinary sale, decorated with a wedding party and blessed by the church. . . . Poor Mr. van Schoenhoven! . . . Thirdly, the layout of the house would make it simple to get to that room at night with a rope ladder, if I only knew where to get a rope ladder. That girl with the pointy collarbones, who's thought up an escape to a desert island, isn't having a pleasant life. . . . Not pleasant . . . She's unhappy in the territory of the rich. . . . Almost no one can be happy who's within the range of an observer's eyes. . . . Maybe there, beyond where the eye can see, beyond that damn tollgate, beyond the Moscow gates, where we are not, somewhere in the sticks, in that blessed "there," there is salvation for poor Mr. van Schoenhoven.

50

TEARING HIMSELF AWAY FROM his diary and tossing the book aside, he attacked a clean sheet of paper frantically, as if it alone contained a cure for a new and sudden ache, and setting to with his pen and scattering ink spots, he let himself go, becoming more and more heated.

> You have, of course, been informed of my visit to your house. Mr. van Schoenhoven, whom I ignored a bit due to differences in age, circumstances, and so on, has suddenly appeared before me and has been shadowing me for over a month now.

He crossed out the clumsy lines, good only for a Christmas joke, and began anew.

> Lavinia, I was at your house. Whether your mother recognized me or not is not the issue. The years do their work, and, suddenly, thinking of you has become a great need. The important part of my life is over, and I've only realized it now. Actually, empty regrets are nonsense. I should leave you alone and not disrupt the smooth flow of family life, to which you are becoming accustomed, but it is out of my hands.

And he crossed that out, too.

> Every evening, no matter what the weather, I have the driver stop across the street from your house, and I watch the windows without any hope of seeing your silhouette on the blind. The desert island that you fantasized about so desperately is becoming, funny as it seems, the subject of serious consideration on my part. I see its shape, sense its dimensions, and feel its soil under my feet. And I see you!

And he crossed that out. He got a fresh sheet. The house was quiet, with a distant conversational rumble reaching him once in a while—the spy and his helper discussing the events of the day. Of late, Afanasy's severe and hostile glances spoke volumes and confirmed Myatlev's suspicions, but the prince had stopped feeling like an inhabitant of Petersburg and had so long ago buried his household in his consciousness that he had neither the strength nor the desire to combat whatever might come. He was like a man rushing to his carriage so that he can collect a large inheritance and dropping a few bills from his pocket on the way.

> Where are you, Mr. van Schoenhoven? I was at your house. But

261

you did not come out to greet me. Now that you are quite grown up, we could talk of so many things together, but you are not in Petersburg. This city takes everything from me. Thank God that you have not become a hope; it would be terrible to lose it.

His ruthless pen destroyed everything as soon as it was created. He imagined Mr. Ladimirovsky opening the envelope and his eyes greedily pouncing on the prince's hurried and belated confessions. "What's this?" he asks. "Ah, that's Prince Myatlev. You remember my childhood attachment?" "But why is he writing now and in this tone?" he asks, controlling his irritation. "I haven't the slightest idea," she says. "A joke, perhaps, I certainly never expected anything like this." "So, then, it needn't be saved—you, I hope, weren't planning to save it." "I don't care," she says, looking at the letter in bewilderment, "I don't care."

My dear friend, my priceless friend, Mr. van Schoenhoven. What's happening to me resembles madness. I'm coming down with an illness. I am not at fault in your regard. Perhaps I'm idealizing you, but I see you all the time—and so beautiful that I can't stand not hearing your voice.

Now he knew that he wouldn't send the letter, and therefore he stopped thinking about Mr. Ladimirovsky.

Petersburg without you is dead and horrible. The only place I could hope to hide is the desert island you invented in a marvelous, unrepeatable, insightful moment.

He rang for Afanasy, but the valet was in no hurry to fly to him with angelic smile, and when he did get there, he was conspicuously drunk. He paused in the doorway, looking almost human through the efforts of Mr. Sverbeyev, Aglaya, and, probably, the new ideas that had taken possession of him, dressed in a gray jacket, with a raspberry vest peeking out. He stood, swaying slightly and staring at his master with his usual reproach. Behind his back the vague outline of the spy showed in

262

the dark, his emaciated face barely visible, and the smell of alcohol spread through the room. The two of them stood there, with the air of masters disturbed inopportunely, and Myatlev thought that he still didn't have the strength or desire to teach them a lesson on account of their insolence and kick them downstairs. "Ohmygod," he heard deep inside, "what is this!" But he controlled himself and said, mustering a mocking laugh, "Would you be so kind, respected sir, as to prepare my evening clothes for the theater?"

In answer Afanasy swayed and said nothing.

"I should take a stick," thought Myatlev, walking to the window, "or a sword—and show them."

"Your Excellency," Mr. Sverbeyev said with a show of obsequiousness, "there is a spot on your frock coat."

"Afanasy," Myatlev asked in a high voice, losing patience and ignoring the spy, "where did the spot come from, you swine?"

"From the air, sir," Mr. Sverbeyev answered respectfully. "The dust and mud, sir." And then he ordered Afanasy, "Go get some vinegar and don't forget the brush, His Excellency can't wait."

And Afanasy rushed downstairs with drunken joy, and Myatlev heard clattering on the steps, the stairs groaning underfoot, and Aglaya's clucking. Indignation was seething in Myatlev, but the figure that appeared before him was so unbelievable, and everything that was happening seemed so unreal, that he wanted to shake his head to wake up. And in a delirium of mist and smoke and clouds, he watched Afanasy's drunken shade flit about and Mr. Sverbeyev shake the ill-fated frock coat, trying to shake its soul out of it, and rub the brush across it, and pant and puff, and wink at the prince, and mutter, "How could we not serve our provider—how could we not obey our master."

The business was dragging on; the invisible spot was not disappearing; and the frock coat struggled to escape the villain's clutches. Suddenly Mr. Sverbeyev, breaking off the hustle and bustle, spoke, presumably addressing the frock coat. "We'll show you. You just take it. Bow and scrape—you won't break. I like it when I'm bowed to smoothly and low, one hand scraping the floor—I do it myself. What's the difference between plowing the earth and kissing your feet—"

"Get out of here!" Myatlev shouted as though from afar, but no one heard him.

And Mr. Sverbeyev went on, "Those who despise others for bowing with their backs bent don't see they are well served by those bent backs. They call the ones with bent backs all kinds of bad names, like, for instance, hypocrite, bootlicker, and so on, but they don't understand that it derives from social custom, from the laws governing behavior between people, and not from a bad character. He who is unwilling to bow to his brother despises the human law, and you get lumps for that. And getting lumps, you become bitter and sink so deeply into hatred that you will never get out. This spot should be removed with acid, Your Excellency. Vinegar isn't strong enough. And it's time for a new frock coat, too. A new one—" And he tossed away the lifeless body of the frock coat.

Meanwhile, Myatlev was picturing a steppe overgrown with bluebells and chamomile, a setting sun, a marvelous freshness in the air, a dustless road after a brief shower, and a fast carriage floating along it; and himself, lolling on the seat in a light shirt open at the throat and a traveling jacket; and nothing ahead of him but that open field and the flowers and the stillness, and the smell of smoke from up ahead— Ohmygod!

When the unsuccessful battle with the spot had ended, the drunken company left the prince's room, and a steady, unintelligible aria from the courtyard reached Myatlev's ears and faded away.

Of course, if Mr. van Schoenhoven were here, if the girl with the pointy collarbones were here, so wise, with tumbling curls, if she were here—

Dear Lavinia, I've reread your letters and understood that your life . . .

And crossed it out.

You know what a man as old as I feels when it's autumn in Petersburg, when the greater part of his life is over, when you alone reign in his thoughts, and you are inaccessible . . . offense . . . protect your . . .

And crossed it out.

Have you no plans to return? Isn't it time? To drop into our park and leave a trail in the new snow, leaving blue tracks that will melt by morning. . . . I know what they've told you about me. That I ruin women. Here's how that slander got started. Baroness Fredericks, of whom you must have heard and whom I did not particularly want, preferred the cold embraces of a certain monarch to me. . . . No, she was not being calculating, but she had no choice. Thus he became the cause of my pain.

And crossed that out, too.

That woman committed suicide, knowing that her days were numbered. Consumption. You must not believe the vile rumor that I drove her to it. . . . What nonsense! There was no other creature in the world for whom I was prepared to do everything. . . . And do you know how her consumption began? Again it was he who made her life unbearable, and she . . .

He rang again and called for some vodka. Mr. Sverbeyev arrived and explained that Afanasy could not move because of "colic in the stomach." The spy reeked more than ever. He tried to start a conversation with the resident of the third floor, but Myatlev waved him away and he finally left. After a few glasses, the prince was feeling much better. He took a dueling pistol from the wall and went downstairs. The door to Afanasy's room was wide open. The treacherous valet was lying on a cot and pretending to be sick or asleep when he really was vilely drunk. The table was piled with dishes and leftovers. Myatlev noted that they were using his best china and that the dirty leftovers of a peasant meal were spreading over its ancient dark-blue glaze. Mr. Sverbeyev was napping, head on the table. Aglaya was not there. On the table next to the meditative spy lay a familiar envelope, blue and decorated with a hand-drawn monogram—

only Mr. van Schoenhoven would go to that much trouble. Redheaded Aglaya appeared. He showed her the pistol, and she froze in the doorway. Myatlev grabbed the envelope and calmly went upstairs. Behind him he heard voices and hissing, the clatter of dishes and pathetic prayers. The envelope, luckily, was not empty, even though it had been opened. Evidently they were interested in its contents.

> If only I had just a word from you! Is something wrong? It looks as if we're finally leaving. If you only knew what a rush I'm in! Of course, like any person not overwhelmed with good fortune, I'm wary. What awaits me in Petersburg? . . . I wish I could know that I will be able to see you from afar and guess that everything is well with you. Write to me. As for me, pretending is depressing. It's worse than autumn rain in the country. I had hoped to hold out, but I couldn't. Who's in the mood for fencing?

He couldn't have hoped for more frankness. Mr. van Schoenhoven was wringing his hands and not pretending to be happy. Myatlev wrote a few words feverishly:

> My priceless friend, certainly I'm waiting for you, always . . . hurry . . . I'm waiting for you.

He sent it by express mail in the morning and felt for the first time how lonely he was.

51

EVERYTHING, EVERYTHING THAT HAPPENED after that was my fault, but neither God nor the court could punish me, and I didn't dare punish myself because of my indecisiveness and my hope that this sad tale would have a happy ending.

I loved Prince Myatlev too much and therefore pitied him, and therefore bustled about imagining that my suggestions were curative and marvelous. Marvelous Georgia, from which I was cut off, was in my every breath. And my every word was drenched with it, like a piece of freshly baked bread drenched with the fat and juices of lamb shashlik, and, reveling in my childhood memories, I brought agitation into the soul of a suffering man, inflamed him, disturbed him, and propelled him toward the fatal hour. I swear that everything I did, either intentionally or by some wild intuition, I did out of love. Only love guided me, guided my exclamations, whispers, tears, gestures, silences, and fevers. A man who is suffering because he is out of touch with reality does not always understand what is happening to him, and the sense of impending disaster pursues him and deepens his pain. He is ready to do anything to escape it, and that may lead to destruction. The lucky ones who do understand either become anarchists or arm themselves with irony. Myatlev didn't understand. He simply experienced unbearable pain, and when I carried on about Georgia as though it were paradise, my exuberant paeans settled in his heart drop by drop, intensifying his hope of finding salvation in a journey there, and even I came gradually to imagine God only knew what as I talked to him about my homeland.

In the mornings, when the first avalanche of blue fog slowly and silently falls from the mountains and the boiling cascades of waterfalls and rivers appear, dizzyingly transparent and as eternal as our life, the sensation of personal immortality makes you strong, calm, and unhurried.

Now in Petersburg, in that damp and drafty nest, everyone moves with unnatural haste along paths they themselves laid down, and they rush, and push, and become ciphers not only for others on the street but for themselves as well. And that all comes from the sense of the brevity and transitoriness of life. That's the reason for the feverish tempo, the convulsive and irritating speech. But in Georgia, when you feel immortal, you take on a bird's lightness, a boar's confidence, a snake's wisdom, and the implacability of the snowcaps on the peaks; and everything divine moves within you artlessly, and everything human drains away; and you don't stand in awe and delight before all this perfection, like a sad Petersburg dacha owner before a sunny meadow, you simply breathe it all in, without thinking about it.

In the mornings transparent swirls of cool mountain air surround you—innumerable; the aroma of the hearth, the thick yellow bread, the spices, the guttural sounds of birds, people, and rivers; the rivers of wine bursting up from the ground; the earth, trembling in the light wind; and finally, the wind, blending all of this into a single sea; and finally, the sea, brimming up to this earth, covered with whitecaps, overflowing with life, remembering Jason and iridescent with the scales from the Golden Fleece . . .

I swear that only my love moved me to this old and enticing spellbinding, and Myatlev clung to that variegated, aromatic, and proud hope with fierce desperation. And the voice of my beloved Maria, my Maro, called to him, too, and with such clarity and effect that it seemed she lived right there in the crumbling wooden fortress, love and compassion incarnate.

. . . And in the evenings a lavender haze slowly envelops the mountains, the trees, and the faces, and the pink trout becomes deep purple and mysterious; somewhere the overripe orange star of a campfire bursts into flame and grows larger, and the sounds of constant music come closer; the lacework of the balcony, further carved by worms, becomes even lacier and more mysterious than it is in daylight, and the milky muslin on the windows and doors becomes more transparent, revealing the interiors of the rooms and the motionless figures of their occupants, looking as if they were painted. Music, and the proud call of the mountain deer, and the squeal of the wild boar, and the bubbling of the water, and the monotonous strumming of the *chonguri*—what else could God invent better to comfort the northern sufferer, straighten him out, instill in him a feeling of immortality, and cure him through love and harmony of his pernicious predilection, his blind need to save himself from others through flight, anger, or temporary insanity?

I was certain of this, and thereby I hastened the catastrophe, and there is no excusing me. However, if we forget the pathos and stop imitating the neurasthenic ladies in provincial drawing rooms, every man, as they say in the Orient, begins to die from the moment he appears on earth, and dies when and how it pleases higher powers, no matter what precautions he may take, no matter how many gallons of curative waters he may guzzle, and no matter what conspiracies he may enter into. And there was some benefit or use, however temporary, in my mad tales, for Myatlev, inspired and intoxicated by hope, fought like a young man passionate in belief, and turned from a recluse into a man of action, illuminating his last love with a glow that made me want to shout and preen with pride over his having managed to overcome himself and appear before his beloved not in pilgrim's tatters but in the bronze armor of a conqueror.

Of course, all this happened later, at the height of autumn, and now it was merely gathering strength, and gloomy colors did not as yet predominate in the picture. It was the end of September. Caravans of happy vacationers slowly wended their way back to Petersburg, still remembering the freedoms of country living. The sky was insistently blue, and there was no sad autumnal bleakness in it. The falling leaves swirled constantly, but the movement was still merry and even lighthearted.

An old-fashioned, peeling mail coach, the likes of which you will not encounter now in the deepest provinces, stopped on Znamenskaya Street near Mr. Ladimirovsky's house, and Mr. Ladimirovsky got out of it. He was dressed in a dusty, wrinkled traveling costume but, unembarrassed by it, began giving instructions to his hovering staff in full view of the passersby. And until all the suitcases, bundles, and baskets were in the house, no one else left the carriage. When the baggage had been taken care of, he opened the door himself, and Evdokiya Yuryevna, stiff and dazed from the trip, crept down onto the pavement. Lavinia came next. She was pale and tired, too, but looked around her with a lively interest, as though seeking someone in the group of idlers who were watching, but they were only the usual Petersburg crowd.

At first, half-blinded by the sudden appearance of colors, faces, and windows, she saw over the shoulders of the curious the familiar, long-awaited features, vague and unreal, the gaze half-glued to the sky, alienated and full of ennui. She reeled in that direction, but Mr. Ladimirovsky caught her with the displeasure of a businessman forced to drop important matters for trifles.

"I'm tired," she explained, still staring into the crowd.

His hand held her elbow tightly, and she wanted to pull away in front of everyone. He always grabbed her like that, his fingers clenched, whenever he was displeased. "You've behaved as you wished once again, and that interferes with my plans. After all, I'm doing it all for you. I want *you* to be happy." He would berate her without changing his usual manner of speaking: almost in a whisper, calmly and politely, confessing his setbacks and disappointments, while his fingers pressed harder and harder, leaving dark marks on her white arm. "What's the matter with you?" she'd ask, and he would come to his senses and blush. But you can't be bewildered every time so rhetorically and monotonously. The time will come to be incensed and to shout, "Watch what you're doing! You're hurting me!" "Lavinia," he explained once in sorrow, quietly, "I really did fall into a state where I didn't notice I was doing it. You've been making me unhappy for a long time, and I can't myself understand how it is that I hurt you." The dark bruises on her white arm lasted for five days. Strolling in the old, run-down garden in the country, he would take her arm, and she could no longer chat calmly; his fingers with their hot, hard cushions were constantly, agitatedly moving, feeling for something, smoothing, measuring, asserting themselves, until she would pull her arm away. "You are placing me in a bizarre situation," he would say, trying to justify himself. "You forget—you seem to think, that I—you imagine, that I— Your fantasies will come to a sad end. Why do you lock your door against me and Evdokiya Yuryevna when you're simply reading? You promised— Are you hiding something?"

"I'm tired," she explained, still staring into the crowd.

Eyes of every color and caliber—black, hazel, blue, green, and faded, eyes of students, clerks, workers, old women and beautiful young girls—all stared at her, anxiously and in anticipation (they were all hoping for a scandal), as though in a daguerreotype; the fluctuating faces with their changing features kept her from finding the one face she wanted to see, now gone forever. She would even have called out his name if she had one shred of certainty that he was there and that the crowd would not laugh, seeing that pale beauty, the mistress of a house on Znamenskaya Street with a bombastic driveway, seeing her, the lucky young woman with an admixture of secret Polish blood, screaming out meaningless words, the empty name of a nonexistent lady killer, invented by her in a dream.

And what would you do if that marvelous, exquisite, sad, thirty-five-year-old man, laughable in his fear of seeming laughable, despised by your milieu and secretly adored by you, so secretly that it could easily be detected; if that old man, until now inaccessible as the most distant star, cold as January, who never answered your letters and preferred his yellow-toothed piano and his dark stories with some pretty young fools— What would you do if that thirty-five-year-old conqueror suddenly wrote those two lines to you, that one line, a few words: "Priceless friend, I'm waiting for you, always"? What would you do then?

"Do you remember," she wanted to ask Mr. Ladimirovsky, "do you remember how you would lock me up in the house in the country with your disgusting female custodian so that I wouldn't do anything foolish?" But she didn't scream this at him because then she would have had to explain to the crowd why Mr. Ladimirovsky was forced to keep her under lock and key, and why he wouldn't even let her go outside alone. He asked her not to: "Don't go out alone, so that people won't think that I've abandoned you." "Why don't you abandon that, so that I'll think it's gone out," she would retort. He couldn't understand; he'd run out into the fields, come back wringing his hands, lock

271

himself in his room, counting, measuring. "What did you say to me? I didn't understand." "What could I have said? I don't even remember," she would reply, looking past him. And it would end there, only to start again. "Are you locking me out, Lavinia?" "Ah, of course not. I don't lock my door. Did you try to open it?" "I can hear the lock click—" How could she explain to the crowd that in those fleeting hours she was writing letters filled with touching accounts of her idyll and honeymoon joys, sending them into the void, to a nonexistent address, to an unknown prince. Poor Mr. van Schoenhoven.

She walked from the carriage to the door with her head held high, a fixed smile on her pale face, and before crossing the threshold she looked at the crowd challengingly. And again Myatlev's clear, calm face appeared before her: the spectacles, the sunken cheeks, the high brow. Yes, yes, priceless friend, I am waiting for you— But the vision wavered and disappeared without a trace. There was only the crowd, which grew larger, filling up Znamenskaya and the neighboring streets.

"Well, well," said Mr. Ladimirovsky impatiently, "let's go, you need to rest. Let's go, I say."

Under the roof of the cold, unfamiliar house, she felt no better. "Ah, this isn't exhaustion, not at all," she wanted to say, but she didn't dare mock an old man. All the servants, she thought, had a single face. The rooms all resembled one another. She missed the dear unfinished spots, the familiar broken things, the dark corners, some disorder, the immortal smells of her childhood. But was it this that seemed cold to her? And to top everything, Madame Tuchkova descended upon them, adding to the icy atmosphere with her all-too-contemporary beauty. "Who is this woman?" thought Lavinia, touching her cheek to the aloof parental cheek offered her. Without planning it, husband and mother insisted in the most kindly terms that the young traveler go up to her room to rest and freshen up. She left. There, among the chairs freshly upholstered in her favorite greenish silk, under the ceiling painted by an unknown genius, within the walls that for some reason reminded her of the crowd downstairs, Lavinia heard a voice say, "Priceless friend, I'm waiting for you, always." She was not surprised. With a lightness of step long forgotten, she ran to the window like little Mr. van Schoenhoven. The crowd had gone. Across the street, under the sign of a red pretzel on a bright blue background, stood Myatlev in a black redingote, hatless, shamelessly staring into her window. It was beginning to rain.

52

[From Lavinia to Myatlev, from Petersburg]

I must describe an amusing scene for you: no sooner had the wagon that had sent me into a near-stupor stopped than a crowd gathered, and among all the possible Petersburg mugs I saw you. I was going to hurry over to greet you, as is accepted among decent folk, but my husband, worried for my health, dragged me into the house. I resisted, but went, my head turned in your direction, and you melted away. And so, with my head turned around on its axis, I entered my house. *Maman* appeared and ordered me to rest—that is, to get out of the way so that she could converse dramatically with Mr. Ladimirovsky—but as soon as I got into my room, I saw you again. You were looking at my window. Isn't that amusing?

My life in Petersburg is beginning. I've been ordered to prepare for a ball at the Anichkov Palace. I'm very happy as a result and laugh constantly, and apparently more than necessary, since Mr. Ladimirovsky has seen fit to speak to me about it— that is, to express his puzzlement at my behavior in the sense that others see this as a great honor, etc. I didn't even have time to rest before he dragged me out in the carriage—to buy hats, and some fabulous cover-up, and a boa, the likes of which "Tatishcheva herself never dreamed of." He held my elbow for the duration of the trip, fearing that I would fall from weakness or joy, and now I have bruises above the elbow. . . . In general, his love for me knows no bounds. It is overwhelming. It does not fit into my frail, pathetic heart and spills over.

My priceless friend, I'm tired of pretending! You know perfectly well that I don't see sunlight without seeing you. What do I want? To beat a path to your porch again and tell you "what Tatishcheva has never dreamed of." But how can it be done? That's the question. . . .Perhaps you could abduct me? Since I am suspected of youthful irresponsibility, they keep a close watch on me. *Maman* keeps demanding that I tell her "the whole truth": am I corresponding with you or not? And since I was brought up in the best possible manner, and always tell the truth, I always say no. But she, also brought up in the best possible manner, finds it hard to believe me. "You do not love your husband, that wonderful man, as you ought," she says in a mysterious whisper. "Ah, *Maman*," I reply loudly, "everyone knows that I married for love. You assured him of that yourself. He knows from you that I'm madly in love with him. What else could he want?"

My priceless friend, I can't pretend any longer. And, I swear, I'm not in the mood for jokes. The mournful call of the horns and the splatter of rain, and the half-light and half-darkness—that's the state of my soul now!

53

Now was not the time, gentlemen, for rope ladders and similar absurdities. Now he had to decide what to do quickly and seriously. Where could they meet? What would you have done? My evenings with Myatlev stopped being our usual indolent, marvelous, friendly, and slightly tipsy occasions and turned into hurried, tormenting, and most unusual strategy sessions. I had to moderate the prince's temperamental fantasies. He was in a hurry, in a frenzy. I'm amazed that I, not the world's most accomplished fatalist, turned out to be calmer, more controlled and sober. For example, that ill-fated rope ladder came up again—damn it! I had to expend great effort to turn him from his fruitless and base idea. What did the ladder have to do with anything? "The ladder will decide a lot," he said on a wave of inspiration. "First of all, it's the easiest. The important thing is to catch hold of it at the top—getting up and climbing down are simple. Secondly, it's expedient—you don't have to wait for favorable circumstances. And finally—" I confused him by asking what he intended to do, once he had climbed up that ladder and finally saw the other man's wife leaning out the window. He became depressed. We rejected the ladder. We rejected other nonsensical plans that came along. The only thing left to do was wait for the ball at the Anichkov Palace so that there, by dint of certain ruses, he could try to talk with our prisoner. I took this upon myself. I said, "I'll bring Ladimirovsky together with Fredericks on some economic issue, and meanwhile you and she—"

Here his imagination flared up again, but with less confidence. He offered to be my driver. We would—that is, he would—while his "master" was frolicking inside, he would get the Ladimirovsky coachman drunk, and then I would offer my carriage to the distressed Ladimirovskys, and charm the gloomy monster en route, and receive an invitation to their home.

He didn't know what would happen then.

Meanwhile, rattling her spoon in a blue cup and nodding agreeably to Mr. Ladimirovsky's peace-making table chatter, Lavinia was making her own plans to reach that beckoning shore. At first, as usually happens, she built a fantastic raft to get there, and then finally a light and usable one . . . *In the home of an unknown and secret confidante, or female friend, or distant relative, mute benefactress, in a room without windows, the elegant, impetuous figure of the prince rises toward her from his armchair. Somewhere in the distance, monotonously and almost constantly, there is the ring of a clock, or of crystal, or of bells, and she manages to say the most important thing to her precious friend in those pitiful moments of stolen freedom—"Long live freedom!"*. . .

"I'm a pathetic man," Mr. Ladimirovsky joked and complained in a whisper so as not to disturb the evening quiet. "I'm racking my brains to make you happy, to keep you from being bored, but I can't come up with anything. I see that you are bored." She smiled nobly and rather aloofly. "We could go abroad, perhaps. Would you like that?" She shrugged. . . . *Or at the ball at the Anichkov Palace she secretes herself behind a column and then races down especially empty passages, corridors, and stairs (she had never been at the Anichkov, so it was easy for her to imagine all the convenient routes), hearing the happy and anxious patter of her own heels, races to the one private spot where no one ever goes, races and can see from a distance Myatlev's silent shadow lurch in her direction and freeze . . .* Mr. Ladimirovsky noted a fleeting happiness on her face and thought that they really must go abroad, as soon as possible!

"Yes, yes," he added quickly, "you'll like it there, the climate is gentle, for instance, in Italy, and there's the blue sea . . ." *She nodded, picturing how she makes her way back down the same rambling corridors and quickly returns in time for the cotillion, and how this same man who is sitting opposite her extends his hand to her, and they . . .*"In Venice, for instance, there are canals. I've been there. I've told you about it. You enter a completely different world."

She abandoned her fantasy and looked him in the eyes, thinking that she was not committing any sin because the strange and marvelous disease she had was incurable and that Venice was just nonsense—but so were the corridors of the Anichkov Palace. It had to be done this way: she would simply visit the Tolstoys, or the Volfs, the Baryatinskys, or the Goncharovs, and then, as planned, she would accidentally run into Myatlev—yes, it was just that simple, and all those fantasies and complications were demeaning. Everything had to be done simply and naturally. She wasn't the first, and she wouldn't be the last.

And so that was what she was thinking, enjoying her discovery, without a suspicion of the monologue Madame Tuchkova had delivered to Mr. Ladimirovsky before his peace-making tea.

"You must appreciate the complexity of your situation and understand my trust in you. Listen carefully. In my youth I was untamable, willful, and even sneaky. Lavinia is my daughter. All her exceptional qualities, which allowed me to agree to your proposal without fearing that she might compromise you, all her qualities notwithstanding, she is willful, too. What can you do, it's her nature. It reveals itself rarely and abruptly. From time to time she needs a chain, which I've put on her." She laughed. "If she gets it into her head to do something—well, something, you know—don't be fooled by her modest and quiet ways. Remember that there is a flame glimmering within her. We Bravuras— And therefore, don't get too involved in your wonderful work. I can see that you are saddened, but don't be. This will pass in a year or two." She laughed. "And she will be so devoted and docile, you will find her boring. It all depends on you, for what can I do? I'm nothing now. I'm smoke, a mirage, the past, her childhood. You are her god now, but until some things are finished, you should not see her as a completely mature woman. She is still a child—she still, unfortunately, is guided by her heart and not her mind. That, as you know, is touching but uncertain, and while it will soon pass, you must—you should— well—don't make a fool of yourself, my dear." She laughed again, amazing her son-in-law for the nth time with her radiance, divinity, beauty, and contemporary spirit.

And then, bussing her daughter's perfumed brow, she left; and that was good, because at evening tea and alone, if you didn't count the empty presence of Mr. Ladimirovsky, it was easier to plan the coming meeting, to measure a bridge, construct a raft, run down nonexistent corridors of the palace, hide at her nonexistent confidante's, and finally, then, laughing at all this childish nonsense, pick the only possible path and concentrate on it.

"I don't spend enough time with you," Mr. Ladimirovsky whispered. "But all my work is for you—for you and your happiness—that's whom I do it for. And in a year, say, we'll be able to move from here closer to the center of town, to Million-naya Street or even Morskaya. I've seen a house with a large garden, the way you like, and they also have—" She smiled at him; when he wasn't grabbing her elbow with the intensity of a mortally wounded man and with a contorted face, he was quite tolerable and even pleasant. "And still, it is important for you to realize that you are completely grown-up now and that you are no longer under your mother's eye and that you are in charge. Your mother, I've noticed, seems to curry favor with you in some matters."

That naive encouragment didn't inspire delight in Lavinia. "We Bravuras," she could have said, "have never curried favor with anyone." But she didn't say it, for just then she realized what she had to do.

"Does Venice have a Police Bridge?" she asked, glowing.

"Why a Police Bridge, of all things?" he laughed, secretly suspecting that the non sequitur could be hiding the usual mockery for a man she didn't love, and that he would have to become angry again or even stamp his foot to nip it in the bud.

"I'm going to my room," she said, rising. "I have a headache."

"Is that flame her mother hinted at spreading?" he thought, watching her leave quickly and gracefully, not like the last few times.

I know your situation and possibilities. All our plans to meet in the next few days are too unrealistic. Let's not endanger our longtime friendship. I suppose that the only thing is to wait for the ball at Anichkov. I'll find a way of talking with you there. I trust you are as courageous as always. Of course, two weeks of waiting can bring on despair, but you and I, tempered by waiting and worse, will be firm.

Unable to think of anything and truly ready to fall into despair, we sat up until late at night, and Myatlev, in order to justify his forced inactivity somehow and to soothe his rampaging conscience, wrote his letter without any idea of how he would get to talk to Lavinia at the ball. His own reputation didn't bother him. The opinion of society, convinced of his sins and incorrigibility, had stopped bothering him a long time ago, but he was afraid to approach Lavinia in front of the world. Even the slightest hint that they might be acquainted could do her a disservice and bring on God only knew what kind of consequences. He had to begin everything from scratch; there was no past at all, and the future didn't peek through the stormy autumnal fog.

But still you should have seen my friend. Could you have believed a week ago, looking at that depressed and wary man, that he could be thus transformed? And where did he find the strength? The fire was raging within him and never showed—not in his gestures, not in his voice, not in his gait—but everything around him had changed: Afanasy, as sober as a judge, hurried to perform his slightest wish at the mere wave of his hand; the spy disappeared somewhere; the lackeys cleaned their feathers (they must have bathed). Aglaya put on a new blue poplin dress, down which streamed her thick red braid. Everything was swept, cleaned, and ennobled by a human touch. The past was forgiven and forgotten. I was overjoyed seeing it all. It even looked as though Myatlev was composing again, and that paradise had descended upon that damned house, dissolving the salt of disillusionment and ennui.

To this day I can't understand how his hidden fire was transmitted to others. But I swear it was.

Sing on, heavenly pipes, all-penetrating, proud. It's sad that your melodies cannot be heard and a pity that they're so short.

I spent the night at Myatlev's. My bed was marvelous—fresh and airy. We couldn't fall asleep, even though we were exhausted, and we spent some more time building ineffectual craft to get us to Mr. van Schoenhoven's shore, each sillier than the last. Finally it grew quiet. We were too tired to talk. My lids began to shut. The familiar ghost in the attic broke another beam. The old nails crept out of their places. But it was all beyond our ken and sounded like a lullaby.

The following morning did not bring us comfort; on the

contrary, the light made our plans seem unrealizable; the ideas that had seemed quite practical in the middle of the night looked like the most ridiculous nonsense. We couldn't even believe that two grown men could have fooled themselves that much, inventing such stuff.

And to top things off, it was pouring rain. The dead leaves fell more thickly. Despair reigned in nature and extended to people. And only Myatlev, who had gained some color while he slept, greeted the morning the way one finally greets the shores of the Promised Land.

But dark forces continued their work. Everything that was meant to perish rushed inexorably toward that end, everything that was doomed to despair awaited that hour with angelic patience. The emboldened ghost no longer confined its perambulations to nighttime but continued its ravages during the day, and we could hear its screeches, and the crash of falling rafters, and the scrape of the nails. And Afanasy, in a gray frock coat pulled on over his bare chest, barefoot and aged, begged us to give him a pistol to shoot "that damned monster."

Apparently, something was about to happen, if not today then tomorrow; something had to burst free; the festering wound had to open.

And only Myatlev was energetic and blinder than ever—ohmygod!—and his light hand raced along the page of his diary like a jumping puppet at the fair.

I feel I'm clairvoyant. I foresee everything that is happening. I've never known my senses to be so acute. It is sunny in Moscow, and that's not hard to guess. Von Müffling is drinking brine for his hangover and hiding the mug behind his books. Mr. Kolesnikov is mechanically rubbing his sleeping wife's back and going over his meeting with Dubelt again. Only Lavinia escapes my vibrations. I can't remember her face. I don't understand how all this happened—everything that has been happening to me. And compared with it, everything else is so meaningless: the autumn, von Müffling, the Hobbler's sufferings, the government, Asia,

Africa, the price of salt, even ships, even my own future, and certainly my past.

This slipped out from under his pen; the pen broke, and a big inky spider spread over the paper; the door opened, and Afanasy, bugging his eyes desperately, whispered hoarsely and in terror,

"You have visitors."

I realized that I would be needed, for something very serious was brewing. I was prepared for the worst, and from the way that I stood and tightened the belt of my uniform, Myatlev guessed what was happening.

"Send them all," he said merrily, "to Hell."

"Impossible," Afanasy whispered. "There's a lady—"

Sing on, pipes. It's said that your melodies cannot be heard, and it's a pity that they're not eternal.

There was silence. Myatlev waved his hand, as if catching a mosquito. Afanasy silently flew out of the room and disappeared so quietly that not one of the rotten floorboards creaked underfoot. Then the door flew open, and a young woman entered, throwing us into panic and delight.

I had known her as a child.

If the incomparable Gainsborough were alive, he naturally would not portray this lady among the strange blue mountains of Palestine, overgrown with thin scrub and flat fig trees, from behind which peer out sleek, languorous lionesses with heavy equine croups and tongues resembling crooked sabers and eyes that belong to Babylonian captives; he wouldn't have recourse to a medieval landscape, either: a shard of a blue lake and a fluffy forest touched with a lavender haze—the sanctuary of saints and beggars—an ancient castle, reminiscent of the craftsman's heavy boot, an exquisite doe that does not exist in nature but is nevertheless alive and stretching her thick lips to nibble at a calico leaf; and he wouldn't waste time searching for bright colors, good only for painting a roast beef or a southern sea as glimpsed by a native Eskimo. No, with his innate tact he would spend a long time mixing black, red, blue, and white, until the canvas would be covered with the delicious twilight of late September, with the barely palpable reflections of the crimson, gold, and straw-colored leaves floating off into the distance; and then he would paint her portrait, and she would be standing in the half-darkness of a still room, as though in the half-darkness of an English park.

I personally prefer the less perfect portraits by Rokotov or Levitsky, and that's how I see her, peering out from these imperfections, suddenly, like the sun emerging from the clouds, the familiar, wary, mysterious young face slightly aloof (just enough to keep from seeming funny), suffused with kindness, the face of some inhabitant of our sad earth from yesterday, yester-year, a recent or a long-ago Lyubushka, or Sashenka, or Verochka, or Annushka, or Katenka, who loved, believed, wait-ed, who was proud of some new lace cap or the attentions of some young fop, and who thought that she was immortal.

And so she paused on the threshold, and I have neither the power nor the words to describe her and how she stood there.

Beauty is a simpering artificial word—I think I've mentioned that already—touch it and it falls apart. And I don't want to imitate our contemporary fine writers, who use the word both where it's appropriate and where it's not. I've seen beautiful women in my day—God grant them every happiness. But as for the lady who entered the room, the word "beauty" had no application there at all—she was not beautiful.

She was wearing a black, sodden mantilla of bizarre cut, with a hood pulled almost over her eyes. Her face had nothing extraordinary about it—just a young face with high cheekbones. There was almost nothing left of Mr. van Schoenhoven, for hardworking, inexorable nature had changed everything, spar-ing perhaps only the gray, wide-set, deep, and too attentive eyes under their dark and not very neat brows and the boyish, stubborn, chapped lips, not very highly valued by connoisseurs of female beauty. The rest belonged to a lady who had already, as they say, drunk from the cup of life. Of course, her sip had been a small one, but the bitter drink had rinsed her soul and probably made her shudder.

And yet there was something about her—I swear it, gentlemen—something that rooted you to the spot, making you gasp, clapping your hands in awe or jumping up like a high-school boy, arms at your sides. She was slender, even thin, and not too tall; when her cape gaped open, the touching bones at the neckline of her gray daytime dress and her long smooth throat could be seen; when she moved her arms, the cape caught on her sharp elbows. I've seen beautiful women, Lord bless them, but this was something quite different.

I return to the incomparable Gainsborough. When you stop say, before, his portrait of Mrs. Graham, it is not the ornamental column to your right or the heavy cascading folds of her satin dress that capture your attention. And certainly it's not the trees in the distance behind her that attract your agitated eye. You gaze directly at her face with an unfamiliar longing—yes, with longing and delight. You are amazed by her proud small head, her pouting lips, and her majesty, and her total dissimilarity to the women you know, and her inaccessibility, for you know that staring beyond you into distances known only to her, she could turn her face to you and would still remain the same, intended for another world, another love.

But I'm not telling you all this to stress the external resemblance between the charming Englishwoman who lived a century ago and the former Mr. van Schoenhoven—Heaven forbid. I just want to say that, while not resembling each other at all—the Englishwoman is obviously rounded in face and body—these two women had something in common.

I will permit myself one more comparison, delving now into the seventeenth century. When Jan Vermeer was painting the head of a girl, certainly no beauty, half turned to us, with a white collar and a gaze filled with sorrow and reproach, and perhaps even condemnation, which you naturally take personally, since it is so masterfully done, when that Dutchman was painting that girl's head, he did not imagine that a century later

283

a beauty unknown to him and not resembling his girl would pause in some marvelous spot on a foggy bank in Albion, and that another century later, in Petersburg, the former Mr. van Schoenhoven would make me want to connect all of them with an invisible thread. Of course, he didn't imagine it, but the thread exists, gentlemen, and I can summon many more examples if you are tormented by doubt for I can see how that silent reproach, cold inaccessibility, bitterness and triumph, weakness and abandon and love all blend into one throughout the centuries.

And she stood before us, a mysterious Carmelite of royal blood who had decided to break her vow and defile herself by assuming the person of a simple secular woman. But to each his own, though one cannot speak of free will when everything—every gesture, every step, every breath—everything hung on the hair of fate, and that hair was thin and insecure.

When she had rejected all the ways of seeing Myatlev, despair (despair, note, and not caprice) told her the simplest and last way. Mr. van Schoenhoven's courageous heart did not skip a beat, and in the morning, as soon as the trotters had carried the councillor of state away to his office, she grabbed the black mantilla as she used to take the old embroidered jacket, slipped out after him, and hailed a cab.

They ran after her—she could hear footsteps and heavy breathing, entreaties and moans—but the driver, luckily, was a good one. It was pouring. It looked as though there was no going back.

And she stood before us.

54

September 1850

And she stood before us!

What had happened? It turned out that there never was a Mr. van Schoenhoven. But I had known this young woman all my life, and all my life I had longed for her, and all my unhappiness had been caused by our forced separation. I think she was saying something in a strange, low, drawling voice, but at first I couldn't understand a thing; I don't remember, but her voice comforted me, I could feel that. And I tried saying something to her—I think something like "Don't worry" or "You're completely safe here"—and I think I tried to help her off with her wet mantilla. Then she told me she was here only for a minute or two, to see me, to hear me, to make sure . . .

Amilakhvari tiptoed out and shut the door. I swear, I couldn't see her at first; I only guessed that she was here, nearby. I think I asked her to sit down, and it was only by a vague change in the light, by a movement in the air, that I guessed that she had perched on the edge of the chair; and I managed to say once more, "You're completely safe here."

How strange: total darkness, as though you are falling endlessly into a dark well and you sense the nearness of the stone walls by their gravelike chill, but you know, you're certain, that you can't be hurtled against them and that there is no bottom and that this painless, safe descent will continue forever, and you lose your breath, and it's terrifying and wonderful.

And suddenly I heard clearly: "Do you hear me?"

The well ended, and light exploded before me.

She was sitting on the edge of the chair in a gray foulard dress, a thin fist pressed to her chest, and looking at me closely and in puzzlement.

"—and that was the only way," she said, "that I could think of. Do you hear me?"

Then their conversation became smoother, purposeful, and strangely businesslike and even calculating. Whether it was the lack of time or the weather, I don't know. Sometimes they would forget themselves and, like sleepwalkers, staring at each other, they would try to discourse with gestures, sighs, and silence. They discussed their unenviable lot, two little people thrown at each other not by personal whim or lust, but by fate, and it's not a good idea to joke with fate.

... Two carriages set out at the same time from points A and B and moved at different speeds toward each other. In the first carriage, drawn by a pair, was a man wearing a dark coat and a gray fuzzy hat; he was freshly shaved, no longer young, and spectacles adorned his long face. In the second carriage, drawn by four horses, sat a woman. She was young, beautiful, and her traveling hat had been blown away by the wind, so that her luxuriant dark chestnut hair was revealed, parted in the middle and pulled back smoothly. The first carriage traveled at the rate of nine miles per hour and the other at twelve. At the point where they would have met, both carriages overturned, due to the error of the road inspector who had failed to have a bridge that had collapsed repaired in time. The coachmen died, carried away by the current. In an open field, far from any villages, the passengers met—the man and woman, previously unacquainted, or so it seemed at first glance. The question is: Where did they meet if the entire distance traversed equaled 120 miles, and what was the subsequent fate of the inspector? ...

Lavinia laughed sadly.

"I'll save you; don't give up hope," Myatlev said.

"Please don't rescue me," she asked, "just don't turn me away, and everything else will follow. You'll have every opportunity to be convinced of how wonderful and fantastic I am. I tried for many years to show you that, but you were unmoved." And she wept.

"Don't cry, Lavinia," he said, "we should—"

"Yes," she said, "but what, what?"

I was allowed to return. We were sitting in a row, and the damned time flew.

"A den of conspirators," Myatlev said.

"Believe me," Lavinia drawled, "this is the most noble plot ever conspired."

. . . The carriage was moving from point A to point B. The new road inspector was very diligent and fast-working, and all the intersections and bridges were in excellent shape. There were two people in the carriage: a not-young man in spectacles with a long, astounded face and a pistol under his coat, and a young beauty who had stepped from a canvas by the incomparable Gainsborough. She was afraid of nothing. The carriage was moving at great speed and reached the mountain pass in less than a week. The question is: What is the name of point B if the distance to it is 1,320 miles, and whom do you have to be not to take advantage of such a marvelous excuse for a journey? . . .

Lavinia was no longer laughing. She didn't take her eyes off Myatlev.

"This is probably the only realistic thing to do in our position," he said sadly.

A long silence ensued.

"Where did you turn up the call of horns, the half-darkness, and so on?" Myatlev asked unexpectedly. "You wrote that in your letter. Did you invent it?"

"It's from Nekrasov," Lavinia said, and grew frightened at the change in his face.

"Could it be this: 'Remember the horn's mournful call, the splatter of rain. . . .' "

"Yes, yes," she said in amazement.

Poor Mr. Kolesnikov! If he only knew how poor Mr. Nekrasov had tormented Myatlev! What powers that crusading poet with the thinning hair, penetrating gaze, and gaunt face must have had if the horns he heard pursued Myatlev like fate!

Suddenly she rose abruptly, and we helped her on with her

287

cape. Afanasy ran for a coach. We went downstairs in a sad, muted file, and red-haired Aglaya studied the unexpected guest over a centaur's shoulder.

October

A wondrous idea! Aneta Fredericks—that's who can help me. I sent her a note today. There'll be an answer tomorrow, and we'll meet. My idea may be unwieldly, but it's not fantastic. If she, a competent, sober lioness, takes Mr. van Schoenhoven under her protection, we could never find a better way to meet.

At first I was ignited by Amiran's suggestion. I almost turned my soul inside out. But there are so many "ifs" in the plan, as many as there are guards in a prison, and at least you can bribe guards, but the "ifs" are implacable. If Lavinia weren't married, and if her *maman* adored me, and if the fearless Mr. van Schoenhoven agreed to travel to Georgia with me, and if I could tear myself away from the stale comfortable pillows of my house . . .

No, that's just a delicious dream, not worth my attention or, actually, worth thinking about just before falling asleep. And yet I went down and bought some excellent guides to the Caucasus so that I could envy the lucky ones fate smiles upon.

October

It's been a week, and still no word from Aneta. Amilakhvari assures me that she's in Bavaria. What the hell does she need in Bavaria! Time is passing, and Lavinia and I are not meeting. Of course, I won't be able to get near her at the ball because my name is anathema at their house.

I myself destroy everything that Providence constructs so painstakingly. Some demon whispers in my ear, and, instead of dying as far as everyone is concerned, just dropping through a hole, so that there is no more talk, I rush into the witch's house with the brazenness of a boy, purchase a worthless painting of the martyred Sapega, and pretend that I don't know her. . . . Why? And what if in the middle of the ball, standing there with my silly hopes, that same demon forces me to declare myself, shout nonsense, grab Lavinia by the hand, slap Mr.

288

Ladimirovsky (for what?), and tear the so fragile thread? . . .

I ought to become a flattering Jesuit, a cold-blooded adventurer, exuding compliments and promising incalculable good to anyone who calls me his own. I must prove to them all that I am as harmless as a lamb, as obedient as a dog, and as dependent as a slave, and then put on my uniform, get rid of Mr. Ladimirovsky with hired help, get in good with the witch, get her to beg me to save Lavinia, and then, grabbing Mr. van Schoenhoven, lock ourselves up evenings in my fortress (first having it repaired and installing a new fence), and then with that slender, exquisite, long-awaited goddess I'll laugh at them to my heart's content and stick my tongue out at them.

And it was fruitless of me to try to depict her looks by referring to the work of famous masters so as to make them a little clearer to you. For it was Alexandrina who stood before us! Those were her eyes staring at Myatlev, and her voice, low and drawling, sounding like distant music, and it was her thin fist pressed against her chest, as though in self-defense.

55

THE TINY HOPE OF seeing Lavinia alone, without witnesses, crumbled at the October ball. Her husband was always by her side. Myatlev moved in wide circles like a wandering star. He would come so close to the forbidden couple that he could make out the crimson roses on Lavinia's white dress and Mr. Ladimirovsky's bristly round head, and then he would move so far away that the young woman turned into a small white spot like a sail on the horizon threatening never to return. People stared at Myatlev with poorly disguised curiosity and surprise. And only Aneta Fredericks, not giving in to the influence of the times, nodded at him joyously, like a sister. "What luck," he thought, "she's here!" And he made his way behind the Frederickses to the half-empty sitting room. His appearance at the ball, it turned out, gave them great pleasure. "You can't even imagine how pleased we are to see you."

"What made you give up your usual seclusion?" the baron asked. "I think you did the right thing—long overdue."

"I've missed you," Aneta confessed. "You haven't changed— as though we had seen each other just yesterday."

"Just yesterday," the baron seconded with unfeigned awe.

At first Myatlev didn't know how to talk with them, but the old, red-haired gentleman-in-waiting went off somewhere, and Aneta said to him kindly and confidingly, "Dear Seryozhenka, let's agree on this: there was never anything between us—all right? You were very young then. It was a long time ago. Now you are no longer young and have had plenty of time to think about the meaning of life. Do you remember what I wrote to you once? That I make a better friend than mistress? Remember? It's the truth. In that sea of gapers you are probably the only one I can deal with without pretense. But don't be proud of that; just value it—all right? Does that console you?"

"Completely," Myatlev laughed. "You have consoled me. I'm delighted by you."

The white sail sprinkled with white roses flashed by at a great distance. Flashed by and disappeared.

"Do you know young Ladimirovskaya? She's lovely, isn't she?"

"No," Myatlev said in fear. "No, I don't know her. Why?"

"Ah, just a bit of gossip," Aneta said professionally. "The tsar noticed her, and immediately after that—and no one missed this—Count Alexei Fyodorovich danced with the young seductress—"

"It must have happened before I got here," Myatlev said, and blushed.

"—And do you know what the count says in such situations?"

"No," said Myatlev, hopelessly trying to appear indifferent, "but I can guess." ("I guess my letter was lost," he thought.)

"Precisely," Aneta laughed. "Oh, nothing improper—on the

290

contrary—but very persistent! Oh—"

"It can't be," thought Myatlev, "not again!" And he thought that the world was emptied of people and that he in his helpless spectacles stood at the edge of a chasm and HE was there on the other side in his Izmailovsky Regiment uniform, and there was no one else, just the two of them in the whole world, and it was time for the last duel. "I won't let him have this one—"

"Aneta," he said in an uneven whisper, "I need your help." And he told her everything.

"Poor Seryozhenka," she said sympathetically. "Ah, you faker. I'll try to do something, I hope I'll succeed. But I must comfort you: the Ladimirovskys are gone, which means that Count Alexei Fyodorovich was not convincing enough. You can believe that. But it doesn't mean that the enticing offer won't be repeated."

Myatlev blushed again. His thoughts were rambling.

"I must stop this," he said in an unexpectedly thin voice, gasping. "No one else can—it's up to me." And he left Aneta. Lavinia was nowhere to be seen, and that cooled him off slightly. He returned to the ballroom. All the people seemed steeped in a milky fog, including Nicholas, squeezed into a tight uniform and chatting matter-of-factly with an overdressed ambassador.

Suddenly someone next to Myatlev said in a slimy bass, "Just think, the Ladimirovskaya beauty could have been more compliant."

A tall Horse Guards' officer whom he didn't know was talking with his friends, and he was planning to continue, but all he did was gasp as Myatlev's elbow jabbed him in the side.

"Prince," the officer managed to get out, "what's the matter with you?"

"You stepped on my foot, sir," Myatlev said calmly, bowing slightly.

"Perhaps you did not like what I said about Madame Ladimirovskaya?"

"I do not know the lady."

"Then accept my apologies!" the officer said angrily.

"I do not."

The next morning the very duel took place with which I began my memoirs.

Days passed. Rumor had it that the Ladimirovskys had left Petersburg. However, Myatlev, racing down Znamenskaya Street at a mad speed, saw the famous trotters in front of the house and the councillor of state himself climbing out of the carriage. He was worried by Lavinia's silence and particularly by Aneta's, but Baroness Fredericks had not forgotten her promise. In November he received from her a scented letter in a blue envelope.

Dear Seryozhenka, pay attention to what I'm hurrying to tell you, even if it's been somewhat delayed. I was away, and our business was therefore held up a bit, but I have managed to begin a relationship with your charming Pole, and it turned out to be much simpler than I had expected. Let that console you. The couple have been to our house several times. Even though my baron makes a face whenever he sees that possessor of innumerable head of cattle, he bears up well. He knows everything and out of love for me and respect for you (and old friendship!) he is prepared to tolerate him as much as necessary. Your L. behaves marvelously, and I'm making her my protégée not only out of sympathy for you (believe me) but because I like her. So, she carries herself marvelously, and her husband, poor fool, plays up to the baron, which is very obvious.

Now to the important thing. Your beloved is coming to visit me in the morning, and alone! I managed to extract the promise from the owner of the trotters. He wasn't too pleased with the idea, but he didn't dare argue with me. "Why shouldn't she come visit us?" my baron said. "Women need to whisper together once in a while." "I have nothing against it," the husband replied with a sour smile. "To visit you is a great honor." We settled on Thursday at eleven. I hope that you are well and can come whisper, too.

How should it be done! You should come earlier, at least a half hour. That's important. And another thing: I'm not ruling out the possibility that our landowner in Byelorussia (to judge by his sour agreement to let his wife out alone) will send a valet or maid with her on some handy pretext or, even worse, have one of his shepherds watch the house. I don't like to think ill of people, but love, as you know, is more serious than politics, and it never hurts to be prepared for anything. Otherwise, imagine how it will look! You drive up undaunted to the house, and everything is exposed! Therefore, my dear friend, don't come from Italyanskaya Street, whatever you do. Leave your carriage on Nevsky Prospect and walk along Sadovaya until you get to the freshly painted red gate. Someone will be waiting for you there. And one more thing: you are mistaken in worrying about Lavinia. In total contrast to you, she is calm, determined (particularly when she became sure of my concern), and, most important, loves you deeply, and that's better than solid fists, a deep voice, or high rank.

Myatlev was inspired by her letter.

56

I can't stand it anymore. And here, with a chill in my neck, I had to lie in bed at home with compresses and in great pain, and even on my bed of pain I heard about the terrible things which that man is up to and which certainly didn't help me get well any faster.

Perhaps he's a French spy—that's why he finds everything here so repugnant. Just judge for yourself what his outward appearance alone says about him, not to mention his actions, and the women he's destroyed so easily who could have been ideal mothers in other hands.

A True Patriot Since Childhood.

[From an anonymous letter to the court minister]

Interlude

"As for ladimirovskaya," said Alexei Fyodorovich Orlov, "she's simply too young to figure all this out. You only saw her at a distance, but I was right next to her. Of course, she is adorable, but there's something of a baby chick about her, without her full strength yet. The feathers are normal, but the arms, scrawny neck, the expression of her face—well, she's just—"

"Nonsense," Nicholas I interrupted, "have you nothing else to talk about? I don't even remember her. Just five pounds of crinoline and other foolishness. But you, Count, you were disturbed by her willfulness, admit it, I could see." He laughed. "On the other hand, what would have happened to her? I wasn't going to swallow her whole. You muffed it."

"In a year or two she may pass them all. She'll be a new star."

"In a year or two where will we be, Count?" Nicholas was silent for a while and then said, "It was mishandled."

This was a pleasant break in their business, even though Nicholas had had a feeling since early morning, an unpleasant feeling, whose cause he couldn't understand.

They were sitting alone in the emperor's study. The count, in uniform and full regalia, was seated on the edge of a raspberry armchair, and Nicholas sat on his camp bed, which was covered with a gray soldier's blanket, wearing his Simeon Regiment uniform without epaulets. The study was small, with only two windows—one opened on the courtyard, and the other on the embankment—and it was narrow, and so the iron bed placed crosswise added some width to the room. Early evening showed through the windows. One of them was slightly open, and Count Orlov was conscious of a draft on his side, but he did not let on because he knew that the tsar would say, "Stop babying your-self!" And so, to avoid hearing those words, he said nothing and covertly and futilely tried to cover his side with the palm of his hand.

"By the way," said Nicholas, "that Ladimirovskaya must be brought closer to court. These proud young things have a good effect on society. They naturally irritate our old foolish women, but they ennoble them, too, and it wouldn't hurt them to think about their morality, either, and she is a worthy example for them all."

"Of course, sire," Alexei Fyodorovich agreed. "You and I are at the age when we must worry about that as well." He noted the smile on Nicholas's face with pleasure. "In the old days—say, ten years ago—I could easily chat with a young girl about a certain subject, but now, I swear, I break out in a cold sweat."

Their friendship went back many years, and there were affairs that they remembered and that they had forgotten, and they were able to understand each other without words or with just a few hints, particularly when it came to women. Of course, Alexei Fyodorovich always played Cupid in these affairs and was very adept at shooting arrows into the hearts of the chosen victims. Occasionally it would happen that the arrows were returned—some victim would not appreciate the attentions of the tsar. To his honor, I must add, he never became angry the way most men would, but, on the contrary, was even engulfed in surprised delight when a lady did manage to prefer her own husband to the seductive interest of the sovereign, and he would say to the count, "She certainly let me have it. What a villainness!" And he would laugh.

Everything was going well, except for a few misfirings, without which, by the way, no one has ever managed to function. Everything was going well, and yet something had been bothering him since morning without giving him any rest. It was as if a runner appeared at the height of some festivity and waited, silent and unobtrusive, at a respectful distance for an opportunity to bring fateful news.

"Well, all right," said the emperor, "all cats can't live in a dairy. What else do we have?"

The next item on the agenda was secret external affairs. The count relayed the reports of scouts and secret agents all over the world. All the reports were comforting, and they all confirmed the emporor's initial suppositions.

"You sent for aides-de-camp Istomin and Isakov earlier to give them a briefing before their departure," Orlov said. "They're waiting."

"Get them," said Nicholas, and stood up abruptly.

The young aides-de-camp came in together in full dress, bowed simultaneously, and stood at attention.

"Forgive me, friends, for catching you unawares," he said to the young men, "but your mission, as you know, is highly secret, and no one must be able to guess your deadlines or time limits. And now it's time. You leave immediately. You'll be in Constantinople within the week. Your mission, as the Turks must be made to understand, is a friendly one. You report to General Grabbe. He will be giving banquets and balls, and you, you take care that you don't lose your heads. The most important thing is your work, and your work is this: you"—he turned to Istomin—"will study the Turkish fleet, when General Grabbe can arrange it, and determine its capabilities and what the Turks have prepared for in the way of war at sea, as well as the reinforcements on the Bosporus and landing sites on the Black Sea. And you," he said to Isakov, "will do the same in regard to their ground forces. Be alert. If they start to talk about Moldavia and Wallachia and the threat of our troops there, tell them that the tsar as the center of power answers for everything himself and that you make no decisions. Behave as modestly and cautiously as possible, so as not to arouse any suspicion. That's all. Farewell and Godspeed." And he embraced and kissed each of the officers and sent them off, calling after them, "Watch out that you don't fall in love with Turkish women. They say they're beautiful."

Things were going well. They were all working hard, all his subjects, loyal to him to the grave; they did their duty with exemplary exactitude, and those who were living under false names in foreign countries, the chameleons, the heroes, those wonderful darlings were also ready at any moment to risk their lives for duty. Things were going well everywhere. Everywhere that the state needed them, the troops were victorious—in Transylvania, and the mountains of Dagestan, and Moldavia. Everything functioned like a well-oiled machine, if you didn't count the small bunch of sick and weak malcontents who were mired in their personal caprices, defective personalities who thought themselves exceptional when they were actually nonentities, pathetic egotists, useless, good only to serve as laughingstocks, like Myatlev, the memory of whom filled the tsar's soul with bitterness, grief, and regret.

"By the way, what's Myatlev up to?" Nicholas asked unexpectedly. "What has he been doing since his wife's death? Preparing for his next scandal?"

"He seems to be living quietly," said the chief of the political police. "And you shouldn't worry about him—he's old, his time has passed, perhaps he'll fool around with a chambermaid or two—"

"I suppose so," the emperor agreed.

It was all going well. The mechanism he had created was functioning perfectly. All its parts had been thought out and planned and handpicked; the atmosphere of the empire was clean and fresh; his children had grown up and looked at him with delight. But in that case, what was it that he couldn't shake, what had been bothering him all day, like a dangerous disease that hadn't yet revealed its symptoms but was already sending signals of anxiety and irritation to the brain? Poland? But the Polish business was just one more difficulty without which history does not exist; and besides, difficulties didn't depress him, they moved him to action. The Myatlevs? But could they possibly have any meaning in such a huge state? Then what was it? What? Could it be the letter to Paris, sent from the French Embassy, which had been cleverly intercepted and copied and handed to him this morning, and which contained among all the diplomatic nonsense those vile lines that had so stung him? Could it be the letter? Could it be those lines that called the mighty state he had created nothing more than a colossus with feet of clay, in which some vicious, unpunished liar and coward called the army a motley and ineffective mob led by nonentities, and said that the habits of Genghis Khan's days still reigned, and that bribery, bootlicking, and thievery were rampant, and that the self-flattery of Russia's leaders bordered on insanity? What a bastard! Nicholas pictured that pen pusher and liar, besmirched with ink, trembling with vile passion, a small, puny man with a red nose and sneaky, beady eyes, heavily powdered to cover up his festering pimples.

"What a bastard!" he said to the count. "Where did he come up with all that?"

"I pay no attention to lies," said the count.

"Maybe it's all true?" the emperor asked, fixing his big blue unblinking eyes on Orlov. And he laughed. "You can go. I thank you."

The old lion scurried out of the study like a fox. Nicholas waited a few minutes and, buttoning his uniform, left, too. The unpleasant feeling had not left him, but he knew how to pull himself together. He walked down the hall, one hand inside the front of his jacket, duty and will incarnate, and the tall sentries at their posts followed him with burning eyes.

57

HE DREAMED OF THE red gate and the snow-covered path, the lantern in the trembling hand of the silent valet, the quiet, unused entry on the side of the backyard, the smells of the leftovers from the masters' dinner, the sheepskin coats and bast shoes, the resonant, empty yellow back hall. The strange sensation of being in Aneta's house, in a part of it where her tactful shadow doesn't flicker, doesn't remind you of her existence. The yellow hallway, steps up (one, two), the polished parquet, the fig trees, a different world now, one turn, another, the receding figure of the valet with the now-superfluous lantern, and the easily opening door, and Lavinia, abruptly rising to greet him. The day before yesterday, yesterday, today. And it was always the same—a light, barely perceptible sense of guilt and persecution, guilt toward no one nor for any reason in particular, but all-pervasive: in the air, in their hurried dialogue, in the candle flames, in the rustle of her dress. And always the same thing: "I was lucky today—Mr. Ladimirovsky was leaving for his club and told me that if I was planning to go to the Frederickses', I should not dare, as I did last time, to leave the house without my furs and catch cold. I had to lie and say that I didn't feel like going and that I probably wouldn't go, even though I was dying to come, and that it wasn't polite to come so frequently—the second time this week—and so on. I've discovered that stealing is easy and shameless. The first time is hard, and then you don't even have to think about it."

Or: "No luck today. Mr. Ladimirovsky let me go reluctantly, and I even felt sorry for him and said that I would not go—it's no great joy, I was getting a little bored by it, and it was more important for him to be happy. He looked at me as if I were mad—you should have seen him—he probably doubted my sincerity, he probably even thought there was something going on, but then he tossed back his head proudly and laughed. And it wasn't very hard for me then to steal what belonged to me, isn't that right?"

Or: "No luck today. *Maman* decided to visit us, to lecture me, as usual, on my coldness. 'You, Lavinia, are sawing the branch you're sitting on.' '*Maman*, it's you who are sawing the branch I'm sitting on.' 'We Bravuras always amazed our chosen men with passionate hearts and fierce fidelity.' 'And we Ladimirovskys,' I said, 'amaze our chosen men with passionate hearts and fierce fidelity, the *chosen ones*.' She pretended not to hear and said, 'Then why this regime of coldness and despondency in your home?' 'How should I know, *Maman*?' 'And you alone benefit from the kindnesses showered upon you, and the rest of the people around you just suffer from your coldness.' "

Or: "I was lucky today. I lied and my conscience isn't bothering me. What do you think, what will happen in the future? See how thin I'm getting: skin and bones. *Maman* is bewildered and even in despair and keeps saying, 'I just can't imagine what's happening to you! The honeymoon is long over. Do you need iron? Does it hurt here? How about here?' 'Ah, *Maman*, it's marvelous being so thin; it's so easy to move, and I'm in no danger of anyone else making any claims on me.' 'Lavinia, you are a fool. He looked at you the way he never looks at anyone; he lowered himself in offering you his protection; if you were wiser and more generous, you would not dare to call the sovereign's kindly disposition a claim.' "

Or: "I was lucky today. I thought, 'How am I at fault?' And I didn't see any of it as being my fault. I set out for the Frederickses' with a light heart, not feeling like a thief, but some kind of change is under way at our house, a chill, and they are looking at me inquisitively. Could they have noticed something? Maybe I've given myself away through an impolite joy in my eyes or some happy gesture? Would you like me to kill them all and we'll move to faraway Okhta? Yesterday Mr. Ladimirovsky took me to see the Obrezkovs. Do you know them? You—oh, please, don't visit them, for if I see you there, I'll fling my arms around your neck and there'll be a scandal. Abduct me, my priceless friend, this is intolerable."

Or: "Today I had no luck—ah, not a bit. If it's like this now, how will it be when I'm old? They are irritated that I'm not nicer to the tsar. '*Maman*, but he's old!' 'Lavinia, you are a fool. When you tore around town after your robber'—that's what she calls you—'you didn't stop to think about his age.' And again, like a thief from the Haymarket, I look around, creep around, make eyes at the policeman, punishing myself. What I'm doing is bad, it's bad, and I can't stop myself, I must see you and touch you, and steal. God, how long will this go on! I'm losing my strength."

Or: "This morning I awoke in total despair. Suppose I run into Alexander Vladimirovich's study, where he is sitting at his desk in his robe, and tell him everything. Let it explode. And then when all the reproaches, insults, threats, demands, hysterics, and terror are over, with a clean heart, I'll throw myself on your neck. I know that you are strong and unhappy, and you will understand and take pity and protect me."

And so today, passing the red gate, Myatlev immersed himself in the damned endless nirvana, where sadness and anxiety rather than sweet dreams envelop the soul. And looking at the thin shoulders of that unbelievable young woman, he thought once more that she was the one whom he would never give up to *him*. Enough. That was it. "He took away Aneta, destroyed Alexandrina, and I won't let him have this one." Whenever she smiled in confusion or happiness—and sometimes it was not clear which—it was like the triumph of the morning sun, and the muffling darkness was gone, and everything would be all right as long as he never let go of those warm, trembling shoulders and he tried to guess how long he could refuse happiness.

Their meetings were brief and infrequent. Almost momentary: the clock chimed somewhere in the distance, and its thick warning did not penetrate the door. There was no Petersburg, no Nevsky Prospect, no Fontanka River, no innumerable loyal citizens and occasional mockers, and there was no wheezing monster peering from the bushes, and no clumsy Sverbeyev, and no taboos; there was nothing until they were disturbed by a discreet scratching at the door, until they awakened from their dream, for illusions were only for children and blind men, while madmen, surrounded by a growling pack of dogs and trained by the Petersburg climate to live with a backward glance, had no need of illusions; there was no room for illusions when it was time to go and the horses had been waiting, and Mr. Ladimirovsky was out there, in another world, nervously scratching his head, reviving the memories of his young tormentor's unnatural behavior and shuddering when Madame Tuchkova shared her suspicions with him or perhaps an excess of satisfaction about it all.

And this time, when the scratching at the door threatened to turn into banging, they began to say their farewells, their feet back on the ground, seeing the room again, saying the last few meaningless words, touching each other, hugging, kissing.

Suddenly Lavinia said, "It's intolerable. I'm ready to do anything, but this can't go on. I'm ready to tell him. After all, what could possibly happen?"

"Definitely," Myatlev said, confused, not thinking, not realizing, "definitely."

And according to their ritual, they separated; the former Mr. van Schoenhoven went into the depths of the house where darling Aneta was waiting for her with wonderful kindness, like a faithful lady of the chamber, and Myatlev went out through the yellow hallway, where the smell of sheepskin coats would disguise his traces.

He decided to torture himself for his indecisiveness and weakness and had the coachman drive along Italyanskaya Street past the Frederickses' house. The nervy trotters of Mr. Ladimirovsky stood in front of the familiar front porch. "What if I stop and go in?" he thought, and his madness was about to play a mean trick on him. He even managed to call out to the coachman something desperate about a ruined life, something childish and cruel.

"I can't understand you, sir," the coachman laughed, turning toward him and slowing the horses in front of the lighted porch, looking at the prince with either love or condemnation. Myatlev came to his senses in time.

"Move!" he shouted. "What are you stopping for!"

The next day he received a letter from Aneta.

Dear Seryozhenka, something's happened. I don't understand any of it, but something happened. We were sitting quite normally, having tea, when it happened. They both grew very pale—apparently they had said something to each other, I don't

302

know what—and they rushed off, and your antagonist could barely control himself and didn't look me in the eyes any longer. Perhaps she told him everything to put an end to this situation, I don't know. In any case, my intuition tells me that something has happened, and something to do with you and with her. Perhaps you told her to, you madman? Now you'll be up to your old tricks again, thinking of rope ladders and what have you.

Aneta was not exaggerating, as we later found out. When Myatlev left the Frederickses' house, the hosts invited their guests to tea. They were sitting around a large round table rather insouciantly, and the old gentleman-in-waiting, his eyes shut as usual, was expounding, as usual, the superiority of the Russian method of government, tried and true, compared to the slapdash and libertine business of other civilizations. Regal Aneta sat by the samovar, and her hands were like those of a choirmaster as, barely touching the cups, she set them floating across the table in a circle, to the quiet music of a winter evening and her own pleasant murmur. Mr. Ladimirovsky was directly opposite. His dark-brown suit, blinding shirt of Dutch cloth, and bloody red foulard tie sparkled, emphasizing the yearning of yesterday's unimportant Muscovite to turn into a pedigreed Petersburger. That was just what Aneta was thinking, for Mr. Ladimirovsky's new brilliance suggested nothing more, unfortunately, than a readiness for countless changes and ambition gnawing at him like a worm. "Oh," she thought, "he won't forgive Lavinia's extreme cruelty toward the tsar." And she watched the councillor of state, feeling nothing for him except routine hostility; and everything about him seemed insignificant, lackeylike—even though the cattle breeder handled himself impeccably and freely—and ugly—even though Lavinia's husband was rather handsome and attractive and the white cup with blue flowers rested confidently in his hand (as opposed to Myatlev's).

In this charming triangle only Lavinia seemed uncomfortable, her thin hands barely touching the cup for fear of being burned. Her smile was estranged, and the candles were not reflected in her gray eyes. They were impenetrable and cold, concealing, thought Aneta, something unanticipated and bad.

Finally the conversation turned to less lofty themes. Instead of high-flown speech on the destiny of nations, they exchanged simple, everyday, touching words about themselves, the house, the lifeline in the palm, the brevity of life, prejudices, cuff links, goose giblets, taffeta, poor taste, migraines, faith, infidelity.

Suddenly Lavinia turned to her husband and whispered so that he alone could hear:

"I've been meeting a man—I love him—"

"Yes, yes," Mr. Ladimirovsky said to Fredericks, "truly, faith, and goose giblets, and migraines—" And then to Lavinia in a whisper: "You're mad. Why are you lying?" And then to Aneta: "By the way, speaking of migraines— Speak of the devil." And he nodded at his wife.

As soon as they got in the sleigh, he said, "Whom have you been meeting? Why are you lying?" And he grabbed her elbow. "What have I ever done to you?"

"Alexander Vladimirovich," she said primly, "I should not have said anything. But it's intolerable to hide and lie—isn't that right?"

"What have I done to you?" he shouted.

"God," she said, "let go of my elbow." And she cried. "Forgive me."

"I don't understand why you're lying. What have I done to you?" He squeezed her elbow harder. "When the tsar delicately expressed his interest in you, you were insulted, and then, it seems, there's this going on—so that's how it is. Why did you tell me this?"

"Ah, let go of my elbow, it's disgusting!"

At home they ran off to their separate corners. The situation was irredeemable. One word had turned everything around. At midnight he entered her room without knocking. She was sitting at the window, her fists on her knees. Mr. Ladimirovsky was calm and said by rote, "Now everything must change. The honeymoon was over a long time ago. I'm sending you to the country."

He waited for an answer for a long time and was about to leave, slamming the door, when she said smoothly, in a low drawl, "You misunderstood me. I've been meeting this man, and I love him. What does the country have to do with it?"

"What?" he shouted stupidly. "What do you mean, what? I'm doing it all for you, for your own good! Do I worry about myself? Until you learn to think like a real wife, I must do it for you, it's my cross, my duty, my burden; while you run around, satisfying your whims, wallowing in happy egotism, thinking yourself the lady of the house, I go without sleep and I hold you up by the elbows so that you don't fall down and break your neck. Do I worry about myself?" And he ran out of the room, slamming the door.

She continued to sit, staring dully out the window. An hour passed, and another, and then he returned without knocking.

"Let's do this," he said calmly, as if nothing had happened. "Let's think this through."

"All right," she said unexpectedly.

"Let's not kill each other, let's wait, the morning is wiser than the evening, a stitch in time—make hay while— You go to bed and get some sleep, and in the morning you won't even want to think about it, honestly, you'll see."

As soon as he left, she threw off her wrinkled visiting dress and snuggled under the covers.

The miserable cattle breeder, convulsed with anger, roused the servants meanwhile, had the horses bridled, put on his fur coat, and raced over to wake Madame Tuchkova.

"What have you done to me? Whom did you force on me?" he was planning to shout at her. "You said, you promised, you swore. Here's the value of your promises!" But he also thought that almost anything could be going on in the mind of the young girl, and he couldn't pay serious attention to everything she said—that would mean demeaning himself, bringing himself down to her level. She has been meeting— Whom? It was impossible. Whom? Whom? Who could it be? Who? Myatlev? Nonsense. Who else was there? No one. Impossible. Delirium. And how disgusting this was. Racing through the Petersburg night— Ugh. What have I done to her? I should whip her, send her to the country, and lock her up there. She's lying, that's all, she's a liar. Her mother warned me—her mother, mother, mother—

His vulgarity calmed him down. Madame Tuchkova dressed instantly, like a fireman. Even though the councillor of state had cooled off considerably during his trip, his intuition told him not to show it and, on the contrary, to appear even angrier, to let loose his misery on the Polish woman, let her save the day, alone.

"You must have misheard her," Madame Tuchkova cried in horror. "How did it happen? Where? What did she say? She just said so? Pull yourself together. This is nonsense."

"*You* pull yourself together, madame."

Almost wearing out the horses, they flew to the damned house on Znamenskaya, to the house that had been so carefully and lovingly painted, decorated, furnished, and draped, and that had brought no happiness. They flew along, each thinking to himself that Lavinia was long gone, without a trace, and that she was flying along in a rented carriage to the devil knew where, into an abyss, dishonor, shame—

"She's just a child; God is merciful," Madame Tuchkova exclaimed with poorly disguised doubt.

"That's what I'm afraid of," said the councillor of state, trying not to believe himself.

"But I warned you about her fantasies. How could you believe that she would actually—that she really—with someone—" said the witch with poorly disguised doubt.

"I don't think that," Mr. Ladimirovsky replied, not believing himself.

Lavinia awoke and saw two familiar, mournful silhouettes by her bed and remembered. Suddenly she pitied them. And herself. And suddenly she thought that nothing could be changed, that she and Myatlev could never be together, and that was fate. Higher powers had to intervene. But where were they?

"Lavinia," her mother said, "child, what have you made up?

You've upset everyone. Alexander Vladimirovich is beside himself from your outburst."

Then Lavinia thought that even if the higher powers did intervene and everything moved the way they wanted it to, she wouldn't have the strength to climb up on that overhanging cliff. What were the higher powers? Just a phrase, that's all they were. Perhaps your thin arms with their thin, bloodied fingers could have supported you, but the higher powers had no time for your foolishness.

"This is no fantasy," thought Mr. Ladimirovsky, his gaze resting on the estranged face of his tormentor. "No, this is not fantasy, and that face is not the face of a liar." And he couldn't possibly have thought of Gainsborough or Rokotov or Levitsky as he tried to understand that face, so calm, so removed from his husbandly doubts. "And if it is a fantasy, then she's had it for a long time, too long to make it go away—"

"I think that we had better go away, travel a bit," he said. "After all, nothing has happened, just some nonsense—"

And Madame Tuchkova laughed in relief, pretending that everything was over, behind them. But, standing over her daughter's bed, she remembered—and it wasn't at all comforting—little Lavinia in someone's ugly embroidered jacket running through deep snow, stubbornly, her long neck stretched out, unswerving, like a bee toward honey; and then her being slapped in the face but still repeating her flights; and the young Prince Myatlev, about whom they were saying terrible things, was the honey; and the persistent bee kept flying, flying there, knowing she would be beaten, punished, locked in her room— Yes, yes, she kept on flying. And the years don't stand still. And how will you stop the bee?

"Of course, it's all nonsense," said Madame Tuchkova, not believing herself. "Really, you should go away." And she didn't finish because Lavinia's gray eyes, mocking and cold, were fixed upon her. "Are you mad?" the witch shouted, losing her courage. "Are you still delirious?"

"Madame," said her daughter's husband, "don't shout, don't

307

make things worse. It's just a fantasy. We'll leave right away. And that's all."

It grew cold in the room. Snow fell. Long blue footprints stretched out on the floor. Mr. van Schoenhoven, raising his cardboard sword over his head, said with horrifying cruelty, "I love him. You know who. You're the ones who are making up fantasies . . . nothing can be changed . . . fire . . . tollgates . . . unhappiness . . ." And she lost consciousness.

58

March 12, 1851

They've hidden Lavinia away with such artistry that I can only fall back in amazement. What a crime! Where are you, Mr. van Schoenhoven? Amilakhvari lost his impeccable self-control and staged a scene blaming *me* for everything. It seems that instead of picking up Lavinia without a second thought and galloping in a carriage away from the Frederickses' house, far from Petersburg, beyond the tollgates, into a mountain cabin, I betrayed the poor girl and turned her over to the hands of talented torturers, lightly, playfully, like a typical Horse Guards' officer, just as I did with that sad victim with the big gray eyes whose cries still sound reproachfully and destroy this old three-storied wooden hut.

March 15

Could they possibly have found the old rusty chain and put it to use once again? Poor Mr. van Schoenhoven!

There was a heartrending gnashing yesterday just before morning. I thought that the house had collapsed. Afanasy brought an architect who, like Dr. Schwanenbach, crawled along the walls and ceiling, listening to every board, then shook his head and announced that the illness was fatal and that he knew of no way to revive my family nest, however much I hate it! I had

Afanasy hire some carts, prepare for the trip, pack up all the books, mirrors, statues, and take them to Mikhailovka until better times. Now the house is in an uproar. Men are trampling the parquet. Cassandra showed up and said that she was sending over some Italian architect famous for saving some tower in Florence and that he's planning to return the house to its former beauty with the aid of some magic salve or other. I made believe that I was very happy, and thanked her, and promised to think about it. I understood from her attitude that the story about Lavinia had not yet reached her beehive. However, my hasty gratitude brought on nothing but suspicion from her. And then, to allay her fears and doubts, I announced that I was even planning to return to work in the department—the Devil tugged at my tongue! She naturally did not believe me and gave me a look of horror, but still a slight sympathetic vibration went through her soul. I must have quiet until I undertake some action.

March 29

The ice is breaking on the Neva, a bit early, but very turbulently. What disaster! I couldn't find Madame Tuchkova, or Kaleria, or Mr. Ladimirovsky himself and his trotters in all of Petersburg. The only thing I did discover, with Amilakhvari's help, is that the councillor of state has taken an extended leave from the Postal Department for reasons of health.

They've probably all gone with Lavinia to take turns guarding her, along with the regiment of grenadiers, and an artillery battery, and some adept combat engineers.

And it was not I but Amilakhvari who went mad and hired two stern thugs who for a generous fee are tearing around Petersburg and sniffing around without a hope of success.

I can hear the rattle of chains and the voices of Mr. van Schoenhoven's tormentors. My friend is probably right. I should have been more decisive, done at least something in this case. After all, I'm lusting after the void, anyway, so why not?

Really, why not? I'm afraid to speak of love. Now, after all this, I'm afraid. I've had it. Could I turn away now? I'm trying to be calmer and more controlled. When your destiny is truly entrusted to you, you should break with the habits of the past.

No, Prince Sergei Vasilyevich, your future does not promise a pleasant stroll. I see hardship and sadness. And perhaps for just once in your life . . . Pull yourself together. . . . Overlook the weakness and indecisiveness and shyness of this no-longer-young criminal with the long face and spectacles. . . . And for once in your life . . . Force him to extend his hand to help someone else. . . . And be quiet about your feelings: don't chop words! Don't calculate. Make a decision; be firm and courageous. As for love, it's not for us to judge it. Just don't cool off, don't weaken, don't betray her. . . . For once in your life . . .

April 18

This is truly unbelievable! I'll start at the beginning. I was awakened this morning to learn with joy and horror that Madame Tuchkova was asking for me. With horror because who wants to encounter a witch, even the most modern one, after everything that has transpired; and with joy because she was alive and in Petersburg and I could strap her to a bench and whip her until she told me where her daughter is or died, and there would be one witch less in the world. I had her brought into the rotunda, into the dust and disarray. Then I came down. What a she-wolf! She could at least inquire as to the fate of Sapega—not a word. As though she were seeing me for the first time. Oh, these modern she-wolves! The ones of the past were ready to swoon, clasp their hands, become suffused with color to their bellybuttons. This one didn't even twitch an eyebrow.

SHE: Kind sir, extreme circumstances force me to disturb you so early in the day.

I: Please sit down, madame. Afanasy, dust off the chair! How can I be of help?

SHE: I am the widow of General Tuchkov. However, that has no bearing here. Perhaps you remember, Prince, long ago, some seven or eight years ago, a certain young boy used to visit your house (I don't understand what attracted him), a small boy with a toy saber—

I: A toy sword?

SHE: Of course! Then you remember? You remember him?

I: No, not at all.

SHE: But you just—

I: A coincidence. There was no boy, madame. There was no boy; I'll swear to it.

SHE: There was no boy, that's true, because it was a *girl* dressed as a boy. In any case, the point is that the girl secretly came to this house (actually, I don't insist, it might have been the one next door)—

I: Probably next door—

SHE: Probably next door— Yes, yes. So please allow me to tell you a very short story, Prince, for I would like to think of you as an intermediary in my argument with your neighbor, to bring you up-to-date, so to speak, since you maintain that the boy—that is, the girl—did not visit you but your neighbor. So, Prince, in the house that you and I mean, there lived a man—not young, debauched, and a great egotist. There were terrible rumors always going around about him. They said, for instance, that he seduced young, foolish girls and then, with the help of his faithful servant, drowned them in the Neva; that he became intimate with certain noble ladies, married them, and when he had gotten his hands on their wealth, did away with his victims through the most horrifying means; that the most desperate brigands gathered in his home, and at such times it was no longer foolish young girls who were in danger but cities and governments. Of course, rumors are rumors [*Laughs.*] but there was something going on in that house, and you should have heard something about it as a neighbor. So, the mother of this girl swore that her daughter would not enter that house, and you should know that the mother was not a woman who cast her words into the wind but one who knew her value, for nature had generously endowed her with clairvoyance, and she was a witch; however, a vow alone was not enough, for the girl in this story resembled her mother in stubbornness, willfulness, and disobedience, and whereas these traits in the mother had helped her arrange a better life for her daughter, in the girl they seemed horrible. You, Prince, are a man of great nobility, and you surely can

311

understand the mother's suffering. [*Laughs.*] But the mother's interdictions were useless, and just then a man appeared, rich, handsome, strong—without any rank, it is true, but with great potential—and the mother decided that she had to save her wayward child. I won't hide the fact that the girl's madness, which she called love, did not cease, but it's always easier to control a married woman, isn't it? There are always methods, ways to hold her down. [*Laughs again, even though it sounds more like a sob.*] Why am I telling you this? The point is, dear sir, that the fate of these two women is important to me, and I would like you to hint to your neighbor that all his plans are in vain, for the mother is so full of zeal and determination and is so desperate that it is terrifying to contemplate.

I became incensed and said that the rumors about my neighbor were highly exaggerated and that my neighbor was known for his unheard-of persistence and relentlessness; that if he loved the witch's daughter, then he would hardly allow the girl to be teased, forced, and mocked; and that attempts to hide her would lead to no good, that was certain.

SHE: So you think that that monster will not repudiate his filthy intentions?

I: I'm certain of it, madame. It's not a good idea to joke with love, madame.

She turned green at those words, and the design she had been tracing on the dusty surface of the card table turned into an intricate pattern. "What terrible dust," she said, holding back her tears, as though pitying me, "how can you live like this?" I took to drink to cover up the taste of her visit.

April 22

It seems it's spring! That always encourages success. In all the excitement I hadn't noticed its arrival. Everything is simpler and clearer. And here's the first swallow: Amiran's rogues tell us that the Ladimirovskys have returned to Petersburg as though nothing had happened, and have taken up their old life, except for the fact that Lavinia is in seclusion. But that's only half a problem.

312

Aneta has offered to call on them. Perhaps something will come of it.

April 24

Success! Success! Finally, after that long silence, a few lines from Lavinia: "I'm ready to fall at the feet of Anna Mikhailovna for her kindness. Once again she has saved us. I've been miserable without you; they tormented me; where is the way out? I'm to blame for it all, and now it's too late to complain. But at least walk past my windows so that I can look at you. . . . They won't let me near you for at least a hundred years. *Maman* is writing tearful complaints to the Heir. And all this could lead me to real despair if not for the quiet hope that God is merciful and that something will happen."

God is merciful. I can't wait anymore. A hundred years! Who has a hundred years—I may have ten left. And as they pass I will be afraid to ask myself: What have you done to correct the unfair whim of fate? I was given Mr. van Schoenhoven. He's been mine since ancient, prehistoric times! I can't wait! While it's spring, while I have the strength and the remnants, however feeble, of human dignity and a tiny hope for salvation, I must use them. No fantasies. O Aneta, prophetess, treasure chest of hopes, friend, matchmaker, be blessed for all time! I immediately sent Lavinia a note: "Our only salvation is flight. Far away, forever. If you are up to it, write me. I'll prepare everything."

April 26

What a story! It's a sign for me to get ready to go. The last loads have left for the country. The house is empty and dead. Sverbeyev has disappeared. Afanasy appeared at noon, mouth agape, terror in his eyes. I can't stand the sight of that pig. He bumped around the doorstep, unable to utter a word, pointing at the door and mooing. Finally I shouted at him. He began weeping and said, "Your Excellency, they're all gone."

"Who? What are you babbling about?"

"All of them. There's no one left. The chef, and the coachman, and the gardener—"

"Where did they go?" I shouted at the fool. "What about their things?"

"All gone." He wept more copiously. "They took their things

and left. And the valets left—I got up to give the orders this morning, and they were all gone. There's no one here. How will we live?"

I checked their quarters and their duty posts. They had all left for an unknown destination. Only Afanasy and Aglaya remained, frightened and cowed.

It's a sign. This signals an end to my indecisiveness. Amilakhvari sees it that way, too.

"The important thing is that that pig doesn't find out," I told him, meaning Afanasy.

Lavinia has agreed to everything: "Thank God, I'm prepared for anything! Command me." That's easy. Life is wonderful. I see everything with amazing clarity, and so I can command: Take nothing, we'll buy everything on the way. We leave as soon as Amilakhvari gets the orders for the relays he has requested in his own name.

May 3

Afanasy is weeping openly. Has he guessed? I say, "Stop, you buffoon!" And he says, "How can I, Your Excellency, they're all gone, like mice. Another beam broke today." What a fool.

It looks as if everything is well planned—just a few details to take care of. The relays are arranged. Today, when I went to Amiran's to pick up the papers, I ran into all my old acquaintances, as if they had conspired to see me. Near the Kazan Railroad Station I saw Lieutenant Katakazi in civilian dress and with a swollen cheek, and he waved to me as if I were a drinking companion, the idiot. Von Müffling was strolling along the Moika River. He didn't see me. Writer Kolesnikov was running across Nevsky in his uniform. He saw me and ran all the faster.

We've decided on May 5! "Under any pretext that you can manage, be sure to be at Gostiny Dvor by noon. Amilakhvari will be waiting for you in a carriage at the end of the Perinnaya Line from noon until two."

I must really be in love if I've finally decided to do this, be this daring. And if I'm daring, then I must be in love.

O Aneta, God grant you all the happiness in the world!

59

[To His Excellency Count L. V. Dubelt]

Your Excellency!

You were kind and generous enough to permit me, a mother mad with grief, to give you the details of this affair.

On May 5 my daughter, Lavinia Ladimirovskaya, wife of Councillor of State Mr. Ladimirovsky, asked me to accompany her to Gostiny Dvor to do some shopping, since she was afraid that if she went alone she would be open to the insulting pursuit of the infamous Prince Myatlev, who has not given her any peace for many years.

We arrived at noon and agreed, as usual, that if we were separated in the crowd we would meet by the poster column on Nevsky. And it did turn out that, engrossed as we were in shopping and examining the many wares available, we lost each other, and I went to the decided-upon spot to wait for her. I waited with mounting anxiety for over two hours, then hailed a cab and had him hurry to her house on Znamenskaya Street. But my daughter was not at home. Mr. Ladimirovsky and I waited for her until evening, and then, in desperation, thought of going to Prince Myatlev's house. My soul shrank at the thought that the old debaucher, usurper, and plain thief could have abducted my daughter and brought her to his horrible den, and could now do what he willed with her. But no sooner had we approached that gloomy spot than what we saw brought us to greater despair. Instead of the famous house, there was only a huge pile of lumber, and the surrounding area was covered with dust and plaster; the man's servant was sitting by the gate right in the dust and weeping bitterly. My heart bled. Wasn't it enough that he had abducted my daughter—did he have to kill her in the ruins as well? "What happened? Where's your master?" I asked the weeping servant. He explained that Prince Myatlev had left that

315

morning, saying only, "Farewell, Afanasy." And an hour later, thinking over his master's words, which he had never heard spoken before, the servant heard a horrible cracking, and managed to run outside, and that den of iniquity crumbled before his very eyes and turned into nothing. Here Mr. Ladimirovsky, who had been silent until then, suddenly laughed bitterly and said that the only possibility was that the prince had taken our Lavinia and brought her to the house of one of his gang members or to his estate. I felt so relieved when I realized that there was no one in the house, except for one maid, who will lie there for the ages now.

So, Your Excellency, these are the circumstances of the horrible event that has befallen us. Of course, the disappearance of my daughter is not the most important thing that could be brought to your attention, but her disappearance is linked with the name of a man who has angered the tsar many times, and that's why I presume to disturb Your Excellency, for Prince Myatlev is not merely an insolent jester, but a rabble-rouser, a sower of immorality and all sorts of evil. And knowing your omnipotence, I beg you, find my daughter and tear her away from the clutches of that scoundrel.

Your Excellency's humble servant,
E. Tuchkova, widow